THE FLOWER GIRL

Until Death Brings Us Together

C. S. M. Beaten

TotalRecall Publications, Inc.
1103 Middlecreek
Friendswood, Texas 77546
281-992-3131 281-482-5390 Fax
www.totalrecallpress.com

ISBN: 978-1-64883-254-3
UPC: 6-43977-42543-0

Library of Congress Control Number: 2023937625

FIRST EDITION
1   2   3   4   5   6   7   8   9   10

To TJ, Elvis, Marley,
EJ, Mozart and Ludwig

Author's Bio

The Flower Girl is one of three novels I plan to publish. I have a Master of Social Work degree and undergraduate degrees in social work and psychology. Experience working with adults with mental illness and in child welfare and completing three novels have helped me hone my writing skills.

Two songs that influenced my writing of this book are Led Zeppelin's *Achille's Last Stand* and George Harrison's *My Sweet Lord*. *Achilles Last Stand* is one of my favorite songs.

The song, to me, is about humanity's quest to know and death freeing one's soul from the constraints of earth. Upon death, there is no need for mythology, such as the myth of Achilles, to make sense of our experience, as with death comes enlightenment and, finally, the knowledge of what awaits us. Death is Achille's last stand.

Acknowledgements:

I appreciate the encouragement and support of my brother Brad, my sister Sherri Arsenault, and friends.
Steve Shilson, Cover Design, Straylight Films.
Sigrid Macdonald, Editor, Book Magic.
Bruce Moran, Publisher. TotalRecall Publications, Inc.

About the Book

Death: the unknown, demons, good spirits, love, going close to Heaven, and coming back. Grief, loss, the promise that things work out in the end between Tyler and Aaron, a teenage girl and boy, lifelong friends who talked about getting married one day. Who, at the time of Tyler's death, were starting to see each other differently, from childhood innocence and doing what children do to beginning puberty and seeing each other in a more romantic way.

This book is about hope, loss, and faith.

Introduction:

Aaron stared into the star-filled sky, thinking about what was and about what might be again. How far does the star field go, and what is at its opposite side if one exists, he wondered. Heaven is there, so it is said.

One day he will know what becomes of the physical when no longer seen.

He thinks about his childhood best friend, Tyler. A beautiful girl in looks and spirit, a tomboy at heart, yet a lover of flowers.

There was no past without her as she had always been there.

Time pushes on, never stopping, blindingly forever on its course, not knowing where it has been or where it will go, guided only by that, which created it.

Every day seems like the last and a premonition of the next. Normalcy placates until tragedy strikes, and then all is altered in some way.

The past is beyond being undone as time keeps its course, as all but time passes, save for the supposed houses of the holy.

Chapter One
The Flower Girl

Tyler Page stormed toward her bicycle, embarrassed and angry, anxious to get away from the diamond after her ballgame finished. Today her junior girls' softball team got blown out, and she was hitless, and she made two unforgivable errors for good measure. Manager Hitch gave Tyler and the rest of the team a good talking to after losing twenty to six; Tyler hated losing, to begin with, and being called out by Mr. Hitch for swinging at wayward pitches and for the errors only added to the pain. She had to get to her friend Aaron Richards' house, needing to tell him about her dreadful morning.

Aaron woke at dawn, roused by a disturbing dream that began with him climbing a spiral staircase in a house he had not been in before. Each floor he passed was elaborately decorated and filled with antique furniture, oil paintings, Victorian-style lamps, and unique odds and ends. Floors were carpeted or surfaced by floorboards; area rugs and walls were wallpapered, painted with pastel colors, or cloaked in wood.

Upward he went, wary of being confronted by someone or something angered by being disturbed from their peace. Aaron climbed six levels before reaching the house's top floor; he passed several rooms before arriving at an elevator. The elevator plummeted after he stepped inside, dropping so fast he seemed on the verge of plunging to death before the elevator finally slowed. Its door opened and revealed a dank basement with concrete floors and cinderblock walls painted different drab shades of gray.

Desperate to find a way out of the house, Aaron hurried toward a metal door at the end of a narrow corridor, which opened into a dark, forbidding room. But there was no turning back. An evil presence pursued him.

Illuminated by daylight pouring through a crack in a wall was a coffin, he realized, upon arriving closer to it. Until opening its lid, he assumed the coffin contained the body of his long-dead grandfather. Instead, it held the corpse of his friend Tyler Page. Aaron startled awake after Tyler's corpse opened its eyes and stared at him.

Images of Tyler in a coffin flashed through Aaron's mind as he sleepily watched cartoons later that Saturday morning. Fourteen and thirteen years old, respectively, he and Tyler lived next door to each other and were best friends for as long as either could remember. They shared everything, but Aaron, not wanting to upset her, decided to keep the strange dream to himself for now. The following day marked the first anniversary of her grandpa's death, so Tyler had enough on her mind without being told about a stupid dream.

Still wearing her softball uniform, Tyler knocked at the back door of Aaron's house a few minutes after twelve. Usually, she showered and changed before stopping by after softball games unless she played well and was anxious to tell him about it. But a glum expression on her face confused Aaron. Looking sullen, Tyler whispered, "Hello," when she entered the house. Aaron held the door open for her.

"I'm assuming you must have had a good game..." he said, following Tyler to a table in the kitchen.

"What makes ya think that?" she asked him, before Aaron could tell her.

"Because you're still wearing your softball uniform," Aaron replied as they sat opposite each other. "Usually... usually, you go home to shower and change before coming over." He yawned, gazing into Tyler's blackish-brown eyes. "Pardon me... I'm tired because I woke up too friggin early. I got up at six and couldn't go back to sleep."

"How come you woke up so early?"

"I don't know," he lied, staring at the table, unable to look Tyler in the eye, feeling bad for not being honest with her. "Anyway, usually, you shower and change before coming over unless you played a good game and are pumped up to tell me about it. But you look sad."

"Yeah, you're right about the going home and changing thing, but I played horribly today, and my whole team sucked. We lost big time... You know how I hate having a bad game... I'm bummed and just wanted to talk to you."

"I could tell something was bothering you by the look on your face. I know when you're upset about something."

"Just like me with you," Tyler said, removing a yellow baseball cap from her head and placing it flat on the table. Her dark brown hair was tangled and knotted. "I can tell when you're upset about something, too... So, do I look okay? I bet I look nasty. I know I'm all sweaty, and my hair must look pretty messed up... I've been too lazy to shorten it like I usually would by now to help keep me cool in the summer."

"You look a little grungy." Her uniform consisted of heather gray pinstriped pants and a matching jersey, and the cap was stained by dirt, grass, and sweat. "Your uniform needs a good cleaning. Let's put it that way."

"I hope I don't smell."

"Not really," he said, despite a hint of body odor and a faint, musty smell emanating from her.

"What does not really mean? You can be honest and tell me if I stink or not."

"You smell kinda funky," he felt compelled to say.

"Yeah, well, it's hot out today, in case you haven't noticed," she curtly replied. "I'm so sorry that I stink."

"You don't reek that bad," Aaron kidded. "You asked me if

you smelled, and I told you the truth... I don't care how you look or smell."

"I'm sorry for being nasty." Tyler patted his hand. "I'm just wound up because I'm so frustrated."

"Don't worry about it," he told her.

"We got thrashed," she huffed, placing her softball glove, propped under an arm, beside her cap. "We got creamed... We got beat so bad it was stupid. My team lost twenty to six."

"It sucks to lose that bad," Aaron said. "I would be bummed out, too. Don't you guys have a mercy rule like stop at fifteen runs, or do you just keep piling up the runs?"

"No, we don't, and I'm glad we don't," Tyler replied. "But whatever... it is what it is... It's okay when we kick the crap out of another team, but it's not as much fun when it's the other way around." She frowned, rubbing her eyes. "Our manager, Mr. Hitch, wasn't happy, but neither were my teammates or me," she continued. "He yelled at us after the game and said we sucked. Basically, he called us losers. That ain't right. We're just girls trying to have fun, but we're always stressing, thinking he's gonna yell at us if we do something wrong."

"He really did all that?" Aaron asked her, struggling to believe the man's alleged behavior.

"Pretty much," she maintained.

"That's not right for a grown-ass man to talk like that. You're right — that ain't right."

"Well, he didn't straight out say that we sucked and call us losers, but that's pretty much what he insinuated."

"Well, that still ain't right," Aaron opined. "What's his problem?"

"I wish I knew," Tyler said with a sigh. "He's different. I never had a manager like him before, which is saying something since I've been playing softball since I was six. It's like he thinks he's managing the Tigers instead of a girls' Little League softball team," she said, referring to her beloved Detroit Tigers.

"Managers I've had before were easy-going and nice, but this guy gets uptight and intense. Sometimes he gets all wound up and angry when we mess up… He's nice enough most of the time, but I don't like it when he gets all upset." Tyler planted her elbows on the table, pressed her hands into her face, and stared at the hat and glove above webs of spread fingers. "Anyway, I didn't get a hit when I usually get two and made two bone-headed plays. One time, an easy grounder I should have snagged went through my legs, and the other time, the ball bounced off my glove and almost bopped me in the noggin." She ran a finger along the webbing of her glove, looking at it wearily. "That was pretty embarrassing.

"It didn't help that there were lots of people watching, besides players on both teams and managers and coaches. I wanted to crawl into a hole and die because I felt so embarrassed... Some people in the bleachers laughed when the ball almost hit my head."

"Stuff happens, and people can be ignorant," Aaron remarked empathetically. "Whoever laughed wasn't nice. It sucks that you didn't have a good game and had to put up with morons, but you have to let it go."

"I know," Tyler sighed. "But if it were you, you'd have to admit it would be hard."

"I would have felt the same way you do," he acknowledged. "I'm just trying to make you feel better."

"I know you are, bud," she replied as she patted his hand again. "You're my main guy. You're always there when I need you like I am for you."

"Did your manager say anything when you made your errors?"

"Not right away, but I knew he wasn't happy. He gave me an evil eye after the ball bounced off my glove and probably when it went between my legs, but I didn't notice. He said some of us played quote-unquote carelessly when he basically yelled at us after the game. I wasn't the only one who messed up... I'm sure I'll hear about it again at our next practice."

"What do your folks think about your manager? They wouldn't be pleased with the guy yelling at you and making you and your teammates feel like crap. I would kick his ass if I were your dad. I wish I could do that."

"You're not going to kick anyone's ass," Tyler chuckled. "Big ole tough guy."

Besides punching a kid's two front teeth out during recess in grade one, Aaron used words over fists.

"He doesn't really yell at us, but he talks loud," Tyler continued. "But, whatever, I don't talk to my parents about Mr. Hitch. There's no point, and I don't want to be a suck about it; anyway, they probably won't care. You know they don't bother coming to my games anyway, which bums me out... But the season's over in a few weeks unless we somehow make the playoffs, and I'm counting down the days. All I can do is hope to have a normal manager next year... Hopefully, 1980 will be a better softball season for me because this one sucks."

"What if you luck out and end up having the same guy?" Aaron joked.

"That's not funny," Tyler moaned. "Don't even say that!" she said, shaking a finger at him. "If that happens, I'll make a point of saying to whoever is in charge of the league that I don't want to play for that man again. If the people who run the league won't listen to me, I'll just quit playing."

"That would be sad if you don't have a better manager, because you love softball. I'm sure they won't force you to play for him if you don't want to, though."

"We'll see what happens," she sighed. "I'll keep my fingers crossed... So, what are you doing this afternoon?"

"I've got nothing going on," Aaron replied.

"Me neither."

A loud noise came from the room above them. "What's that?"

Tyler asked him, looking at the ceiling.

Aaron said his parents were moving furniture around, doing a major spring house cleaning. They were going to be away a lot over the summer, spending the odd week at his grandmother's cottage on Lake Erie and going on a road trip to Maine in August, where they would stay at a resort for two weeks.

His dad was a physics professor at the University of Windsor, and his mom worked in the office at a school bus company, so they had most of the summer off.

"I like the trips you guys go on," Tyler said. "Last year, you went to California, and the year before that, you drove around northern Ontario for a month, where you stayed for a bit at your grandparents' place on your dad's side. You guys are always going somewhere cool."

"You must be getting pumped up about the big trip you're going on in a few weeks," Aaron said.

"I can't wait!" Tyler yelped. "We've been doing the 'spic and span' thing, too, trying to get everything clean before our trip, and besides that, I've been painting the room in my basement that will be my new bedroom."

Tyler and her parents were going to Ireland, where her mother's family came from, and then to England, where her father was born, for a month, at the end of July. She had been to England twice with her family to visit her paternal grandparents, but this time she was going without any of her seven siblings.

"I can't wait to fly on a jet again… but I'm a little nervous about going to Ireland with all the bombings over there."

"That's in Northern Ireland," Aaron told her, knowing Tyler referred to a series of bombings across Northern Ireland early that spring. "You won't have to worry about that where you're going."

"Oh… okay."

Tyler and her parents would spend a week in Ireland and then three weeks in England, two weeks visiting various areas, and one week at her grandparents' place visiting with them and other relatives who would be coming over for a family reunion. She focused on being in London because that's where her grandparents lived and her favorite rock bands were based. Meeting David Bowie, Paul McCartney, or Jimmy Page from Led Zeppelin walking about would be nice. Tyler wondered if she and Jimmy were cousins since they shared the same last name. It would be cool if they were.

The trip would be the second time she went to England to visit her grandparents and the eighth time she saw them, as they came to Canada and stayed at their house every other year. They were going to spend a week at her grandparents' house, and this time around, she wanted to see Abbey Road Studio, where the Beatles recorded their albums. She wanted to see that and Buckingham Palace again because, as she said about the first time she saw it, "That was pretty cool to see."

"Let's do something to get your mind off things," he suggested."

"You always have a way of making me feel better just by being you!" Tyler exclaimed. She smiled, and her eyes returned to their typical smiling selves, indicating her mood had lifted. "I'm assuming you're not grounded still, are you?" "No. I'm free now!" Aaron cried.

"I can't believe you got grounded for a night because you missed curfew one measly ole time," Tyler said. "You usually get home on time."

"I know," Aaron agreed. "Wayne kept me out too long, and I had no way of calling them to let them know I was running late."

"You can't blame Wayne for... You made yourself late, Mister, not Wayne."

"I know," Aaron agreed. "Wayne doesn't have a curfew. He stays out all night if he wants... I've seen him outside on the street at midnight."

"My eight o'clock curfew on weeknights and ten on the

weekends is good enough for me," Tyler said. "I don't have anywhere to go after dark… So, what were you guys doing that you had to be out past nine?" she asked him, nine o'clock being his weeknight curfew.

"We rode our bikes to the west end. Wayne has a friend who lives out there… I misjudged my time. They were waiting for me when I pulled in at 9:30 p.m."

Wayne, Tyler, and Aaron became friends when they were toddlers. Wayne lived across the street from them. Wayne was a good friend but not as close as Aaron and Tyler were. He often spent time with himself, and there were times when sometimes he stayed in his house. Aaron and Tyler wondered why Wayne would do that. It was like he was grounding himself.

"So, have you gone out anywhere today?"

"I was going to play basketball with Wayne this morning at Oakwood," Aaron said. Oakwood was the grade school he, Tyler, and Wayne went to before graduating a week ago. "But Wayne couldn't play. He had to go to his uncle's house because one of his cousins turned sixteen today. There's a big party for him."

"I hope someone throws a big party for me when I turn sixteen."

"I'm sure your parents will," he said. "If not, I will."

"That's so like you," Tyler gushed. "So, is Wayne going to see that car dealing uncle of his? The rich one who owns the car dealership?"

"Yeah, the one Wayne says will give him a car when he gets his driver's license."

"Man, I hope someone gives me a car when I get my license! That would be sweet," Tyler said.

"I wouldn't mind if someone gave me one, too," Aaron agreed. "My dad is still mad at Wayne's uncle because of that car he sold us." The car, a brand-new model, was a lemon. His father managed to exchange it after taking the car back to the dealership a ridiculous number of times for repairs.

"It's only right that they gave him another car," Tyler said, aware of his father's problems with the car.

She turned away and sneezed for the second time.

"Bless you," Aaron said.

"Thanks," she gasped. Aaron pushed a Kleenex box in front of her after Tyler sneezed a third time. "Thanks," she said as she sniffled, pulling a tissue out of the box.

"Your allergies are bugging you, eh?"

"Good guess," she replied and chuckled after blowing her nose. "What was your first clue, Dr. Obvious?" Tyler smiled. "It's from pollen, grass, and dust from the infield... The outfield was covered by pollen, and the grass was just cut before our game. Hmm... That's probably why I played so bad. Maybe my allergies messed me up?"

"Yeah, go with that if it makes you feel better."

"I think I will," she said, maintaining a straight face. "And it could be true."

"It's that bad time of year again for you."

"It's always that time of year for me," Tyler groaned. "You know all the stuff I'm allergic to... Dogs, dust, grass, leaves, mold, pollen, milk, tomatoes, and other things." She balled the tissue, tossed it into a trash container, and sneezed.

"Bless you again," Aaron said.

"Thanks again," she replied while sniffling. "My allergies are so messed up. The allergy shots and antihistamine I take don't seem to help much."

"At least you're not allergic to flowers."

"Yeah, thank God for that!" Tyler exclaimed. "You know how I love flowers, especially purple daisies. You know I always have a bunch of them in my room."

"Oh, I know you do, Flower Girl," Aaron said. Flower Girl was a nickname her father gave her when Tyler was little because she would put the flowers in her hair that her mother gave her from the flower garden in the backyard of their house. Aaron called Tyler that sometimes, too, because of her dad and because she kept daisies in her room and helped her mom maintain the garden.

He called her Flower Girl more often after Tyler wore two daisies in her hair in a giddy mood one day a few years back. That made him think of the 1960s song from The Cowsills about a girl with flowers in her hair.

"That time you walked around with daisies over your ear all day was funny..." he told her. "You get so silly at times."

"I was in a silly, happy mood, and I want to feel that way again!" she yelped. "And right now, I need to do something to get my mind off things."

"I knew, I knew, I knew, I knew she had made me happy," Aaron sang, not doing a good job of singing the song. "Flowers in her hair, flowers everywhere... I love the Flower Girl... Oh, I don't know why, she simply caught my eye. I love the Flower Girl. Was she reality or just a dream to me?"

"Okay, okay, you can stop now," Tyler chuckled, her face flushed.

"Does that embarrass you?" he asked her.

"Kind of," she replied.

"That could be your theme song."

"Yeah, you're right."

"What do you want to do to help get your mind off things?" he asked her.

"Let's go to the fort and organize our baseball and hockey card collections," Tyler proposed. The fort she was referring to was a six-foot-high room on top of a shed in her backyard with a door and windows. Her father built the room for Tyler when she was eight, and she and Aaron often whiled away time there. They kept a collection of hockey and baseball player cards in the room. A few cards were from the 1950s and 1960s and were kept in Ziplock bags to preserve them.

"I don't feel like sitting around and doing that right now,"

Aaron said. "I've been stuck in my house for a week. Let's go outside. I feel like going for a long bike ride somewhere."

"Can we do that on Monday? Let's go over our collection."

"But you're upset about your softball game. How will going over our baseball and hockey cards make you feel better? If it were me, I would want to do something else."

"I know, but I just found out that the 1979 Windsor sports card show is coming up next week at the Cleary Auditorium... We have duplicate cards we can trade for ones we don't have. I always wanted to get a rookie Reggie Jackson card, and you always wanted to land a Bobby Orr card. Maybe we can trade for them or buy them? We'll probably find a lot of other cards we don't have there, too, which we might want. They'll have the latest Topps baseball and hockey cards."

"You're such a guy," Aaron said. "You're more into collecting trading cards than my guy friends are." Tyler scowled at him playfully as her eyes continued to smile. "You know what I mean."

"I'm just a girl who's into collecting hockey and baseball cards," Tyler asserted. "We haven't gone over our collection forever. Would you be okay doing that?"

"Okay," Aaron said, reluctantly acquiescing to her request.

"Cool," she said. "And when we're done, we can go swimming in my pool if my mom goes out somewhere. She probably will."

"Why do we have to wait until your mom leaves?"

"My dad chlorinated the pool before he went to work this morning. My parents don't want people in the pool for at least eight hours after they chlorinate it," Tyler said. *"You know their eight-hour rule when they chlorinate the pool,"* she sang.

"They must have a good reason for their rule because they've had it forever," he suggested, yawning yet again. "The water's probably toxic. Chlorine is pretty much like bleach. It can soak into your pores, which can't be good."

"My dad shocked it at seven-thirty, Mister Sleepy-head, and it's now..." Tyler looked at her watch. "It's getting near twelve-thirty, so that's like close to five hours ago. The chlorine level should be okay by now. Anyway, we'll kill another hour easy, sorting through our cards."

"Their eight-hour rule does seem a bit much," Aaron declared.

"They think chlorine is like Agent Orange," she said. Agent Orange was a cancer-causing herbicide the United States military used in the Vietnam War to kill jungle foliage. "I've snuck into the pool right after my dad chlorinated it and never ended up losing skin or getting rashes or anything nasty. I don't have cancer as far as I know."

Aaron claimed he had gotten a nasty sore last summer when they had been swimming too soon after the pool was chlorinated. That never happened. He was kidding, but for a moment, Tyler thought he was serious.

Aaron chuckled.

"You're lying," Tyler yelped. "You would have told me about that." She slapped his hand. "Anyway, let's go," she said, rising from her chair. Tyler grabbed her hat and glove and began toward the back door. Aaron started after her. She slammed the door closed to impede his progress after stepping outside.

Tyler was a good twenty feet in front of him when Aaron left the house and in the fort when he caught up with her. "What took ya so long?" she gasped, catching her breath.

"You shouldn't have closed the door so hard," he admonished her. "That wasn't cool because my mom probably heard it." Aaron went to the wall opposite the fort's entrance.

"You know my mom loves to ride my ass," he said after sitting on the floor. "She's going to yell at me when I get home if she heard the door slam. She'll go on about how the door could have broken and ask me why you slammed it... My mom's gonna be mad at you."

"I didn't mean to make a scene," Tyler said. "Please tell her that I'm sorry. I was just trying to slow you up. I hope she's not mad at me and I don't get you in trouble. I'm sorry, Aaron. As you said, that wasn't cool."

"It's okay. Don't worry about it," Aaron told her. "I'm used to my mom yelling at me. She says one of my middle names is trouble, but that should be your middle name."

"How do you figure?"

"You always cause trouble and get away with it. That's how."

"I do not!" Tyler yelped.

"Yes, you do," Aaron said. "Remember that little incident during recess a few months back?"

"What are you talking about?" she asked him.

Aaron replied, "You went into the bush with some other kids." The bush, called Oakwood Bush because it bordered the eastern and northern edges of the school's property, was out of bounds. Students were prohibited from leaving the property during school hours. "Everyone but you got caught by Ms. Olsen," he said, referring to a woman who monitored the schoolyard during lunch and recess. "Ms. Olsen took them to the principal's office, and they got the strap."

"I can't believe they still allow the strap in school," Tyler said. "Like that's so sad that a principal can beat kids up by whipping them. That should be left for parents to do."

"I agree, but nice try to change the topic. You wanted to go into the bush and got the others to go with you."

"Okay, whatever," she muttered. "I can't help it if I got back on school property before they did when I saw Ms. Olsen walking toward us," she said. Ms. Olsen was a senior citizen volunteer who helped teachers monitor the schoolyard. "I told everyone she was coming, but they didn't listen 'cause they were too busy talking or just ignored me. I snuck back onto the school property when Ms. Olsen went into the bush. The others waited until she came over and caught them... It's not my fault they got caught."

"That's true," Aaron agreed. "But Ms. Olsen would have seen you if she wasn't half blind."

"Yeah, maybe," Tyler contended. "She was nice enough, but Ms. Olsen could be such a nuisance, always butting her nose into our business… And she was old and creepy looking with her cat eyed glasses from the sixties. You know old people scare me."

"Yeah, but she was just doing her job," Aaron said, speaking in the woman's defense. "She's a yard monitor, and they're supposed to get into kids' business if they act up or leave school property like you did."

"I suppose," Tyler conceded.

"You were lucky no one ratted you out."

"Yeah, I was," she agreed. "I lucked out on that one."

"And there was that time you stole money from kids at school."

"When? I never stole from anyone."

"Yes, you did."

"Tell me when," demanded Tyler.

"You did that in grade two when you charged people twenty-five cents to tell them a secret based on something you made up. It was funny, but still, you stole from people."

"Oh, come on, man!" she exclaimed while turning a radio on. "I wouldn't call that stealing, and that was so long ago. That was just innocent childhood hijinks."

"Innocent, my ass," Aaron said. "You made up a story about Arlene Maysome." Arlene was a snotty classmate he and most of their peers did not like. "You told people you had a secret about her but would only tell them what it was if they gave you a quarter. And then you told them some out of this world story."

"But that's not stealing," Tyler insisted. "I never forced anyone to give me money. I just told them a little white lie, and they paid me for it."

"You lied to take their money, so how is that not stealing? The judge would say you took money under false pretenses if you had to go to court. You could have gotten busted for fraud and even thrown in jail if you were older."

"You don't need to be so over-the-top dramatic. I didn't think of it as stealing. Like, give me a break, man; I was only seven..." Tyler paused to reflect. "But you could be right," she said finally.

"Damn straight, I'm right," Aaron declared, chuckling. "And yeah, you were only seven, but you knew better. You told people Arlene pooped her pants when you were hanging out with her... It wasn't a nice thing to do, but it was funny. Me and most of the other kids in our class got a laugh out of it."

"Maybe I did know it wasn't right, or maybe I didn't," she said. "Maybe the devil made me do it? Yeah, whatever, I knew I shouldn't have done that... But I made seventy-five cents, which was pretty decent back then, and things were going good until Arlene found out after people started teasing her about what I told them. Remember she wanted to fight me after school? You know how I hid in the school until a quarter to five, figuring she would have gone home by then and that the coast was clear? Thank God Arlene wasn't waiting because I would have had to defend myself... I would have kicked her ass and felt bad about it, and my parents would have kicked my ass once someone from the school called them."

"You would have kicked her ass," Aaron agreed, confident that Tyler, stronger and taller than Arlene, would have won. "It all worked out. Arlene went home, and the kids you took money from let it go."

"I made up for it. I apologized to Arlene after she cooled off and gave the money back, so it was all good in the end. What I did wasn't nice, but I made up for it."

"Yeah, but would you have paid them back if you hadn't gotten caught?" he asked her. "I'm just kidding... I know you would have."

Tyler replied, "I would because, you know, my conscience would have kicked in and made me feel guilty... What I did wasn't cool, but that was a million years ago." "Give me a break already!" she exclaimed. "And I just had my tonsils out and was taking some pain medication. I remember that because it made me tired and feel weird."

"There are lots of other times you've gotten away scot-free with stuff," Aaron continued. "Like…"

"I suppose," Tyler said, cutting him short before he could cite other examples. "But you're no perfect little angel yourself, mister. You've done naughty little things and didn't get caught. Anyway, let's change the topic," she said, retrieving a shoebox containing their cards from a shelf. Tyler knelt, placed the box in front of her, and looked at Aaron. "You know, my-guy? I'm starting to feel a bit weird about coming up here."

"How come?" he asked her.

"Kids hang out in forts," she replied, placing the box's lid on the floor. "We're going to be in high school in September."

"I know what you're saying," Aaron said. "Maybe we are getting too old to hang out here."

"We have decent rooms in our houses where we can hang out when it's cold out," she suggested. "Maybe we can lounge around on couches and watch television or whatever, like most other people our age do… But I like having a place where I can be by myself, so I'll probably still come up here when I need to, to think about things… Me and you have spent a lot of time here, but we are getting a tad too old for this. People will think it's weird if they find out that we hang out in a fort."

"Probably," he said. "But since when do you care about what people think? You never have before. You always do what you want as long as it doesn't hurt anybody, and I love that you're a free spirit… You have too much confidence to be worried about what people think."

"That's true." Tyler chuckled, staring at the box. "I always do what I want to do because that's the way I go. That's the way I play… Always have and always will."

"What's so funny?" Aaron asked her.

"Do you ever wonder about… about what our folks think we do up here?"

"No, not really," he replied.

"Maybe they think we're being naughty," she said and grinned.

"Like doing drugs or smoking?"

"Maybe, but I'm not thinking about that," Tyler said. "There's no reason for them to think that we're getting high or smoking cigarettes because we're not stupid like that… And anyway, they would smell cigarette smoke on us, and I'm pretty sure they could tell if we were stoned."

"Well, what are you thinking?"

"Aaron, Aaron, Aaron," she sang. "Do I need to spell it out for you?"

"Yeah, please do."

"Come on, Beaver Cleaver," she said, referring to a boy in an old 1950s television series whose family they thought was the epitome of impossibly wholesome and lame. "Making out, silly," Tyler sang again. "You can be so naïve sometimes," she huffed. She began pulling cards from the box. "I'm talking about… like making out, dude."

"We've been coming up here forever."

"That we have. We've always been tight," Tyler said. "Remember when my mom told us that we were like two pieces of a puzzle that fit together because we always hung out?"

"She must have noticed that you followed me around like my shadow," Aaron said as he chuckled.

"You've followed me around like my shadow, too," Tyler countered.

"We've known each other as long as we've known ourselves," Aaron noted. "We kiss now and then, but so what?"

"I like doing that," Tyler said. "And that's so true about how we've known each other as long as we've known ourselves… I dig that. That's a cool thing to say."

"What got you worrying about what they're thinking?" he asked her. "Where did that come from?"

"A few of my girlfriends have asked me if you and I are boyfriend and girlfriend and if we make out. That got me thinking that our parents might think the same thing. They might think we're going at it out here."

"And what did you tell your friends?"

She giggled. "I told them maybe." She blushed.

"Maybe what?"

"Both," she chuckled. "But we are boyfriend and girlfriend. We don't think of it that way, but we are. We've always been boyfriend/girlfriend."

"What did they say?" he asked her, nodding.

"They just smiled and went on talking about something else."

"That would be funny if our parents thought that we're making out in here all the time, but they probably do," Aaron said with a laugh as he stroked Tyler's face. It never dawned on him what their parents were thinking about their relationship. As Tyler said, they were boyfriend/girlfriend. They had always been that.

Tyler grinned at him. "You're a big boy now, and I'm right behind you. You and I are going to get married one of these days."

"No one should care about what we do up here," Aaron said. "It's no one else's business — we're not doing anything wrong." Tyler smiled coyly at him. "We're just hanging out."

"Maybe we should make out now," Aaron said.

"Yeah, let's give people something to talk about."

"Let's go for it," he half-jokingly said. He kissed Tyler's lips and pulled her closer.

"I was just kidding," she said while touching his chest. She closed her eyes and leaned toward him.

Aaron planted his lips against hers, and they kissed again.

"Okay," she said after a moment of kissing. She pushed Aaron away. "We need to work on our hockey and baseball card collection."

Aaron smiled. He had always found Tyler attractive. They kissed many times before, but today was different. He was more aroused than ever.

Aaron asked Tyler how many cards they had in their collection and if she had counted them lately. Tyler said no, but there were three hundred and two cards the last time she counted seven months ago.

Aaron suggested they do a count; she was right; they had exactly three hundred and two cards. He was not surprised she was right because she had an excellent memory, as did he. They knew each player in their collection, where they were born, their birthdays, and career stats.

"We should separate the baseball from the hockey cards," she suggested. "I'll do the baseball cards, and you can do the hockey cards. After that, we'll separate them by teams."

Not caring for a song that came on the radio, she changed the station to one playing the single version of Heatwave's hit song 'Boogie Nights.' "Oh, my God! I love dancing to this!" Tyler yelped and pushed their piled cards against a wall. "We gotta dance!" she exclaimed, turning up the radio volume. "Hurry up," she told him, grabbing Aaron's hands and pulling him off the floor. "That's my favorite dancing song, and it's almost over."

"Alright," Aaron moaned. Though he didn't care to dance, he allowed her to lift him without resistance.

"Got to keep on dancing, keep on dancing… got to keep on dancing, keep on dancing," Tyler sang along with the song as they danced. She shuffled left and right in sync with its refrain. Impressed with her disco dancing and the way Tyler moved her feet and swung her arms, Aaron tried to emulate her moves.

They continued dancing, albeit less fervently, as a Lovin' Spoonful song played next. "Do you believe in magic in a young girl's heart?" Tyler sang, pointing at her chest. "How the music can free her whenever it starts. And it's magic if the music is groovy..."

Their fun ended when her mother yelled Tyler's name. "Oh, not now, Mom," Tyler moaned, lowering the radio's volume. She went to the door. Aaron followed. Mrs. Page stood at the bottom of a series of steps leading to and from the fort.

She wore her usual summer dress, sandals, and a floppy straw hat that somehow managed to stay over her big, permed hairdo.

"Hello, Aaron," Tyler's mother said.

"Hello, Mrs. Page," he responded.

"I need to go out and pick up a few things," she told Tyler. "I shouldn't be too long. I'll be back in an hour or two."

"Are you going grocery shopping?" Tyler asked her mother.

"Not today. I'm doing that on Tuesday."

"But there's hardly anything decent to eat," Tyler protested.

"We have lots of food," Mrs. Page said. "You'll be fine without junk food for a few days. You need money to buy food, and we won't have any until then... So, how did your softball game go? You never came into the house to tell me about it and let me know you were home. I only knew you were up there because of the music blasting from your radio."

"Oh, I forgot to report to you," Tyler snidely remarked. "Anyway, we lost if you really want to know."

"Again?" Mrs. Page asked her daughter, not acknowledging Tyler's challenging retort. Tyler rolled her eyes, clearly annoyed by her mother's response. Tyler hated losing and talking about it even more unless she chose to. "You girls lost again?"

"Yes, Maw; we lost again."

"That's too bad, honey," her mother said. "I'm sorry I haven't seen you play this year. I'll make sure I come to your next game. Your dad would probably have come out to watch you play today if he hadn't been working." Tyler's father worked in

Detroit across the Detroit River from Windsor, Ontario, where they lived.

"Don't worry about it, Mom," Tyler muttered in a condescending tone. She and Aaron watched through a side window as Mrs. Page approached the flower garden. "She could have come out today or at least driven me to my game," Tyler bitterly spat under her breath. "That's BS that she's gonna come to my next game. He won't either, even if he isn't working... I don't know why she even bothered asking me how my game went. It's not like she cares about what I do," she sighed. "And why did she have to say 'again'? That's so negative."

"At least she asked how your game went," Aaron noted. "That's a bit of interest."

"True, I'll give her that," Tyler said. "But they never come out to watch me when I play sports," she continued. "I've been playing softball and soccer forever, and my parents only bothered to watch me play a few times — same thing when I made Oakwood's basketball team. Neither of them came out to see me play, even though I was one of the top scorers last year in the WDSBJAL," she groaned, referring to the Windsor District School Board Junior Athletic League.

"Anyway, you would think my dad would at least see me play soccer a few times since he taught me how to play. And he's got plenty of time to coach my team... He just likes coaching guys' teams, but whatever. I'm the only one left who plays in the youth league, so it's not like he has seven other kids to worry about."

"That's not cool," Aaron said. "I don't get why your dad doesn't do that."

"At least he's taken me out to the soccer complex a few times to teach me things like freestyle tricks and different types of kicks. But that's all we've done together, just him and me... We do that, but he won't coach my team," she groaned. She was confused by that.

She giggled.

"Whoa. My daddy is too much of a big bad man to coach a 'whittle girls' soccer team!" Tyler sang in a mocking tone of voice. She giggled again, amused with herself.

"That's too funny!" Aaron laughed.

Aaron knew Tyler was frustrated by her parents' lack of interest in her athletic pursuits; they disappointed her. Still, he was surprised by the flippant way she spoke to her mother. That was not like her.

"And you wonder why I sometimes feel like I was a mistake," she huffed. "Case in point."

"I hate it when you say that," Aaron said, as Tyler had said that before.

"Are you staying up there?" Mrs. Page asked Tyler after she returned to the shed.

"Yes!" Tyler sharply replied without bothering to go to the door to engage her visually. "We'll be up here for a while." She made a face at Aaron and shook her head.

"Don't be snippy with me," her mother said. "That's not nice."

"What do you mean?" Tyler asked her mother, speaking in an innocent tone of voice. Tyler put a finger in her mouth as she grasped her throat like she was gagging.

"You know what I mean," Mrs. Page said. "And stop making faces at Aaron... I can see your shadow, so I know what you're doing. You have your hands around your throat like you're gagging, I assume because you're mocking me."

"I'm sorry, Mom," Tyler said. Her face reddened out of embarrassment; Aaron knew.

"We'll sit down and chat later," Mrs. Page promised. "I don't know what's going on with you, but we'll find out."

"I'm sorry," Tyler told her again. Mrs. Page walked away when Tyler went to the door to talk with her. Tyler tapped her mouth with her right hand as if to slap herself. "I'm probably going to Hell for that one!" she muttered.

"You might," Aaron chuckled. "You're supposed to honor your parents."

"It's not funny," she groaned while giving Aaron a light slap on his shoulder. "I respect them most of the time, but they bug me sometimes, and I just can't help it... There goes that devil again, making me do bad things!" she chuckled.

"Man, I would never get away with talking to my parents like that," Aaron said under his breath, watching Mrs. Page storm toward the house. "She was nice."

"I shouldn't have done that," Tyler said. "I feel bad for talking to her like I did, and now she wants to talk to me. That's not gonna go well."

"Just apologize for talking to her like you did and for mocking her," Aaron suggested. "Maybe she'll go easy on you."

"I said I was sorry," she sighed as her mother entered the house. "I don't like getting nasty with my parents or you, like I sometimes do... I told you my mom slapped me in the face when I said that I hated them in front of their friends because my parents always break promises. I shouldn't have said that; it humiliated them in front of company. That wasn't cool, but my mom slapping me in the face and leaving a mark that didn't go away for a few days wasn't cool either."

"I forget what brought that on," Aaron said.

"We were supposed to see a movie, but they backed out when friends of theirs called, and she invited them over," Tyler reminded him.

"Yeah, I remember now. I would have been angry, too."

"My mom and dad frustrate me so much, sometimes," Tyler continued. "They always had other things to do whenever I asked them to watch me play when I was doing well in basketball this year, and that hurt. I love my mom and dad with all my heart, and I'm sure they love me, too, but it would be nice if they were at least a little bit interested in the things I do. You know how that bugs me, how sad that makes me feel. And it's not only sports… I don't think they ever ask me how I'm doing in school. They didn't go to my grade eight graduation, and they haven't bothered to ask how I feel about attending high school… It really hurt that they didn't go to my graduation… They only want to know who I'm hanging out with, what I'm doing with them, where I'm going, and when I'm coming home… They probably don't even know I go to school."

"I get that you're upset with them, but my ass would have been kicked if I talked to my mom the way you just did," Aaron said.

"Well, they should at least make an effort. I'm telling you… I'm betting that I was a mistake."

"You weren't a mistake!" Aaron groaned. "Stop saying that."

"You don't know if I was a mistake, but I appreciate your trying to make me not think that… I'm the youngest by six years of eight kids. What's that all about?"

"Maybe they held off on having more kids because kids are expensive, and seven kids is a lot to take care of. Your folks probably needed a break… One diaper change after another, dealing with all that crying, and then to go through it again two years later when the next kid is born."

"Some of us are three years apart," she said. "But I hear you… I would want a break, too."

"You just want their love and approval," Aaron said. He felt terrible for her. It was obvious that Tyler was ignored at times.

"And time, and to be noticed," Tyler added. "Like, hi Ty, how was school? When's your next game? Maybe we'll come and watch. Geez, at least try… They always went to everyone else's things… At least it seemed that way."

"It would be hard to juggle that many kids and grandkids, and all the things they had going on, not to mention work and taking care of the house, the laundry, shopping."

"I get that, but my dad seems to have lots of time to coach a guys' soccer team with kids he barely knows," she replied while pulling up beside him. She began to caress Aaron's hair. "And it's just me now. I'm the only one still at home. But they want to know where I'm at, who I'm with, and when I'm coming home, so that's cool. I'm probably just being a suck ass." She chuckled while moving to sit in a different spot. "I'm probably missing all the attention I got when I was a baby. Maybe that's why I feel so needy."

"I don't think you're being a suck ass." Aaron hugged her. His situation at home was different. Without brothers and sisters, he had more than enough attention from his parents. More than he cared for.

He knew that Tyler loved it when one of her brothers or sisters came over, especially the ones with kids. She liked hanging out with her nieces and nephews and helping her mom care for them while she was babysitting. That was one benefit of being the youngest of so many siblings. Odds were there was a little kid around a few times a week.

Her father was often away from home in the evenings, and on weekends, he was working or coaching his soccer team. Other times, he was tired and needed time to himself.

"Anyway, I'll apologize again to my mom when she sits me down to talk, but I'll probably get grounded," Tyler huffed. "You know why I'm upset with her... And I don't think she's actually planning to go to my next game... We'll see, but I'm not holding my breath."

It made Aaron uncomfortable when Tyler got into it with her mom. He liked her mom; she said interesting things and had a wicked sense of humor, like his mom. Mrs. Page and his mom were good friends. But he was not better at biting his tongue with his mom either. Like Tyler, he was trying to stop doing that.

"Anyway, you sometimes get into with your mom, too."

"You're right."

Tyler smiled at him. "I know I am... Ugh, parents can be so

annoying! She and my dad claim poverty and talk to me like I'm stupid. They say money doesn't grow on trees when I ask them to buy me stuff." She paused. "I shouldn't say that because they are taking me to Europe, and that's probably going to cost them $5,000 or $7,000 or more... Maybe I should get a paper route or something and make some cash..."

"But anyway, my dad is a senior manager at the, and she's a nurse. They must make good money, yet here I am without anything good to eat."

"You're far from starving," Aaron said. "If I went through your kitchen, I would find lots of food. There must be something to eat."

"We have veggies, chicken, ribs, and junk, but no Kraft Dinner or SpaghettiOs, the stuff I like," Tyler replied.

"It could be worse," he said. "You could be a poor starving kid living in Africa or some other place where they don't have enough to eat."

'You're totally right," Tyler said. She smiled at him and chuckled. "By the way, I'm just making that up. We have food... I just wanted to see what you would say." She snickered. "I wanted to see if you would take my mom's side, and you did. It doesn't matter if you did or not. I just wanted to see."

"Hardy, Har, Har," he groaned. "You got me. You know what they say about paybacks though?"

"No, tell me," she said, knowing fully well what he meant.

"They're a bitch." Aaron shook his head and smiled. They like to kid each other, telling little white lies and then the truth after some amusement was had.

"I do want burgers, though, and the Kraft Dinner or SpaghettiOs," Tyler said while going to the window, where they had watched Mrs. Page walk to the garden. "We can go swimming after my mom leaves," Tyler said, looking at the pool. "I wish she would hurry up and go 'cause I need to cool off. I feel so hot and grungy."

Aaron looked at the above-ground pool after joining Tyler at the window. Its blue water looked inviting, as the air was uncomfortably hot and humid. "I want to go into the pool, but I don't like the idea of it still being saturated with chlorine," he said.

"The water should be fine by now," she told him. "Anyway, a little too much chlorine never killed anyone, as far as I know."

"I suppose," he sighed. "But what about our cards? We haven't sorted them out by teams like you wanted to do."

"We can do that later if you're okay with that. I just want to go swimming. You wanted to do something besides sitting around."

"Where are you going?" he asked her as Tyler backed toward the doorway.

"I'm going into the house to put my bathing suit on," she replied. "Are you going next door to get your bathing suit?"

"I'll wear my shorts," Aaron said.

"No," Tyler said. "You better go home and get another pair of shorts because the ones you're wearing might still be wet when you have to leave. My mom might notice they're wet."

"I gotcha," Aaron replied.

He hurried home and pulled on another pair of shorts over the ones he wore. Tyler passed him as he re-entered the backyard on her way back to the fort. She wore dark shorts and a black T-shirt he knew she put on to conceal her bathing suit.

Aaron looked over a tall fence through a window after they returned inside the fort, at Mrs. Page's car, anxiously waiting for her to leave. Tyler knelt beside him. Her body odor was noticeable and offended his nostrils. "You still smell a bit," he had to say.

"Give me a break already, would ya?" Tyler yelped, slapping his shoulder. "I wanted to tell you what went down at my game today, so I came straight here… It's because of you I stink."

"How is it my fault?" he asked her.

"Damn straight, it's your fault," she replied.

"You could have gone home and showered if you wanted to," Aaron said. "I didn't stop you from doing that. Don't go putting it on me, for you stinking up the place," he kidded.

"It's not necessarily your fault, but in a way, it is," Tyler said, chuckling. "You're my go-to guy when I'm bummed about something. If not for you, I would have gone home, showered, and changed, but I was anxious to talk with you because I was so upset."

"I'm just messing about you smelling. I don't care," he said.

"I know. Same here," Tyler replied. Tyler pulled a band off her arm and put her hair in a ponytail. "Anyway, like we always say, we accept each other unconditionally, no matter what... even if one of us is stinking up the place."

"What's taking your mother so long?" Aaron wondered aloud after a fair amount of time passed.

"She was about to leave when I left the house," Tyler told him.

Mrs. Page finally appeared in the driveway. "Well, it's about time," Tyler huffed.

They watched as her mother entered her car. It seemed like forever before the car reversed. The car slowly pulled away after backing onto Askin Avenue, the street their houses were on.

Tyler hurried out of the fort after removing her shirt and shorts while Aaron pulled off his shirt and outer pair of shorts. He followed Tyler toward steps leading to its deck, climbed them, and jumped into the pool, yelling, "Geronimo," as she had. Angst about swimming in thick chlorine succumbed to her lead, and his desire to cool off took precedent.

The water felt refreshing, regardless of how toxic it might have been.

Tyler moved away after he broke the surface beside her. "Let's play Marco Polo," she suggested. "You can be it."

"How come I'm it?" Aaron protested. "I'm always the first to be it when we play Marco Polo."

"Maybe most of the time, but not always," Tyler replied as she chuckled. "Maybe it just seems that way. Someone needs to be it, so stop whining. Now turn around and start counting," she told him, gesturing for Aaron to turn around by making a U-shape with a hand.

"Whatever," he muttered. Aaron began counting to ten. "One, two, three, four, I owe Ty for almost hitting me with my door. Five, six, seven, eight, she's lucky her face I do not break. Nine, and she had best be gone 'cuz I'm saying ten; she's lucky I don't kick her in the ass end." He turned around and started toward the middle of the pool, trying hard to keep his eyes closed. "Marco," he said.

"Polo," Tyler yelled. Aaron failed to touch her after leaping toward Tyler's voice. That happened a few more times before he touched her foot.

Tyler touched him shortly after he caught her. Soon after, Aaron made her it. And so, it went on as the lifelong friends alternated between making each other it.

"I'm done," Aaron announced after a long while had passed. Tired and bored with Marco Polo, he climbed out of the pool, sat on the deck, and rubbed his eyes. "The chlorine is bugging my eyes," he remarked as Tyler sat next to him.

"Rubbing your eyes is only going to make them feel worse," Tyler advised.

"What else am I supposed to do? They're irritating the crap out of me."

"Try not to rub them. You can dry your eyes with a towel when we get back to the fort."

"You could have brought a towel when we went to the pool."

"I didn't think of it," she told him. "By the way, my eyes feel fine. They don't bother me at all, just so you know."

"Yeah, well, lucky you," Aaron retorted.

"Geeze, your eyes are totally bloodshot," Tyler said, looking at him. "Weird, eh, how mine feel fine?"

"You already said that," he said. "Your eyes are barely red. Nothing ever seems to bother you."

"I must lead a charmed life," she surmised. "I didn't find the chlorine all that bad."

"You must lead a charmed life," he agreed.

"I usually do," Tyler replied. "Your eyes always get red when you go swimming in a pool. Your eyes must be super sensitive to chlorine."

"Yeah, you're probably right."

Tyler stood up, walked toward the steps, and descended them. Cuddles, one of her two cats, basked in the sun as Aaron followed her toward the fort. She sat on the ground, petting Cuddles and rubbing his belly. Her attention to Cuddles drew her other cat Elvis from under a shrub, no doubt wanting a taste of similar affection. Aaron continued toward the fort, focused on drying his eyes.

"Oh, Scrumptious, you're so jealous," Tyler said as Aaron reached the shed. That was a nickname she gave Elvis, his orange and white coloring making her think of a Creamsicle, her favorite treat.

"You probably confuse Elvis when you call him that."

"Oh no, he'll answer to both. He likes both his names."

Tyler's attention to her cats ended after the sound of a car door being closed came from the driveway. Mrs. Page had returned. Tyler followed Aaron into the fort. He crawled inside to avoid being spotted by her mother.

"Can you turn around so I can get out of my bathing suit?" she asked him while Aaron dried off with one of several towels she kept in the fort. He obliged. "You can turn back around now," Tyler told him after she removed her bathing suit, dried off, and pulled her shorts and shirt back on. She scooped his shirt and dry shorts off the floor and tossed them to him. "Here, put these back on."

"Now, you turn around," he asked her. He put the dry shorts and his shirt on.

Tyler wrapped her bathing suit in the towel she used to dry off. Next, she placed it, along with Aaron's towel and his wet shorts, behind a trash bucket. "I'm going to wash the towels, my bathing suit, and your shorts tomorrow when my parents are out of the house; at some point, they're both going to go out somewhere," Tyler said while combing her hair. "I can't bring them into the house now to wash them because my mom is going to get into my business and ask me what I'm doing. I'm already in trouble for being snotty to her... I'll for sure end up getting grounded if she finds out I went into the pool, and I'll probably get double the time you did because of bringing you with me."

"What if your mom notices water on the stairs and the pool deck?" Aaron asked her.

"I never thought of that!" Tyler exclaimed. "That's a good point. Oh well, I guess I'll just have to deal with it if that happens."

"The water should evaporate soon enough with the heat and the sun," Aaron surmised.

"I hope so," Tyler replied. "Oh, well, I don't care. "I'm not going to worry about it because I'm already in trouble, so whatever happens, happens... Anyway, I won't have a chance to wash our stuff and the towels until at least Monday because my parents and I are going to church tomorrow morning. Then me and you and the guys have a game in the afternoon," she said, referring to a game of soccer they planned to participate in. "And my parents and I are gonna be busy after dinner. The towels, my bathing suit, and your shorts will be okay after I wash them. A little mildew won't hurt them."

"So, are we going back to sorting our cards by teams and figuring out what cards we want to trade?" Aaron asked her.

"I'm not in the mood for that now," Tyler told him. "I'm bored with that. We can do that another day. Let's play chess instead if you're okay with that."

"Whatever," he said, sounding disappointed. He had been stoked to finish sorting the cards. "We really should finish sorting them since we already started, and you were all hyped up about doing that before next weekend."

"I hear you, but I'm in the mood to play chess. You want me to get my mind off the horrific softball game I had today. We're out of school now, so we'll have every day next week to finish counting our cards. Playing a few games of chess will be just the ticket to help me feel better."

"But we're just going to have to start sorting them all over again," he said, worried their card sorting efforts would go to waste.

"I'll keep the cards together," she assured him. "We have all day Monday to go through them if I don't get grounded for the way I talked to my mother." Tyler returned the shoebox to the shelf after they placed the cards inside it. Then she grabbed a box containing a chess set and put it on the floor. "I don't blame you if you're scared to play chess with me since I usually beat you," she taunted, unfolding the chessboard. She grinned.

"Yeah, yeah," Aaron groaned. "I'm really scared... I'm ready for you because I'm onto your strategy, which is pretty much the same as mine since I taught you how to play... You're going to lose! I'm going to kick yer ass."

"Aaron, you've been so patient with me," Tyler remarked as they placed pieces on the chessboard. "I've been bossy with you today, and you put up with it. I'm not my normal self. I'm sorry about that."

"It's okay," he said.

"I mean it, though," she insisted. "You wanted to go out on our bikes, and instead, you came over here to go over our card collection. You danced with me and were iffy about going into the pool, yet you still went swimming. Now I want you to play chess while you want to go back to sorting the cards... I love and appreciate you, man!"

"I know you do," he said.

"I've been so irritable lately," Tyler continued. "I felt bad for snapping at you when you said I smelled and for being snippy with you and my mom. I wish I hadn't done that. I don't ever want to make people feel bad, especially you and my mom."

"I was surprised by how you talked to her," Aaron said. "That's not like you."

"I'm stressing out because of how I played today, my parents, and tomorrow is the first anniversary of my grandpa's death... It's hard to believe that it's been a year already."

"He was so nice to me." Tyler's hand trembled as she dabbed at the corner of her eyes. Tears fell. Aaron held her. "He was interested in things I did. He watched me play sports, and you know, we liked doing things together."

"You guys did a lot of things together," Aaron said as he hugged her. Tyler figured that her grandpa tried to make up for the lack of attention she received from her parents.

"I'm okay now, Aaron, thanks," Tyler said while moving away. Her eyes were red and watery. She wiped at them with the sleeves of her shirt and took a deep breath. "But besides my grandpa, I'm stressing about changes I've been going through."

"What kind of changes?"

"Girl changes. I don't want to gross you out, but I've been having times of the month, if you know what I mean, and it's been freaking me out... And if you haven't noticed, my breasts are growing... It's a bummer thinking that I'm becoming a woman because I'm not ready for it. I still want to be a kid. I don't want to grow older right now. I like my life the way it is, and I'm scared about the future."

"I worry about the future, too, because the world is so messed up."

"I worry about the world's future too, but I mean my own future," she said. "It would be nice to have kids one day, but I don't want to be responsible. I just want to keep doing what I do and be nice about it."

"Not having to worry about having a job and paying bills is nice, but being an adult has its plus side," Aaron said. "At least we'll have a lot more freedom."

"I know, but I just feel anxious for some reason I can't explain," she groaned. "Like I said, I like how my life is now... And yeah, the world is messed up. My dad always told me I would find out how cold the world could be as I grew older. I just want to stay young and not have to deal with it. I feel so anxious about what's to come. It makes me want to cry when I learn about bad things that happen, like all the murders in Detroit and how kids live in poverty."

"I like how my life is too, but life goes on. You just have to flow with it is my take on things," Aaron declared. "I've gone through my puberty changes, and I'm okay with it... It freaked me out when I started getting hair where I never had it before. I'll never shave my armpits again or that spot above my little Mr. Friendly," he said, referring to his crotch. Aaron told her about a misadventure he had, shaving those spots when he was uncomfortable with his body's developing state. "I kept itching until the hairs grew back."

"I cringed when you told me you itched all over after shaving down there," Tyler said. "I haven't thought about shaving body hair yet, but maybe I will if I start looking like a wolfgirl, which I might because my skin's so white and my hair is so dark."

"I'm okay with having pubic and body hair now," Aaron said, chuckling, amused by Tyler's wolfgirl comment. "I like that I'm finally becoming a man, as long as I don't start looking like a wolfman."

"You're too blond and fair-skinned ever to have to worry about that," she surmised. "No one's going to notice body hair on you unless they have telescopic, superhuman vision..."

"At least I barely have any on my legs, chest, and arms," he said.

"I might look like an ape or something, because I'm so white.

"I worry about how things will be between us when we get older," Tyler told him. "I don't ever want to lose you. We've been tight forever, and I want us to stay that way."

"We'll always be tight as far as I'm concerned," Aaron assured her. "You are a major part of who I am and always will be."

"And you're a major part of who I am," she said. "But what if you become interested in other girls?"

"That's not going to happen. You'll always be my girl."

"And you'll always be my guy. But what if you start liking other girls?"

"That's not going to happen."

"I hope not," Tyler hummed, looking at a crucifix on her silver necklace. They were Christmas presents from her grandpa.

"But what if you start liking other guys?" Aaron asked her.

"Never, ever will I like other guys better than you," she replied. "Thanks for going through the cards and for swimming and dancing with me, by the way..." She put the necklace under her shirt. "You're such a sweetheart and have always been a sweetheart, you know... You're so awkward dancing, but you get a nice groove going once you start moving."

"You know I'm not a dancing kind of guy," he said.

"I know, but you can bust a move, man. You've got a groove going on once you get going. You're a good dancer, bud."

* * * * *

They played three chess matches. Tyler won the first, checking Aaron's king on her tenth move, and the second match ended in a draw. Frustrated after losing the third, Aaron sent chess pieces flying, swiping them away in anger.

"Take it easy, man," Tyler chided him. "Take a chill pill, dude."

"I should have won that game," Aaron angrily spat, hating to lose. "I messed up when I tried to check your king a few moves back. I had him trapped but screwed up by letting you out of it."

"You went after a pawn I sacrificed that you shouldn't have taken," she said.

"Maybe," he muttered through gritted teeth, looking at his watch.

"Well, you did. I wanted you to take it, and you did. That's how I was able to get out of it. You've got to give me some credit for that."

"I guess," Aaron said, angry with himself for falling into her trap.

"I played well," Tyler insisted.

"You played good games," he begrudgingly admitted. "You know I hate to lose just as much as you do."

"Losing is as much fun as getting a cavity filled," Tyler laughed as Aaron put chess pieces in the box. "We're both competitive, but someone has to lose. Today was just my day to win. Maybe the next time we play will be yours."

"Are you done playing?" she asked him. Tyler knew he had to leave by five; Aaron had told her he had to go with his parents to his aunt and uncle's house for dinner. "Don't you want to play anymore?" Tyler taunted.

"I want to play another game, but I have to leave because it's twenty-to-five," Aaron said.

"Well, you better get going. You don't want to be late," she suggested. "Since you just got done being grounded and all, you don't want to go through that again. God forbid you show up a few minutes late."

"Tell me about it," he complained.

"Where are you guys going?" she asked him.

"I just told you. We're going to my aunt and uncle's for dinner. It's my uncle's birthday," Aaron replied. Fond of his aunt and uncle and their older children, Kim and John, he did not care for their youngest son, Jeff, whom Tyler knew. "I don't like going there because of you know who."

"Jeff?" Tyler asked him. She smiled.

"Yeah, Jeff. You know I don't like him…. You're messing with me. You're asking me questions that you already know the answers to."

"Ya, I'm messing with you," she confessed. "I know you never liked Jeff, and I don't like him either because you told me he's a pain, a goof, and obnoxious. I think the same thing too, and I've only met him twice. He didn't even look at me after I said hello when I met him."

"Oh, well," Tyler said, laughing.

"What's so funny?" Aaron asked her.

"I'm just thinking about how you're not having a good day," she replied. "First, your eyes bugged you from the chlorine. Then I kicked your butt in chess. And now you hafta go and hang out with your favorite cousin."

"You can be as smug as you want about beating me in chess, but I'll kick your ass next time," Aaron warned her. He could have added to Tyler's list of bad things of his day; he did not mention the drama that might occur with his mother because Tyler had slammed the back door. But that was best left unsaid as Tyler felt bad for doing that. "Just you wait and see. And don't forget that I was the one who taught you how to play chess."

"I just got lucky today… somehow I managed to make the right moves," Tyler said. "I know you're not happy about losing, but it's only a game."

"Ha, ha," Aaron said. "You don't need to be modest about it. You know exactly what you're doing… and that's pretty awesome that you seem to think a few moves ahead."

"I think three moves ahead and sometimes four, which isn't too shabby for someone who hasn't been playing all that long," she declared.

"Anyway, I'll get you next time," Aaron promised on the way out of the fort. "I'll see you later, Flower Girl," he said after reaching the ground.

"Good night, bud," Tyler bid him.

Aaron looked at her after reaching the driveway and waved. She waved back. How he loved The Flower Girl, he thought while crossing over the front lawn of Tyler's house.

Chapter Two
Friends

"What took you so long?" Aaron asked her, when Tyler arrived at his house at five to one o'clock Sunday afternoon. He was on the verge of going next door to see what was happening, as she was running late. "We're supposed to be at the soccer field by one. I started thinking you got grounded."

"Nope," Tyler said. "I'm sorry about being late. I just finished lunch because we got home from church later than usual."

"So, what did your mom say about you talking back to her?" he asked.

"She said she was hurt and asked me not to disrespect her like that again," Tyler replied.

"That was it?" Aaron asked her.

"What? Did you expect her to beat me or something?" she snickered as he left the porch.

"No, I didn't expect her to beat you! I'm not trying to be funny because she's slapped you before."

"She knew I felt bad enough as it was. We had a good talk. She knows I love her and that I only acted like I did because I was upset that they don't seem interested in what I'm doing."

"What did she say about that?"

"She denied it. They're interested in everything I do, so she claimed. She said she has a lot to do, with eight kids who need her and has to do a lot of babysitting and stuff."

"That's good that you guys talked things out. I can see that. You have a lot of brothers and sisters, and then there's your nieces and nephews."

"Yeah, I guess, but she's not always as busy as she says."

"And don't forget, Joe was twenty by the time I was born, and

Janice was eighteen," Tyler said, referring to her oldest siblings. "Anyway, asking me how my life is going and coming out to see me do things once in a blue moon isn't asking for much."

"That's true," Aaron replied. "That's good that you guys talked, but that sucks that your mom keeps denying things and never apologized for not going to your games."

"By the way, my mom didn't say anything about you slamming the door," Aaron told her.

"That's good that it didn't become a big deal. Maybe she didn't even notice."

"I dig those sunglasses you're wearing," he remarked. Tyler sported black, Ray-Ban Wayfare sunglasses. The sun, sky, and Aaron's face reflected off the dark black lenses. They were so dark it was impossible to spot her eyes.

"They don't look goofy, do they?"

"Not at all. The glasses look cool. Where did you get them?"

"In Detroit, when my mom and I went shopping there last week."

"They look expensive."

"They're Ray-Bans," Tyler said as they reached the street. "They were on sale for forty-five dollars American, which is like forty-eight Canadian with the exchange rate."

"And you complain because your mom didn't have enough money to go grocery shopping until Monday," Aaron said.

"What makes you think I didn't buy them with my money?" Tyler asked him.

"Easy, you don't have any money. The only money you have is from your six-dollar weekly allowance."

"Okay, so I didn't necessarily buy them with my cash, but I could have," she insisted. "You know I'm good at saving my allowance... But whatever, my mom bought them for me."

"You look like a rock star, a female Mick Jagger, a white female Stevie Wonder, or a blues musician. Toss a beret on you, and you'd be all set."

"Jazz guys wear berets," Tyler said. "Guys who play the blues wear derby hats. I don't know what I'm talking about, but I think that's the case."

"Derby, smerby, whatever. I don't know."

They began walking down a graveled lane leading from Askin after passing two houses, one where Wayne lived at the corner. They referred to the lane as the stone road. The road cut through woods called Oakwood Bush, passed the school, and ended at a highway. They played soccer on a field inside the schoolyard.

He glanced at Tyler, looked down the road, and became lost in thought. He thought about the kissing they had done the day before. He liked it, and so did she.

Still, he worried that the inevitable was coming and that their relationship would change as they got older. It had been on his mind over the last year. Puberty was changing things. Tyler was prettier now in his eyes than she had ever been. Would they still be tight as they pledged they always would be, or would they become attracted to someone else and go their separate ways? He wanted to tell her how he was feeling, but wary of risking their friendship, he would wait for now to see how things played out.

"I hope the guys aren't going to be mad because I made us late," Tyler said, taking him away from his thoughts. "Probably, everyone is waiting around and wondering where we are."

"They shouldn't be angry with us — everyone's been late before."

"True," she sighed.

"Andy's bringing a cooler of ice water," Aaron told her.

"Well, that's good… it'll be nice to have some cold water to drink," she said, kicking at a stone and sending it skipping along the road. Her mind seemed to be elsewhere. He knew she was thinking about her grandpa.

"Are you okay?" he asked her.

"I'm good," Tyler replied. "I'm happy my grandpa died quickly. It was horrible for us, but he probably didn't suffer a horrific death, and that's a blessing. I'm grateful for his sake."

"I don't plan on dying for at least a hundred years or so, but when I do, I want death to be quick," Tyler continued. "It might be selfish to think that way, dying before people can say goodbye to me, but that's how I want to go."

"What about you?" she said to Aaron. "Do you ever think about how you might die?"

"No."

"Never?" she asked him.

"No, I never have. I don't like to think about death."

"Death is so scary," Tyler said as she kicked a large stone down the road. "I wonder what it's like to die and be dead. What if there isn't a Heaven? I know there is, but still. What if you end up just being in the ground after you die? What if you rot away, or if your spirit stays in your grave, and you can see life go on without you from there? What if that's going on with my grandpa? Maybe he's just stuck in his grave watching life go on," she wondered aloud.

"There's a Heaven," Aaron declared. "You have to keep the faith... And people start rotting not long after they die, so I guarantee he's not down there looking on."

"I'm certain, too, that there's a Heaven, but sometimes, it's hard to have faith," Tyler whispered. "I hear about bad things happening to people I know and strangers on the evening news. I also read horror stories in the newspapers, especially my dad's paper, with people getting murdered every day in Detroit and living in poverty. Sometimes life seems so hard and unfair... not for me, but for others.

"Oh, well, I can't get hooked on all that unless I want to get depressed... Let's talk about something else because I'm feeling sad enough as it is. Unless you want to talk about your grandpa."

"No, I'm okay," Aaron said.

"It sure would be nice to have a little more Heaven on Earth... Oh, well."

He was just about to tell her about the dream of her in the coffin, having debated whether to do so, with her mind on her grandpa. It seemed perfect timing, with her talking about death, but maybe not. She had enough gloom on her mind.

"I'm going to my grandma's later," Tyler continued. "We're going to the cemetery to visit my grandpa and then to her place for supper. I've been to his grave six times and cried each time. Hopefully, it'll get easier someday… I hope I don't bawl my eyes out and embarrass myself."

"I'll be thinking about you," Aaron told her, gazing into the bush, a mix of trees, grasses, and ponds. The bush was their playground in younger years, where they had spent many a summer day climbing trees, catching crayfish and tadpoles, and doing whatever. They reached a wildlife sanctuary inside Oakwood's grounds farther down the lane. A large pond and feed bins constantly replenished by student volunteers drew ducks, geese, and pheasants to the sanctuary.

The soccer field was adjacent to the sanctuary. Wayne and their other friends, Andy, Carl, Scott, Allen, and Allen's twin brother, Steve, were at the field when Aaron and Tyler arrived. Allen held a ball stained by earth and grass. Tyler apologized for running late.

"I love your sunglasses," Carl commented to Tyler.

"Thanks," she replied. "That's if you mean it." Carl often made sarcastic comments.

"Of course, I mean it," he said. "They're cool. I like 'em."

"Well, thanks."

"They look just like the sunglasses that Roy Orbison guy wears."

"Whoever he is," Tyler huffed.

"You never heard of Roy Orbison?" Carl asked her. "Roy Orbison is a singer who's been around forever."

"Maybe I'm dumb," she groaned. "I heard the name, but I don't know much about him."

"I'm not saying you're stupid." Carl gave Tyler an unsure look, apparently caught off guard by her comment. "Relax. I don't know much about the guy either, just that he wears glasses like the ones you're wearing."

"I'm sorry," she said to Carl while hugging him. "I'm feeling a little sensitive today."

"You're probably thinking about your grandpa. He died a year ago today, I think."

"Oh, Carl, that's so awesome that you remembered that," she sighed. "You're so sweet. And, yeah, I'm thinking about him."

"Are you doing okay?" he asked her.

"Yeah, I'm alright. Thanks for asking," Tyler replied, nodding. "I miss him so much." Her voice cracked as she spoke. Aaron hugged her in a comforting effort. "Thanks, Aaron," she haltingly whispered, clearly attempting to hold back tears. "I'm going to be alright," she assured him after pausing.

"I know how it feels," Scott said. "It sucked when I lost my grandpa."

"Yeah, I know," Tyler softly remarked, stepping away from Aaron.

"So, where did you get your sunglasses?" Andy asked her.

"At the Fairlane Mall."

"I like 'em. I want to get me a pair."

"Thanks," she said. "Anyway, I haven't played goal forever. I want to play goal today."

"That's cool," Allen said. "I'll play goal for the other team."

It was Andy and Wayne's turn to captain each team of four players, which meant they picked the teams. Steve tossed a coin to see which captain won the opportunity to begin selecting players. Andy picked Tyler first, the only one of the group that played in a soccer league, as she was the best player of the eight, and then Aaron and Scott. As captains, Andy and Wayne got to pick heads or tails in a coin toss to determine first possession of the ball at kickoff and what side of the field they wanted to start on. Wayne won that toss.

Steve arrived at midfield and looked at his watch. "It's almost fifteen minutes after one," he declared. "Okay, so because it's hot, are we going to play a full hour and twenty minutes as usual, or do we want to go with ten minutes a period and stop at a quarter past two?" Steve asked the others. No one answered. "Okay, we'll go the usual hour and twenty minutes." "We'll stop at twenty-five to three," he added while digging at his crotch.

"Itchy balls, eh?" Wayne chuckled.

"Turn around and do that, man," Tyler said, feigning offense. "No one wants to see you scratching your privates."

"Yeah, there's a lady here," Allen chimed in.

"Thank you," Tyler said. She smiled at Steve. "Do whatever you need to do. I'm only messing with you."

Steve smiled back, as he placed the ball on the ground. "Let's rock and roll, he said, while jogging backwards to his side of the field.

The game began after Wayne kicked the ball to Carl. Scott caught up to Carl, who ran as fast as his skinny legs could take him toward Tyler. Carl passed back to Wayne, whom Aaron covered. Aaron stepped toward the ball as Wayne hesitated.

It was a trap as Wayne moved the ball after Aaron committed and fed it back to Carl. Pushed forward by momentum, he fell after kicking at air and watched helplessly as Carl closed in on Tyler. Carl moved to his left, kicking the ball hard and upward at the net. Stepping forward and good at narrowing angles, Tyler smothered the ball after knocking it down.

The game continued with the ball mainly in Allen's half of the field. The heat became oppressive. Everyone was wiping sweat from their foreheads and eyes. Aaron wished he had voted for playing for an hour.

Tyler made the best play of the game when she kicked the ball with authority halfway across the eighty-yard field, where Andy received it in full flight on the right side. Andy, who could run fast, arched toward the center of the field and kicked the ball over Allen's shoulder into the upper right corner of his net. Allen had no chance to stop it.

Tyler jumped up and down and clapped in glee at placing the ball so well and Andy delivering; Aaron, Scott, and Tyler high-fived each other. Aaron hugged her tight and turned away, smiling, happy and proud of her, and pleased that something good had happened to her on this day. Andy ran to Tyler, picked her up, and told her that was the best pass he had ever seen. Tyler stretched her arms out in triumph.

Soaked in sweat, stiff, and dogged tired, Aaron and the others were happy when time ran out. The final score was three to one in his team's favor. Better yet, he scored two goals against Carl's one as an unstated competition existed between them. Aaron was the second-highest scorer behind Tyler the previous year, but now Carl had assumed that spot, and Andy was right behind him. Tyler remained number one.

Years of playing soccer and practicing with her dad paid off. The boys were in awe of her footwork with the ball and the power Tyler had when she kicked it. They also liked watching her juggle the ball and do other freestyle tricks when she had time to warm up before games.

"That pass you made was amazing," Allen told Tyler as the friends gathered under a tree around Andy's cooler. "You couldn't have placed it better."

"Thanks, Allen!" Tyler replied. She smiled as they friend-hugged each other.

"Yeah," Carl said. "That was sweet!" he exclaimed as he and Tyler high-fived.

"I stopped you pretty good a few times," Tyler chimed at Carl. She had reason to boast, having made several saves against him, some of which were spectacular. With an innate knack for positioning herself well, Tyler excelled at goaltending.

"You got lucky there, Tyrone," Carl said. He and Tyler liked poking fun at each other, and he called her Tyrone in his own fun because Tyler had told him she did not like it. He derived Tyrone from Tyronious, one of her more common nicknames. Sometimes he called Tyler 'Tex,' a nickname she acquired because she was born in Texas. She was okay with that name. "Anyway, I went easy on you," Carl claimed. "I wouldn't have wanted you to break a nail or something." He looked at Andy and laughed at his blatantly sexist-tinged comment.

Tyler, who had a habit of biting her fingernails, glared at him.

She threw a hand in his face to show him that her nails were short. "My nails are probably shorter than yours are," Tyler crowed. She punched Carl's shoulder and ran away from him.

"Candy ass chickenshit." Carl laughed, taking a few steps after her.

"We should play later after dinner when it's hot like this," Andy suggested.

"I hear ya," Allen said. "I'm dying out here."

"I'm down with that," Tyler said after returning to the cooler and sitting beside it. Thinking that the confrontation with Carl was over, she had put herself in a vulnerable position should he go after her again. Sure enough, he walked over and gave her a playful kick in the side as she rolled away. Tyler rose to her feet and kicked Carl's right knee moderately hard.

"You two need to calm down," Andy told them.

"Ya, let's chill out," Tyler told Carl.

"Agreed," Carl replied.

They hugged in an affectionate reconciling manner, and then they sat down next to each other.

"What if we start playing earlier before the heat kicks in?" Andy proposed.

"I can't play on Sunday mornings," Tyler declared.

"Oh, that's right," Andy said. "Your folks make you go to church."

"They don't make me go to Mass," Tyler told him. "No one

makes me do anything… I do what I do because I want to."

"I'm busy on Sunday mornings, too," Scott said.

"What? You also go to church?" Carl asked him.

"Sometimes," Scott replied. "What's that to you?"

"Who cares if we go to church or not?" Tyler said to Carl. "I love God and feel connected to Him, and maybe Scott does as well. But whatever. As Scott says, it shouldn't matter to you."

"Come on, Tyrone. I'm just messing with him," Carl said.

"Stop calling me Tyrone!" She stood and arched her foot, acting as though she were going to kick him again, and then went over to where Aaron was sitting and sat beside him. "That's a stupid nickname, and I never liked it. I've told you that!"

"Okay," Carl promised. "I'm not going to call you that again."

"What if we play on Saturday morning?" Andy suggested.

"I play softball Saturday mornings," Tyler advised. "That's until the second week of July or longer if my team makes the playoffs. We probably won't, but if we do, I could have a game anytime during the day and in the evening, too."

"Okay, let's play on Sunday evenings," Andy proposed. "We could start at six."

"That works for me," she said.

"Me, too," Wayne told him.

"And me," Steve said.

"And me," Scott agreed. "I usually don't have anything going on, on Sunday nights."

"I'm okay with that," Carl said.

"So, where did you get Tyrone from anyway?" Tyler asked Carl. "You've been calling me that for a while now. It didn't bother me at first, but it's getting old."

"I heard it in some movie," he replied. "A guy in the movie was named Tyrone. What's wrong with calling you Tyrone?"

"Tyrone is a black guy's name, that's what. I'm not black, and I'm not a guy. And besides, I told you I don't like it."

"Tyrone could be short for Tyronious," Carl chuckled.

Everyone except Aaron and Tyler laughed. "Ha, ha, ha," she said, glaring at Carl. "You're a clown, Carl."

"Well, I'm out of here," Andy said after getting to his feet. "If you guys want more water, you better get it now because I'm dumping out the cooler."

"I'm fine," Allen sighed. "I'm leaving, too. I have to help Carl fix his bike."

"Screw you, you do," Carl angrily spat, no doubt embarrassed, the proud person that he was, that people would think he was not able to fix his bike. "Don't be telling people I can't fix my bike... "You invited yourself over to my house to supposedly help me fix my bike. I don't need your help."

"Whatever," Allen replied.

Andy emptied the water cooler after Aaron refilled the plastic cups he and Tyler drank from.

"Well, I'm off," Carl announced. "Goodbye, Tyronious," he bid Tyler. "You know I'm just kidding," he said. "I won't do it again."

Allen, Andy, Carl, and Steve started toward the stone road. Scott walked in the opposite direction toward his house across Cabana, a primary road that fronted Oakwood. He had to get home to cut grass on the large expanse of property his house sat on.

"Yeah, see ya later, Tyronious," Allen yelled at Tyler. "I'm just kidding," he added.

"Whatever!" Tyler yelled back, looking at him. She shoved her thumbs in her ears, waved her fingers, and stuck her tongue out.

"Don't let Carl and Allen get to you," Aaron suggested. "They're just messing with you."

"I know," she sighed. "They're both so silly. Silly boys, those two are."

"I think they're calling you Tyrone and Tyronious in an affectionate kinda way. They might have been trying to get your mind off your grandpa."

"Probably, that could be true," Tyler replied. "Maybe they are doing it in an affectionate way, but Carl sometimes gets to be a little too much. He can be so sweet, like how he remembered today was the anniversary of the day my grandpa died and asked me how I was doing. But I don't like it when he calls me Tyrone. It bugs me... It's like he's making fun of me for having a guy's name." "I don't think he means it that way," Aaron said.

"You know I've always been sensitive about my name. I like it, but I don't know about any other girl named Tyler."

"There must be a few," Wayne surmised. "I knew of a girl named Toni and another one named Bobbie. I like your name, and it fits you to a T because you are a bit of a tomboy. Tyler seems like it could be a girl's name to me."

"Well, thanks," she replied. "I do like that my name stands out; that's pretty cool... At least my parents didn't name me Stanley or Frank."

"That would be something," Aaron mused.

"What are you guys doing later?" Wayne asked them. "The 'Muppet Movie' just opened. It's playing at the mall tonight."

"How 'bout we watch it sometime next week?" Tyler suggested. She put her sunglasses back on while staring at the ground; she had removed them before playing net to avoid breaking them. "I'm going to my grandma's tonight."

"I still can't get over that it's been a year since my grandpa died. I was so upset... I cried and cried... I began to think that I would never stop crying... It was just so sudden, so out of the blue, when he died. It's not like I had a chance to prepare for it... it just happened. I talked to him the day before on the phone. He was going to take me to a Tigers game the next Friday night... I miss him so much. I wish I could have seen him one last time, but I'm glad he died suddenly. I don't think he suffered because he died in his sleep... I just hope he didn't."

"We were so close," Tyler continued. "We did a lot of things together. My mom said he hurried home from work when I was a baby, and my grandma took care of me when my folks were at work. He took me to Tiger and Red Wing games, and we liked taking long country drives together. He called me his little princess." She took a deep breath and exhaled. "I wish I'd had a chance to say goodbye to him."

"There might be a way you can do that," Wayne claimed.

"How so?" she asked him. "What are you talking about?"

"Do you know what a séance is?" he asked her.

"Duh. I know what a séance is. I've heard of them, but I don't believe in them. I don't think there's a way of contacting people after they die. Séances are nonsense."

"I thought the same thing until my sister told me she and her friends tried one," Wayne said. "It seemed to work. At least that's what my sister told me."

"Don't play around with her," Aaron told him. "She's upset and doesn't need to hear made-up stuff."

"It's okay, Aaron," Tyler said. "I want to hear about it."

"I'm not lying," Wayne contended. "I'm just telling you guys what my sister told me. I'm not making nothing up."

"Okay, so tell us what happened when they tried the séance," Tyler asked him.

"My sister said they started to do a séance in the basement at my house," Wayne replied. "Supposedly, the light in the room went dim. A face began to form on the television screen. They freaked out and stopped the séance, and the image went away." He paused. "I don't think she was lying. I could tell she was bummed out when she told me about it. She's always straight up. My sister always has her nose in her university books. She's a nerd and doesn't play around because she's too uptight for that."

"Okay, Wayne," Aaron sighed. "Whatever you say."

"I'm just saying what my sister told me."

"And you believe that?"

"I don't think she was lying," Wayne said. "She seemed pretty serious. I'm not saying I believe it or not. I'm just telling you guys what she told me."

"How did they learn how to do a séance?" Tyler asked him.

"You know Old Man McFarren, who lives on Normandy Road?" Wayne asked her.

"That kooky, creepy old Englishman who lives in the house at the end of the road?" she said, looking disappointed. "That's the guy you're talking about?" Every kid in the area knew of the man: a local legend, because he was weird and reputed to have a mean and nasty disposition.

"Yeah, him," Wayne said. "My sister claimed he taught them how to do one."

"So, they just went and talked to the guy?" Aaron asked him. "No one I know has the guts to go up to that house."

"My sister knew his daughter from high school," Wayne claimed. "They hung out together. His name is Zachary McFarren."

"I can't believe that man has a daughter," Tyler hummed. "I would hate to be her based on what people say about him."

"Yeah, I couldn't believe he had a daughter either," Wayne said. "She doesn't live with him anymore... My sister went to see her at her house. McFarren said she went to live with her mother the last time my sister tried to visit her... A guy in their class was killed in a car accident, and my sister, the girl, and their friends were all bummed out about it. They wanted to communicate with the guy. The daughter said her father knew how to do a séance and supposedly gave them a list of words to say and instructions on how to do one. They started the séance, but like I said, they stopped because their friend's face started forming on the TV."

"Does your sister still have the words?" Tyler asked Wayne.

"No," he replied. "A friend of hers had them and took them with her when she moved or got rid of them."

"Well, I want to contact my grandpa if it's possible," Tyler said. "I want to talk to the man. He might be creepy and all, but if I have a chance to say goodbye to my grandpa, I would love to do it. Doing that would make me feel so much better, even though I'm not sure if it's good to try a séance or not."

"You actually want to see him?" Wayne asked her. His eyes grew large. "I don't know if I want to meet with the guy."

"Yeah, why not?" she huffed. "It's not like the guy's going to kill us or something. Your sister supposedly saw him, and he never hurt her… She came out alive." Tyler chuckled nervously. "But I understand if you don't want to see him. Aaron and I can go over there by ourselves, right, bud?" she said, looking at Aaron.

"Do I have a choice?" Aaron asked her. Regardless of what Tyler said, he had to go with her as there was no way he would let her go there alone.

"Not really," she said. "I don't want to go there alone, and you're my main bud. You're not afraid of the big bad old man, are you?"

"No," Aaron reluctantly replied. He looked at Wayne. "Well, come on, man, are you going to come with us? You better because you're the one who brought this up and got her thinking about going there."

"I'll go with you guys," Wayne affirmed. "I'm not crazy about it, but I'll go if Tyler wants to see him."

"Cool," she said. "It'll be kinda fun to go to the guy's house. It'll be a rush because it'll be suspenseful to see how he reacts. I would feel so much better if he knew how to do a séance, and I could say goodbye to my granddad… So, you guys are *really* okay with going to see him?"

"If you are," Aaron said.

"And what about you?" Tyler asked Wayne.

"Let's do it," Wayne replied.

They passed the school on their way to McFarren's house and started down a lane leading from the school to Cabana Road. After crossing Cabana, they started onto a narrow path in a field abutting Scott's property. A path, traversed by foot, bicycle, and motorcycle tires that ended at Talbot Road.

Scott, busy cutting grass, waved at them from a riding mower. Aaron, Tyler, and Wayne waved back at him. "Scott must be wondering where we're going," Aaron surmised.

"He probably figures that we're going to the store," Tyler reckoned.

The Double D convenience store, the only convenience store within reasonable biking or walking distance from their neighborhood, was across Talbot, opposite the path. Double D occupied space above a Y-shaped intersection between Talbot and a road called Huron Church Line on its right. Normandy Road was half a mile down Huron Church Line.

The group followed the path to its end. After they descended a slope, they crossed Talbot and continued onto Huron Church Line toward Normandy Road. A rural road, Normandy, cut through farmland. McFarren's house was the last one before Normandy ended. A path leading from the road led into a forest.

"I don't think I told you guys this, but last summer, Scott and I had an encounter with McFarren," Aaron told them.

"Scott told me about it," Wayne said. "You mentioned that to me, too."

"You told me," Tyler reminded Aaron. "You said he stepped out from the hedges in front of his house, and you guys ran into the woods."

"Damn straight, we did," Aaron replied. "He stared at us with mean-looking eyes, holding the biggest hedge clippers I'd ever seen. I had the strangest feeling that he could look right through me."

"Aren't you exaggerating a little?" Tyler asked him.

"I'm telling you, the clippers looked like they could take down a small tree," Aaron said. "I'm not saying he could look right through me. It just seemed that way because of the way he stared at me... There was some weird look in his eyes that's hard to explain. It sent chills through me."

"He gave you a real mean look," Tyler said. "That's what you told me when you first told me the story."

"The guy was probably having fun with you guys," Wayne declared. "Scott said the same thing when he told me about the encounter. That it felt like the guy was looking right through him."

"Maybe you guys were just scared," Tyler surmised.

"Maybe," Aaron replied.

"Scott said he gave you guys a Clint Eastwood look," Wayne said.

"What do you mean by that?" Tyler asked him.

"You know that look Clint Eastwood gives when he's pissed off and about to shoot someone in his cowboy and *Dirty Harry* movies?" Aaron said. "When he gets all squinty-eyed and gives people a nasty look? Well, it was like that."

"Oh, I got you," she replied, pulling her sunglasses off. Tyler pointed her finger at him, making like she was holding a gun, squinted, and grimaced to conjure a mean stare. "This is a .44 Magnum, the most powerful handgun in the world, and it can blow your head clean right off," she snarled, quoting a line from the first *Dirty Harry* movie.

"Alright, put your gun away and chill," Aaron said. Tyler put her sunglasses back on.

"McFarren was probably just effing around with you guys," Wayne suggested. "He must know people think he's weird and scary. He was probably only trying to play up to his reputation."

"It seemed like he was messing around because he laughed at us as we ran into the woods," Aaron said. Whether McFarren was playing around or not, the look he gave them was chilling.

It honestly felt that McFarren looked right through him, perhaps at his soul, Aaron thought. He and Scott did not believe the McFarren was having fun as they ran, worried he might go after them. And yet here he was with Tyler and Wayne, on the way to his house.

"You don't think McFarren will go mental on us?" Wayne asked Tyler as they started onto Normandy Road.

"How would I know?" Tyler groaned. "I've never even seen him before."

"Well, you tell us," Aaron said to Wayne. "You said your sister talked to the guy. Your sister must have told you if the McFarren acted crazy. You probably know more about him than we do."

"As I said, if either of you guys doesn't want to come, that's fine," Tyler said. "You don't have to," she told Wayne.

"Oh no, he needs to come with us," Aaron insisted. "You're the one who told her about the séance," he said to Wayne, glaring at him. "We wouldn't be going there if it weren't for you."

"Relax, I'm going," Wayne said.

"Don't be mad at him," Tyler said to Aaron. "Wayne was just trying to be helpful."

They passed the last house before McFarren's, which loomed on their left. The A-framed peaked roof of his house rose between maple, oak, and spruce trees as they continued past a small field between the houses. An ominous tinge, perhaps from tree shade or fear, likely a combination of both, darkened the house.

"What if the McFarren knows we're coming?" Aaron asked Tyler and Wayne, wondering if the McFarren was looking through a window just below the peak. "Maybe he's watching us from that window?"

Tyler stopped as they were about to walk in front of the house. Aaron and Wayne stopped with her. She looked at them. "Are you guys still okay with this?"

After much discussion regarding whether they should proceed, Tyler finally said, "Well, guys, let's do it. And it's not like your sister hasn't been here before. Nothing bad happened to her." She looked at Wayne.

"Not that I know of," Wayne told her. "My sister didn't

mention anything about the guy doing anything wrong to her or trying to keep her and her friends from leaving."

"I'm sure the he's a nice old fart," Aaron sarcastically remarked.

"He might be," Tyler hummed. "None of us have talked to him. Maybe he's not as nasty as people say he is."

They started up a driveway in front of the house, Tyler in the lead, with Aaron and Wayne trailing a few steps behind. A cat hissed before darting behind a hedge as Tyler climbed steps leading to the McFarren's front porch. Unfazed, Tyler reached the front door and pressed a doorbell buzzer. The door opened as she reached toward the buzzer to press it again after a minute passed. She rested her sunglasses on her head.

"What do you want?" McFarren looked at Tyler and asked in a stern voice. She looked at him in silence: fear, Aaron assumed, rendering her unable to speak.

McFarren was taller than Aaron expected, looking to be about 6'3". His hair was a matted shock white, and he wore Colonel Sanders type-glasses. He had an unkempt beard on the longish side.

"Well, you better get on if you're not here for a reason," McFarren said, now casting his stare toward him and Wayne. "Kids like you come by and ring my doorbell and take off," McFarren growled. "I'm tired of your little game of ring and run," he said, looking Aaron in the eye. "Young lady, you and your two friends must think you're something else, ringing my door and having the nerve just to stand there and look at me," the man said to Tyler. "I'm going to find out who you kids are and talk with your parents and let them know you're a bunch of hooligans up to mischief."

"My name is Tyler, and this is Aaron," she said while glancing at him. "And this is Wayne..." "This might sound dumb, but we came to talk to... to... to... you about doing a séance," Tyler told him, stuttering. "We heard you knew how to do one."

Who told you that?" McFarren asked her.

"My friend here says that you taught his sister how to do one," she replied, glancing at Wayne.

"My sister said you know how to do a séance," Wayne mumbled, his voice trembling and barely audible.

"Speak up, boy," McFarren told him.

"My sister was a friend of your daughter's," Wayne said, speaking clearer. "She's probably full of it, but she said you taught her and some of her friends how to do a séance."

"What's your sister's name?"

"Lisa."

"Oh, Lisa," McFarren said. "I remember a girl named Lisa who came around to see my daughter. A pleasant girl she was. I haven't seen your sister since my daughter moved away to live with her mother out west."

"So, what's this séance business about, dear?" McFarren asked Tyler.

"We would like to try one, sir," she said. "I want to say goodbye to my grandpa, who died suddenly last year after a heart attack."

"Well, come on in then," the McFarren said, holding the door open. Aaron's heart skipped a beat. McFarren seemed to confirm what Wayne's sister claimed. Aaron stared at him as the three friends filed into the house, wary about what they might be getting into. "Take a seat," McFarren said, pointing at a couch in his living room.

Dust clung to the air, and the walls and carpet needed a thorough cleaning. Aaron noticed that Tyler's hands trembled while she stared at McFarren as the friends sat on the couch. Tyler grimaced while arching away when he tried to put his hand on her shoulder. She blushed.

"Don't be shy, sweetheart... I'm not going to hurt you," McFarren told her. "It's hard to lose a loved one," he said, sitting across from them. "God knows I've gone through that too many times to count… Death might seem final, but trust me, it's just a starting point to a better place."

"Your grandfather, I'm sure, is somewhere watching over you and wanting you to be with him when your time comes… There *is* a way of communicating with him… Have any of you tried to do a séance before?"

"I never have," Wayne stated.

"Me neither. That's why we came to see you," Tyler uttered hoarsely after sneezing. Her voice crackled. The dust bothered her allergies, Aaron knew.

"How about yourself, son?" McFarren asked him.

"I haven't tried one either," Aaron replied.

"Oh well, can't say that I expected you had," McFarren said. "To do a proper séance, you need to be in a dark room. There can't be any outside light in there, no outside light whatsoever. Could you grab that book there?" he asked Wayne. "It's on the top shelf behind you."

"That one right there?" Wayne asked, pointing to the only book on the shelf.

"That's it, boy; that's the only book up there," McFarren replied sarcastically. He thumbed through the book's pages after Wayne handed it to him and stopped where two folded sheets of paper were tucked inside. "You will need these," McFarren said, giving the sheets to Tyler. "One sheet has a pentagram on it. Instructions and words you need to say are on the other."

She unfolded the sheets and glanced at them as McFarren, Aaron, and Wayne watched. Aaron noticed as a confused expression formed on Tyler's face. She appeared to be taken aback.

"You need to post the sheet with the pentagram on a westerly wall," McFarren advised after she handed the sheets to Aaron. The sheet with the pentagram depicted a goat head on it, and as the man said, the other one had instructions and the words to be spoken.

Aaron read the words:

I speak to the spirits while doing this rite. I speak to one named while I cite these words. To communicate with (him or her) is what I seek, as there are words I've neglected to speak.
While in the clouds, the ground, and walking upon this earth, my aim is not to disturb you in your flight.
Dawn is to light as dusk is to night.
Forge the joy of your present place so as to bless me with your presence.
Bless me with your presence.
Bless me with your presence.
Bless me with your presence; I am with all my might.
To see you again, pray to make things right.
Bless one with your presence.
Oh, loved one, bless me with your presence.
Bless me with your presence.
Repeat…

"You need to put a table under the pentagram like the instructions say," McFarren continued. "You need two candles, one black, and one red, and candleholders to hold them in place. Put the black candle on the left side of your table and the red one on your right and light them. You need to put a silver chalice between the candles. Wear black clothing; otherwise, the séance won't work."

"Light the candles," McFarren instructed as Aaron tucked the sheets into a pocket of his shorts. "If you do it in a room with windows during the day, you need to cover them with a thick, dark blanket. Once you light the candles, someone needs to read those words I gave you aloud. There's a space where you can state your grandfather's name. Did you notice that, honey?" he asked Tyler.

"I noticed," she replied.

"Do you kids have any questions?"

"Not that I can think of," she said, her voice cracking after she sneezed again.

"What is a chalice?" Aaron asked McFarren.

"It's like a wine glass," Tyler told him. "Only it's made of tin or steel."

"That's right," McFarren said. "Any other questions?"

Aaron had another question but, wary of irritating McFarren, it seemed best not to ask. How did McFarren know how to do a séance? That would be good to know, he thought, as he watched Wayne shrug when McFarren looked at him. And he was curious about the goat head.

"Well, you kids need to leave now because I have things to do. If other people want to learn how to do a séance, you can share the sheets or direct them to me. I'll have no issue with that."

"Will do," Tyler said, leaving the couch.

"I will, too," Aaron and Wayne replied in unison.

The boys followed Tyler outside after the friends bid McFarren goodbye. "Thanks for coming with me, guys," she told them.

"No, problem," Aaron replied.

"You're welcome," Wayne said.

"McFarren wasn't so bad," Wayne stated as they stepped onto Normandy Road. "The dude seemed perturbed when we showed up but lightened up after Tyler told him why we came to see him," he noted while they walked homeward bound.

"He had no problem telling us about the séance, which was cool," Tyler said. "He seemed pretty nice overall. I didn't mind talking to him, but I didn't like it when he tried to touch me."

"Maybe he was just being affectionate," Wayne suggested.

"Affectionate?" Tyler asked him. "That's pretty gross."

"Some people like touching people when they're talking with them."

"Yeah, but I'm a kid and don't even know him, so he should

have kept his paws to himself," Tyler huffed. "But he was nicer than I thought he would be, and he sounded like my English grandpa, with his Cockney accent."

"What does Cockney mean?" Wayne asked her.

"It's the way people in the East End of London speak," Tyler replied.

"I want to look at the sheets again," she said to Aaron.

Aaron handed her the sheets. Wayne stared at her as Tyler looked at them. "Can I look at the sheets?" Wayne asked Tyler, after a moment passed.

"I'll let you look at them when I'm done; just hold your horses," she told him.

Wayne read the words to be spoken aloud after she handed the sheets to him. "The words are pretty out there," he declared. "The line where it says, 'While in the clouds, the ground, and walking upon this Earth, my aim is not to disturb you in your flight' is cool and creepy."

"'The words are creepy and all, but the goat head creeps me out the most," Tyler remarked. "That makes me think of satanism."

"McFarren said we had to wear black clothes," Aaron said. "What's that all about? And I wondered about the goat head, too."

"And what about the candles and a table against a westward wall?" Wayne said.

"It's probably all ceremony hocus pocus nonsense," Tyler surmised. "But maybe that's needed for it to work?"

"Do you still want to try the séance?" Aaron asked her.

"I think I do, but I'm leery because I don't know if trying a séance is a good thing," Tyler replied. "Can you hold onto the sheets? I don't have pockets." Aaron took the sheets, refolded them, and returned them to his pocket. "Thanks, bud," she said, placing her sunglasses on the bridge of her nose.

Chapter Three
Lord, I Want to Be with You

Aaron and Tyler rode around Oakwood School the following day, peering through classroom windows. They were biding time before riding their bikes to somewhere they had yet to determine.

"Do you feel like riding out to Holy Redeemer?" Tyler asked him. A Catholic seminary on the southernmost edge of Windsor, Holy Redeemer was a thirty-minute casual bike ride away from Oakwood. The diamond she played her softball game on Saturday was behind the seminary. "We can hang out at our usual spot on the bleachers and talk," she suggested.

"Okay, but I can't be late getting home for supper because I'll hear about it," Aaron said. "I don't need the drama, and besides, my mom is cooking my favorite... chicken dumplings. . She made me promise to be home by six-thirty. You won't see me again because she'll kill me if I'm late."

"Hardy har har," Tyler groaned. "It's only two o'clock, so we have lots of time. We can hang out at the baseball diamond and then go to the Double D and hang there for a bit. I promise you'll get home on time. I don't want you to be incarcerated again or have your mom kill you."

"Okay, but I didn't bring any money with me."

"Don't worry. I'll treat," Tyler offered. "I'll buy you a pop, a chocolate bar, a bag of chips, or whatever you want."

"I would have brought money if I had known we were going to hit the store."

"That's okay. You can treat me another time if you want."

"Okay, thanks," Aaron said.

They began down the lane in front of the school, toward Cabana.

"My sister and I are going to Devon Heights Mall tomorrow night," Tyler told him as they reached Cabana. "Did you want to come with us?"

Which sister?" Aaron asked her. "You have five."

"Sandra," she replied.

Sandra, the sibling six years older than Tyler, was the last of her siblings to leave the family home after getting married that Spring.

"Yeah, I'll go with you guys," Aaron said as they crossed Cabana during a gap in traffic. "There's a new hobby store there that I wouldn't mind checking out," he said upon reaching the path leading toward the store. "Supposedly, they have lots of model train stuff."

"Are you still buying stuff for your train set?" Tyler asked him as they rode. "You have the biggest train I've ever seen. What else could you possibly need?"

"I wouldn't mind adding a few more boxcars," he told her.

"You had fifty boxcars the last time I counted them," she said, having tallied his boxcars a few months before. "And you have four engines... Isn't that enough?"

"Now I have fifty-five boxcars and another engine," Aaron proudly announced.

"That's not enough?" she asked him. "Fifty-five railroad cars and five engines seem like a lot to me."

"You don't understand because you're not into toy trains," Aaron told her. "With train sets, you never stop adding trains and stuff... It's addictive because you always want to buy more. It's like with our card collection... You know how we want to keep adding to it."

"I suppose," Tyler said.

"We're both addicted to growing our collection," he said.

"That's true," she agreed.

"We love adding to it and trading to get cards. I'm the same way with my trains."

"I guess," she said.

"And what about you?" Aaron asked her.

"What do you mean?"

"You always want more clothes," he teased.

"Maybe, but that's what girls do," Tyler countered. "We like adding to our wardrobe, but I don't go overboard buying clothes like other girls do. I'm going through a growth spurt, so I don't get too crazy about buying things. They'll only last a while. I don't buy more clothes than I need and never will."

"Whatever," he said.

"Yeah, well, whatever is whatever," she said, giggling. "I wear clothes I buy and don't shove them into my closet and never wear them like some of my friends. You can check out what I got if you want to... Some of my favorite T-shirts are faded and worn because I wear them so much. I can't wear shabby clothes, and I've gotten two inches taller over the last four months."

"I know," Aaron replied.

"I've outgrown most of my clothes."

"Okay," he said. "Whatever... some guys like to collect trains."

"Yeah, I get your point," Tyler said. "But I'm not over-the-top about buying clothes. I like to change things up just like you do with your choo-choo trains. I think it's cute, you playing with your train set. You're such a little boy with that."

"Grown-ass men have train sets," Aaron told her. "A friend of my dad's, who is in his upper forties, has a train collection twice the size of mine. I've seen his collection, and he's the reason I got into it. The guy builds mountains and hills out of papier-mache and makes shrubs and trees. He's artistic... The mountains he builds look like the real thing."

"Well, isn't that something?" Tyler remarked.

"I might still have my train set when I'm eighty, and I'll still add to it if I do," Aaron declared.

"That's cool — whatever makes you happy," Tyler replied,

ringing a bell attached to the handlebar on her bike. It gave off a barely audible, tinny sound. "This bell is so useless. I can barely hear it, let alone anyone else."

"I tell people I'm coming when I ride up behind them," he said as Tyler repeatedly rang the bell.

"I do the same thing." She laughed. "Why bother putting this thing on the bike? It's completely useless."

They reached Talbot Road. Talbot, a four-lane highway, was a road in name only. It funneled traffic from Highway 401 to the Ambassador Bridge and vice versa through residential neighborhoods. The busiest border crossing between Canada and the United States, the bridge carried seventy percent of truck transported goods between the two countries. It connected to major freeways, Highway 401 via Talbot on the Canadian side and Interstates I-75 and I-96 on the American side.

The sound of truck traffic on the highway changed depending on traffic flow. If the intersection lights were green, there would be a steady hum, and when the lights turned amber or just turned green, the sound of various truck gears shifting down or up dominated. Askin was half a mile away from Talbot. With only the bush and Oakwood School as sound barriers, truck traffic could be heard all day and night.

Aaron liked hearing truck sounds at night when he had his window open. The sound lulled him to sleep as he wondered where the trucks were from and where they were going. Having spent many an hour along the highway, he could tell what make of rigs they were by the sound of their engines.

They rode south along Talbot's freshly paved eastern shoulder. "I love it when I can ride hands-free," Tyler said, crossing her arms. "The pavement is so smooth, you barely feel a bump..." She grasped the handlebars, anticipating a draft from a group of approaching trucks. "I was thinking about that séance," she yelled as the trucks roared past. "I decided I don't want to try it."

"What made you change your mind?" Aaron yelled back.

"It's just way too weird," she said. "The words and that pentagram and having to wear black clothes and light candles weirded me out, especially that part with the goat head. Like I said, it seems satanic to me, and the words say it all. I don't know anything about devil-worshipping, but I know goat heads are involved. I don't know what I'm talking about; I just remember that from somewhere."

"The goat head weirded me out, too," Aaron said. "Goat heads do have something to do with satanism. I remember seeing that somewhere, too."

The connection between goat heads and satanism occurred in their formative years, in news reports about devil-worshipping that was somewhat popular in the late 1960s. Though too young to understand what they saw at the time, they subconsciously absorbed it. The connection was buried somewhere deep.

"Those words made me think of Ouija boards," Tyler yelled as another truck passed. "You know how they say Ouija boards can conjure up evil spirits? I think that a séance might do the same thing, so I figured it was better not to try one."

"What about contacting your grandpa?" Aaron asked her.

"I think there's something dark about it," Tyler replied. "I don't know what I was thinking, but it just doesn't seem right, and I know my grandpa wouldn't want me doing something like that. He'd roll over in his grave."

"I'm sorry about you and Wayne coming with me to meet Mr. McFarren. He wasn't all that bad, though, other than being nasty with us at first... I'll just keep contacting my grandpa in my heart and through my prayers. This might sound corny, but I can feel his presence."

"I don't think that's corny. I get what you mean. I feel my grandfather's presence."

"I feel like I'm talking to him when I pray at night."

"You still do your bedtime prayers?" Aaron asked her. Tyler

told him she prayed at night years ago.

"Yup, every night," she said. "Don't you?"

"Sometimes I'll pray when I go to bed if I'm upset about something," he replied. "But I don't pray every night."

"Well, I pray every night. "Protect us, Lord, as we stay awake; watch over us as we sleep; that awake we may keep watch with Christ,' and so on," she hummed. "That's a Catholic prayer my grandma taught me when I was little, and I've been saying it every night ever since, unless I'm sick and forget... So, what did you do with the sheets?"

"They're still in the shorts I was wearing yesterday," Aaron shouted as a line of trucks began to pass.

This was Monday, and a holiday, so the heavy volume of truck traffic surprised Aaron. Typically, truck traffic was light on these days. Neither spoke while continuing toward Cousineau Road; they both needed to rest their vocals, their voices hoarse after repeatedly yelling at each other. They turned onto Cousineau.

After starting on a lane leading to the seminary a short while later, they continued to where it split into two separate ones. One lane led to a parking lot in front of the seminary while the other wrapped around it and continued toward the baseball diamond. They began talking again after starting on the one leading to the diamond.

"I love coming here," Tyler stated. The seminary was surrounded by acres of well-kept lawns bordered by farmland, Talbot, and Cousineau Roads; Tyler and Aaron considered it and its triangular-shaped grounds an oasis. "It's so peaceful, despite traffic noise from Talbot Road. This is a place where I've always felt close to God."

"Me, too," Aaron said, looking at shrubs, trees, and the back lawns. "It's a different world out here. Coming here is like getting away from everyday reality."

A pinwheeled design with a bell tower at its center, the

seminary was a complex of five connected, four-story buildings and a chapel. Remarkable in size, the seminary was equally impressive in its unpretentiousness. Adorned with drab, tan-colored brick, and of mid-twentieth-century modernist style, the seminary was designed by a world-renowned architect, Tyler had told him.

Windows in the chapel, the first building they passed, were composed of opaque block glass. Tyler had attended a few weddings in the chapel and spent time there while she attended a three-day Catholic youth retreat at the seminary. She told Aaron the glass block windows, boring as they were, served a purpose as they diffused sunlight and directed it toward the chapel's altar.

"The building looks drab," Aaron opined. "That's partly what gives it its character, but if I had designed it, I would have made it more cheerful."

"It's probably designed to reflect the simple, boring lives priests who live there have to lead," Tyler surmised.

"What's does it look like inside?" Aaron asked her.

"It has a few nice points, but mostly it's as unimpressive as it looks on the outside. It's bland, dull, and purposely depressing... All the walls are painted a yellowish-white, and fluorescent lights give off dreary yellow colors. But the chapel is beautiful if you can believe it."

Tyler arrived at the bleachers where they liked to sit. Aaron stopped behind her. She hopped off her bicycle. They climbed the bleachers five levels and sat on the top bench. A statue of Jesus Christ facing the diamond, with arms outstretched in an embracing manner, stood at the bell tower's base. A bright white cross atop the tower contrasted sharply with a cloudless, icy blue sky.

Aaron thought God felt close due to the seminary's trapping-less, unobtrusive yet peaceful appearance and remote location. He stared at the cross and reflected on the painful reality of life.

On how sweet childhood ignorance had withered away as war, poverty, and other horrors came to light. But the seminary and its back lawns, bordered by crop fields and Talbot Road, remained unchanged from when he had first known them. Tranquil and peaceful.

"It's so serene here, even with traffic noise from the highway," Tyler commented.

"Yeah," Aaron agreed, looking at a grove of trees to their immediate right. A small graveyard surrounded by a ring of evergreens contained remains of priests who died while serving at the seminary. "It would suck to be a priest because you can't get married," he said, considering such a life to be a lonely one. "I never understood why priests couldn't get married and have a family... And then when priests who live here die, they're buried in a little obscure cemetery and forgotten."

"I wouldn't say that they're forgotten," Tyler replied. "The other priests probably visit their graves, and there must be family and friends who visit them... Any cemetery is lonely because nothing is going on other than people visiting dead people. People don't typically hang out in cemeteries to have picnics, take pictures, and throw Frisbees around and stuff."

"Yeah, I guess you're right," Aaron agreed.

"In terms of not getting married, I guess the idea for priests is that they're married to God," Tyler surmised. She fell silent while looking up at the sky.

"What are you thinking about?" he asked her.

"This is creepy, but do you ever think about how you might die?" she asked him.

"Not really," Aaron replied.

"I do." Tyler let out a heavy sigh. "I don't sit around dwelling on it, but I think about dying every so often."

"How come?" he asked. "We have our whole lives ahead of us. We have lots of years to live unless something unexpected happens."

"I started thinking about dying after my grandpa passed," she said. "So, how would you want to go when the time comes?"

"I would like to die in my sleep," Aaron said. "Supposedly, you don't feel anything."

"That's the way I would want to go too, just like my grandpa did," Tyler huffed. "My grandma found him dead beside her after she woke up in the morning. She didn't notice anything during the night... I hope he didn't feel his heart attack," she said weepily, gazing at the seminary. "But maybe he did. Maybe he woke up after the heart attack but couldn't say anything? Who knows if people die without knowing about it in their sleep?

"Talking about dying is depressing," Tyler groaned. "Let's talk about something else... So, how did it go at your cousin's last night?" she asked him.

"It was the same old, same old," Aaron replied. "My parents, my aunt, and my uncle argued like they usually do, but I barely saw Jeff, which was good. This time, they argued about taxes. My aunt and uncle said old people shouldn't have to pay taxes, and my parents said they should, just like everyone else... They argue about the dumbest things."

"I don't think that's a stupid argument," Tyler said. "I agree with your aunt and uncle because most old people don't have much money to live on. They paid taxes all their lives, so why shouldn't they get a break after they stop working? It's only fair, especially if they live in poverty and can't pay their bills... I've heard some old people eat dog food just to survive because they can't afford to buy regular food, and that's no joke. That happens, and it's so sad to think people have to live like that."

"Since when do you care about old people?" Aaron asked her. "Old people scare you."

"That's true, but that's because they make me think about getting old and dying, but I'm going to grow out of that," Tyler replied. "And just because old people scare me doesn't mean I don't respect and care about them. We're supposed to respect our elders, even though some smell like mothballs," she said with a chuckle. "That mothball smell is something, but the idea they're close to dying bugs me the most."

"You've got a point there about the mothball thing — lots of old people smell like mothballs," he said. "There must have been a big problem with moths back in the day... And yeah, I think their days are numbered whenever I come across a person sixty years or older."

"That's what I'm saying! The older you get, the closer you are to death... I'm not scared of the afterlife because I know there's Heaven. It's the dying part that scares me."

"Yeah, well, I try not to think about dying," Aaron said. "Like it might pop up in my head every so often, but I don't dwell on it."

"Me neither," she said.

Aaron asked Tyler how everything had gone at her grandmother's the night before and when they went out to the cemetery. She said that it was okay. She had cried but hadn't gotten hysterical like she usually did.

"I thought about things we did together while I looked at his grave," Tyler replied. "Maybe I'm getting used to seeing it, so doing that is not as traumatizing as it was before."

"Does your grandmother creep you out because she's old?" Aaron whimsically asked her.

"No. It's different with her."

"Why?"

"It's just different, you know."

"But she's old," Aaron noted.

"I love my grandma, but I worry about her because she probably doesn't have much longer to live. Obviously, I want her to live forever... But, whatever, it was fine at her house after going there, considering the day and all... We sat around after dinner and talked about my grandpa. Then we watched the Tigers game."

"The Tigers lost again," Aaron said.

"They sucked," Tyler groaned. "They blew a five-run lead."

"I watched parts of the game. That new center fielder they traded for made two bad errors."

"Did you see the play where he dropped that fly ball?" she asked him. "I could have caught that... The guy had the ball covered. It was soft, and he positioned himself well, but it popped out of his glove like that stupid ball did to me the other day and rolled to the base of the right-field wall."

"I saw that and couldn't believe it," Aaron said. "How could a major league baseball player make such a bad play? I'm not good at baseball or softball like you are, but I'm pretty sure I could have caught that ball, too."

"The ball went way up toward the lights, but I could have caught it with a basket catch," Tyler said.

"What's a basket catch?" Aaron asked her.

"It's when you hold your glove out in front of your waist and let the ball drop into it," Tyler told him. She outstretched her hands and clasped them to demonstrate what she was talking about. "You make your glove like a cup and put your other hand under it to keep the ball from bouncing out."

"Have you ever made a basket catch in any of your games?"

"No, but I did it twice during our first practice this year," she said. "Mr. Hitch gave me an evil look after the first one and talked to me after the second one. He told me to smarten up."

"Did you drop the ball?"

"No, I caught it both times. I'm pretty good at eying the ball and positioning myself."

"So, what was his problem?"

"Mr. Hitch said I was doggin' it by not going under the ball and catching it properly, that I was showing off... It looked like he was mad at me because his face got so red. I thought he was going to start yelling and get all nasty, but thank God, he never did. He told me not to do it again. He said doing a basket catch was sloppy; if I stepped the wrong way, the ball could pop out of my glove and make it harder to throw back to the infield. I got his point, but the guy's way too serious. I like making basket catches because it makes things more challenging for me, and I'm good at it. I wouldn't do that if there was anyone on base... Mr. Hitch thinks he's managing the Tigers. He doesn't play around."

"He needs to chill out," Aaron said.

"That he does," Tyler agreed.

"Speaking of the Tigers, who do they have scheduled to pitch tonight?"

"Pat Underwood," Tyler replied. An avid Tiger's fan, she could recite the names of every player on their roster, their stats, birthdates, where they lived during the offseason, and where they were born. "Underwood has been pitching awesome lately. Hopefully, they might actually win a game because they've been losing like crazy over the last month. I like Underwood, and he's a decent pitcher."

"He's a decent pitcher," Aaron agreed.

"Yeah, and besides that, I think he's cute... He looks like Ringo Starr."

"That's funny," Aaron said. "I never noticed until you mentioned it."

"It's eerie because he and Ringo could be twins."

"Maybe Underwood could take over for Ringo if The Beatles ever get back together and Ringo doesn't want to join them," Aaron joked.

"Did you hear the latest news about The Beatles?"

"What about them?"

"They might get back together," she said.

"Come on, Tyler, people have been saying that ever since they broke up in 1970. You want them to get back together, and I do too, but it's been nine years since they broke up. If they were ever going to get back together, they would have done so by now."

"You're being a downer," she uttered. "It could happen...

Don't be like the guy they sing about in 'Nowhere Man:' Dark and depressed and not appreciating good things that are going on."

"I'm not trying to be a downer," Aaron said. "I want The Beatles to get back together as much as you do, but I'm just being realistic. Lennon and McCartney hate each other. It just ain't gonna happen."

"Yeah, but it might be true this time," Tyler insisted. "A guy on the radio last night said 'The Beatles' were in a studio cutting a new album and were planning to go on tour."

"Was the guy Brian Epstein?" Aaron asked her. Brian Epstein was The Beatles' long-dead manager. "A dead man talking on the radio is as likely as them getting back together."

"Ha, ha, you're so funny."

"Them putting out a new album and going on tour is as likely as seeing the Easter Bunny, or Santa Claus, or a ghost."

"You never know," she said and smiled. "It could happen… The Beatles putting out an album and going on tour, that is…, not seeing the Easter Bunny or Santa."

Aaron joked about them possibly seeing the ghost of a priest who supposedly walked around the Seminary and the Seminary grounds. He died after a tree fell on him and became a ghost, according to what an older girl at the youth retreat told her. The girl made the story up, Aaron suggested. Ghosts might exist, he believed, but the chances of seeing one, if they did, were slim to none.

Tyler could not decide if ghosts existed or not. According to the Bible, a priest said ghosts could not exist because the immaterial soul and material body don't go back together after death until the resurrection. But the Bible also mentions angels, demons, ghosts, and spirits. And some people believe ghosts appear for their own or a divine reason.

She was beginning to lean toward ghosts existing after her grandfather died, certain she could feel his presence. Her mother believed she could feel his presence, too. Her father was skeptical.

"Hey, Tyler," a familiar-sounding voice yelled from behind them before Aaron replied. They both looked toward the voice, which belonged to Arlene Maysome. She rode a bicycle toward them on a path. Arlene entered the seminary property via a cut in a fence bordering Talbot Road, he surmised.

Tyler waved at her.

"Oh God, not her," he muttered.

"Be nice," Tyler whispered while elbowing his arm.

"I can't stand her," Aaron whispered as Arlene drew closer. "The chick makes my skin crawl. She's mean, nasty, and a witch, and nobody likes her."

"She's not the nicest person," Tyler agreed.

Arlene arrived at the bleachers where they were sitting. A bat with a baseball glove hanging from it lay over the handlebars of her bicycle. "What are you guys doing out here?" Arlene asked Tyler.

"We're just hanging out," she replied. "What brought you here?"

"I'm meeting Kathy and Tina," Arlene said. Aaron knew Arlene, Kathy, and Tina as they were classmates of his and Tyler's at Oakwood. "We're going to bat a ball around." The three girls played on a team in the same league as Tyler. "So, how's your team doing?" Arlene asked Tyler.

"We're still in seventh place," Tyler replied. "You should know that. Don't you look at the stats they give us each week?"

"We're still in first place by a few games," Arlene spluttered, her voice laced with smugness. "So, you guys are probably out of the playoffs since only the top six teams make it," she said. Arlene smirked, looking at Tyler as Aaron glared at her. He wanted to erase the smirk off Arlene's face.

"I know your team is in first place, and only the top six teams get to play in the playoffs," Tyler said. "But there's still two weeks left, and we might win the last three games. We'll see what happens."

"Do you want to practice with us?" Arlene asked Tyler.

"No, because I'm hanging out with Aaron," she replied.

"Are you sure?" Arlene asked her. "The more you practice, the better you get."

"She said no," Aaron barked at Arlene.

"Whatever, Aaron," Arlene snarled. "Who asked you?" She rolled her eyes at him. "Don't stare at me," Arlene said as Aaron glared at her.

"Well, stop smirking then," he said.

"Thanks for asking if I wanted to practice with you," Tyler said.

"Suit yourself," Arlene grumbled. "I'll talk to you later."

"I hate her," Aaron muttered under his breath, watching as Arlene began toward the bleachers opposite the one they occupied. "Arlenie is a weenie," he said.

"She's messed up in the head, so try not to hate her or talk bad about her," Tyler said. "She doesn't know any better, so don't let her bother you… It's not good to hate people… Hating people only zaps your spirit."

"Why do you bother with her?" Aaron asked Tyler. "You've been hanging out with her on and off forever."

"I feel sorry for her, that's all," she replied. "She doesn't have any friends."

"That's because of her attitude," Aaron surmised. "She's never been very nice, and she smirked at you after smugly saying your team was probably out of the playoffs. I would never hit a girl, but that pissed me off. I wanted to smack the grin off her face."

"Just relax," Tyler asked him. "She doesn't bother me because I know Arlene's attitude, and I don't let her get to me."

"What was I supposed to do if you practiced with them?" he said. "Why would the mean little thing even ask you to practice with them? Was I just supposed to hang around and watch?"

"Arlene's inconsiderate because she's so wrapped up in herself," Tyler said. "Arlene doesn't get along with humans," she chuckled. "She doesn't know any better... But I don't want to talk bad about Arlene behind her back."

"Why not?" Aaron asked her.

"Because it's just not nice," Tyler replied. "I know you're only venting because you don't like her. You hardly ever talk bad about people."

Arlene sat in the grass, her back toward them, after reaching the opposite bleachers.

"Arlene was being smug when she asked you what place you guys were in," Aaron opined. "You showed me stat sheets Mr. Hitch gives players on your team each week, including what place teams are in. Other managers do the same. Arlene just wanted to rub it in your face that her team is in first, and you guys are in seventh place."

"Maybe she is caught up in actually being happy that her team is in first place," Tyler suggested. "I only asked Arlene how her team was doing to make conversation. She doesn't bother me because I don't let her get to me... It's not worth it."

"You're a better person than I am," Aaron remarked.

Tyler shook her head and called him a sweetheart. She explained that since her grandpa died, she decided it wasn't worth letting negative people drag her down and steal her sunshine. Tyler told Aaron that she used to let Arlene do that to her, but now she just left Arlene and her attitude alone. Arlene's not evil, Tyler concluded. She's got a good side, she explained to Aaron, but she's always had a chip on her shoulder. If Arlene talked to Tyler, she talked to her. Otherwise, Tyler didn't go out of her way to talk to Arlene anymore.

"You go to her house now and then. Why do you bother?" Aaron asked her.

"Not as much as I used to," Tyler replied.

"You went there two weeks ago," he said.

"Yeah, but I didn't go by myself," she told him. "I went with my friends, Jessica, Jayme, Kristen, and Courtney. Arlene bought the latest Supertramp album, so we went over to listen to it. That's all... I don't necessarily enjoy being around her, but it's not like I hate her. I feel sorry for her because she doesn't have any friends. Arlene doesn't know she turns people off because of her attitude."

"Why is she so nasty and negative?"

"Her parents aren't the nicest people, and they're stuck up, so maybe Arlene gets her bad attitude from them," Tyler surmised.

"I heard that her parents are rich."

"They are. That's probably why they're stuck up," she suggested. "Her dad owns a mold company that makes parts for the big three." Tyler referred to the Detroit-based automakers, Chrysler, Ford, and General Motors, as the big three. "Her family is always going on cool vacations. They went to Hawaii over the March break, and they're going to Europe this summer...

"You guys are going to Europe, too," Aaron said. "Maybe you'll see Arlene and her family there," he chuckled.

"You never know," Tyler sighed.

"With any luck, they'll go to Northern Ireland."

"That's not nice!" Tyler replied, looking at her feet, trying not to grin.

"Yeah, that's not funny," Aaron agreed. "I feel bad for the people there, with the bombings and the shootings."

"Why are they doing that?" she asked him. "They show cars there and other things all blown apart on TV occasionally. It's very sad."

"I'm not sure. It's a Catholic-Protestant thing, I guess."

"Anyway, do you want to go to the Double D now? I'm tired. I need to eat something or else I'm gonna crash." Tyler looked at her watch. "We have time to get a little something to eat and hang outside the store for a bit before you have to get back to your house."

"Yeah, let's get out of here," Aaron said, looking at Arlene.

"Suddenly, I feel like I need to go somewhere else."

"Just try not to let her get to you."

"I can't help it," he moaned. "She's evil incarnate."

"Seriously, Aaron? She's not evil. Arlene isn't that bad... She can be nasty, but she doesn't know any better... Believe it or not, Arlene has a nice side."

"I try to stay away from her, but she always ends up coming near me," he said. "And now she shows up out here in a place where we want to get away from everything. It's like I can't get away from her."

"Maybe she likes you," Tyler chuckled. "Maybe Arlene has the hots for you," she kidded.

"Ya, ha-ha-ha," Aaron said as they climbed out of the bleachers. "If she likes me, she has a crazy way of showing it. You know Arlene has always been snarky whenever she talks to me."

"See you later," Tyler yelled to Arlene after they reached their bikes.

Arlene waved at both of them, much to his surprise. Driven by a desire to be polite, Aaron awkwardly returned her wave. Maybe Tyler was right, he thought. Maybe Arlene did have a shining for him. Ugh! Nonetheless, proper manners dictated he return the friendly gesture.

He followed Tyler along a path leading to an opening in the fence where Arlene entered the seminary grounds. Tyler stomped on a pedal of her bike after taking a bump hard. "Stupid chain," she grunted, grimacing.

"What's wrong?" Aaron asked her.

"My chain slipped," she told him. Tyler backpedaled and stomped on the pedal again to force the chain back onto her rear sprocket. After making a sound reminiscent of a deck of cards being shuffled, a clicking sound suggested that the chain had returned to its proper place.

"Did you fix it?" he asked her.

"Yeah, it's okay," Tyler replied.

They continued toward the highway until her front tire became ensnared in a rut. Tyler veered into a patch of tall grass and tumbled. Her bike landed on her.

Aaron hurried to where she lay, worried that Tyler was hurt. "Are you okay?" he asked her.

"Yeah, I'm fine," Tyler said, laughing. "That was kind of fun, actually."

He grabbed her hands and helped Tyler to her feet. "You're so silly," he remarked, amused by Tyler's cavalier response. "You got thrown off your bike, and it's no big deal."

"I didn't get hurt, and my bike seems to be okay, so it's all good," she replied, wiping grass off her clothes.

"This has been quite the adventure, trying to go to the stupid store, and we haven't reached the highway yet," he said. "Your chain came loose. Then you end up falling and landing on your back, and then your bike ends up on top of you."

"Yeah," Tyler replied, laughing. "It's been quite the little adventure for me, hasn't it? But it's all good. There's nothing like adding a little drama to spice things up."

Aaron recalled when Tyler fell from a tree in Oakwood Bush and broke an arm just under its elbow. The sight of bone protruding from her arm was the grossest thing he had ever seen. "Remember when you fell out of the tree and busted your arm?" he asked her. "I felt so bad for you. You cried all the way home."

"I was out of my mind with pain… You would have cried too if that happened to you."

"Damn straight, I would, but you said something funny," he told her. "Just like now, after wiping out and landing in the grass," Aaron said. "Like, don't you feel sore at all? You landed hard, and your bike landed on top of you."

"I'm a little sore, but I'm okay," Tyler assured him. "So, what did I say after I fell out of the tree?"

"You said it was good that you didn't land on your head because you only had a few brain cells and couldn't afford to lose any."

"I really said that?"

"Yeah. I couldn't believe it. You were in agony, yet you tried to be funny. Girl, you don't know how much I respected that because I wouldn't have been joking around if it were me. But that's how you are."

"I was probably close to going into shock," she said, mounting her bike after they returned to the path. "I don't think I meant to be funny because there was nothing funny about it. That was bad... The pain was horrible, and I was probably out of my mind because my arm felt like it was going to explode."

"I tried not to gag because I didn't want to freak you out when I saw the bone sticking out of your arm," Aaron told her. "I wanted to help you stay calm."

"You're so sweet," Tyler declared as they resumed riding toward the highway.

"Well, I try to be," he chuckled.

"That was so messed up when I fell out of the tree," she said. "A branch I always used whenever I climbed the tree broke after I stepped on it... I tried to grab another branch, which was the last thing I remember doing before falling and passing out."

"I freaked out when you passed out — I thought for a second that you were dead until I realized that you were still breathing. Your eyes were closed for a few moments. It took a bit for you to say something after I kept asking if you were alright. When you finally looked at me, you looked scared. Then you grabbed your arm and realized that it was broken."

"I was so freaked out when I felt my bone where it shouldn't have been," Tyler groaned. "I don't know how I didn't barf after I felt the bone and saw blood on my hand. I almost passed out again."

"I don't know how I didn't barf or pass out myself," Aaron said. "That was horrible seeing blood streaming down your arm and the bone sticking out of your skin. I wouldn't wish that experience on anyone."

"Not even Arlene?" Tyler joked.

"Not even her," he replied.

"At least the chain didn't come loose again after my most recent misadventure," she said.

"I have to take a whiz," Aaron told her after they began along the highway. "I'm going to take a pee in some of those bushes along the path that leads to Cabana."

"Why don't you use the bathroom in the store?"

"It was disgusting the last time I used it. There was crap in the toilet and poop stains on the wall."

"Really? That's so gross."

They ascended the slope after they reached the path and continued toward a cluster of trees. Aaron went behind a tree to respectfully hide from Tyler's view to take care of business. While heeding nature's call, he reflected on how Tyler's perspective on life darkened after her grandpa died.

After Aaron relieved himself, he and Tyler continued toward the store. Leading the way, Tyler descended toward the highway without slowing as a steady stream of transport trucks approached. Aaron assumed that she would stop at the last possible moment as she had done before. Tyler had a bit of a daredevil in her.

"My brakes aren't working!" she yelled in a panicked voice.

Blood and flesh sprayed as a truck slammed into her after she rolled onto the highway and knocked her into the air until she landed on grass on the hill. Aaron ran to where Tyler had come to rest, knelt, and held her hand, sobbing uncontrollably. Blood streamed from her eyes, ears, and mouth. He stroked her face to comfort her as Tyler moaned. In shock, he begged her to stay alive while focusing on every breath she took as her moaning grew softer and stopped. She stopped breathing soon after.

By then, an ambulance siren grew closer from farther down the highway and became ear-tremoring loud as it pulled up beside them and stopped. Someone tried to talk to him, but Aaron was too shocked to speak. All he could do was stare at his friend and sob harder than ever before as a white sheet draped over her quickly became red with her blood in spots.

That's the last thing he remembered before passing out and going into a catatonic state, which he didn't come out of until the following day.

His mother told him that Tyler's aorta separated from her heart, and she bled out, according to her brother Brad. "Tyler is home with her grandpa now, in Heaven," his mother said. Tyler died instantly, according to her brother.

"No, she didn't," Aaron told her. She was moaning until she stopped breathing. Tyler was in utter agony.

He told his mother that Tyler died a horrible death, just as she feared she would.

He couldn't shake the guilt that came with thinking he should have checked her brakes. Why didn't he do that? If he had, she would still be alive.

Chapter Four
I Loved the Flower Girl

Aaron listened to doves singing their mournful songs outside his bedroom window as they did every morning while he was lying in bed and staring at the ceiling. At that moment, their songs symbolized the irrelevancy of life as life and the world carried on without regard to Tyler's or anyone else's passing. One minute he and Tyler were riding their bikes, and the next, she lay dying beside the highway. Tyler's time on Earth had passed, he thought, feeling a wretched sense of emptiness. He felt angry at God for allowing her to die. And yet life and the world carried on.

The nightmare of Tyler lying in a coffin haunted him; it was always there to pop in during a lull in a stream of other disturbing thoughts and things he had seen. It might have helped him forget about the dream if he had told her about it when she returned to being her happy self. Tyler probably would have asked where he thought the dream came from, and that would be about it.

Somehow the dream, their talk of death, wanting to contact the dead, and Tyler's death had to be connected, or was it just coincidence?

* * * * *

Six days had passed since Tyler died. Aaron remained holed up in his bedroom, venturing out only to attend visitations at the funeral home and Tyler's funeral, which took place the day before. Thoughts of trying to contact her through the séance came to mind as he lay alone in his misery.

Some days there was a need to open the bedroom window to let a breeze in to cool the room when it became too warm. He lay in bed and listened to truck traffic noise that came in with the breeze, today being one of those days. Many trucks were passing the spot where Tyler died; he could tell by the direction from which their now haunting sounds came.

The truck drivers would have no idea what happened there as evidence of the accident would have been cleared away by now. Doves, trucks, and everything else carried on. 'All we are is dust in the wind.' 'Nothing lasts forever but the earth and sky', he thought, as the Kansas song "Dust in the Wind" played in his head.

Wayne stopped by to see him each day and tried to plant a seed to coax Aaron out of his melancholic state. Finally, today, Wayne persuaded him to leave the house to meet with the other guys. The friends were gathered in the bush at a small clearing where they often hung out. Everyone was anxious to see him, according to Wayne.

Aaron noticed that a moving van was parked in Tyler's driveway as the boys stepped onto the front porch of his house. "They're not wasting any time," Wayne remarked, referring to her parents.

"No, they sure aren't," he agreed. Aaron watched, almost paralyzed by sadness, as men carried furniture out of Tyler's house. "My mom told me her parents can't live in their house anymore, and they're getting their bedroom furniture because they're staying with one of Tyler's sisters right now," he said. "They're going to pack up the rest of the house at the beginning of August, but, well, you know..." Aaron looked away from Wayne, needing a private, tearful moment. "That's hard to think about, man," he said upon regaining composure... That's my second home. I have a lot of memories in that house."

"I can't imagine what her family must be going through, especially Mr. and Mrs. Page," Wayne said as they walked toward the stone road. "Losing a child... wow, that's just too much."

"They're not good, according to my mother," Aaron told him, staring at his driveway as they walked toward Askin.

"I feel so bad for her mom, her dad too, but he didn't have the kind of relationship Ty had with her mom," Aaron said. "Tyler got snarky with her mom sometimes... She got attitudinal with her the last time we were in her fort and felt bad about it right after... They had their moments. They had a love-hate relationship, but they did love each other. They had a special bond.

"The big thing Tyler didn't like about her parents was they didn't have much interest in what she was doing. It bothered her that they never went out to see her play sports and ask her about school and stuff like that."

"They had a strange relationship," Wayne noted.

"Yeah, they did," Aaron agreed. "Tyler didn't like fighting with them. She always felt bad when she was mean to them."

"She said her parents probably didn't even know she went to school. That was pretty funny," he said with flat effect.

"Yeah, that's funny," Wayne said, slightly laughing. "That was cool that they were going to take her on vacation without the others. That would have helped them get closer."

"It would have meant a lot to her," Aaron said. "She was really looking forward to it. She just wanted their love and attention and to have time alone with them."

"It's so hard to believe she's gone," Wayne said. "Man, I just can't believe it... Are you doing okay, buddy?"

"No, how about you?" Aaron replied.

"I've had an empty feeling in my stomach that's starting to go away, but I can't stop thinking about her and what happened," Wayne replied. "It makes me sick to think about it. There's no way I'll ever go down that path again. Seeing that spot..." Wayne stopped speaking mid-sentence as they reached the street. He sneezed and wiped tears from his face.

"I've been feeling the same," Aaron said. "I can't look at her yard or her house. I would break down if I did."

"I miss her so much," Wayne said. "A part of me is gone now. She was always around us, and now…"

"I feel dead inside," Aaron replied in a shaky voice. "It will never seem real. Whenever I hear the doorbell ring or someone knocking, I think it might be her. I get all teary-eyed whenever someone comes to the house, and that's probably going to happen for a long time."

"It will help both of us to talk with the guys," Wayne said. "Especially for you because you haven't been out."

"We'll see what happens," Aaron said, doubting that talking with their friends would lift his shattered spirits. "It will be good to talk about it, but I don't know if that will help me and you feel better… But it might help the guys to talk."

Neither spoke for a moment as they passed Wayne's house after reaching the stone road.

"I can't believe you got lost right behind my place," Wayne said, referring to when Aaron got lost in the bush just behind the house.

"What brought that up?" Aaron asked him.

"I'm just thinking about the old days," Wayne replied.

"Yeah, I was terrified," he replied. "That was the first time I ever stepped into the bush. I was three. I waited for the lady who babysat me to take a nap and then snuck out the door… She probably didn't even notice I was gone."

"You had a couple of hippies babysitting you back in the day," Wayne remarked. "I remember them. The one girl Jenna always wore a bandana and brought her long-haired, bandana-wearing boyfriend, Richard, with her, who never took off his sunglasses."

"I liked them," Aaron said. "They were mellow and easygoing, which was cool. And they always wore colorful clothes."

"They probably smoked some grass before they came over,"

Wayne chuckled. "That might be why they were so mellow."

"Probably," Aaron said. He wanted to laugh but could only force a grin. "Yeah, that dude never took off his sunglasses. It was funny only seeing these round polarized sunglasses looking at me when we talked."

Aaron recalled when he and Tyler played war games and built forts in the bush when they were younger. Childhood innocence, indeed, had ended. Life, as he had known it, died with Tyler.

"Tyler should be here with us; instead, she's in the ground in some cemetery," Aaron muttered. "It's like a bad dream you can't wake up from."

"Everyone loved Ty. She was so sweet," Wayne lamented. "She liked you better than anyone because you were boyfriend and girlfriend."

"Tyler loved you, too."

A bizarre sense that Tyler waited with their friends was hard to shake. Maybe she was still alive, Aaron fantasied after reaching a path leading to the clearing. Perhaps the last week had been a terrible nightmare, he wanted to believe. He knew this had to be a delusional thought.

"Who's all going to be there?" he asked Wayne.

"Carl, Allen, Scott, Steve, and Andy," Wayne replied.

"Aaron boy," Carl solemnly said. A talker, usually more words would follow, but greeting Aaron was all Carl could muster.

The friends gathered for a group hug and then sat on logs they used as benches.

"I feel bad because I teased Tyler about her name the last time we played soccer," Carl said after an uncomfortable period of silence. "Now I feel bad about calling her Tyrone because she said she didn't like it. I was kidding with her, but now I wish that I hadn't done that."

"Try not to worry about it. Tyler knew you were just messing with her."

"Was she mad at me?" Carl asked him.

"It didn't bother her," Aaron lied. "You two always liked to pick at each other. She liked that."

"I called Tyler that, too," Allen said.

"You called her Tyronious," Aaron corrected him.

"Well, it's basically the same thing," Allen opined.

"Don't bum out about it because Tyler knew you guys were messing around," Aaron said.

"So, she was okay with me?" Carl asked Aaron. "I hope that she wasn't pissed off at me."

"She wasn't pissed off with you guys," he assured Allen and Carl.

"Well, that makes me feel better," Carl said. "But I'll always feel bad for teasing her... I loved everything about her. She was tough, generous, and sweet."

"That she was," Aaron agreed.

"That was so sad to see her in that white coffin," Allen sighed. "I just couldn't believe it... She was so full of life; then there she was, stiff and pale. She had no color to her face. It broke my heart to see her like that."

"Me too," Scott said.

"I'd never seen her in a dress before," Carl said. "She looked beautiful. I liked how her hair was combed back and the white headband they put on her."

"The daises they put between her hands was a nice touch," Steve added. "And the two roses over her left ear."

"Ah, she was something else... It's funny how she loved hanging out with us doing guy things, like building tree forts and playing road hockey, and then there was the girl side of her who loved flowers and cooking with her mom... She sure loved her daisies."

"That she did," Aaron agreed. "And it wasn't just daisies. Tyler and her mom had a flower garden with daisies, roses, daffodils, and other flowers Tyler had to pronounce the names of because I couldn't pronounce them. That's no doubt where the two roses came from."

"She looked so ladylike," Allen remarked. "I never saw Tyler in a dress before, either."

"I've seen her in dresses many times," Aaron said. "She'd wear a dress if there was some special thing going on at church or when she went to weddings and her grandpa's funeral."

"I felt really bad for her because she was so sad and upset when her grandpa died," Wayne said. "She had such a hard time with that. And now she's gone... At least they're together again."

Wayne began to sob. Aaron reached over to him. They hugged.

"The three of us grew up together since we were babies," Wayne continued, looking at Aaron. "It's like the world's... well, it's just not like it should be, and it will never feel that way again." He cried a little more. "It's just too weird. I expect to see her every time I go outside, but it's not going to happen. She's never there."

The friends fell silent, each needing a moment to digest the reality that they would never see Tyler again.

"It was crazy how many people came to see her at the funeral home," Scott remarked. "The visitations I went to were packed, and you couldn't fit another person in the church for her funeral service."

"A lot of kids from school were there and most of the staff, including Ms. Olsen, the volunteer lady," Aaron said. "Her softball and soccer teams went to one of the visitations. And all of her girlfriends I know of were there."

"She had a ton of friends," Wayne noted. "She had that magnetic personality of hers. Everybody liked her..."

"I can't think of one person who didn't," Aaron said.

"That was nice of her parents to ask us to be pallbearers," Wayne said to Aaron, the two of them having joined three of Tyler's brothers and one of her nephews, who was three years older than her, in the honor of carrying her coffin. "It was unreal carrying her coffin. I felt like I was in a trance while trying to keep myself together."

"The Hearst creeped me out. Black Cadillac hearses look so gothic and make me think that one day I'll be in one... The opening at the back of her hearse was larger than I thought it would be, and the inside seemed so tall and narrow... The rack, the curtains, the lantern lights, and the black felt on the ceiling and walls gave me the chills.

"It was hard to put Tyler inside something like that."

"I felt so bad for her mom and dad," Carl said. "They were crying so hard, and her brothers, sisters, and grandparents... I was afraid her mom would faint when she walked toward the limousine after the service. Tyler's dad had to support her because it looked like she was going to fall."

"I've never seen anyone cry as hard as she did," Aaron said, dabbing tears. "Mrs. Page is like my second mom. I hated to see her so distraught."

"Bringing Tyler out of the hearse was just as hard as putting her inside it," Wayne declared after giving Aaron a quick hug. "That's when it hit me that we were about to walk away from her, and that would be it. We would never see her again."

"I almost dropped my part of the coffin when we reached her grave because I was shaking so hard. "That's the first time I've lost someone close to me. Tyler was so young... It just doesn't seem fair."

"What you told us at the funeral was unreal," Scott said. "About that dream you had about finding Tyler lying in a coffin... Did you tell her about it?"

"No, I never got to," Aaron said. "I didn't tell her because she was thinking about her grandpa, so the timing wasn't right. But I was about to tell her on our way to Holy Redeemer."

As he told the others, Tyler was focused on death that day, and just as he was about to tell her about the dream, she wanted to change the topic because it was depressing her.

He told them about him, Tyler, and Wayne going to see Mr. McFarren, because she wanted to learn how to do a séance to talk with her grandpa, but she changed her mind.

It was out of character for her to want to try a séance, to think about doing something 'dark,' they agreed. It seemed opposed to her convictions. To the deep relationship they could tell, though she strived to keep it to herself, she had with God. She thanked God a lot. Sometimes she talked about trying to give God good things to see as He looked at the world, to offset the bad. Tyler thought God would not be pleased if she attempted to contact the dead.

Some of the others connected Aaron's dream and Tyler's focus on death and wanting to try the séance to her death. Death, death, death... It seemed to be coincidental. The consensus was that he and Tyler both had a premonition about her death.

Wayne said he wondered why God let bad things happen. He talked about a recent article in the about a serial killer who murdered six women and a thirteen-year-old girl, in Ypsilanti, and Ann Arbor, Michigan, in the late 1960s.

He found the murder of the girl to be deeply disturbing. She had been abducted while walking alongside a railroad track, trying to get home before dark, and driven to an abandoned farmhouse where she was brutally murdered. The police officers who saw her body said they were still affected by what they saw.

Then he talked about another thirteen-year-old stabbed to death near Chicago two months ago after a man walked into her house and tried to rape her. He said a lot of bad things keeps happening, and it was never going to end.

Steve wondered why God allowed children like Tyler to die so violently. He said he could not stop thinking about the horror Tyler felt just before the truck smashed into her. He wondered what was going through her mind when she saw the truck just as it smashed into her.

Aaron wondered where God was, too.

Aaron described some of what happened. How terrifying it was for Tyler when her brakes failed and she realized there was no way to keep from going onto the highway. He said she looked away just as the truck hit her, was pushed into the air, and landed on the side of the road. He left out the part of watching her blood and flesh spraying in the air and that she moaned in what had to be absolute agony before she went limp, deciding not to tell them everything he saw. That would have only upset them more.

He said he thought there was a chance Tyler was still alive since the truck did not hit her square and she landed on grass, but there was no way of saving her. He told them that blood streamed from her mouth, nose, eyes, and the side of her body where the truck hit her. And that the cause of her death was an aortic rupture.

"At least she's with her grandpa now," he said. Most of the others said they thought the same, except for Wayne. He stared ahead in silence.

"What about that séance?" Allen said.

"What about it?" Aaron asked him.

"Do you still have those sheets he gave you?" Allen asked Aaron, having told them what was on the sheets and how the séance was supposed to be conducted.

"You want to try it?

"Seriously? To contact Ty?"

"I've been thinking about it," Aaron replied while kicking at the earth with a heel. "And now I want to try and contact her," he said, on the cusp of tears. "I can't stop feeling so horrible about what happened. We were just being us... She fell hard on the ground before we reached the highway after her tire got stuck in a rut..." He grimaced and shook his head. "The bike landed smack on top of her after she ended up in the weeds, or grasses, whatever they are, in the field. I thought she hurt herself because she and the bike fell pretty hard, but she laughed and said it was kind of fun."

"That's Ty," Wayne said.

"That has to be why her brake became loose," Aaron said. "Fuck..., fuck, I wish I had checked it. Damn! I beat myself up over that. She might still be alive if I just checked her brakes."

"But why would you think to do that?" Wayne said. "I wouldn't have. You have to stop blaming yourself for that."

"That's right," Carl said. "I've hit ruts there before and got knocked off my bike, but I never thought I had to check my brakes."

"I've never had that happen to me, either," Scott said. "And I've fallen off my bike a few times going down that path. Once your front tire gets in those ruts in the mud, when it's dried, it's pretty much fifty-fifty you will wipe out."

"Yeah, you guys are right," Aaron said. "The bike seemed fine after she got the chain back in place... Now I want to have a chance to say goodbye to her, like she wanted to do to her grandpa."

"Getting back to the séance, Tyler didn't want to do it because there was something wrong about it," Allen said. "You guys always thought along the same way."

"I did feel the same way, but people do séances all the time, so they can't be all that bad," Aaron observed. "It's different because now I'm the one regretting being unable to say goodbye. I miss her so much." "You said your sister and her friends tried the séance, and nothing bad happened to them," he said, looking at Wayne.

"The face of the guy they were trying to contact began forming on a TV screen in the room they tried it in," Wayne said.

"That's pretty creepy," Carl remarked.

"It freaked them out so much they stopped doing it."

"Who were they trying to contact?" Carl asked Wayne.

"A guy friend of theirs who died in a car accident," Wayne replied.

"So, who wants to try the séance with me?" Aaron asked the assembled.

"I'll do it!" Andy enthusiastically replied.

"Me, too," Wayne seconded. "It would be nice if we contacted her, but it would be pretty weird."

Allen, Carl, Scott, and Steve agreed to participate somewhat unenthusiastically, as evidenced by their somber tone. Carl said it would be sad to see Tyler in a different way. Steve thought it was best to remember her as she was, saying that was better than if they saw her as an apparition.

"When do you want to try it?" Wayne asked Aaron.

"We could try the séance today if you guys are up to it. We can do it in the rec room at my house. My parents aren't coming home until after eight tonight, which gives us plenty of time."

"What about black clothing and the black and red candles and a silver chalice?" Wayne said. "Do you have that?"

"I have lots of black clothing, but I don't have a silver chalice, and I don't think there are any candles in my house," Aaron replied.

"What are you guys talking about?" Carl asked them.

"That's the stuff we need for a séance," Wayne told him.

"We need to have black and red candles and a chalice, and everyone has to wear black clothes," Aaron advised. "And we'll need to cover the two windows in my rec room with blankets. McFarren said you had to block outside light."

"My mom has one of those silver chal... chalices, whatever ya call 'em, and has as a drawer full of candles and candleholders," Andy said. "There are a few black and red ones in there."

"I don't have black pants or shirts," Wayne declared.

"I'll find some for you," Aaron said. "We're the same size, so I got you covered."

"I don't have black pants," Allen said. "At least I'm wearing a black shirt."

"I have a pair you can wear," Aaron told him. "We're probably the same size. It doesn't matter if they're too tight or too loose."

* * * * *

Andy began toward his house, a few houses away from where Scott lived, while the others made their way to Askin. Aaron, Wayne, and Allen continued to Aaron's place, while Andy, Carl, and Steve went to their homes to change. Wayne and Allen went to Aaron's recreation room in the basement.

Aaron looked away from a window that faced Tyler's backyard, while climbing a staircase on the way to his bedroom to retrieve the sheets, black clothing, and change clothes. It was hard to look in her backyard, where they had spent so much time. The first and only time he had done that since she died brought on a flood of tears. He cried so hard it was a struggle to catch his breath.

He went to a table where he left the shorts containing the sheets. Panic set in after finding a pocket where both sheets should be empty. Unbeknownst to him, his mother emptied its pockets while preparing to wash dirty clothes piled in a laundry basket beside the table. Finding them suitably clean, she laid the shorts back on the table after placing both sheets in another pocket — relief set in upon finding them.

Aaron grabbed two black pants and a black shirt and began downstairs after changing clothes. He fought off the fear of trying to communicate with an unknown world while entering the recreation room. Wayne and Allen placed a table against its west wall and draped thick blankets they had taken from a couch over both windows.

"How does it look?" Wayne asked him, regarding their setup.

"It looks good to me," Aaron replied.

The front doorbell rang after taping the sheet with a pentagram above the table. Aaron found Andy, Carl, Scott, and Steve on the front porch. "Come on in," he said to the guys as they walked into the house, and he held the door open.

"I got everything," Andy announced. "The chalice is a bit tarnished, but I suppose that shouldn't matter." "So, who's going to read the words?" he asked Aaron.

"I'll read them," Aaron said, confident of being able to do so without succumbing to emotion.

He led them downstairs and into the recreation room, where they joined Wayne and Allen, who had changed clothes in an adjacent room. A tick past three o'clock, how long the séance would take was anyone's guess. But at least they had five hours to do it, Aaron thought, watching as Andy lit both candles after placing them in candleholders. Aaron turned the overhead lights off after Andy placed the chalice. Shadow and light danced as flames flickered while opening the sheet with words that had to be spoken.

He nervously began to say the words, then said Tyler's name, and continued to utter the séance words while struggling to read in a faint, wavering light. A television screen glowed, on which an image of Tyler's face began to form. Aaron blew the candles out, unable to continue after reading three-quarters of the sheet, suddenly distraught and overwhelmed by nerves. The screen went dark.

"Why did you blow the candles out?" Andy wanted to know. "Damn, man, Tyler's face was starting to form."

Aaron hurried toward a light switch, without responding to Andy's question. An abrupt brightness of fluorescent overhead lights stung his eyes while looking back at the television. Wayne looked up, and Andy buried his face in his hands. Carl, Steve, and Scott stared at the screen.

"Oh, man," Wayne moaned. "Did you guys see Tyler's face beginning to form?"

"I saw it!" Andy exclaimed.

"Me, too," Carl said.

"I saw it, too," Scott declared.

"That was unbelievable," Allen and Steve said.

Aaron looked at Wayne, whose facial expression indicated that he was disappointed. "Why did you stop?" Wayne asked him. "You wanted to see Tyler, and it seemed to be working."

"I'm sorry, but I didn't like what was happening," Aaron replied. "Seeing her face form freaked me out."

"That freaked me out too, but man, I wanted to see what happened next."

"That was pretty wild," Carl remarked.

"It was too weird," Steve said. "I'm glad you stopped reading the words," Wayne said.

"Do you guys really think that was her?" Carl wondered aloud.

"I think it was," Aaron sighed, feeling a sense of dread. A chill weaved into every fiber of his being despite sweating as his heart raced. "I wish I'd never brought up the idea of trying this."

"The face looked like Tyler's," Wayne commented, noticeably trembling.

"I'm sorry I stopped short, but I just couldn't go through with it."

"It's okay, buddy," Wayne assured him. "I understand."

Chapter Five
The Phantom Horseman

Aaron left his house at eleven-thirty, the morning after attempting the séance. Regret and guilt for having tried it weighed heavy while riding down Askin toward Cabana Road. Houses lined both sides of the street. Far from being in a socializing mood, thankfully, there were no friends or others he knew on a talking basis in their front yards. He felt bad for having disturbed Tyler from her peace.

He was heading to Holy Redeemer Seminary in need of feeling close to God. Anger directed at Him for allowing Tyler's death had lessened somewhat. Once there, Aaron planned to ask to be forgiven by God for being bitter and Tyler to forgive him for trying to contact her.

A soothing southern breeze blew after starting east on a sidewalk on its north side after reaching Cabana. Aaron wondered if Tyler rode the wind on her eternal travels while pedaling hard toward Mount Royal Drive, a street that ended at Cousineau Road. He began south upon reaching Mount Royal Drive and passed Toby Redd Golf Course, an 18-hole championship course named for a legendary Windsor-born professional golfer. He and Tyler played a 9-hole Par 3, next to the main course, a few weeks before she died.

Holy Redeemer's bell tower and the cross above it came into view while nearing Cousineau Road. Bells in the tower that loomed over houses tolled. They tolled at noon to let people within hearing distance know God had a place nearby.

After reaching Cousineau Road, he continued east a short distance before arriving at Holy Redeemer and then rode toward the baseball diamond. He climbed the bleachers, sat where he and Tyler liked to sit on the top bench, and recalled their awkward conversation about death and ways to die. While looking at the seminary, he wondered if she somehow unknowingly knew she was moments away from dying. *God, forgive me for being bitter toward you,* he prayed while looking at the statue of Christ. *Tyler, I'm sorry for trying to contact you through the séance,* he said, looking at the cross.

Tears began. There was no need to do one, as Tyler said regarding her grandpa; he felt her in his heart. A sense of Tyler's presence began as the shock of her dying subsided.

* * * * *

While Aaron talked to God and Tyler, Wayne walked through Oakwood Bush hunting birds, squirrels, and other small animals with a pellet gun. A loud ping said that he missed his mark after firing at a crow perched in a tree. Wayne watched as the crow flew away, his gun a cheap one-shot affair. He put another pellet in the gun.

With enough pellets for an hour or so of trying to kill for killing's sake, he continued deeper into the woods until noticing movement in the underbrush. He stopped and aimed at the movement. A large rottweiler emerged about twenty feet in front of him, on the path he was on, and bared its teeth.

Too scared to succumb to fear, to stand in place, adrenaline upped to high mode, Wayne considered climbing a tree. But the lowest branches of nearby trees were too high to reach. Logic, though sensing he should run, said it was best to walk back toward where he had come.

Not wanting it to sense fear in his eyes, Wayne tried not to look at the menacing beast on his way to the stone road. An idea of smacking the rottweiler in the head with his gun to stun it ended after deciding that would only stir the beast to attack him. Hitting its head with the lightweight gun would be as effective as trying to smash a rock with a stone.

The rottweiler snipped at his ankles after reaching Oakwood

Lane. On the verge of being paralyzed by fear, Wayne continued toward home as the beast followed. A sense of its presence ended. Relief washed over him as he looked behind him and saw that he was alone.

* * * * *

Aaron wondered if priests and seminarians residing in the seminary took time to stare at the statue of Christ. If they sat where he sat and grieved for family members, friends, and other loved ones who died. Regardless of their position in earthly life, all living things passed. Kings and queens, popes and presidents, dictators and prime ministers, rich and poor, and priests and their congregations.

He walked toward where priests were buried, needing to see their graves. The southern breeze blew brisker with every step, and darkness set in. Maybe a giant stepped between the sun and earth, he thought in the wilds of his mind, after reaching the graveyard.

Tower bells tolled, trees bent, and grass, leaves, dirt, and litter flew, pushed by a sudden howling wind. A giant horse guided by a robed rider stepped out of a now murky, early post-dusk-like darkness as he looked in the seminary's direction. Transfixed by what he was seeing, Aaron stood in place and watched as the horse trotted at a slow pace and its rider began toward him.

The horse and rider, who held reins around the horse's neck with hands resembling claws, passed close by. The rider stared ahead while pursuing a southern course. Through dark-and-debris-obscured vision, Aaron watched as the horse and rider disappeared.

Debris fell dead still after the wind calmed and the darkness gave to light. Tower bells rang softer and less often before falling silent. His spine throbbed, juiced by fear. Leaving his and Tyler's now former hallowed place, given what had just occurred, could not happen fast enough.

Scared and despondent, finding it odd and sad to now fear his and Tyler's peaceful place, Aaron hurried to his bike. He wondered if it all had been a hallucination—the sudden intense wind, darkness, rider, and horse while starting home under a hot mid-afternoon sun. If so, every sense experienced it. Tracks, grass matted by hooves, did not exist beyond where the horse and rider came into view.

Two men hauled boxes into the seminary from a truck parked in its receiving bay. What would they say, he wondered while pondering whether to ask if they noticed the sky go dark and the howling wind? They might respond by questioning what he was going on about or just stare blankly at him like they thought the poor kid had lost his mind.

Desperate to be alone to process what happened, he strived to get home faster than what was physically possible. No one else would be home; his parents were out with friends. A Les Paul guitar he learned how to play five years back and a Marshall amplifier were in the basement. Playing guitar might help soothe his tormented soul.

Aaron mourned the loss of a world once known while riding home. The place where he and Tyler sought solace no longer existed, and life once full of innocence, belonging, promise, joy, and predictability now felt empty and uncertain. Tyler was dead, and the life they planned to live together died with her. In dark moments, he wondered if life was worth living. It seemed that his life had become a catastrophe.

Finally, he arrived home; the journey seemed to take forever.

The first thing he saw after entering the room where the guitar and amp were was a big, orange bean-bag chair. That was Tyler's chair, the one she used to sit in when she would watch him play new songs he had learned or old ones she liked. She was his biggest fan.

Every so often, she would sing a few verses, if she knew the words, or make them up.

She had just been in that chair a few days before her death, listening to him play "Listen to the Music" by the Doobie

Brothers, one of her favorite songs. Sometimes she talked about trying to get good at playing piano, like her English grandma who taught her how to play a few songs on the largely unused baby grand in the basement of her house. She began practicing the piano part on "School" from Supertramp to play for her grandmother during her visit. She said she would not get the song perfect, but at least it would be presentable.

It was hard not to eye the chair after he settled into his usual spot. He picked the guitar up and wrapped its strap over his head and then around his shoulder, brushing aside some of the long hair he had sported in the back over the last year, letting his hair grow a bit on the shaggy side to sport a rock guitarist look. He began tuning the guitar, plucked away at the chords, one by one, all the while focused on the chair. He figured there was no point in moving it to another room, out of eyesight, because there would still be an empty spot. And it would be time-consuming for him to set up playing somewhere else, moving the amplifier, a Wah Wah and fuzz pedals, and some chords. He would be half an hour into playing by the time his parents came home.

Instead of soothing his soul, playing guitar might torment it more, he thought while staring at Tyler's chair. But he tried. He gave it a good effort but gave up after playing a couple of songs, realizing he could not focus, consumed by Tyler's absence and what happened at Holy Redeemer.

Maybe hearing music might help, he thought. He eyed the George Harrison "All Things Must Pass'" album beside a turntable behind him. That record contained three discs he tried to master, as Harrison was one of his favorite guitarists.

He decided to play "My Sweet Lord," his go-to song when feeling sad. Harrison anguished about wanting a relationship with God, about wanting to see Him, rather than accepting His existence through blind faith. Aaron thought about meeting deceased loved ones again when his time came while listening to the song. "I really want to see you... really want to be with you,"

Harrison sang as Aaron stared out a window at a deep blue spot in an otherwise clouded sky. Tyler now existed somewhere unseen beyond the blue, he thought.

He looked at a photo album containing pictures of him and Tyler. The first photo was of him at five years old, standing in front of a Desoto his father owned, which he vaguely remembered. It's toothy chrome grill and headlights formed a monster's face, in his childhood mind. In another photo, he and Tyler stood next to each other in front of a lion exhibit at the Detroit Zoo. They would have been five years old, per a date stamp on the photo. Tyler wore her softball uniform after returning home from a game in another picture.

He stared at the last picture of them together, taken by her mother, shot in front of Tyler's house two months before she died. In a defiant mood, not wanting to pose properly per her mother's request, Tyler stared aside as they had an arm wrapped around each other. Tyler looked so cute, wearing a red and white checkered long-sleeved shirt and the sun lightening her dark brown hair. He wished that she had looked at the camera.

"My Sweet Lord" continued playing. From a perspective above its wayside, he watched as the funeral procession behind the hearse, carrying his soul mate to her grave, wound along a winding road beside Lake Erie. He pictured the statue of Christ and then the cross above the seminary's bell tower as the song faded.

* * * * *

"Are you okay?" Aaron asked Wayne after answering knocks on the front door. His now dearest friend stood on the porch. Wayne's face was pale and his eyes wide open.

"I'm okay now, I guess, but I wasn't a while ago," Wayne replied. "You wouldn't believe what just happened to me," he said after the friends sat on the porch. "I saw a huge rottweiler when I was hunting in the bush. It stepped out of the woods onto the path I was on and walked toward me... The terrifying thing showed its teeth!"

"Oh, my God!" Aaron exclaimed.

"It followed me after I turned around and began to walk away," Wayne, noticeably shaking, continued. "I almost wet myself as the thing stayed right on my heels after I reached the stone road and walked toward my house. Thank God it never attacked me before it disappeared after following me down the stone road... I was never so scared in my life... You know how big dogs scare the crap out of me to begin with? I could only stare at first because I was too scared to move. Thank God I didn't lose my nerve and was able to walk away... There was nothing behind me when I looked back at the stone road after reaching my place. I was glad it was gone, but how could something that huge disappear into thin air?"

"Ain't that something?" Aaron said.

"Yeah, ain't that something?" Wayne tersely replied, paraphrasing Aaron's comment. "I'm not lying, man. I thought the thing would rip me apart. I almost shit myself."

"Well, I believe you," Aaron told him. "I really, truly do."

"If you told me something like that, I would think you were either screwing around or lost your marbles," Wayne said. "But I'm not making this stuff up... Like I'm glad you're saying that you believe what I'm telling you, but I don't believe it myself. Like you can straight out tell me if you think I'm full of dodo or that I should go see a head doctor. I might tell you that if you told me something like that happened to you." Wayne took a deep breath. "Oh, my God, I don't know what happened," he continued. "I know what happened, but I don't know what happened, if you get my drift. Like this monster-sized, beast of a rottweiler follows me, than it just vanishes... It was out of this world, man."

"Something crazy happened to me today, too," Aaron said. Wayne gave him a cautious look as though he braced for a smart-ass response to the experience he just shared. "I'm serious."

"Okay," Wayne said. "So, tell me what happened to you."

"I didn't laugh or say you were a liar, so don't be doing that to me," Aaron told him.

"I won't... I promise," Wayne replied. "We'll shake on it." They hooked fingers in a 'you can trust me' handshake. "But if you mess with me because of what I told you, I'm gonna kick your ass."

"Let's just be straight up with each other," Aaron groaned, irritated by his buddy's threat of causing bodily harm. "But something did happen to me today, and I want to tell you about it the way you told me what happened to you... It bugs me, man, that you don't believe that I believe what you told me."

"I'm sorry, man, but you know it's hard to believe that the stupid rottweiler could just disappear," Wayne said. "I'm extremely sorry, Aaron. I believe that you believe me... So, what happened to you?"

"I rode out to Holy Redeemer to think about things," Aaron said. "I've been angry with God for letting Tyler die... I went there to ask God to forgive me for thinking like I did and Tyler to forgive me for trying the séance."

"Aw, man, don't feel bad about trying the séance. And everyone is upset and probably feeling angry about what happened to her. I've been feeling angry at God myself."

"I went to where Tyler and I sat in bleachers at the baseball diamond before she died and thought about what we talked about," Aaron continued. "She talked about death and dying. We had what I thought was an awkward conversation about what we thought was the best way to die. That was such an odd conversation... It seems even odder now."

"That's pretty ironic," Wayne said. "Hopefully, Tyler was alright, mentally wise. I hope our girl wasn't talking like that because of being depressed."

"Tyler was bummed about her grandpa dying as you know, but she wasn't depressed," Aaron assured him. "I could read her pretty well. She was just talking... We talked about death every so often after her cat Taffy died when she was ten."

"That's good," Wayne said. "I remember how upset she was when her grandpa died. I felt so bad for her."

"Every so often, we talked about what happened to animals and people after they die," Aaron said. "But we never discussed the best way to die until we sat in the bleachers that day. I thought about that while sitting in the bleachers today, and I wondered if she somehow knew that she was about to die because that conversation was so weird. I felt bad thinking that because I knew she had no idea what would happen."

"Maybe she did," Wayne submitted. "I've heard that sometimes people sense they're about to die before they die. Maybe that happened to her, or maybe she was just thinking about ways to die because she was dwelling on her grandpa's death?"

"But the one thing that disputes that regarding her is that Tyler was acting normal," Aaron told him. Aaron's eyes threatened to water, desperately missing his mate. "If Tyler had any notion that she was about to die, she sure didn't show it... So, getting back to what happened to me, I went over to where priests are buried. You know the graveyard at the seminary? I needed to go there for some reason. The wind began blowing hard, and the sky got dark... By the way, did it get dark and windy in the bush?"

Wayne said no. He told Aaron that it had been sunny, and there was only a slight breeze.

Aaron said that it had gotten really dark, like nighttime was coming, but that was nothing compared to what happened next. He assured Wayne that he was not screwing around... "I believe what you told me happened to you, so I hope you believe me after I tell you what happened to me," Aaron declared.

"Whatever happened can't be any crazier," Wayne supposed.

"I'm going to tell you what I saw, and you can let me know what you think when I'm done," Aaron said.

"I'm listening," Wayne told him.

"Like I said, it got windy and dark, like almost nighttime dark, and bells in the tower tolled," Aaron began. "Grass and stuff blew around... Now, this is where it gets even weirder because a horse and robed rider appeared out of the darkness. No kidding around, the rider had claws for fingers as it held the horse's rein while they passed in front of me. They continued before disappearing back into the darkness. The wind stopped blowing, and it became light out again after they disappeared... So, what do you think about that?"

"That's pretty wild, man," Wayne replied.

"I believe what you told me, and I hope you believe me, too," Aaron said.

"What happened to us?" Wayne wondered.

"Your guess is as good as mine. All I know is I saw what I saw."

"Man to man, me too," Wayne said. "It's going to be a long time before I go into the bush again."

"I don't know if I'll ever go back to Holy Redeemer," Aaron said. "It's sad because that was our spot when Tyler and I wanted to get away from life... That place means a lot to me."

"I never told you this, I haven't told anyone, but I had the strangest dream two days before she died. I was running around this place that I couldn't get out of, and something that seemed evil was chasing me... I went into this room, and there was a coffin in the corner. I went up to it, and Tyler was inside.

"That dream... well, it was more like a nightmare, ended when she started knocking on my door. She came by still wearing her baseball outfit and all, because she just had a game, and she was so upset she had to come straight over to vent about it."

"Did you tell her about the dream?" Wayne asked.

"No, I didn't want to..." Aaron began. Tears came, thinking about what he was going to say next. "I didn't tell her, because I didn't want to freak her out," he spat in between sobbing and gasping for air.

Wayne patted Aaron's leg and then hugged him.

Aaron hugged him back.

Chapter Six
Demonville

Waves crashed against Lake Erie's shore as Aaron drifted to sleep on a night during a week he spent at his grandmother's cottage on Ambassador Beach, a month after Tyler died. Without air conditioning, shutters propped open for the most part were closed only when it rained. The uninsulated cottage was inhabitable only in the warm months. It lacked a shower and bathtub, so he had to bathe in Lake Erie or go to his aunt's nearby home.

He walked along a street through a comfortable-looking, middle-class neighborhood in the dead of night, in a dream. A sweet smell of rainwater clashed with the stench emanating from worms in gutters. Picket fences and hedgerows fronted most of the sleepy houses. Porch lights were on in some, but most of the houses were dark. No one other than himself was around.

An odd sense of being an intruder, of being in a place he had no business being, set in.

Cars were parked alongside the street and in driveways. It was 1979, yet every car was from the 1940s and 1950s era. What appeared to be a shipping label was affixed to a car's rear window parked in a driveway. Curious, he attempted to get closer to the label but could not read it without the benefit of light.

Headlights broke the dark as a car turned onto the street. Aaron sought cover behind a tree as instinct suggested whoever was inside the car would bring him harm should they spot him. Evil seemed to be on its way. The small of his back went numb, and his stomach tightened, fearing he had been spotted.

The hum of a car engine and tires slowly riding over asphalt began. Brakes squeaked as the car stopped in front of the tree.

Aaron swallowed hard, and his heart rate gathered speed. He worried that a goon or two or maybe more were about to appear on either side of the tree to confront him.

A few moments passed before the sound of tires riding pavement resumed as the car started away. His heart just began to calm before the brakes squeaked again. Headlights illuminated a nearby house after the car pulled into its driveway, where it stopped for a moment. The headlights retreated as the car reversed and started back in his direction. Perhaps the driver dropped someone off or picked someone up. The car passed and continued away.

Wary of leaving his cover, Aaron stayed behind a tree for a good while, until deciding it was safe to leave. He reached the sidewalk and started to run in the opposite direction of where the car had gone. After running a fair distance, he slowed and hurriedly walked toward an intersection. He ran across it to avoid being spotted by whomever was inside the car if the car lurked nearby. Sure, enough a car engine roared. A shadowy bulk sped toward him from behind. Headlights came on.

He reached a wrought-iron fence bordering the sidewalk and continued through an opening into a field of waist-high grass and weeds. Tall grass, weeds, debris, and uneven ground combined to slow his progress. A sound of car brakes being applied came from the road while noticing a building that appeared to be a mansion. Someone or something trampled through the weeds behind him while hurrying toward the massive house. With broken windows and an absence of inside light, it appeared abandoned. Thought of trying to engage the pursuer in reasonable conversation gave way to better judgment. He continued toward a set of doors, desperate to find a place to hide.

A cold wind that felt like demon breaths slapped his back while entering the mansion. After nudging through darkness, he went into a closet-sized room to hide. He picked up a two-by-four to use for self-defense.

Dread of having been pursued by evil ended upon waking. Relief came after Aaron realized he was safe in his grandma's cottage. What a strange dream that was, he thought.

Chapter Seven
Shay De Blasio

The first day of high school arrived too soon as far as Aaron was concerned, the summer of 1979 having passed quickly. Vincent Massey Secondary School, which assumed students from five elementary schools, had nearly five times as many students as Oakwood did. He wondered how he would find his way in a school with so many students.

Allen and Steve arrived at his house ten minutes later than they were supposed to. "What took you guys so long?" Aaron asked them. "We're going to be late now."

"It's our mom's fault," Steve hummed. "She forgot to wake me up."

"Nice move, blaming your old lady," Carl said.

"Have you heard of an alarm clock?" Aaron asked Steve.

They began down his driveway after Aaron locked the front door of his house.

"He was supposed to get me up," Alen claimed. "We've been sleeping in the same room lately. I depended on him to set the alarm."

"We can still make it in time if we walk fast," Steve suggested.

"So much for taking our time and getting there early," Aaron said. Though no one admitted it, the four were nervous about starting high school. They had planned to arrive early to get a sense of the place to ease their nerves before their first class.

"I'm sorry about being late, guys," Steve said. "I know we wanted to get there early."

"It is what it is," Aaron said.

"I hate school," Carl muttered. "This sucks! I wish we had another couple of weeks of summer vacation."

"Me, too," Aaron sighed. "Being stuck in class is like being locked up in prison."

"It's going to be different at Massey," Carl said. "We're not going to know many people. It's not going to be like it was at Oakwood, where we knew everyone. I think Massy has over a thousand students."

"Are you a chicken shit?" Allen snarled. "Are you scared?"

"Chicken shit my ass, butthole," Carl snarled back. He gave Allen a look to kill. "I'm just saying there's going to be a lot more students there."

Despite being good friends, Carl and Allen delighted in pushing each other's buttons.

"Chill out, you guys," Aaron grumbled. Burdened by sadness that Tyler was not with them, he had little patience for petty bickering.

"Are you guys thinking about Tyler?" he asked the others. "She should be walking with us."

"I was feeling the same," Carl said. "That's why I was bugging Allen. I'm trying not to think about it."

"Me, too," Allen said.

"I didn't want to say anything because I know it's hard for you and all of us," Steve said to Aaron.

"Tyler was really looking forward to going to high school. She wanted freedom to pick her classes and wanted to be on the soccer, softball, and basketball teams. The Massey soccer coach knows her dad, and he was saying she might have been the best player on the junior team."

"I could see that," Aaron barely heard Steve say. Emotions spiked when he talked about what she might have, what might have happened. "I'm gonna stop talking," Aaron said. Tyler was right beside him, he imagined. She should be right there, but all he saw was his shadow.

Aaron walked the rest of the way in stone silence, at times trying to smile to keep from crying. He looked up at the sky, deep into the blue, to the left of the lonely moon, which was still in the sky for some odd reason, toward where Heaven should be. Tyler was up there somewhere with her grandpa, without a worry about the grind and the pain of daily life. It would be nice to be that way.

It seemed odd, but he was jealous that she was at peace and not feeling the crushing depression that had darkened his life since the accident. Sometimes he thought about joining her. They would be together again, and the pain would be gone, but suicide was not an option. That would anger God, and he might not get into Heaven, so there would be no seeing Tyler again. And his parents would be devastated, and Tyler would be too, if that were possible in Heaven.

He would, as Mr. Page sometimes jokingly said, "Keep a stiff upper lip and carry on." That would be hard, but he had no choice but to do so and be brave about it.

Aaron, Carl, and Wayne, who walked to school with Scott, were assigned to the same homeroom class, while Allen, Andy, Steve, and Scott were assigned to a different homeroom. His homeroom teacher, a large man with a military buzz-cut, bore a menacing expression that screamed that he was a no-nonsense kind of guy, Aaron thought. The man's name was Mr. Simpson. Sure enough, as his haircut and expression suggested, Mr. Simpson had been a sergeant in the United States Army during the Vietnam War. Students were to address him as 'Sir' when they called upon him, Mr. Simpson advised the class.

Desks, five across and six rows deep, were assigned in alphabetical order. Wayne, his last name being Anderson, was assigned desk one of the first row. Carl ended up in a middle row, and Aaron was assigned to a desk in the fifth row.

Aaron looked around for familiar faces as Mr. Simpson reviewed class rules and *his* expectations. Besides Carl and Wayne, a few classmates from Oakwood and two kids he knew from around south Windsor were in the class. Three girls were teammates of Tyler's, two on her soccer team and one on her softball team. He met other teammates of hers in the hallways who introduced themselves to him, or he recognized them from team pictures Tyler showed him and from Tyler's funeral.

He became close to three of her teammates from softball and two from soccer. They all talked highly of Tyler and how much they missed her. Tyler spoke about him often, the girls said. A few of them said it was obvious that she adored him.

One of the girls on her soccer team was not surprised when he told her about the perfect kick she made to Andy, how it dropped in front of him while he was in full stride. Tyler was good for two goals a game, she said.

The girls on her softball team agreed with Tyler's take on Mr. Hitch that he was too hard on his team. One of the girls said Mr. Hitch and Tyler got along like fire and water. He was stern and by the book, whereas Tyler always wanted to have fun, like when she caught the ball basket style.

September 22nd, Tyler's birthday, fell on a Saturday that year. He went with her parents to visit her grave and brought purple daisies, which he placed in an urn beside her gravestone. That was a difficult day. Tyler would have been fourteen. By now, three weeks into the school year, she would have been settled into high school and playing on the Junior Girls' soccer team.

He thought they would be talking about their new experiences and what they hoped to accomplish while looking at a mound of settling earth above her grave. He came close to vomiting at the thought of her lying below him. Tyler should be alive, enjoying her life, not dead and alone. It just seemed so unfair.

"I hope you're okay and with us," he told her, looking at the sky.

The school year dragged on. Aaron noticed he did not laugh like he used to, and nothing was funny as the emptiness of her not being there remained as intense as it did when she died. Instead of healing, he seemed to miss her more with each passing day.

Christmas that year failed to liven his spirits. He still loved Christmas, but he felt ho-hum about it. He did not decorate his room as usual and begrudgingly helped his father string lights around the house, which he usually loved doing.

He continued to go to Holy Redeemer, deciding that seeing the horse and rider would not stop him from sitting in the bleachers and reflecting on life. He was no longer emotionally able to take the Talbot Road route, so he used Mount Royal Drive to get there. Sometimes, he cried while looking at the cross atop the bell tower, imagining Tyler somewhere beyond the sky behind it.

Her softball league replaced the old backstop on the diamond with a new one they dedicated to Tyler. A plaque with 'Dedicated to the memory of Tyler Page 1965-1979' etched on it was attached to the backstop. He looked through tears when he read it.

The first anniversary of her death came and went. It was the same as any other day. She was gone, and he missed her, and the empty feeling remained.

The summer passed quickly, as usual. School resumed. Mr. Simpson was his homeroom teacher again.

Mr. Simpson proved to be more down to earth as the previous school year went on. He set the standards he expected at the beginning of the school year and backed off as long as they were met. Be on time, be respectful to each other, listen to him and no one else, and sing, not mouth, the words to "O Canada." If you did that, then he liked you. For him, respect begot respect.

A girl who eerily resembled Tyler sat at the second last desk in Wayne's row. Her hair was black instead of dark brown, but her facial features were disturbingly similar. Her name was Shay De Blasio, Aaron learned as Mr. Simpson checked attendance.

Shay approached him in front of the school a few days later. "How's it going?" she asked him. Carl, Allen, and Wayne were there, but Shay only looked at him, and Aaron noticed. So did the others as they dispersed, leaving Aaron and Shay alone. "So, what do you think about Mr. Simpson?" she asked him. "He's a stern guy… he doesn't play around. He needs to relax."

"I had Mr. Simpson as my homeroom teacher last year," Aaron replied. "He can be a total hardass if you don't follow his rules, but if you do, he's pretty chill. He's trying to set the tone and will lighten up if everyone follows his rules… Get to class on time, be nice to each other and respect him, shut up and all that, and he's fine."

Shay giggled. "It freaks me out the way he talks — Mr. Simpson seems so mean, and the way he looks — like he's seriously pissed off about something."

Aaron chuckled. "I laughed to myself last year when he told us that he was a sergeant in Vietnam because of his haircut and the way he talked. He looks like a drill sergeant, and then, sure enough, he said he was a sergeant in the US Army."

Shay laughed and tapped his shoulder. "I thought the same when he went on about that today!" she exclaimed. "I had to bite my lip to keep from laughing."

"It's the same old spiel, just a different year."

"Was he a sergeant in Vietnam? I didn't think Canadians were over there."

"He's American, from New Jersey, and moved here five years ago when he married a woman from Windsor," Aaron replied. "If he wasn't a sergeant there, then he's a damn good liar… He talks about it every so often and last year showed us a picture of himself in uniform."

"I think the guy still thinks he's in the army and that we're his little soldiers," Aaron said, recalling Tyler say Mr. Hitch saw her team as his own little Marine troops.

"That's hilarious! He probably does."

"Could you imagine if he yelled out 'Attention!' when he returned to our classroom after stepping out and caught us all talking with each other?" Aaron asked her. "I would die."

"That wouldn't go over well," Shay replied.

"I haven't seen you around before I saw you in class," he said.

"I moved here in August from Toronto," Shay told him.

"That's gotta suck, moving from Toronto to boring old Windsor."

"My dad took a job here. That's why we moved here."

"Where?" he asked her.

"He's an accountant at Chrysler's in Detroit."

It had to be close to nine o'clock, the time their class started. Aaron feared incurring Mr. Simpson's wrath for being late. Tempted to look at his watch, he refrained, worried doing so might be construed by Shay as a sign of disinterest in her.

Shay looked at her watch. "It's getting close to nine," she declared. "We better pick up the pace. The guy's gonna be pissed if we're late."

"Yeah, I was thinking the same," he said as they hurried up a flight of stairs toward their homeroom on the second floor.

"So, have you always lived in Windsor?" Shay asked him.

"Yeah, in the same house," Aaron replied.

"That must be nice to stay in one place," she remarked as they reached the second floor. "I've moved about four or five times."

"How come so much?"

"My dad's old company moved him around all over the place," Shay said. "Before Toronto, we lived in British Columbia and Alberta."

It was two minutes to nine, according to a clock above the door, when they arrived at their homeroom. Aaron slowed to spend a final private moment with his apparent new friend. Shay slowed with him.

"So, where do you live?" he asked her.

"On Church Street. What about you?"

"On Askin, near Cabana Road."

"I think I've been down that street," she said. "That's the one next to a bush, right? If it's the one I'm thinking about."

"Yeah, that's my street," Aaron said. "That bush is called Oakwood Bush."

"My mom and I drove down your street when we were checking out the area just after we moved here. I saw a stone road that went into the bush. The road looked so pretty and peaceful, with forest on either side of it."

"The road is officially called Oakwood Lane, even though there's no street sign for it," he told her. "Everyone calls it the stone road. It's right by my house."

"I've wanted to check out the bush," Shay said.

Aaron took her comment as an invitation to ask if he wanted to go with her. "I'll go with you if you want," he offered. "I know Oakwood Bush like the back of my hand. I walk through it all the time and spent a lot of time in it when I was younger."

"Okay," she said. "That would be cool."

"Just let me know when you want to go there."

"Why don't we go tomorrow after school?" Shay suggested. "Unless you have something going on."

"No, I got nothing going on, so let's do it," Aaron happily agreed.

* * * * *

Shay Lynn De Blasio was her full name Aaron learned as they started toward Oakwood Bush. After leaving Massey, they continued to the end of Liberty Street, the street Massey fronted, to where Liberty ended at Askin. From there, they continued along a path leading into the bush that crossed over a sidewalk that led to the stone road.

"What's with the sidewalk?" Shay asked him as they began walking in toward the road.

"There're two sets of sidewalks in the bush," Aaron told her. "There's a sidewalk we passed that's hard to see because it's been grown over and the one we're walking on. There's another set of sidewalks deeper in the bush."

"Any conservation area I've ever been to has trails going

through it, not sidewalks," Shay said. "I don't get it."

"This bush wasn't meant to be a conservation area," Aaron replied. "If the city had its way, it would have been gutted and replaced by houses. It's a wasteland as far as the city's concerned." A swath of weeds and wildflowers and a ditch were to their left. "My dad said some developer cleared trees away to build a street, so that's why there's a clearing there. They were about to cut down another bunch of trees for another street before they realized the ground was too swampy to build on."

"Seriously? That seems pretty ass-backward," Shay remarked. "Didn't they know that before destroying a bunch of trees? That's crazy."

"I know, but that's what my dad told me. That was back in the 1950s... Maybe they didn't do environmental studies back then, or maybe people running the company that wanted to build the houses were stupid."

"It's good they didn't put houses out here," Shay said. "It's so pretty. There need to be more places like this because I've noticed that there are hardly any natural areas in Windsor. They should take the sidewalks..." She stopped in mid-sentence, spooked by a pheasant that flew out of the woods and crossed the sidewalk a few feet in front of them. "What the hell was that?"

"That was a pheasant," Aaron told her. "The bush is full of them. Pheasants are dumb. They don't know enough to get away until you're right on them... So, what were you saying?"

"Oh, I forget. Hmm... Oh, I remember," she said. "I was about to say the city should take the sidewalks out and put in real trails."

"That's a nice idea, but the city would never do it, at least not anytime soon. They won't spend the money."

"That's too bad because it would make for a nice conservation area."

"At least there are a few footpaths," Aaron noted. "I spent a lot of time out here when I was younger, like I mentioned yesterday. I always came out here with Wayne and Carl and my other friends Scott, Allen, Steve, Andy, and Tyler."

"I know Wayne and Carl. Have I seen the other guys?"

"You might have seen me with Scott, Allen, Steve, and Andy. Tyler was a girl."

"Like acted like a girl or was a girl?" Shay asked.

"Tyler *was* a girl," Aaron replied.

"The only Tyler I ever knew or heard of was a guy."

"Her parents named her Tyler after a town she was born in," Aaron said. He chuckled while recalling Tyler's sensitivity to her name. "She liked her name, but then on the same hand, Tyler didn't because she thought Tyler was a guy's name."

"I like Tyler as a name for a girl," Shay opined. "So, how come you refer to her in the past tense? Did she move away?"

"Tyler died last July," he told her.

"Oh, my God!" Shay exclaimed. "How old was she?"

"Thirteen."

"Oh man, that's so sad! What happened to her?"

"She got hit by a truck on Talbot Road that's on the other side of the bush. I was with her when it happened. We were riding our bikes down a hill on a path that ended at the highway… Tyler said her brakes weren't working, but I didn't believe her at first, thinking she was playing around because sometimes she acted like a daredevil on her bike. Tyler liked to jump over things and stop at the last minute when we went down the highway. But that time, she kept on going and ended up in the path of a truck after riding onto the road."

"Oh my God, that's so sad," Shay said. "I'm so sorry about your friend Tyler. You must have been devastated."

"I still can't believe she's gone," Aaron groaned. "I'm always thinking about her and about what happened."

"How long did you know her?" Shay asked him.

"Forever," he replied. "We grew up next door to each other. Our mothers hung out together, and we spent all our time at her house or mine when we were real young. We spent every day with each other. She was always there.

"It might sound corny, but part of me died with her," Aaron continued. "We stayed close as we got older. Ty would do anything for me, and I would do anything for her. I don't have a brother or sister, and she was the youngest of eight kids by six years, so we spent lots of time with each other. We were soul mates. It was a situation where we knew each other's thoughts and could finish sentences for each other."

"That doesn't sound corny at all about part of you dying with her," Shay said. "You guys were close. I can't imagine losing a friend I had known forever, let alone watching them die. That's pretty heavy and sad. She was only thirteen like you say. It just seems wrong for a person to die that young."

"I hope I'm not bumming you out," Aaron said. "I don't mean to bring you down. I'm just talking."

"You're not bumming me out, Aaron. It's good to talk when you're bummed out about something… You're a good guy Aaron."

"Aww, well, thank you," he said. "But what makes you say that?"

"Because of what you told me about how you felt about losing your friend," Shay replied. "So, tell me about Tyler. What was she like? What did she look like?"

"She was the nicest person I ever knew," Aaron began. "She always tried to be nice and considerate. Tyler wasn't perfect at that, but she tried to be… By the way, not to creep you out, but you kind of look like her. Tyler had dark brown hair, but your face reminds me of hers, and you have doe-like brown eyes as she did."

"Oh, do I have doe-like eyes?"

"Oh, you do. You have beautiful eyes, if you don't mind my saying."

"Not at all," Shay gushed. "That's nice of you to say."

"Well, you do," Aaron said. "Tyler liked hanging out with the guys and me," he continued. "She was a sweetheart but stood up to people who tried to push her around. Tyler never said a bad word about anyone and would help anyone or animal, for that matter. She had a sweet way of looking at life. Tyler was a total sweetheart."

"She sounds like she was a special person."

"She was," he sighed.

"It's kind of creepy that I look like Tyler, isn't it?" Shay said.

"Yeah, it is creepy," he agreed.

They reached the stone road and began toward Oakwood School. "I walked on this road a million times with Tyler," Aaron noted while watching the traffic on Talbot Road. It felt strange to walk on Oakwood Lane with another girl, he wanted to say.

"That's gotta seem weird to walk on this road with a different girl," Shay remarked. "Is this the first time you've done that?"

"Yeah," Aaron replied. "It's funny you say that because that's what I was thinking," he confided.

"The grade school I went to is down this road. It's called Oakwood School."

"Why would there be a school in the middle of a bush?"

"They began building it when they started putting the streets in; the school is on higher ground. If they built the houses like they wanted to, Oakwood would be surrounded by them… But it's not as though my old school is in the middle of a bush. There are playgrounds around it. And it has a front lawn with a U-shaped driveway that goes around a lawn, which connects Oakwood to Cabana Road…. There's a small crop field between the school and Talbot Road. An old farmer used to grow crops in the field, but nothing's been growing there for a few years now. I guess the farmer got too old to keep using it, or maybe he died."

"Or maybe he sold it to some developer," Shay surmised.

"Perhaps," Aaron said. "He sold the property the school was built on, so he would have had a good chunk of the field at one time. The farmer probably kept working the strip of land by the highway to keep busy while hoping someone would buy it off him to put up a strip mall or something. Tyler and I almost got caught by him when we were running through the field. We called him 'Farmer Dell' because the farmer looked like a depiction of *The Farmer in the Dell* in a book of children's songs we liked to sing when we were little kids."

"That's cute," Shay said.

"The guy looked like a spitting image of the farmer in *The Farmer in the Dell*. He always wore a straw hat, overalls, and a red and black checkered shirt like the farmer in the book and drove an old tractor. He ran after us and came close to grabbing Tyler by the hood of a hoodie she was wearing when he spotted us one day running through rows of corn he was growing. He yelled at us and warned us not to go back there again as we ran away. Tyler wanted to go there a few weeks later, but I didn't want to."

"Tyler sounds like she was a bit of a troublemaker."

"She was at times but never meant to be," Aaron said. "She just liked to have fun by adding a little spice to life."

Waterfowl sounds became noticeable as they neared the school.

"That sounds like a bunch of ducks," Shay said.

"There's a wildlife sanctuary at the school," Aaron told her. "Mr. Sweetman, the first principal at Oakwood, wanted to leave a section of the schoolyard natural and had six-foot high wire fences placed around it. He had lots of little shelters built, where ducks and geese could tend to eggs."

"That's cool. What made Mr. Sweetman think to do that?"

"Mr. Sweetman was a naturalist kind of guy. He cared about wildlife, ducks, and whatever. The school board probably went along with what he wanted, thinking they would have a place where kids from other schools could go on field trips."

They passed a path leading behind the sanctuary. "We could look at the back of the sanctuary if we went down that path,"

Aaron said as he looked at it. "But it's going to be all muddy and watery with all the rain we've had over the last two weeks."

"Maybe we can go down it another day," Shay proposed.

"Definitely," he said, delighting in the potential of spending time with her again.

"They built that barn a few years ago," he told her as they passed a small barn in the sanctuary.

"What's in it?" Shay asked him.

"Animals — sometimes, if local farmers have animals, they want to lend them to the school. There's been cows, pigs, and goats in there before."

"That's pretty cool," she said.

"It works out pretty well, actually, except for the animals," Aaron told her. "Oakwood students get a chance to know young farm animals and tend to them as they grow. The farmers take them back after they're full-grown and have them slaughtered."

"Did you know the animals you helped take care of were going to be killed?" Shay asked him.

"I didn't know that until my teacher told me a few weeks before I finished grade eight," he replied.

They started onto a path in front of the sanctuary and reached the main gate of the fence. A padlock secured it. "Damn, I figured it would be locked," Aaron muttered.

"Well, that sucks," Shay said. "It would have been nice to go in there."

"They started locking the gate after the sanctuary got vandalized a couple of times," Aaron told her. "Sometimes losers knock over the feeder bins and spray paint the barn and the shelters. One night some assholes went in there and killed a few geese and ducks."

"That's pretty morbid," she said. "I've never understood why people can be cruel to innocent creatures."

"I knew some of the morons. Their names were published in the *Windsor Star* after the police arrested them. One of them, a guy I was close to, never confessed to me about doing that, but I wasn't surprised he didn't because what he did was sick and depraved."

"That's sad they had to start locking the place because of morons like that," Shay remarked. "That sucks that a few assholes ruined things for everyone else," she added. "But the fence is easy to climb if you wanted to."

"Because of a few assholes, people are only supposed to go in there during school hours or every other Saturday when the gate is open for a few hours," he said. "Or when Mr. Dennison, a teacher who oversees the place and the barn boys who volunteer to help maintain it, is there... Barn boys are kids in grade seven and above who feed the animals and ducks, build the shelters, and help keep the place clean."

"There were no barn girls?" Shay asked him.

"Some girls helped out, and Tyler was one of them. Barn boys are what the school called students who help out. Tyler had a problem with that, so she called herself a barn girl... I think the school calls them barn helpers now after she told the principal how she felt."

Mallard ducks, geese, chickens, and other ducks waddled to where Aaron and Shay stood. "They think we're going to give them food," Aaron said. "People toss bread and sunflower seeds over the fence to get ducks, geese, and the chickens to come up to it."

"Don't they get enough food here?" Shay asked him.

"They always have food. There are feeders over there... Do you see them?" Aaron asked her while pointing at a cluster of feed bins. "The grade seven teacher and the kids that help him out always make sure they have food and freshwater."

"What do they feed them?"

"A mix of grain and seeds. They can live on that, but it's probably like porridge and vegetables to us. To them, bread and sunflower seeds are like steak and potatoes, I guess. They love it."

The largest goose in a gaggle hissed at Shay. She jumped back. Aaron could not help but laugh. "It's not funny!" Shay exclaimed as she chuckled. Her face went a brilliant red with fright and apparent embarrassment.

"I'm sorry, but it was funny," he said.

"I would laugh too if I was you... But what's its problem? I was just standing here."

"It's a male and the dominant one," Aaron informed her. "He thinks we have food and wants to have it all to himself."

"No food for you, you prick," Shay yelled at the gander. She pointed a middle finger at it. "Screw off!" she told it.

"Oh, be nice. He's just an alpha male doing his thing."

The birds, without an offer of food, waddled away.

"I'm thirsty," Shay said. "I need something to drink."

Aaron told her there was a variety store on Talbot Road and they could be there in ten minutes if they walked at a decent pace.

"Oh, the Double D," she said. "Ya, I know that store. Let's go."

Aaron announced that that had been his grade two room, as they passed a classroom after reaching the school. They cupped their hands to block day glare while looking through a window. The desks and chairs in the room were alarmingly small. "I can't believe I was able to fit into those desks."

"We were all small once," Shay remarked.

They started toward Cabana Road. After crossing Cabana, they continued on the path leading through the field. Aaron dreaded passing where Tyler died.

"Tyler and I spent a lot of time beside the path where it goes down to the highway," he said. "We sat around eating candy or whatever we bought at Double D. Sometimes we laid on our backs and looked up at the sky or played a game we called counting trucks... I miss those days... Counting trucks was something we did to kill time when we were bored and didn't have anything better to do. That was fun, a challenge to see who would win. We usually spent a good hour or two doing that, as one of us counted trucks in the southbound lanes, and the other counted trucks in the northbound lanes for a set amount of time. Whoever counted the most trucks was given two dollars by the loser to buy stuff at the store the next time we went there."

"Usually, we tossed a coin to decide who counted the south or northbound lanes," Aaron continued. "The last time we played it, Tyler insisted on counting trucks in the northbound lanes, which end at the bridge to the United States. I didn't care which lanes we counted since there seemed to be no rhyme or reason to the flow of traffic... Tyler ended up counting twice as many trucks as I did. She told me after that, she figured there would be more trucks heading to the US because Memorial Day weekend was a day away. She figured that American truckers would want to get home to spend time with their families, and it turned out that she was right."

"That was sneaky," Shay said. "Tyler got you good there, eh? I like that. That's funny." "You go, girl," she declared, looking at the sky.

"Yeah, Tyler was quite the girl," Aaron stated. They continued toward the spot where she died. "This is going to be hard," he said after a few moments passed.

"What's wrong?" Shay asked him.

"This will be the first time I've been to where she died since the accident," he replied.

"Are you okay with it? We could cut through the field and go to the highway somewhere else if you want."

"No, I have to do this," he said, steeling himself to pass the spot. "I always used this path... I can't avoid it forever... I'll focus on the store."

"Are you sure? It's cool if you don't want to."

"It's okay," he said. "I have to," he groaned, looking at the ground where Tyler fell off her bike. Tears welled in his eyes. To the left of them was their spot where they sat to count trucks, a slight bump in the field just big enough for both of them to sit on.

Shay asked if he was okay. He told her he was fine, but he needed a minute. He had to cry; there was no holding back. This was their place, his and Tyler's. Now it had the feel of a place of dread. The place haunted him. One minute she was saying it was fun falling off her bike, that it was all good because she and her bike were fine, and the next came the most horrific moment of their lives.

"I can't do this right now," he told Shay, not caring if she understood. He had to leave, and that he did, as he looked at the path and saw himself and Tyler riding up and down it, which they did at least three times a week. That path was a part of them. That path betrayed her. He vowed never to step on it again.

He said he was sorry for changing plans on her. Shay understood, but he did not care if she did or not. He told her how he and Tyler dodged traffic to get across Talbot Road without a second thought. Tears came again as visions played of her lying on the hill their spot was on, on the opposite side of the path, where they would look north to the Ambassador Bridge, visible from their vantage point, despite being five miles away.

They barely noticed the spot where Tyler landed while looking over it, never suspecting the significance it would have in their lives that she would die there.

* * * * *

Aaron and Shay became close and, by mid-January 1981, considered themselves to be a couple. He often considered what Tyler would think about him being with another girl. She would be happy for him, he was sure. She would want him to be happy.

They went steady throughout high school and on to university. He and the rest of the guys continued to be friends. Andy moved to Toronto, but the others remained living in and around the Windsor area.

Dwelling on days long gone, Aaron took a nostalgic solo walk around Oakwood School the day before beginning university. He could picture himself and Tyler waiting to enter the school in line with their classmates before passing a door leading to their kindergarten room in 1970. An innocent time it seemed now, blissfully unaware of the dark world around them. Those were the good old days. Perhaps with Shay, good days of a different kind might lay ahead.

Aaron turned his thoughts to when he sat in the library at Massey, perusing books while preparing to write an essay. An illustration of a hooded, robed figure on a horse stuck out from a book about the supernatural. Geoffrey was the rider's name. Geoffrey was an agent of death, according to the book.

The horse and rider resembled the horse and rider he saw at Holy Redeemer.

Chapter Eight
Texas Road

Teri-Ann De Carlo pulled away from Steve after giving him a goodnight kiss. "Well, good night, sleep tight, say your goodnight prayers, and keep your hands out of your underwear," she sang.

"What are you talking about?" Steve asked her after laughing. He and Teri-Ann were in their third month of dating. Teri-Ann possessed a sense of humor that Steve appreciated.

"That's what my grandmother used to say when she tucked me into bed at night when I stayed at her place," Teri-Ann said. "When I was a kid."

"Yeah, right!" Steve exclaimed. "I doubt your grandma told you to keep your hands out of your underwear. You're kidding, right?"

Teri-Ann smiled at him. "Well, she would say good night and sleep tight and say your prayers," she said. "I added the part about the underwear."

"You're funny!" Steve said, laughing. "That would be hilarious if your grandma said that to you." Parked in front of her house, he looked to see if Teri-Ann's parents were looking on.

Teri-Ann kissed him again as Steve stared at the house. "What's wrong?" she asked him.

"I'm looking to see if your parents are watching," Steve replied. "I don't need your old man to come out here with a shotgun."

"Oh, don't worry about them," Teri-Ann said. "They're not home." She grabbed his crotch and kissed him again.

"Does that mean I can come in?" Steve asked her.

"That would be nice, but they're coming home soon," Teri-

Ann replied. "Anyway, you and I have to get up early tomorrow." They planned to spend the next day at Point Pelee National Park, a forty-five-minute drive from Windsor. She gave Steve a final kiss before they separated for the night.

"I'll come by at ten to pick you up," he said. "Is that okay?"

"I'll be ready," Teri-Ann promised.

Teri-Ann left the car and started toward her house. She reached the front door and waved at him before starting inside. Steve pulled away and began the half-hour drive home after seeing her safely inside.

* * * * *

Highway 18 was dark where it brushed against the eastern reach of the Detroit River as Steve drove home. Texas Road was darker yet. Gravel, for the most part, paved only where it met a major crossroads; Texas Road was as remote as it got in Essex County. No houses, only fields, bush, and a cemetery bordered its two-mile length. The road was supposedly haunted, and bad things happened to people on it, according to local urban legend. A young couple became stranded on the road, according to one infamous story, after their car ran out of gas. The woman stayed in the car while her boyfriend went to get help. She fell asleep. Hours passed. The woman woke to find herself alone. Worried about her boyfriend, she left the car and went to find him. His severed head was stuck on the top of the car's antenna. She ran down the road and found his body impaled by tips of pickets of a wrought-iron fence in front of the graveyard.

"Jesus!" Steve yelled while stopping after his car began to shake and pull to the right. He slammed his door in frustration after leaving the car. Its right front tire was flat, the rim barely above the ground. "God damn it," Steve muttered while walking to the trunk to retrieve a spare tire, jack, and tire iron. He worried that the spare might have gone flat, not having checked its pressure in years. Thankfully, it remained solid.

While picking up the tire iron, he wondered how the flat had been acquired. No potholes or debris had been run over. The tires were in sound shape, according to the mechanic who inspected and rotated them only a few weeks before. He pulled a spare tire out of the trunk and tire iron and jack. Unexpectedly top-heavy, the jack slipped from his hands, straining his right wrist. While uttering a few swear words, Steve grabbed the wrist with his other hand and massaged it. Pain subsided.

Paranoia set in, alone at night on a supposedly haunted road with a nefarious history, while kicking away gravel to clear a spot to kneel. Thoughts turned to the couple. What happened to them was only one of several ghastly things that were rumored to have occurred on the road. Not a believer in ghosts, headless horsemen, and the like, paranoia stemmed from rumor an escaped murderer lived in the nearby woods. The idea a killer might be lurking nearby heightened his senses.

With moonlight as his only source of light, Steve wedged the tire iron under the hubcap and tugged at it. The cap refused to budge. With both hands, he bore down with full weight. The hubcap came loose with a solid-sounding pop.

Thoughts turned to Teri-Ann while removing lug nuts from the tire. Teri-Ann seemed to have it all, looks, smarts and, like him, a quirky sense of humor. Tonight marked their third date, and things seemed to be going well between them. Steve liked her and hoped they might have a future together, though wary after having been burned in prior relationships.

A hard push with the tire iron loosened the first four lug nuts, but the last one came off with relative ease. "Holy shit, the nut job didn't tighten all the bolts!" Steve angrily yelled, feeling anger toward a mechanic who had recently rotated the tires. He would talk to the mechanic first thing in the morning and let the guy know how displeased he was.

A faint sound began after removing the tire. A large shadow moved toward him while he looked in the direction the noise was coming from. He hurried toward the driver's side door to find shelter in the car, not sure what was happening. An object struck him in the forehead with enough force to send him reeling backward while looking toward the noise again. Blood drained into his eyes, blinding him as he began a desperate, aimless, futile trot along the road to get away. Whatever it was that originally struck him slapped his back and then the back of his head. Blood drained under his coat collar and flowed onto his back, and his heart began to ache. Exhaustion sent him to the ground as he carried desperately on to wherever. He strained to see what attacked him as his heart squeezed and then stopped. Only moonlight shared the road with him as far as he could see while taking a final breath.

*****

After Steve's funeral, the friends gathered to come to terms with his death and help his brother, Allen, through a life-altering, difficult time.

Their grief was enhanced as this was the second funeral they had attended together since Tyler's. Memories of her were shared there and whenever they had a chance to be with each other. Each of the friends had been out to the cemetery to see her, usually around the time of her birthday.

Aaron's parents were present, as was Tyler's mom.

The last funeral the friends attended was for Tyler's father; he died a year after Tyler died. They did not know her father well, but all felt compelled to go; they had a bond as they were compatriots of grief. Cardiac arrest was the given cause of death, but everyone knew it was heartache that killed him. He could not overcome the pain of losing his daughter, and his heart gave out.

Aaron spent part of the service with Tyler's mother. They stayed close. He called her every year on Tyler's birthday to help lighten her mood, and his too, by talking, laughing, and sometimes tearfully reminiscing about Tyler and what she might be up to today, and they had lunch every so often.

Tyler would have been proud of her nieces and nephews, they

agreed. She would have nine nieces and seven nephews if she were still alive.

He also connected with her sisters and brothers from time to time. They would ask each other questions, wanting to know everything about Tyler. He did not share things she was not proud of, like making up the story about Arlene or that she sometimes thought that she was a mistake.

The calls to each other became less frequent over time as there was a point where all that could be shared was shared. The youngest was five years older than Aaron, so they were merely acquaintances.

According to an autopsy report, Steve died from massive blood loss. The police were investigating his death as a homicide and were looking for the culprit. No evidence was found, no one witnessed what happened, and no one could guess who the killer might be.

"You guys don't think that road had anything to do with Steve's death?" Carl asked the others.

"You're kidding, right?" Allen asked him. "That's crap what they say about that road. It's a crock about the headless horseman. That's all-Halloween nonsense people on the radio came up with about stupid things that supposedly happened on Texas Road." He referred to tales told by jockeys on a local radio station.

"I don't know, man," Aaron said.

"Oh, come on, Aaron," Allen grumbled. "You don't believe that nonsense, do you?"

"I don't know," Aaron replied. Thinking about the horse and rider he saw at Holy Redeemer, anything seemed possible. "I'm sorry, Allen," he felt compelled to say in light of his brother's death.

"About what?" Allen asked him.

"I do not mean to trivialize Steve's death. I'm not saying I think that any bullshit happened to your brother on that road."

"You're not," Allen replied.

"I think something's going on, on that road, but that doesn't mean it had anything to do with your brother's death."

"It's just a coincidence that he happened to die on it," Allen said.

"Do you guys remember the two guys we met at the New Year's party last year?" Carl asked the others. "The guys who claimed they saw a man vanish into thin air when they walked by the cemetery on Texas Road. They said he was an apparition of a man who hung himself in the cemetery. Those guys probably were messing with us, but who knows?"

"Those guys were smashed and making things up," Allen submitted.

"What about the chick who supposedly found her boyfriend's head stuck on the antenna of their car after it broke down?" Andy said. "Who supposedly found his body impaled by spikes on top of an iron fence in front of the cemetery?"

"The radio jocks always mention that story every Halloween, and I don't believe it," Allen firmly stated.

"What about the family found murdered in their farmhouse on Texas Road?" Wayne asked Allen.

"What family?" Allen asked him.

"The McDonald family," Wayne replied. "Everyone knows about what happened to the McDonalds," he said. "It's legendary. The parents and their three kids were stabbed to death, and their hearts were cut out."

"When did that supposedly happen?" Allen asked.

"In the twenties," Aaron told him. "Devil worshippers supposedly killed them, and that's not a bullshit story. There was an article in the paper a few years ago about the murders on the anniversary of them. The police never identified any suspects, so no one was ever arrested."

"The house where the massacre took place was torn down a year after the murders, but its foundation is still there," Andy said. "I went there with my brother to check it out a few years ago. Dirt and vines covered the foundation, and trees were growing out of it."

"Whatever," Allen groaned. "I still don't believe there's anything weird going on, on that road. It's all bullshit they made up on the radio for Halloween," he muttered after swallowing a mouthful of beer. "I was open to the idea something was wrong about that road, but I don't want to believe that now. I just want to think that my brother died peacefully. It's hard to believe that my brother's dead... I miss him."

Chapter Nine
Time Goes On

Years passed, but time failed to numb the pain of her loss as Aaron continued to be haunted by Tyler's death. Steve's death impacted him, too, but to a lesser, different extent. A part of him died with Tyler, and he had yet to emotionally overcome losing such an integral part of his being. Long ago, Aaron concluded that he had to choose between wallowing in pity or spin a more humorous take on things. He found humor in disparaging himself if that brought a laugh to others but, more importantly, to him.

Respect was not needed or required of anyone other than himself, having matured to come to know that life was too fleeting to live for the opinion of others. Confidence grew to cut through the nuance of life to make meaningful decisions and stick with them without second-guessing himself. If time proved him wrong, he revisited and adjusted decisions per his own dictates, believing that he only had himself and God, if He truly existed, to answer to.

Doubt in God's existence began with Tyler's death. If God performed miracles, why did He not help her? She was faithful and wanted to show God good things. Was there not a way that He could have made the truck run a few seconds slower to allow Tyler time to reach the medium? And now Steve died savagely. Where was God then, and could He not have done something to ease Mr. Page's unending pain?

God did help him find Shay in some way, Aaron thought. He took his relationship with her seriously. In all fairness to her, he never expected that she would take the place of Tyler. But he and Shay developed their own special bond and loved to laugh and have fun together.

Shay earned a Master of Social Work degree over the intervening years, as Aaron went on to graduate from medical school and become a family physician. After ten years of being together, they finally married. With neither caring for extravagance, they held their reception in a back room of Barre's, a tavern they frequented with their friends. Their honeymoon was kept simple, too. Although they had the financial means to travel to some exotic locale, they decided to go on a two-week road trip instead. A road trip that would take them through the Maritimes and on to New York City, where they planned to spend a few days before heading home. But they made a point of staying in nice places.

Their honeymoon trip began at his parents' house the day after they married. He looked at the front yard of Tyler's house while passing it. The memory of chasing Tyler to the fort a few days before she died was vivid.

A familiar-looking man washed his car in a driveway as they started down Cabana Road. Mr. Dean was the man's name. Once with salt and pepper hair and slightly overweight, his hair was now shocking white, and he had grown fat. The passage of time can be cruel, Aaron thought, remembering the more youthful-looking Mr. Dean.

Aaron glanced at the playing field as he and Shay passed Oakwood School, recalling the day he, Tyler, and Wayne sat around talking after playing soccer before seeing McFarren. He smiled, remembering how Wayne's fear of going to see McFarren contrasted with Tyler's ambiguous comfort by the prospect. The look of fear in Wayne's eyes remained priceless.

"What are you smiling about?" Shay asked him.

"I'm thinking about the time me, Tyler, and Wayne sat around talking after playing soccer in the field beside the school," he replied. "That was when Wayne mentioned McFarren who taught us how to do the séance after Tyler had said she missed her grandpa and wanted to say goodbye to him. Wayne regretted mentioning the séance because he didn't want to see McFarren but finally gave in to li'l ol' Tyler after she insisted on seeing him. Wayne told me he felt he had to go because he told her about the séance and couldn't talk her out of it."

Shay knew the story. That Wayne told Tyler the man taught his sister and her friends how to do a séance. That she missed her grandpa and wanted to do a séance to contact him. He had told her why they tried to contact Tyler through the séance and that they stopped after her image began to form.

"I always wondered why Wayne just didn't ask his sister," Shay said. "She knew how to do the séance."

"Because his sister's friend had the sheet the man wrote how to do the séance on," Aaron replied. "Her friend moved away after they tried the séance before he mentioned the séance to us."

"I find that hard to believe that your friend Tyler's image began to form on the television screen when you guys tried to contact her." She paused as they turned onto Talbot Road. "I believe you about what happened, but it's hard to imagine that her face began to appear."

"I'm not bullshitting," he said.

"I'm not saying you are," Shay replied.

"I still don't believe it either," he maintained.

They neared the path that ended across from Double D. Aaron spotted a boy and girl sitting where he and Tyler sat above the road. The girl bore a disturbing resemblance to Tyler and the boy, a younger version of himself. Not paying proper attention to his driving, the car veered toward the medium.

"Watch out!" Shay yelled. Aaron quickly corrected the car's direction. "Watch where you're going," she scolded him.

He looked back at the hill. The boy and girl were gone. "Did you see two kids sitting beside the path?" he asked Shay.

"I didn't see any kids," she replied. "I was looking in the opposite direction… But whatever, pay attention to your driving."

"I will," he promised, disappointed with himself for upsetting Shay. He wondered how the kids could leave so quickly. And damn, the girl looked like Tyler and the boy like a younger version of himself. Maybe his eyes had played tricks on him?

Aaron looked straight ahead as they reached the western extent of the lawn surrounding Holy Redeemer Seminary while dwelling on seeing the boy and girl. He could not look at the once sacred place. That would only conjure painful thoughts.

* * * * *

After exploring the Empire State Building, they walked along a midtown Manhattan to the hotel. Buildings they passed were seedy and pollution-stained. Three to four stories on average, the buildings housed shops at street level and apartments on the upper floors. Signs for the shops, rising along the facades or jetting over the sidewalk, vied for attention. A neon sign stood out with a purple background, yellow lettering, and an image of a woman in fortune teller garb with a spread of tarot cards in her hands. They reached the shop. A sign in a window read 'Palm and Tarot Card Reading by Madame Lisa.'

Obsessed with astrology and predicting the future, Shay would want to see the fortune teller if she noticed the signs. She used horoscopes to plan her days and even suggested their wedding date by referencing their astrological signs. Aaron tried to get her to look at something across the street, but it was too late.

"Oh, look at this," she said while yanking his shoulder and staring at the window. "We have to check this place out."

"Oh damn," Aaron groaned. "Do we have to? That fortunetelling stuff is fake. It's a ruse to make money."

"Oh, come on, Aaron, don't be a buzz killer," she said.

"This should be interesting," he sighed.

A bell rang as Shay opened the door. A narrow staircase was ahead of them, and a large, dimly lit room lay to their right, illuminated by a light bulb hanging from the ceiling and two gaudy-looking lamps. The walls were purple and yellow, like the sign outside. A large table surrounded by green 1960s modernist chairs occupied the middle of the room.

An older woman started down the staircase, gingerly grasping hand railings on either side. "How can I help you?" she asked them.

"We saw your sign and decided to come in," Shay replied.

"Tarot card reading will cost you five bucks," the woman said while leading them into the large room. "Palm reading will cost you ten."

"We'll do both," Shay replied. "Both of us." She looked at Aaron. He rolled his eyes in dismay. "Come on, try it. It'll be fun."

The woman reached a chair at the table and motioned them with a shriveled, aging hand to the chairs directly opposite hers. Shay pulled a ten and a twenty-dollar bill from her wallet and laid them on the table. The woman took the bills and tucked them inside her bra. "Let me see your hand," the woman asked Shay.

She asked questions and followed with broad statements after making a series of guesses. The woman was skilled at her con, saying typical positive things, which Shay lapped up. "Your future will be bright," the woman said while studying Shay's palm. "Your future will be one of romance and material wealth." Shay turned and looked at Aaron, her face glowing. "What's your birth date, dear?"

"July 23, 1965," Shay replied.

"Ah, you have the stamina and determination of a bull. Anything you set your mind to will be yours."

"I always thought you were as stubborn as a bull," Aaron chuckled.

Shay smiled at him. The woman glared at him and grimaced as if she had swallowed vinegar, clearly not impressed by his making light of her work. "Now you," she barked, pointing at the table. "Put your hand on the table." Aaron obliged the woman, winking at Shay as he did, clarifying that he was doing this to accommodate her interest in such nonsense. The woman placed her hand over his. Her hand felt rough, like it had spent a day soaking in salt water. Yet the touch was almost stimulating, a scary thought, this woman capable of stirring pleasure. "What day were you born?" she asked him.

"May 31, 1965," he replied.

A concerned expression formed on the woman's face. "Something terrible is going to happen to you."

"What?" Shay asked.

"I can't say... it's hard to say. But it's not good."

Aaron pulled his hand away.

"You can't say, or you don't know?" Shay asked the woman.

"I don't know," the woman replied.

"Let's get out of here," Aaron said, rising from his chair. He had heard enough.

Shay grabbed his arm. "Come on, Aaron, hear her out."

"You will have bad followed by bad," the woman continued after he sat down again, after retaking his hand. "That's all that I know. It's all blurry. I wish I could tell you more, but I can't. All I see is that something evil is watching you."

"Well, I guess I better stay away from black cats," Aaron quipped. "Come on, Shay." He started from the table, this time leaving for good.

"Thank you," Shay said to the woman.

The woman waved at them as they left the shop.

* * * * *

Fatigue set in—a combination of champagne, road weariness, and not having eaten properly over the previous few days. Aaron drifted asleep on the final night of their stay in New York, in a hot tub he lounged in with Shay in their room. A continuation of the dream from several years ago, where he was trapped inside the abandoned mansion, began.

Though it was pitch-black, Aaron seemed to possess the night vision of a cat. A good amount of time passed hiding in the closet, the point from which the dream resumed. He had to leave the house before dawn to avoid being spotted by his pursuer. He started from the closet, cautious with every step, wary of being noticed. Chunks of plaster lay along the way as he quickly walked toward the front door.

A wall was where the door should be. In a state of panic, Aaron started down a hallway, certain he had gone the wrong way and that the entrance was near. The hallway went on and on, seemingly without an end. No door leading outside was in sight.

"Wake up," a familiar voice said, startled by someone trying to shake him awake. "Come on, Aaron," Shay said. Aaron regained consciousness and opened his eyes. "We better go to bed, Mister," she told him. "You're dead to the world."

"How long did I pass out for?" he asked her.

"About ten minutes," Shay replied. "I let you sleep, but then you began to twitch and were breathing fast like something was wrong with you."

"I had the weirdest dream," Aaron said. "I was inside this abandoned house and couldn't find my way out. I kept going down this hallway that seemed to go on forever."

"You had me worried," she told him.

Chapter Ten
A Texas Town and the Girl in the White Dress

Clouds, leftovers from a storm that took down trees and power lines, followed their cousins, gone somewhere east, as Aaron stood in a remote section of Our Lady of the Lakes Cemetery, where Tyler was buried. The cemetery was located twenty-five miles outside of Windsor on Lake Erie. He made a promise to Tyler on the day of her funeral to visit her grave a minimum of every three months, when he could drive there. He kept his promise and always left six purple daisies, Tyler's favorite flowers, at her grave.

"It's hard to believe you've been gone thirteen years now," he told Tyler while looking at her gravestone after placing the customary clutch of daisies in a vase. 'Loving Daughter and Sister, Tyler Kathleen Tatum Page, September 22, 1965 - July 2, 1979' was inscribed on the stone. A cross and a praying angel of a girl were depicted at its bottom.

A smile formed while remembering how she sometimes complained about her first name. Tyler was to be named Kathleen, after her English grandmother, but her parents' plans changed after she was born eight weeks early in Tyler, Texas, where they had gone to attend a wedding. The name of the town grew on them during the time they spent there while their fragile daughter fought to live in a neonatal intensive care unit.

They decided to name her Tyler to honor the town because of the help they received there: from a gas station attendant who directed them to the nearest hospital to a police officer who happened along who escorted them there to hospital staff who took care of their daughter during her first weeks of life.

Tyler planned to travel to Tyler one day, curious to see what the town looked like, having always felt a connection to a place she had never been. He would go with her; at least, that was her plan.

Aaron scooped remains of daisies left on his last visit and started toward a trash receptacle to dispose of them. There was something odd about the cemetery. It took a moment to realize what it was — that he was alone. There were usually other visitors whenever he went there and at least a few cemetery tenders trimming trees, cutting grass, and digging out graves.

Something moved to his left after arriving at the receptacle. A girl in a white dress, who looked like Tyler, stood in a distant area of the cemetery, near where it backed onto a cliff facing Lake Erie. She waved at him. He waved back at her while wondering what she was doing there alone, unaccompanied by adults.

After depositing dead daisies, he looked back to where she stood. The girl was gone. Had his eyes gone back to playing tricks, like they apparently had done when he saw the girl and boy along Talbot Road?

He walked to Tyler's grave and placed the fresh daisies in an urn. He retrieved a jug of water from the car and filled the urn. Used from when first bringing daisies to her grave, the jug was a dirty white color, having faded from its original bright orange. Of sentimental value, he affectionately called the jug, 'Bug the Jug.'

A thought came that perhaps Tyler may have been blessed to leave this life before it could erode her wide-eyed innocence. She died before coming to know human nature led to blind, self-serving behavior, often without regard to others. Yet pain did find Tyler after her grandpa passed. Desperate to take her pain away, he futilely wanted to do more than merely provide a listening ear and a shoulder to cry on.

Her pain ended, but his remained. Aaron had a cross to bear. Perhaps his pain would end in God's chosen time.

The idealism of childhood ended with him watching Tyler

die. Crumbs of happiness remained, if of mind, to see and appreciate them, yet the pain of her loss was a beast without a master. Guilt came, and he worried as Tyler felt close, she could feel his pain. But there *was* no pain in Heaven, if one existed, he concluded.

A sense of being watched by the girl who disappeared felt strong until he left the cemetery.

Chapter Eleven
A Phantom in the Streets

It was the dark side of dusk when Andy stepped onto Bloor Street and into a raging blizzard. Snow pelted his face. He had to get to the Eaton Centre, a ten-minute walk from where he worked. The hell with the weather. He and Karen had a spat that morning about household responsibilities. Anger close to getting the better of him, he stormed out of their apartment and left for work. Anger lessened, and regret set in after he climbed into a subway car. He broke a promise they had made, not to part ways in anger, but leaving was preferable to saying something he would later regret.

He clock-watched all day, anxious to get home to Karen, to make things right. He called her during morning recess at the school where she was a teacher. They resolved their dispute as Karen accepted his apology for having left in anger and appreciated his rationale for doing so. He promised a special evening that night. He would bring home dinner after going to the Eaton Centre to buy a sweater they saw in a store a week before. Karen loved the sweater and thought it would look good on her, but what little extra money they had was earmarked to buy presents for others. That was before news of the promotion.

People trudged along the sidewalk. Traffic slowly passed. Buses rumbled along, their exhaust fumes held thick, ensnared in the thick driving snow. Streetcars rattled and clanged as they meandered past.

Andy neglected to fasten the top button of his coat, an oversight that allowed snow to pile before melting against his neck. He stepped into an enclosed doorway of a shop to get out of the wind, pulled his gloves off, shook snow away from inside the collar, and fastened the button. He stepped back onto the sidewalk after putting his gloves back on and began toward the nearest subway station after leaving Eaton's where he bought the sweater for Karen. A sense of an unseen presence paralleling him along the opposite side of the street felt strong.

Ringing bells became noticeable as Andy neared a department store, tolled by a man dressed as Santa Claus, collecting money for the Salvation Army. "Help the hungry have a Merry Christmas!" the man asked, passing people as he stood beside a money pot chained to a stand. Andy made a point of helping people in need, but with no cash in his wallet, he could only offer a smile. Santa smiled back. "Help the hungry have a Merry Christmas!" Santa cried out again after Andy passed.

He reached the century-old King Edward Hotel, a stately place built during a time when prominent buildings were erected with financially unrestrained pride. Snow stuck against its limestone edifice and piled atop a row of gargoyles and carriage lanterns above the sidewalk. A hotel footman jabbed a push broom at an awning in front of the hotel to relieve the awning of snow. Andy and the man nodded at each other as their eyes met.

"Bitch of a storm, eh?" Andy commented to the footman.

"And yesterday, they were calling for rain," the footman replied. "Hah!" the man scoffed. "Now, they're calling for over a foot of snow."

Andy looked up after passing the awning to sneak a peek into one of the rooms, only to be blinded by snow. Someone had told him that high-end suites in the place, with a whirlpool, fireplace, and bar, cost an audacious $400 a night. He thought it would be nice to spend a weekend in one of them with Karen to celebrate their upcoming fifth anniversary. With his promotion, they could absorb the cost without incurring undue strain on their finances.

A tall, dark figure stood twenty feet away when Andy looked in front of him. The figure stood among a throng of passing people. No one seemed to notice it.

Andy crossed the street after waiting for a car to pass. The figure began across the street without waiting for another car, which continued right through it. Again, people passed without seeming to notice it after the figure arrived at the opposite sidewalk ahead of him. The figure darted toward him, inhumanly fast, before grabbing Andy's forehead and slammed him against a building. A loud thud sounded when the back of his head struck a brick wall. A brilliant aura and a searing headache ensued.

Concussion drunk, Andy struggled to rise after falling on the ground. People passed, yet no one offered help. He stumbled along until the figure threw him against a wall, shoulder first. Pain shot through the shoulder which Andy barely noticed, stunned by what was happening and close to going into shock.

"What do you want?" Andy asked the figure. It did not respond to his question.

Relieved that help might be near as a police cruiser approached, the cruiser passed despite trying to flag it. Andy looked at the figure that faced him. Its face was masked by blackness.

Andy stumbled down crowded stairs leading to a subway station. Though crowded with people, no one seemed to notice as he called for help. Only after repeated attempts to get attention proved futile did it dawn on him that no one could see him.

Desperate to escape the pursuing figure, Andy hurried toward the platform. No train waited upon reaching the platform. The figure pushed him onto the tracks. Andy stumbled while getting to his feet after landing on his side and striking his head hard against a rail. With nowhere to go, Andy stumbled along the tracks, disorientated, his head swollen and throbbing.

* * * * *

Wayne phoned Aaron to tell him Andy had been struck and killed by a subway train; Wayne learned that Andy died while watching the evening news. A man operating the train said there was no way of stopping before hitting him, according to Toronto Police, a reporter covering the tragedy said. The conductor saw Andy after rounding a curve.

Andy's death ruled death by suicide left many unanswered questions. His wife, Karen, said they had been getting along well though they did have a minor quarrel the morning of his death. They planned on having a baby and were looking for a larger place to live. Andy's career was going well, weeks away from a promotion that came with a generous increase in salary and additional assorted perks and potential bonuses. And he had become obsessed with trying to stay fit. All in all, Andy seemed far from being bent on self-destruction.

Chapter Twelve
An Empty House

With Shay longing to have lots of children, she and Aaron bought a house with four bedrooms they planned to fill in time. Shay maintained a list of names, including Zachary, Julie, Zane, and Tyler, which, at her suggestion, he insisted they not use. They agreed to not learn the baby's gender until after it was born and to name it based on gender and physical features.

They agreed that a child's name had the potential to impact personality and self-esteem. Aaron wanted their children to be proud of their first names, remembering how Tyler felt embarrassed by hers. Why did her parents give her a boy's name? Tyler often wondered, overlooking their reasons.

But Tyler was reluctantly okay with her name despite being named by the happenstance of being born where she was. If her parents felt compelled to name her after the city where she was born, to have been born in Madison, Wisconsin, would have been nice, Tyler had mused. Charlotte, North Carolina, would have been nice, too. Being born in Tacoma, Washington, would have also been good. Tacoma sounded cool for a first name, she joked.

It was hard to imagine Tyler having a different first name. The name Tyler suited her to a 'T' as she was a boy in spirit with her tomboyish ways, yet feminine. He smiled at the thought, the paradox. That Tyler loved girly things, like cooking with her mother and flowers, yet loved playing sports with him and the rest of the guys and always held her own.

He and Shay began trying to conceive a baby, a year into their marriage. Discouraged after two years without success, Shay underwent fertility testing to see if there was a biological reason behind her not getting pregnant. Perhaps a drug might help her along if that were the case, but no drug could help after learning that she was infertile.

Devastated, her outlook on life changed. Always optimistic, a trait of Shay's that Aaron appreciated and admired, her optimism lifted his spirits whenever he sunk to a dark place. Light in her eyes stopped shining after learning she could not produce a child, and her positive outlook disappeared.

"At least we have each other," he told her, as they lay in bed the night of the day Shay received the heartbreaking news.

"I always dreamed of being a mother, and now that's never going to happen," Shay sobbed as Aaron tenderly embraced her. "I always dreamed of feeling a baby grow inside me. I wanted to have a few mini you's and a couple of mini me's. I wanted to have kids that looked like me and you," she sighed. "I wanted to see our faces in our kids. I know I've held you down. You're going to find someone else to have babies with them."

"I would never do that to you," Aaron promised. "It's going to be okay."

"I think you would," Shay said. "You say that now, but..."

"Why would you think I would leave you because of that?" he asked her, hurt by Shay's suggestion.

"I don't," Shay said. "I'm sorry."

"We'll be okay," Aaron said.

"Are you sure?"

"We're going to be fine," Aaron assured her again.

"I don't believe you," Shay said as she pulled away from him. "I don't, I don't, I don't. It's not going to be okay. I know it's not going to be okay. It's never going to be okay," she repeated continually. Shay left the bed and started toward the door. "I have to be by myself," she told him.

Somehow, Aaron knew right then he had lost her. Tempted to follow her, he held back, heeding Shay's stated desire to be alone, knowing she needed to work through the shock and process the devastating news. Shay had a history of abusing drugs and alcohol. He worried she would return to her old ways.

She drank well past the point of intoxication on most weekends. After learning she was infertile, Shay drank to intoxication every day, as Aaron feared she would. She lost her job after returning to work from lunch drunk after consuming one too many ryes and cokes.

He hoped that Shay would want to change after losing her job and get help if that was what it took to curb her drinking. Instead, her alcohol dependence worsened with too much idle time on her hands. It got to where he occasionally found her passed out when he came home after work. One time he arrived home just in time to save her from drowning after she passed out in their hot tub. When he found her, her nose was on the verge of slipping under the waterline.

So sad what Shay had become, he thought.

Their relationship suffered as her drinking worsened. They rarely spent time with each other as alcohol became her lover. Shay did her thing, and he did his.

He avoided going out in public with her because of her excessive alcohol use, as her drunken behavior embarrassed him. Shay slurred words and said outlandish things. Alcohol inhibited her filters as she blurted out whatever came to mind under its influence, sometimes unintentionally insulting people without regard in the process.

Aaron avoided Shay at home, keeping to his study, the garage, the backyard, or anywhere he could find peace. She rambled, talked nonsense, and became hostile and challenging to contend with when she drank. He grieved the loss of the Shay he fell in love with as fond memories of how things once were grew distant, and prayed for her to get better. Long gone were the days when he hurried home from work, anxious to be with her.

* * * * *

Their place was dark upon arriving home from work on a January night in 1999. Aaron looked at neighboring houses to see if they had power, wondering if a neighborhood-wide blackout had occurred. Only their place was dark.

Shay typically left at least the porch light on so they could see their way into the house if either one arrived home after dark. Maybe the porch light burned out? The newspaper was in the mailbox, which was surprising as Shay usually began her day by reading it. Mail remained uncollected.

Footprints tracked through snow, between the porch and the driveway, and bubble wrap and discarded cardboard boxes littered the ground. A shadowy emptiness awaited in the front room after entering the house. Light enveloped the room after flipping a light switch to its 'on' position. His heart raced upon discovering the room had been emptied of its furniture.

Concerned about her well-being, worried that they might have been robbed while Shay was in the house, he wondered where Shay was. Maybe whoever invaded their place bound and gagged her and left Shay helpless somewhere? He called out to her while beginning a search of the house and received no response. Perhaps she had gone somewhere before the break-in occurred, he wondered. Furniture and whatever else was stolen was replaceable. It was more important to know that Shay was okay.

He climbed the staircase to the second level and began toward the master bedroom, looking in rooms along the way. The only room they furnished aside from their bedroom, using it as a place for guests to sleep, was empty. He continued to call out Shay's name and got no response.

Aaron flipped the light switch on after arriving at their bedroom. The furniture in the room remained, save for a dresser that Shay used. It occurred to him, after seeing that, that Shay had left him.

He hurried back to the first floor and went into the kitchen, where he and Shay kept a pad of paper to leave messages for each other. Perhaps Shay had left a message for him, Aaron thought.

After turning its lights on, he continued through the kitchen to the message pad. Sure, enough Shay had written something on it. He picked the pad up and looked at it.

"Dear Aaron," Shay's message began. "We're not close anymore and haven't been for a few years. We never talk because you're never home, and you do your best to ignore me when you are. I've been thinking things through, and I think it's best if we go our separate ways. I still love you and always will, but I just can't go on this way. We can settle things later. My lawyer will be contacting you sometime over the next few days. I'm sorry it had to end this way because I hoped we could work things out. As I said, I love you and always will, and I really want you to be okay." Shay signed her name and drew a smiley face beside it, with the smile reversed.

Anger, sadness, and confusion took hold. The pad fell from his shaking hands. He picked the pad up off the floor, needing to reread the message. How dare she blame him for their problems when her drinking drove them apart, he thought. He threw the pad to the floor in anger after rereading it.

Their relationship was no more dismal than it had been of late. Aaron considered leaving her at times over the previous year and begrudged that Shay beat him to the punch. If he was the one who ended their marriage, he would have told her in advance and not walked out. So, it wouldn't have been such a shock.

At least his den was intact, Aaron was pleased to find after going into it, from where he phoned Wayne to tell him that Shay left. Wayne, always a loyal friend, came over and spent a few hours trying to console him. Aaron knew Shay would be at her parents' place. Angry and wanting to speak with her, Aaron picked up the phone and was about to dial her parents' number before Wayne grabbed the phone. Wayne surmised that it was best to allow time for the shock to settle before speaking with her. Aaron took Wayne's advice, knowing that he was right.

Confused and angry trying to reach out to her in his current state would only make matters worse.

He lay on a couch in the den after Wayne left and tried to sleep, having to work the following day. The night was spent wound by a variety of emotions; perhaps half an hour of sleep was had when his alarm sounded at 7:30 a.m. Unable to think straight, working that day would be a disservice to his patients. Not wanting to leave his patients in a lurch, he decided on the better of two difficult choices, to call in sick. If their time or needs were pressing, other doctors at the clinic could tend to his patients as they covered for each other.

He called the clinic an hour before it opened and spoke with Jen, a woman who managed the office, and he claimed to have the flu. Jen began her workday early to process lab reports and correspondence faxed in overnight and pull the charts of patients scheduled to be seen. He and Jen were close and often confided in each other about personal matters, which made being dishonest with her more difficult. In time, Jen would know what happened.

Jen answered on the first ring. "Dr. Fuhrman, Bernstein, Harmon, and Richards' office," she said.

"Hi, Jen," Aaron said.

"Hey, you, what's up?" she replied. "Are you running late?"

"No, I'm not running late," he said. "I'm sick and can't make it in today. I've been up all night with the flu," he lied.

"Oh, oh," she groaned. "It snuck up on ya, eh?" Jen alluded to a surge in flu cases seen recently in the clinic. "I figured it would only be a matter of time before one of us caught the flu," she said, referring to clinic staff.

"Yeah, me too," he said, feeling bad about lying. "I can't function. I hate screwing people around that are planning to see me today, but I just can't make it in."

"I know you do, but if you're sick, you're sick," she said. "There's nothing you can do about that. Try not to worry about it. I'll cancel your appointments."

"Thanks," Aaron said, too shaken to speak the truth. "If it's urgent, then they can see one of the others... If not, can you see if they can reschedule over the next few weeks? I'm going to work late so I can see them all."

"Will do," Jen affirmed. "Try not to worry about it. You need to rest, but I don't need to tell you that because you're the doctor."

"Thanks," he replied.

"Well, you take care, mister," Jen said. "Hopefully, you'll get better quick."

"I'll be able to shake this thing off if I stay in bed today," Aaron replied.

Aaron leaned into a chair and looked at the ceiling after ending the call, feeling relieved to have gotten over it. He then dialed the number to Shay's parent's house, knowing that Shay's mother was an early riser and would be awake. Mrs. De Blasio answered on the second ring.

"Hi, I'm looking for Shay," he said. "Is she there? I don't understand why, but she left me last night."

"Hi, Aaron, she's here, but she's sleeping right now," Mrs. De Blasio replied. "I know it's hard for you for her to leave you like she did. Shay said to tell you when you called, because she knew you would, that she doesn't want to speak with you right now."

"She doesn't want to speak with me?" Aaron angrily asked her. "I don't mean to be disrespectful to you," he said, mindful of his tone of voice. "I'm just feeling so frustrated."

"She didn't get into details," Mrs. De Blasio replied. "I've always thought of you as a son. I hate being in the middle of this. Between you and me, we know she's been having problems, and you stuck by her, and her dad and I are grateful for that. She said she was angry and upset with you about something but didn't give us a reason. But you know she's not in a very good state of mind right now. Who knows what's going through her head?"

"I haven't done anything to upset her that I know of," Aaron said.

"I'm sure you haven't," Mrs. De Blasio replied.

"So, she didn't tell you exactly what was bothering her?" Aaron asked her. "We haven't been getting along over the last few months, but I figured we would work things out. I really would like to speak with her. I want to know why she just up and left me like she did."

"I know you do," Mrs. De Blasio said. "I want you two to talk, but I can't tell her what to do. I hope you two can work things out."

He angrily slammed the phone in its cradle after bidding goodbye to Shay's mother. A piece of plastic broke off the phone and struck his forehead. Blood streamed from a cut on his right palm after breaking a glass tumbler in his way while slamming the phone. Aaron went into a bathroom and tended to the wound. After soaking up blood with a cotton swab, he sterilized the wound with rubbing alcohol and then covered it with a butterfly bandage. Blood trickled from where the chunk of plastic struck his forehead. He dried that cut with another cotton swab, dabbed it with rubbing alcohol, and then covered the cut with a bandage.

Aaron returned to the den, where he kept a bottle of Tylenol No. 3's with a cup full of water. Shay would have binged on the pills to catch a buzz, so they were locked in a drawer in his desk. His hand throbbing in pain, he swallowed two pills and washed them down before leaving the house to visit with Tyler.

The temperature was five degrees Fahrenheit, according to a thermometer on the porch. Bundled up in a heavy coat, gloves, and a scarf, only his face was exposed to a biting chill while clearing snow that had fallen overnight, from his car. His white Lincoln Continental blended with snow in the driveway, where he parked it in front of their two-car garage. Shay kept her car in one bay, and a boat they owned occupied the other.

Tightened from cold, the car's leather seat crunched as he sat on it. Pain shot from the injured hand while inserting the key in the car's ignition. A clicking noise sounded from the engine as it failed to come to life. The engine roared but fell silent, sputtering after attempting to start it again. It roared to life and kept on running when he attempted to start the engine again, after pausing to allow his pain to subside.

He reached the cemetery at ten-thirty and was pleased to find the main avenue that ran through its center had been plowed. Thankfully, the lane leading to Tyler's grave was also clear, so there was no need to trudge through seven inches of fresh snow. Her gravestone, located eight gravesites away from the lane, slowly came into view. A set of footprints led to and from the grave, he noticed after parking.

After touching Tyler's gravestone, as per his custom upon arriving at it, he told her what Shay had done. "How different life might be if you were still here," he told Tyler while staring at the snow over her grave. For some reason, he thought about how her smiling, angelical face would have long ago gone to bone and dust. "If only you were still alive," he said. "You would never have betrayed me like Shay did."

Cold, becoming too much to bear, he ended the visit well short of the time ordinarily spent at her grave. "I'll see you later," he said to Tyler, touching her gravestone while looking at a clear sky. A strange thought occurred while driving away, that Tyler was trapped alive in her coffin. He sullenly looked toward her grave after turning onto the avenue and was shocked to see the girl he had seen in the summer standing there.

With a pounding heart, he turned around and noticed the girl was gone while he was driving back to Tyler's grave. Only his footprints and those made earlier were in the snow around her grave when he arrived. Maybe ghosts did exist, or the girl was a figment of his imagination, Aaron wondered. Perhaps lack of sleep and the effects of pain medication and emotional duress had combined to form a hallucinatory effect. But he was neither tired nor impacted by the influence of pain medication or experiencing emotional duress, the first time he saw her.

Chapter Thirteen
Devon Heights Mall, Spring 1999

A tall, blonde woman stood at an ATM with her back toward them as Carl and Scott walked through Devon Heights Mall.

Carl looked at the woman. "Man... check out that ass!" he exclaimed to Scott, whispering to avoid being overheard by people around them.

The woman wore form-fitting tights that showed off sculptured buttocks and a tight T-shirt fit snug over her ample breasts. The woman looked at him. "I did that chick," Scott boasted after looking away. "I work with her. Her name is Toni."

"You didn't screw her!" Carl said, continuing to look at the woman who possessed an athletic body.

"That happened last year after our work's Christmas party," Scott whispered. "We had a good time. We flirted big time and went to another place for a final drink when the party ended. We ended up at her place. One thing led to another."

"No way," Carl sputtered. Carl shrugged his shoulders and squinted his eyes at Scott in a doubtful manner. "You wish."

"I'm not lying," Scott insisted. "She works the opposite shift at Chrysler's. I'd seen her before but never talked to her. Man, she's very good in the sack. She really likes it."

"Hello, Scott," the woman said after stepping away from the ATM, as they reached her.

"Hi, Toni," Scott replied. "How are you doing?"

"Fine," she curtly replied. "I'll see ya," the woman said while hurrying away.

"Yeah, take care," Scott replied. Toni obviously did not want to talk with him, and Scott was okay with that. "That was awkward," he told Carl. "She's mad at me because I was supposed to call her, but I never did."

"Right," Carl said with a sigh. "You're playing, right? Why didn't you call her? What's wrong with you, man? She's a real babe. I'd drink her bathwater."

"You're such a horndog, you'd do a cow if no one were looking," Scott said.

"Yeah, I don't know about that," Carl said. He chuckled and then fell silent, waiting for a woman to pass who had entered within hearing distance of them. "What was wrong with her?" he said after the woman passed. "Who do you think you are, Tom Cruise or something?"

"She's nutty as squirrel turds, like Val was," Scott said, Val, a woman he made the mistake of marrying. "Sometimes, it doesn't matter how hot chicks are. With Toni, it was like a pump and dump and head for the hills. I'm not about to go through anything like I did with Val again. It isn't worth it. No way and no how!"

For Val, it was all about wanting her needs and wants to be met. Eventually, her physical beauty took a back seat to her narcissism, so he filed for divorce six months into the marriage. He was really fed up with her attitude.

Toni was as beautiful as the first warm, sunny day of spring, but that evening together, he came to realize she was as narcissistic as Val. Beyond that, she voiced bizarre thoughts, talking about how they could have a beautiful life together despite the fact they hardly knew each other. After leaving her place, he ran for the hills and dared not look back.

Carl's search for a new computer brought them to the mall to a store called Computer Mart. Though a weekday morning, the mall teemed with people as they made their way to Computer Mart. Before reaching the mall's main corridor, they passed stores such as Brief Encounters Lingerie Shoppe, Trendy Wendy's Hairstyling salon, Sitting Bull Steakhouse, and the 'This and That Shop.' Broad and stretching, the corridor went a long distance. Computer Mart was a third of the way down it.

Scott looked at something. Carl followed his gaze to a poster of an actress from the television show *Baywatch* promoting a California vacation package on the window of a travel service office. "I can never understand why people get into that show, *Baywatch*," Scott sighed. "I mean, like what do they do all the time, you know? Oh, my God! Someone's drowning! We'd better save 'em! I don't watch the show, but it's probably the same thing every week."

"People get into that show because of the babes, dumbass," Carl scoffed. "Guys love seeing the gorgeous chicks, and chicks like seeing the hunky guys... It'd be nice if there were a beach around with nothing but hot chicks."

"It doesn't exist, but it would be cool if it did," Scott said. "Where out-of-shape, beer-gutted guys like us could go, but the only women allowed were hot!"

"Maybe they have beaches like that, like in places like Mexico," Carl joked.

"Like in the Club Med commercials where everyone's good-looking," Scott said. "You never see any overweight people in those commercials. Like guys like you where they'd kick you off the beach with that beer belly you got going on."

"Whatever," Carl replied, while patting his beer-bloated paunch. "I'm proud of my belly," he joked. "A lot of time and money went into this."

Kiosks that typically lined the main corridor had been replaced by dozens of vintage cars as the mall celebrated the area's automobile history that week. After passing several less interesting cars, they stopped to look at a '47 Packard. Next, they stopped at a '35 Ford fire engine, adorned in chrome and painted a traditional shade of fire engine red. Next along the way was a Ford Model T.

"You know what Henry Ford supposedly said?" Scott asked Carl as they looked at the Model T. He referred to the Detroit industrialist who founded Ford Motor Company and invented the moving automobile assembly line.

"No," Carl replied.

"You can get a Model T in any color you want as long as it is black."

"Actually, I think I heard that," Carl said. "Henry Ford came by my grandparents' farm a couple of times."

"Really," Scott muttered, under his breath, focused on the dashboard. "So, Henry Ford happened to stop by your grandparents' place?"

"That's what my grandmother told me," Carl said. "She said he traveled all over Michigan, Windsor, and Essex County trying to sell his Model Ts."

They studied the car as they walked around it. So anciently simple. The car was the first produced on a moving assembly line, a process that made it cheaper to build than the individually made, so-called horseless carriage cars that proceeded it. The revolutionary process of making the Model T put the world on wheels; a person of modest means could afford one. Just a basic, simple, pocketbook-friendly means of getting around, the Model T represented a pivotal moment in the industrial revolution.

They were shocked to find themselves alone when they left the car.

"Where is everybody?" Carl asked Scott.

"I have no idea, but this is really weird," Scott replied.

"Did a fire alarm go off, and somehow we didn't hear it?" Carl asked Scott.

"I don't think so because we would have heard it," Scott replied.

"Well, whatever," Carl said. "Let's get out of here."

"I hear ya," Scott sighed. "Maybe there's a gas leak... Or maybe someone called in a bomb threat?"

They hurried back in the direction they had come, their footsteps echoing without the noise and mass of other people to muffle them. An improbable sight greeted them as they left the main corridor and began along the hall that led to the entrance, from which they had entered the mall. A brick wall replaced the exterior doors.

They hurried back to the main corridor and continued toward another set of exterior doors located at the back of an appliance store. They reached the store and began along its main corridor. Something moved along a parallel aisle as they continued toward the exit.

"I swear I saw something move down the aisle next to us," Scott told Carl. "I saw something move out of the corner of my eye."

"I think I saw something, too," Carl said.

Like the doors they passed to enter the mall, a brick wall stood where the doors should be.

"What the hell!" Scott yelled. "What is going on here?"

"Let's try Walmart," Carl suggested.

They left the store and hurried toward Walmart located farther along the mall's main corridor.

No blue shirts manned the entrance to greet them. Music played over the store's sound system, surreal seeming to only play for them while continuing into the people-less Walmart. They turned to their left and walked down an aisle ending near another set of exterior doors, in silence, both too exhausted to run and too confused to speak. Those doors, too, were replaced by a brick wall.

"Jesus Christ!" Carl groaned.

"Let's go to the other exit," Scott yelled, referring to another set of exterior doors on the store's east side. Movement again came from alongside them, this time from behind a series of clothing racks, as they trotted. They rounded a corner and found the exit no longer existed.

They hurried back toward the mall. The icy blue of a clear morning sky loomed over a skylight in the mall's main corridor.

A grand clock that hung from the ceiling in an atrium had stopped at a few minutes after ten. Water spraying and bubbling in fountains were all that moved, other than the friends as they carried on.

A rumbling sound came from a side corridor ahead of them. "Do you hear that?" Scott asked Carl.

"Yeah," Carl huffed. Faint at first, the sound grew louder. "Maybe it's one of those Cushman carts security and maintenance people ride around in."

"It sounds like a worn-out car!" Scott said as the sound drew closer.

"I'm betting it was a bomb threat," Carl said. "Why else would everyone have left?"

The Packard they had looked at emerged and began toward them. Light reflected off its windshield, preventing a look at the driver. Its tires squealed as the Packard accelerated.

They ran into the nearest store, searching for cover and a way out. The car pursued them, smashing through display units until lodging itself on debris. Carl, full of rage and determined to confront its driver, stormed toward the driver's side window. No one was inside the car.

On they ran into the corridor and found a hooded, robed figure astride a large black horse where the Packard had emerged, looking at them. The rider held a halberd with long bony fingers and wore sandals on feet resembling those of a crow. A darkened spot occupied the space where its face should have been.

The horse and rider charged toward them. Scott and Carl ran toward an escalator. Scott, having reached it before Carl, hurried toward the mall's lower level. Carl, struck by the rider's halberd, tumbled past. His blood and other body matter splattered around the escalator before violently rolling to rest at its bottom landing.

Propelled by shock and adrenaline, Scott carried on toward where Carl lay in a gruesome, twisted heap. Blood, tissue, muscles, and brain matter splattered the area around his body, and a piece of spinal cord protruded from Carl's back. Sickened from the sight and nauseated by the stench of blood, Scott carried on as quickly as he was able toward another outside exit.

A teenage boy and girl, having followed alongside him and Carl in the Walmart and appliance store, appeared after reaching the exit and finding it replaced by a wall. "The way out isn't here," the boy said. "You need to go back up the escalator to the main floor's south end. The doors at the end of it are open. They have to leave a way out."

"Who's they?" Scott asked the boy.

As Scott waited for an answer, the boy and girl faded away. Scott recalled that a madman shot and killed a teenage boy and girl while on a rampage in the mall a decade ago while running toward the escalators. Perhaps he had just encountered their ghosts, he thought, trying not to look at Carl while stepping on spray that came from his body.

Relief came upon seeing exit doors after reaching where the boy said outside doors would be open. The horse and its rider arrived behind him. His head smashed through a glass door as the rider's halberd struck him. Blood sprayed from fatal wounds after a dagger-shaped chunk of glass fell and sliced through his neck.

Chapter Fourteen
Pool, Death, and Jack Daniels

Wayne tried to help Aaron back onto his emotional feet in the months after Shay left, just as Aaron had helped him through a recent, difficult divorce. They spent a night reminiscing after Steve died. Both got teary-eyed, but showing such sentimental weakness was okay between them. They spent a night grieving together after Allen died in a bizarre accident on a farm he worked at and another long night after Andy died.

And now Carl and Scott were dead.

The last two days were hard, the former spent together at Scott's funeral and the latter attending Carl's. They spent the night after Carl's funeral at Wayne's house, trying to make sense of the deaths of their friends over Jack Daniels, beer, and pool. They played prolonged games of unfocused pool, the games drawn out by non-stop conversation.

The circumstances of the death of Allen, who died after a thresher inexplicably rolled over on him while fixing it, were too bizarre to believe. That Steve, so young and in good health, succumbed to a heart attack was troubling. The idea that Andy committed suicide when his life seemed to be going well was especially disturbing. That Carl, agile and in good health, would tumble down an escalator was beyond comprehending. That Scott would throw himself headlong toward a glass door, equally so. Also, it was perplexing that Carl and Scott died near each other a few minutes apart, and no one in the mall noticed them.

Out of all their friends who tried the séance to communicate with Tyler, only Aaron and Wayne remained alive. How could that be was something Aaron and Wayne discussed long into the night. Perhaps they were all cursed for having tried it, Wayne said after he and Aaron stopped playing pool, opting to sit, drink, and talk. The idea was too bizarre to comprehend, but they conceded it could be true.

* * * * *

Traffic moved too slowly for Shay's liking while driving home, to a rural house owned by her parents, six months after leaving Aaron. While on a four-lane road and desperate to pass vehicles in front of her, she looked at the inner lane to see if it was clear. A slow-moving cement truck occupied the lane, so she had no choice but to tail it as the road narrowed to two lanes. There was no passing it with a thick line of traffic heading toward the city, but at least the truck reached the speed limit.

Resigned to being stuck in place and bored, she focused on the truck, Detroit Diesel emblazoned on its mud flaps. A length of thick chain securing an auger mixer rattled, swinging to and fro, as the truck barreled over bumps and potholes. A beast that seemed to own the road watching the truck had a subliminal impact. It seemed to connect with a deep unconscious need to be taken care of.

Perhaps Aaron treated her too well, she thought. Every so often, he expressed concern about her alcohol abuse, a topic that got her dander up and always prompted her to deflect in some way. Alcohol abuse altered her personality in a bad way, she realized after being sober for a few months. Aaron tried to tell her that, she realized, when he dared to broach the subject. Now that she was sober and thinking clearer, she grew to appreciate his typical reaction to walk away and leave her alone after saying he did not want to argue. One day she would reach out to him and try and work things out in the hope they could reconcile and perhaps resume their marriage.

The truck's engine growled as the truck, for whatever reason, shifted to a lower gear and slowed. Shay entered the opposite lane when oncoming traffic cleared and passed the truck as its driver accommodated by pulling toward the shoulder. She accelerated to twenty kilometers over the speed limit on a now open road after returning to her lane. The truck picked up speed as she slowed to ten kilometers over the post speed limit. Its image grew in her rearview mirror until the truck arrived within a few car lengths behind her.

The truck rammed her car when she slowed to turn onto a road her house was on. Her car went over a ditch and crashed into a concrete culvert below the crossroad. Shay died upon impact.

* * * * *

Time allowed for healing after Shay left. Initially consumed with anger toward her, in time, anger subsided, knowing Shay's spirit had been overtaken by her demons after learning that she was infertile. The time they first walked through Oakwood Bush together remained a fond memory, Aaron told Wayne as they again grieved another death. Deep inside lived the Shay he fell in love with, and the place she occupied in his heart would be there forever, Aaron said.

Whoever drove the truck that had been stolen from a construction site had left before the police arrived. Tears fell as news of her death stirred a tide of feelings. Hope that they might one day resume their marriage, provided Shay got herself together, died with her.

A detective who came to the house to inform Aaron that Shay had died wanted to know when he last saw her. It could have been a case of a hit and run, but the fact the truck, in working order, had been abandoned near the scene ruled that out, the detective said. That being so, its driver intentionally struck Shay's car, the detective surmised. Next came the standard questions, police asked partners of people killed in a suspect manner. Did he know if Shay was having problems with anyone? Were they having problems after they separated? Why did she leave him? Where was he when she died?

The police ruled him out as a suspect in Shay's death.

He attended Shay's funeral and internment. Shay's parents continued to regard him as a member of their family. Nonetheless, Aaron kept to himself to privately grieve the loss of his mate.

Her parents told him that Shay had been sober for a few months and was thinking clearer. Perhaps they did have a chance of getting back together, Aaron thought, with Shay in a better state. But now, that would never happen.

Frustration grew over time as her murder remained unsolved, wanting the person responsible for her death brought to justice.

Shay was the latest person close to him that was murdered. She had never participated in the séance, which made her different from the others. Maybe the murders had nothing to do with the séance but more with tragic life circumstances.

Chapter Fifteen
And You and Your Sweet Desire

Sunlight filled a cloudless sky as Aaron arrived at Our Lady of the Lakes Cemetery. Summer days often brought stifling humidity in the low-lying water surrounding the area that was Windsor and Essex County. But today, the temperature was moderate, and the humidity was low.

Two F-18 Hornets, having just completed a flyover at an airshow at Windsor Airport, roared overhead and over the lake as he left the car. With the usual six purple daisies in hand, he watched the jets disappear before proceeding to Tyler's grave, where he touched her gravestone. He spent a moment saying hello and reflecting before pulling dead daisies from the vase and replacing them with fresh ones.

He looked around to where the girl in the white dress had been while heading toward the receptacle. The lake lay before him. A large lake freighter was in the distance on the horizon, sailboats and pleasure crafts made their way, and a Cessna flew above them. The girl was nowhere to be found. Maybe she was the Lady of the Lakes, he mused.

"It's been twenty years since you've been gone," he told Tyler, returning his focus to her. "It's hard to believe it's been so long," he told her, barely able to hear himself as another warplane passed.

"I listened to the Heatwave single you liked dancing to," he said after the warplane passed, the song playing on the car stereo on the drive out to see her. Hearing it made him long for the day twenty years ago when they danced to the song in the fort. What he would give to live that day again.

The world had changed so much since the late 1970s, he

mused when he listened to the song. The song took him back to 1977 when the single version was released… Disco, leisure suits, the Son of Sam serial killer, platform shoes, bellbottom jeans, and mood rings were a few of the things that came to mind. He and Tyler never wore platform shoes or bellbottoms, but they did like mood rings, and she was okay with disco if the song made her want to dance.

Music has a way of stirring intense feelings.

The Flower Girl song made him happy while thinking about Tyler when she was alive. Now it made him sad thinking about her as a part of his past, how he missed their time together, how long she had been gone, and the loss of the sweet naivety that came with being a child, full of hope and dreams. Yet he would play the song over and over when he was up to hearing it, wanting to go back to the good times and feel the pain of missing them.

Thoughts of trying to contact her gnawed at him over the last six months after Shay left. He decided to try the séance again after leaving his cousin John's house, after spending the evening celebrating John's birthday. This time it would be completed, despite feeling there was something wrong with trying to contact the dead. Aside from its premise, the séance had the markings of being evil, with its words, the candles, black garb, pentagram, and goat head. But contacting Tyler seemed to be worth whatever cost that might be.

Wayne would not be with him this time. Other than him, Wayne was the last surviving participant of the first attempt at the séance. It was best to leave Wayne out of it, lest something happen to him. This time it would be just him and Tyler. It did not matter what happened to him if he lived or died. He was alone, with no children and no wife. The world would get on well without him.

Whether right or wrong, he regretted losing a chance to contact her by ending the séance short of completing it back in

1979. He wondered if Tyler's image would have materialized on the television screen. Would she have appeared in the room? Could they have spoken with her? Was the séance an ongoing way of maintaining contact with her?

Ten kilometers separated his place from John's, but it might as well have been a hundred while rushing home full of anticipation. Hellbent on doing it, he hurried into his den to the photo album he looked at after Tyler died, where he kept the two sheets needed to complete the séance. The shoebox containing their card collection was beside it.

He placed the sheets on a table that he had pushed against a westward wall. Next, he went to a cabinet where he kept black and red candles, candleholders, and a silver chalice in anticipation of trying to contact her again. His heart panged with an equal measure of anticipation and fear as he placed the chalice on the table and put a black and red candle in holders.

He taped the pentagram above the table after changing into black clothing. With that done, he shut the lights off, pulled a lighter from a pocket, and lit both candles. Fervid anticipation fought growing trepidation as a television screen glowed as he read the words while sitting in a chair. He continued reading as there could be no stopping this time, short of uttering each word.

Tyler's face formed on the screen, which became blindingly bright before returning to darkness after reading each word. He stared at the television while feeling disappointed that no contact with her had occurred. After waiting for an hour or so, dejected, he extinguished the candles and headed to bed.

He dreamed about Tyler. He sat on her pool deck at night and watched an adult version of her emerge from the water. Tyler had grown into a beautiful young woman.

"Hi, Aaron," Tyler asked him. "Won't you kiss me?"

She climbed onto the deck. They kissed. "I've missed you so much," she said after sitting on his lap.

That dream morphed into him and Tyler in their late twenties, married with children. What a good mom she was, he thought, while watching her tend to their one-year-old boy, with blond hair and blue eyes, just like him. Two little girls watched. Twins that both looked like mini-Tylers.

The dream was beautiful, like life should have been. They were doing what they dreamed of doing. Getting married, having kids, and continuing to experience life together.

And then it ended. It took a moment to understand that what had seemed real was not. Aaron woke up emotionally devastated upon realizing what he saw was merely what could have been.

Sweat covered him, and the room was hot. His heart was pounding, and his breath was short. He rolled over to his other side, stared at the wall, closed his eyes, and willed his mind to think pleasant thoughts.

A smile formed while picturing Tyler pulling him off the fort floor to dance with her. And then he remembered the two of them running across the farmer's field, trying to outrun him, laughing nervously, not knowing what he would do if the farmer caught them. There were so many memories and hopefully more to make when they met in Heaven.

Tyler's funeral came to mind. So many people came to see her for a final time. It made him feel good that Tyler was so well-liked, so many people loved her, and that she had left an impact in her short life.

He marveled at how busy she was, playing softball on Saturdays and Tuesdays and soccer on Mondays, going to school, doing homework, helping care for the animals at the Oakwood Sanctuary, learning how to play piano, and attending Mass on Sundays.

Chapter Sixteen
Zachary McFarren

Zachary McFarren watched Edwin Matthews tap the earth with a shovel while smoothening the topsoil of a grave Matthews and his buddy Harry Neal had just refilled.

"Just about done, are we?" McFarren asked Matthews.

Matthews took a final swipe at the ground. "I think so," the fatigued man replied. "That basically does it."

"Well, hallelujah!" McFarren exclaimed as he cast a flashlight at the grave. "I was beginning to worry you lads might take all night."

Harry Neal appeared from behind a tree, pulling up his fly after taking a pee. Neal was angered by McFarren's remark, as he and Matthews had spent the night digging the grave out, only to refill it, at McFarren's behest. Exhausted and sore, he had little patience for McFarren's criticism or sarcasm, whatever one cared to call it.

Other than illuminating it, McFarren offered no assistance when the men unearthed the grave. McFarren handed Neal a sledgehammer. A white coffin came into view after Neal smashed through the lid of a concrete vault.

They left and returned an hour later and found the coffin open and empty. Small footprints, trapped in dew-soaked grass, led from the grave. Neither Neal nor Matthews dared to ask McFarren, who was quick to temper, if he knew who left the footprints. McFarren appeared to be unfazed.

McFarren was an odd sort.

Matthews and Neal often talked about a hunting trip they had taken with him. McFarren sliced its head off after downing a buck. Blood splattered his coat, hands, and face as he cut its throat with a buck knife, yet he did not seem at all bothered. He walked away head in hand and invited Matthews and Neal to harvest meat from the buck's carcass. Stuffed and mounted, the head with its fine set of antlers would make for a good conversation piece, but why give away the meat, they wondered.

A similar incident occurred two days later after McFarren bagged another buck. Matthews and Neal went home with a few months' worth of meat, though neither man had downed a buck. McFarren only wanted the heads.

Time had reached a few minutes before four in the morning when they returned to McFarren's truck.

They first became aware of McFarren six months prior, after he began to regularly appear at the 594, a Legion Hall they frequented. McFarren kept to himself. He preferred to sit alone at a table in the corner of its billiards room.

McFarren was a topic of conversation between Matthews and Neal and other Legion regulars. Everyone wondered why he kept to himself, spending hours at each sitting, rarely uttering a word. People thought it odd he bothered to come to the Legion, where its members came to socialize.

Matthews and Neal were surprised when McFarren placed a quarter on the top rail of their pool table to challenge the winner of a game they were playing. Though neither man cared for McFarren, they felt compelled to drink with him at his out-of-the-way table, from that point on. They began going to McFarren's house for a few drinks after last call.

* * * * *

They drove with McFarren in his pickup truck to his house after filling in the grave. Matthews angled the top of a pack of cigarettes downwards and tapped at its bottom until a clutch of cigarettes came loose. He pulled one out, stuck it between his lips, and waved the pack toward Neal and McFarren, offering them a cigarette, which both men accepted. Matthews lit his own cigarette after giving them a light. The first inhale harsher than anticipated, the cigarette fell from his hand as he coughed. He desperately tried to retrieve it before burning the seat, but his movement caused the cigarette to roll into a crevice.

"Goddammit!" McFarren roared at Matthews. "Find your damn cigarette it! It's burning my seat!"

Matthews burned two fingers while retrieving the cigarette. "I found it," he yelled.

"Did it burn my seat?"

"It might have, but just a little, I think," Matthews loudly groaned. A fingertip-sized hole had been burned into the leather seat.

"Just a little? Just a little, the man says," McFarren angrily muttered. "Do I go over to your house and leave just a little burn in your sofa?" he asked Matthews, who sat between him and Neal. "How about I come around and give your old lady just a little poke? How would that be?" He grabbed Matthews' head and rammed it against the dashboard.

Matthews formed a fist out of McFarren's view and came close to punching McFarren before checking himself. He remembered well bad things that happened after making what he thought was a harmless joke at McFarren's expense. McFarren's face went red after Matthews joked that he was old enough to have fought in World War One. McFarren gave him an angry stare but said nothing. Matthews' beloved dog died after its kidneys failed a few days later, though young and in good health. Within a week, his dog died, his house burned to cinders, and he suffered a bout of food poisoning. Absurd though it seemed, Matthews began to believe that McFarren had put a hex on him.

Matthews and Neal climbed into Matthews' car after returning to McFarren's place.

"What the hell happened tonight?" Matthews asked Neal on the way to Neal's house.

"I don't know," Neal replied. "Did you notice footprints in

the grass after we went back to the grave?"

"Oh, I saw them," Matthews said. "Who made them? Who do they belong to?"

"Your guess is as good as mine," Neal declared. "And who opened the coffin, and why was it empty?"

"You got me there. You didn't open it, did you?"

"No!" Neal angrily exclaimed. "You were right there with me when we finished digging out the grave and climbed out of it. The coffin was closed when we left."

Matthews rubbed his forehead, still smarting from having met McFarren's dashboard. He put the cabin light on and looked in the rearview mirror, curious to see if his forehead was bruised. A part of it looked darker than the rest. Matthews leaned toward Neal. "Is there a mark on my forehead?" he asked Neal, certain that it was bruised.

"You have a badass bruise," Neal noted while looking at his forehead.

"Holly shit!" Matthews exclaimed. "What am I going to tell the old lady?"

"Just tell her someone punched you because they got pissed off because you beat them at pool."

"Yeah, that should work," Matthews said.

"So, what about the grave?" Neal asked him. "What was that all about?"

"That had to be a dream," Matthews contended. "Did we really go to some cemetery and dig out a grave? Maybe the guy put drugs in our beer?" He paused. "I don't know what to think. Maybe we hallucinated?"

"We went to the cemetery and dug out a grave. That was no hallucination."

"I suppose," Matthews said.

"Don't bother denying what happened," Neal told him. "I want to, but we both were there. We both saw what happened."

"I ain't denying nothing. I know what I saw... But why dig out someone's grave? It doesn't make sense."

"Maybe money or jewelry was in there?" Neal wondered. "Maybe McFarren and some other people stole stuff and hid it in there until things cooled down? Maybe there was never a body in the coffin? That might be why the coffin was open when we returned because his buddies removed whatever was in there… But there was only that one set of footprints we didn't make that led from the grave. And they were too small to have been made by a man."

"The open coffin and footprints freaked me out," Matthews stated.

"Me, too," Neal replied.

"Maybe the guy just got out of prison for robbing a bank or something?" Matthews speculated. "Maybe that's why he began showing up at the Legion, out of the blue?"

"Who knows?" Neal replied. "I'm still trying to figure out why we even went to the cemetery."

"Yeah, I'm wondering the same thing."

"It's hard to put into words, but it felt like I had no choice but to go there," Neal said. "I don't remember the dude saying anything about a cemetery. I just remember playing pool. Next thing, we're in a cemetery and digging out a girl's grave."

"Now that you mention it, I don't remember him talking about that either," Matthews told him. "But we drank a lot tonight. Maybe we blacked out at some point. He might have even told us what was inside the grave, but we just don't remember."

"No way," Neal said while shaking his head. "He never told us what was in the grave, and no way did we both blackout at the same time. For us to pass out at the same time is practically impossible. If we did, that would be pretty much coincidental."

"Maybe he did put a little something in our beer?" Matthews said. "He could have done it when we were playing pool, and we just didn't notice."

"Maybe," Neal allowed. "But, whatever, if there was loot in there, he should have shared some of it with us since we did the heavy work. We were the suckers who did all the digging while he just stood around watching us."

"Yeah," Matthews groaned. "All he did was hold the flashlight and bitch at us."

"Do you ever think about why we bother with the guy?" Neal asked him. "It seems like he's there every time we go to the Legion. We always end up hanging out with him and going to his place after last call."

"That's strange you say that because I'm thinking the same thing. I just figured you wanted to hang out with him."

"And here I thought you were the one who wanted to deal with the old prick," Neal said.

"We should just not hang out with the guy anymore," Matthews suggested. "We should just stop going to the Legion for a while. Maybe he'll stop going there since we're the only people he bothers with."

"But I like the Legion," Neal protested. "I like talking with the people there and playing pool. Why should we stop going there because of that old goat?"

"We could just stop going for a while," Matthews said. "Maybe for a few months or so and see if the guy stops going there."

"That might work," Neal agreed.

"Let's just avoid the place for a bit. Like I say. Maybe he'll stop showing up there?"

"Remember that hunting trip we took with him?" Neal said. "Remember the buck heads the old guy took home with him? He said he was gonna hang 'em on the wall behind the bar in his basement, but he hasn't done that yet."

"That's true," Matthews groaned.

"Maybe he's a Satanist?" Neal wondered. "Maybe he used them in some weird-ass ceremony."

"Anything is possible with that old goat," Matthews said, repeating Neal's term for the man.

"And the beautiful girlfriend of his," Neal sighed. "I can't figure out why a hot-looking chick like that would have anything to do with him."

"She's absolutely doable," Matthews hummed. "She's a total babe, and I love her name, Savannah. That's a sexy name."

"I like her name, too," Neal said. "The guy has to be like a hundred and twenty years old, and she's what, like twenty-four at the most? I can't get over that. It's a sin for a young doll like her to be shacking up with an old relic like him, but then she doesn't seem to have much going on upstairs. She's as intelligent as a post, from what I can tell... Chicks like that are good in bed, flighty, horny, and gorgeous. Do your business and send her on her way is what I say."

Both men laughed.

Neal stared at the road on which he lived as they neared it. "You don't need to take me to my house," he said. "Just let me out at the end of my road... I'll walk the rest of the way."

"I can take you to your house," Matthews insisted. "It's not that much farther."

"It's okay," Neal told him. "It's only about a half a mile walk to my place. I feel like walking. Walking helps me sort out my thoughts. We have a lot to think about."

"That we do," Matthews agreed.

"Besides, I could use the exercise," Neal added. "It'll help me sleep better."

"If you insist," Matthews said as they stopped at Neal's road.

Neal stepped out of the car. "My arms feel like they're going to fall off with all the digging we did," he told Matthews through its open window after closing the passenger side door. "And my back is sore."

"My back is sore, too," Matthews said. "Plus, my fingers are killing me from burning them when I tried to get the dam cigarette out from behind the seat." He sucked on the fingers every so often to soothe them as they drove. "And my head hurts from when the old man slammed me into the dashboard."

"I couldn't believe the old man did that," Neal muttered. "I wanted to deck the old goat because it pissed me off. That was uncalled for. There was no reason for him doing that to you."

"Thanks, brother," Matthews said. "But you know how it is if you piss the guy off. Remember the harassment I went through after saying he was old enough to have been in World War One? That all had to be a coincidence..."

"Believe me, I wanted to deck him, too... Anyway, I'll come over later today with a sixty of Canadian Club. We'll get our drink on and talk."

"That sounds good," Neal replied. "Come by around one-ish. My old lady will be at work by then."

Neal waved at Matthews and began walking home, worn and tired, desperately anxious to reach his bed. He looked across a farmer's field at car and truck lights on Highway 401 while contemplating all that had happened that night. Cricket and beetle chatter and the sound of his feet treading on the road's graveled surface accompanied him along the way.

Neal turned around and noticed what appeared to be a person charging toward him. Soon upon him, a man grabbed Neal's throat with a vice-like grip. Neal passed out and died from asphyxiation.

* * * * *

Matthews woke with an unnerving sense that someone other than his wife was with them in their bedroom. A moment passed before his eyes adjusted to dark mixed with dawning daylight, pouring through a window. A monstrous hand grabbed his throat before Matthews was able to react and strangle him to death.

Oblivious to the violence beside her, his wife was undeterred from her sleep.

* * * * *

"Where were you last night?" Savannah asked McFarren. She stood at a stove, stirring a pot of stew, when McFarren entered the kitchen at eleven a.m. Savannah knew that she risked McFarren's wrath by asking the question. The man she knew as Zack had little patience for being questioned, especially by her.

McFarren grimaced at her. Emotionally cold though he was, he found it difficult to harbor anger toward Savannah, a loving, strong, yet vulnerable soul. But Savannah was a mere object to him, of no more significance than his battered old truck or a cheap watch he wore around his wrist. "Don't worry about it," McFarren grunted. He delivered a soft, disrespectful slap to her buttocks in the context of the moment. "How long will it be until that stew is done? I'm starving. I'm so hungry, I could eat a horse."

"It'll be done in forty minutes," Savannah muttered, glancing at a clock on the wall.

"Smells bloody tasty," McFarren said, looking out a window. "It's going to be a scorcher out there today," he said, having heard a weather forecast on the radio on his way home.

"You don't need to tell me that it's going to be hot out today," Savannah told him. "I've already been outside." Her beautifully shaped lips morphed into a grimace. "So, what happened to you last night?" she asked Zack. "I fell asleep at four in the morning after staying up waiting for you."

"I was out," was all McFarren offered.

"Out?" she asked him.

"Yes, out," McFarren sharply replied.

"Doing what?"

"Don't worry about it," he said while patting her head. "I didn't count on being out so late. I would have called, but I figured that you would be sleeping and didn't want to wake you. You should give me a little credit for that."

"I couldn't sleep because I was worried about you."

"I love you too, sweetie," McFarren replied. "I'm sorry about that, and I promise to let you know where I am from now on if I'm running late... Did you pick up the clothes from the seamstress, like I asked you to?"

"Yeah, I got 'em," Savannah said, having dutifully fulfilled his request. "They're in the living room, laid out on the couch nice and flat, just like you wanted them."

"Good girl," he said, pleased Savannah did what he requested of her. "I'll need them tonight." A satanic ritual was on his mind, and the clothes were a crucial part of it.

* * * * *

McFarren and Savannah drove to a beach a forty-minute drive south of Windsor as evening set in later that day, along Lake Erie.

Two detectives stopped by their house to question him about the deaths of Matthews and Neal before they left. Matthews' wife, who suspected that he had been with McFarren, called the police after waking to find her husband dead and a hand-shaped bruise around his throat. Neal's wife also suspected that her husband had been with McFarren when the police spoke with her after a newspaper delivery boy found his body.

McFarren feigned surprise after the detectives told him that Matthews and Neal had died the previous night. He acknowledged having been with them at the Legion but claimed ignorance regarding what might have happened to them. The detectives told McFarren that they planned to talk with him again.

"What do you think happened to Matthews and Mr. Neal?" Savannah asked him as they drove toward Lake Erie. She liked Matthews and Neal, having met them a few times, and was genuinely concerned about their well-being.

"Hell if I know," McFarren replied.

"That's too weird that they both died last night," Savannah said. And you were with them, she was tempted to add before thinking better of it.

"It could be," he said while firmly stroking her throat, threateningly. "What happened to those guys is a coincidence and nothing more."

McFarren parked the pickup after reaching Ambassador Beach, arriving at their destination. They gathered with his fellow Satanists on a remote section of the beach. He forced her to participate in a dark ceremony. The ceremony led to her end as Savannah was the subject of a sacrificial rite.

Chapter Seventeen
Until Death Brings Us Together

Trees obscured the light from a full moon along Normandy Road. Tyler stared at McFarren's house after reaching it and recalled when she, Aaron, and Wayne went inside and how their meeting with him led to their undoing. McFarren, his eyes closed, facing the front window, appeared to be sleeping in a recliner. A hallway leading to a backdoor was behind him.

After reaching his backyard, she picked up a rock to bash McFarren's head in with; he had to die to reverse the harm he had caused. The back door opened and closed without a sound, as she entered his kitchen. She traded the rock for a butcher knife and crept softly toward where McFarren sat, obscured by the back of his chair

Tyler arched the knife over her head after reaching McFarren and thrust it into his neck. McFarren looked at her when she stepped in front of him and then fell out of his chair onto the floor. Blood flowed along the floorboards.

"Get away from me!" McFarren yelled, raising an arm in a defensive posture as Tyler prepared to stab him again. With strength that came from somewhere else, she sent the knife deep into his shoulder and then struggled to get it out because it was stuck. She sobbed in frustration as she wanted to stab him a few more times to ensure the deed was done. The knife was loosening when the room was illuminated by the headlights of a car that pulled into his driveway.

She ran outside and into the woods behind the house after someone stepped out of the car.

*****

Depressed by failing to contact Tyler, Aaron lay on a couch in a Florida room at the back of his house, watching but not noticing what was playing on television. He shut the TV off and listened as a gusting wind rattled windows and rang metal wind chimes on the eves outside as a thunderstorm passed. Though in need of a good night's sleep, he succumbed to a strong urge to look outside before heading to bed. A flash of lightning illuminated someone in his backyard while he looked out a window.

Anxious to find out why the person was there, he continued into the darkness with a baseball bat to use for self-defense after going outside. He noticed the person was wearing a dress and had a young teenager's stature after drawing close. Perhaps it was a developmentally delayed girl who lived in his neighborhood, who had a habit of wandering and getting lost.

"What are you doing in my yard?" he asked the girl after reaching within ten feet of her. She did not respond.

"Are you okay?" he asked her after dropping the bat. Again, she did not reply. "Are you okay?" he asked the girl again. A flash of lightning partially illuminated her face, revealing that she resembled Tyler. "Who are you?"

"Hi, Aaron," the girl said. "Don't be afraid. Please don't be upset with me."

"How do you know my name?" he asked her.

"You know who I am," she said.

A hollow feeling began while staring at the girl. Her voice was reminiscent of Tyler's, and she appeared to match her five-foot-four-inch height and medium frame. Emotional wounds that had never completely healed were ripped open. He wondered how she knew his name and how he knew her. She looked like Tyler, and her voice sounded like Tyler's, but it could not be Tyler. Tyler was dead.

"Who are you, really?" he asked her again. Maybe it was Tyler? Maybe it was her ghost? Maybe this had something to do with the séance?

"I'm Tyler," the girl said. "It's real, Aaron. I'm really here, and

I'm talking with you. I've watched you all the time since the accident and could even read your thoughts if I wanted to. I didn't always do that. But I could if I wanted to."

"Tyler who?" he asked her.

"Tyler Page," she replied. "The Tyler you grew up with."

"Your name's not Tyler Page," he groaned dismissively. He wondered why the girl was playing such a cruel joke. The only plausible explanation was that, for some morbid reason, someone must have put her up to it. But she was wearing a white dress, like the one Tyler was buried in.

"It really is me," the girl said. "I'm Tyler. It's me, Aaron!" she insisted as he stared at her in utter bewilderment.

"This has to be a dream because that's impossible," he said.

"It's not a dream, Aaron," she replied. "It really is me... I need you to believe that. You're my guy. We've known each other forever. I know it's hard, but you must believe that it really is me," she repeated in a pleading tone of voice.

"The Tyler I knew died twenty years ago," he told her.

"Remember when I came to your house all upset after a softball game I played?" the girl asked him. "And then we went to the fort in my backyard to go through our baseball and hockey cards. Then we went swimming in my pool even though my dad laced it with chlorine five hours before... We didn't want to get into trouble for going into the pool, but that didn't stop us. And then we played chess in the fort before you had to go to your cousin's place.

"How would I know about all that if I wasn't Tyler?"

"Oh, my God!" Aaron exclaimed, on the verge of fainting. She had to be Tyler, but how could that be?

"I didn't want to upset you by showing up here like I did," the girl claiming to be Tyler said. "I know it's hard for you, and it's hard for me, too... You couldn't see me, but I've always been close. Like I said, I could watch you and read your thoughts if I wanted to, and also see our friends and my family. I've always been with you in spirit, just so you know… I hope that somehow makes you feel better."

Neither spoke while staring at each other for a moment. Aaron began to shake. "I don't know what's happening, but I'm so happy to see you. I can't believe it," he said, his voice quivering with emotion.

"I know, Aaron," she said. "I have so many things to tell you." She stared at him silently for a moment, which he knew was to help him process what was happening.

"You'll understand."

"You always came to visit me and brought me daisies. You and my dad called me The Flower Girl because I loved flowers, and you called me that more often after I went around wearing a daisy in my hair that day."

"It… it just can't be," he uttered softly in a comforting tone of voice in case it was her. "Are you her ghost?"

"There's no such thing as ghosts because they don't exist," Tyler replied. "Remember when we went to see Mr. McFarren because I wanted to learn how to do a séance so I could say goodbye to my grandpa a year after he died?

"Everything went dark after you and the guys tried to contact me. I left an awesome place and returned to my body in the grave. I couldn't move even though my body somehow went back to a healthy state. I didn't breathe. I didn't seem to need to."

"We just did the séance because we were upset and missed you," he said, now certain though unable to comprehend how he was speaking with Tyler. "I was devastated after you died," he tearfully said, speaking with emotion. "I missed you so much. I had to contact you somehow if I could… Now I feel bad… I wish I never tried to do the séance."

"It wasn't your fault," Tyler said. "You would never have thought of doing a séance if it wasn't for me putting the idea in your head when I wanted to try one for my grandpa."

"You meant well… Remember, I told you I didn't want to do

it because it seemed wrong. Well, now I know that I was right. I was wrong for getting the words Mr. McFarren said we had to say because they are what caused all this. " Tyler crossed her arms and looked at the ground. "Remember how we were all saying it seemed to be satanic, with the goat heads and all? The séance really is evil." She looked back at him. "I heard digging sounds after you finished saying all the words the other night and saw two men with McFarren, digging out my grave." She unfolded her arms. "I love you so much, Aaron, and you love me, too."

Another clap of thunder rumbled through the dark, cloud-shrouded sky. A glow cast from lightning illuminated Tyler's dress. The dress was torn, dirty, and tattered.

"I left my grave after the men freed me from it and spent the last few nights walking to McFarren's house. I walked through fields at night and hid in wooded places during the day so that people wouldn't see me... I went to Mr. McFarren's house tonight, before coming here to see you... Aaron, I was so scared, especially when I had to cross roads and pass through areas while terrified about being seen. It was so weird having to hide from people."

"I feel like I'm going to faint," he said, his knees rattling on the verge of buckling.

"I know it's hard for you to believe what's going on, that it's me and that we're talking," Tyler said. "We were always together, and you were and are and always will be my soul mate... This is all so weird, me being here and us talking with each other."

"Oh, my God, I'm so confused," he told her. "It has to be you, but I just don't get it."

"I know," Tyler softly replied.

"I just can't believe it. I don't know if I'm having an out-of-body experience," he said. "I don't know what to say. I want to believe it, but..."

"You're not having an out-of-body experience, Aaron," Tyler told him. "This is real…"

"Why did you go to McFarren's?" Aaron asked her. "What made you go there?"

"I'll tell you in a bit," Tyler replied. "You'll understand why I have to wait to tell you. You'll see."

"I went on to Heaven after the accident. There really is a Heaven! But I didn't get to stay there," she said, her voice breaking with emotion. "People seemed to be very happy there and did not have things getting in the way of being with each other, but I could only watch."

She told him what she knew about Heaven. That people could be with different people and do other things and be in different places, all at the same time, because there was no concept of time. And the climate was however you preferred. It could always be sunny and warm or nighttime dark and cold, or it could rain or snow or whatever you liked. According to Tyler, you could see billions times a billion, times a few more billion, stars than you could anywhere on Earth.

"But I wasn't happy," she said. "There was no way I could be happy when I saw how upset everyone was when I died. You, and even my parents, were devastated. I watched my funeral, and I saw everyone there. My English grandparents were there, and my parents had to make the funeral later so they could get there.

"They were all upset because of what happened, and my parents really, really, really wanted things to be better between us. Now I know they did love me and beat themselves up for not being there for me like they should have been. Still, I did things I wish I didn't do either, like not looking at the camera for the last picture my mom would ever have of me, the one you were looking at in your basement, just after my funeral… It broke my heart. I wanted to cry, but I couldn't. All I could do emotion-wise was be sad. Nothing else."

"My dad was so devastated he never got better. He just kept thinking about me, and I never ever would have thought I was... Guess."

"I don't know," Aaron said.

"I still never understood why he didn't coach me in soccer until a few months before he died. I know now he thought girls' teams needed girl managers. It's how he felt; I was so upset about that... I don't know why he never told me. I would have understood...

"So, how are you feeling right now, Aaron? I'm babbling on. I want to hear what you have to say."

"I don't know what to say," Aaron said.

"Well, you must be feeling something, like are you confused, happy? Are you happy to see me?"

"Of course, I'm happy to see you... but I still don't know if I'm dreaming or seeing things."

"No, this is real... I'm really here," Tyler said. "I know you bought the plot next to my grave. That was so sweet! That should have happened, and you made it happen, so that you and I would be next to each other when the time came if life turned out the way we thought it would. Man and wife, together forever."

"That's so horrible that you were alive in your grave."

"I was awake the whole time," Tyler said. "I've never not been awake since just after the accident... But being alone in my grave is all done now, Aaron. I'm getting close to going to Heaven for good...

"I felt so bad for you, Henry," Tyler continued. Henry was a nickname she gave him, derived from Henry Aaron, one of the greatest baseball players of all time, who was a household name in the 1970s.

"I haven't been called that for a long time," he said. He wanted to chuckle, but Tyler using the nickname brought back many memories and feelings, all jumbled together. Just the name brought a flashback of when she last called him that, when he and Wayne were exploring a beat-up car someone had dumped in the bush at a spot they hung out near Wayne's house. His sister was listening to a live game broadcast on the radio when Henry Aaron beat Babe Ruth's all-time home run record. That was major news for even the most casual baseball fans; Tyler was listening with muted interest, so it seemed, while clearing away brush to set up a lawn dart range. She was paying attention, though, because she called him Henry for the first time before Henry Aaron could have cleared the bases. "Isn't that something, Henry?" she said loud enough to be heard over the crowd's roar while looking at Aaron.

"You and me were stuck together like glue. We said we were always going to be together... You kept blaming yourself for my brakes not working, and I think you should stop because I could have thought of it, too. I was a big girl," she said again with a chuckle.

"It just goes to show you how messed up things are. I don't know why I had to die so young. You know how I talked about that day and that stupid phobia about old people making me think about death? I ended up dying, and some of those people are probably still alive!

"I still feel sad for you because you watched the truck hit me. You were devasted. You tried to help me, but there was nothing you could do, and you knew it... It's bothered you ever since; other things have happened, and you missed me as much as the day I passed.

"You did the séance two nights ago."

"So there is something bad about it?" Aaron asked.

"Yes, there is. It isn't good! The words are evil if spoken to contact the dead. The séance is just a way to get people to say the words; the only thing that is needed is the words being spoken to contact the dead and someone to say them. You don't need the black clothes, candles, chalice, or any of that.

"I'm here because you did it, but I'm not blaming you, and

I'm not going to blame Wayne either. I was the one who talked you guys into coming with me. You know I would never have gone to see him by myself... I knew you guys would come with me.

"I've prayed to be forgiven for getting the words and sharing them as they were evil," she told Aaron. "Now I want you to ask God to be forgiven for saying the words to contact me," she told Aaron. "We'll be together again if you ask for forgiveness for saying them. Trust me. You'll see."

Aaron did as Tyler asked. He prayed to God and asked to be forgiven.

"I'm so happy you did that," Tyler told him when he finished. "And just so you know, you're not gonna die for a few more days at least."

"How do you know that?" he asked her.

"Because people get a black aura around them just before they die. It starts as a black mist a few days before a person dies and gets more intense. It takes three days for the aura to form fully. You're okay for the next few days because there's no mist around you."

"Thank God I at least have that going for me," he said.

"I know what you're saying because no one wants to die," Tyler replied. But the life you have after dying is so much better. It's the dying part that sucks..."

"I want to show you and tell you things that will be hard to believe and understand. I want to take you somewhere, but I need to explain a few things before I do."

Aaron was trying to make sense of what she was saying. "Where would you take me?"

"I'll tell you. But the first thing is why I didn't get to stay in Heaven. Oh, Aaron, it seems so much better there. People weren't caught up with all the trivial stuff of life there like they are here."

"What do you mean by saying it seems so much better?"

"Because I was having an out-of-body kind of thing, because I just had this feeling that I was coming back, to here... I was there, but I wasn't. I could only feel sadness, and I didn't think people were sad in Heaven... And then I went back to my body after you guys tried the séance."

Aaron could only stare at her, unable to find a meaningful word to say while feeling a surge of guilt for having ever bothered with the séance. "It's okay, Aaron," Tyler said, feeling what he felt. "Try not to feel bad. It wasn't your fault. None of us knew what the purpose of the séance was."

"Thanks for trying to make me feel better, but no matter what you say, I won't."

"But I was the one who insisted on doing one," Tyler said. "I know you're gonna feel what you're going to feel, but none of us knew any better. The main thing is that Heaven really does exist," she continued. "There's no way I can explain how beautiful it is.

"I'm here, now, Aaron," she hummed. "It would have been better if we met in Heaven, though ... We talked about whether there was a Heaven, and there is, Aaron, and we will meet there someday and be together forever."

"But it won't be the same," Aaron said. "You're still a girl. I'm a full-grown man. You would be my daughter, I guess..."

"You can be any age you want in Heaven, Aaron. We can go back to where we were and be that way forever if we want, or we can both be adults. It's our soul that matters. We started seeing each other differently... I was always attracted to you, the way you looked, because, as I said, you were very handsome, but it's more than that. We knew what the other was thinking without asking, how we were feeling, what we were doing... I see now that what was inside us kept us as tight as we were... I liked how I looked, and I could be that kid again if I wanted, but like I say, I can be any age I want to be, and so can you.

"There's a reason why I'm here." Tyler looked toward the field momentarily, like she was gathering her thoughts, and looked back at him. "A spirit named Abigail came to see me every so often in a vision."

She paused for a moment in case he wanted to say something.

"Abigail is a blonde-haired, blue-eyed lady spirit who always wears a silky blue tunic when I see her," Tyler continued as Aaron stayed silent. Tyler paused again to allow Aaron a moment to collect his thoughts. "This is all too much for you, and I'm sorry it has to be like this, but it does, and it sucks.

"I know it sounds kooky for me to say a spirit came to see me, but it's true, just like me standing here talking to you... There are a lot of spirits mentioned in the Bible... I trust the one I saw because it all makes sense, I guess. One thing for sure, the words in the supposed séance are evil because we saw that.

"Abigail came to see me right after I went back, and she's the reason I can see you and my family and all of my other friends and know what you were thinking. So I could always know what people were doing and thinking when I wanted to. So, I wasn't completely alone... And Abigail is why I know you and I will be together forever because she told me so.

"She told me all about the séance. What it's about, and that some things need to happen because of it. She said it's the words that matter, not the séance itself, which is all for show. It's fake.

"I need to show you how the séance started and what it's all about so you understand," she said. "I also want to tell you that I did something before I came here that I had to do, and I want you to understand why and what you need to do."

"I can't explain it, so I'll need to show you," Tyler said. Aaron stared at her in silence. "Aaron?"

"I heard you, Tyler," he said. "I'm so confused. I'm in a daze, trying to take this all in."

"You'll understand," she said in a halting voice. She dabbed at her eyes to wipe away tears.

"What's wrong?" Aaron asked.

"I'm okay," Tyler said. "You'll understand."

"I'm going to take you to see Mr. McFarren to see how the séance started. You can watch him and even go inside his head to know what he's thinking and feeling. I'll be there with you. So… are you okay with that?"

"Ya, yeah," Aaron replied. "I guess I have to be."

"You know how everyone called Mr. McFarren Old Man McFarren because he was old and creepy? Well, he really is old," Tyler said. "He was born in 1605, just so you know... Like as in the year 1605. Trust me, Aaron," she asked of him. "I need you to take my hand, so I can show you how the séance started and what it's all about." He merely stared at her and nodded. "Come on, Aaron. I'll come to you, but you need to look away from me because I don't want you to see me up close… It'll be okay. It's me, Tyler."

Her hand felt warm, not cold, and clammy as expected after hesitantly taking hold of it. His soul mate and all that was around them meshed into a foggy twilight, which they passed through until reaching a cobbled lane. Fog obscured the light from lanterns illuminating its way as Aaron rode the air, hovering a few feet above the lane.

"Bring out your dead," a man driving a wagon drawn by two horses cried out.

Unable to avoid making contact with the horses, he braced for an expected collision that never came. Instead of colliding with them, he passed through the horses and man and continued into a cloth-covered wagon. Yellowed complected corpses were placed in an orderly fashion along its floor.

A man walking along the lane came into view after passing through the wagon. Aaron continued toward him and then slowed to match his slow, labored pace. The man wore a long coat, hat, gloves, and a scarf.

"It's Mr. McFarren," Tyler said.

Aaron looked in the direction of her voice. She was nowhere to be seen. He was alone.

Aaron recognized the man as McFarren. McFarren brought a hand to his sweat-sodden yellow complected face and coughed.

Rats passed underfoot, but he did not seem to notice, or if he did, he showed no mind of their presence.

A man approached and tipped his hat, an unspoken way that men acknowledge each other. McFarren returned the favor. The man started across the lane after noticing McFarren's unhealthy appearance. Other people he encountered along the way also made a point of avoiding him.

McFarren retrieved a key from his coat and inserted it into a door that opened into a comfortable abode. After closing the door, he walked toward a fireplace, placed his gloves on a table, and then put logs in the hearth. He poured liquid over the logs from a container. Fire erupted after he struck a match.

McFarren placed his coat, hat, and scarf on hooks and warmed his upper body and then his hands when the flames subsided at the fire. A rose-colored rash was around his neck. 'Ring around the Rosie,' a singing game played with Tyler when they were little, came to mind.

'Ring-a-round the Rosie, a pocket full of posies, Ashes! Ashes! We all fall down,' they gleefully sang before collapsing. Played in blissful childhood innocence, he learned in later years that their seemingly innocent game derived from a nursery rhyme about the plague that ravaged mid-1600s London. People stuffed their pockets with posies believing doing so spared them from the plague. 'Ring around the Rosie' referred to a rose-colored rash formed on the necks of the stricken.

Aaron was able to read McFarren's thoughts and glean a sense of his history. On the verge of dying from bubonic plague, McFarren feared not being able to complete a play he was close to finishing more than death itself. A bookkeeper by trade but a playwright in spirit, McFarren was close to finishing what he considered his best work. A play worthy of playing at London's King's Theater, its premier venue, he was certain. This would be the play about a family that left London to escape the plague. Confronted by villagers fearing plague was coming with them, the family sought refuge in deep woods, striving to live in unfettered peace.

Such a play would lead to riches and acclaim and give credence to his passion. He slaved away at writing and became a hermit, shunning family and friends in the process. Now staring death in its face, he only longed to leave a legacy. His son and daughter could reap whatever riches came from his labor, wealth no longer an aspiration.

"Should have stayed in me diggings," McFarren exhaustedly mumbled after entering a bedroom. He wet a cloth with water from a bucket and used it to moisten dry, leathered lips while sitting on a bed. That done, he placed the cloth on the rim of the bucket, sprawled out, and closed his eyes.

Time passed. A man and woman entered the room. Neither gave a hint of noticing him as Aaron stood in plain sight. The man and woman were McFarren's son and daughter.

"Father's fast asleep," McFarren's son said. "Shall we wake him?"

"Nah, let's not disturb him," the woman suggested after staring at her father for a few moments. "I shall return in the morn to see of his well-doing."

"I'll add a log to the fire," the son said as the woman stared grimly at their father. Sparks fluttered as a flash glow illuminated the room. McFarren's children left after a burst of fire subsided.

The house returned to its state of peace after his children left, save for silence disturbed by fire crackle and occasional gasps McFarren made. McFarren looked at a churning sea, in a dream, at waves exploding to their end against a cliff he stood on after an unknown desideratum compelled Aaron back into his mind. A massive wave ended with tremendous ramifications after crashing, followed by an even larger one that shook what was below as it broke. A wave of equal size followed, prompting McFarren to step well away from the cliff. Where he previously stood dropped into the sea. McFarren rode a horse along a path in a forest in a second vision. "He's coming, he's coming," Tyler's voice said. Sunlight filtered like water finding downward points through trees. Air-colored fluorescent green misted above the forest floor. A path he trod was dark ahead where tree cover thickened.

A bearded man of tall stature with brown hair stepped from behind trees as McFarren was feet from reaching where the path became dark.

"Good day there," the man said. "Might I have a word with you, my man?" he asked McFarren.

"Who are you?" McFarren wanted to know, wary of being in the company of a thief. A reasonable assumption, the forests known to teem with robbers.

"You can call me Geoffrey," the man said. "Please do not regard me as a thief, as you no doubt are."

"Why shall I not?" McFarren asked him. "How could I not assume you to be a man of such cloth?"

"A logical inclination to have, a man of your wherewithal; however, I assure I am not of such ilk," Geoffrey said. "Mr. Zachary McFarren. You are a man of sound intellect and a thorough judge of one's character."

"How do you know my name? We have never met before that I know of."

"Our paths have crossed," Geoffrey said.

"Well, your memory serves you better than mine. You are not familiar to me, and I never forget a face."

"I know you well, more than you could ever know," Geoffrey said. "But how that has come to be is of minor importance overall in light of things. My understanding is that you're in a bit of a fix," the man said, looking into McFarren's eyes.

"How do you mean?" McFarren asked Geoffrey.

"Now, let's not be coy, Zachary," Geoffrey replied. "The sickness is within you, and death is near, yet the best play you have written remains unfinished. Not a very favorable state of affairs, I would say." The man who called himself Geoffrey smiled sheepishly. "That's if you asked for my opinion." McFarren stared at him in cold silence. "I can help you through your predicament," Geoffrey said.

"What predicament might that be?" McFarren asked him.

"Again, with the coyness," Geoffrey hummed. He chuckled softly. "To move on past your sickness is the predicament I speak of."

"How could you possibly know if the sickness is inside me?"

"The sickness is all over you, my friend, and I can smell it, for Christ's sake! You're a yellowed, sweating, walking, stinking corpse to be. Quite a pathetic sight, you are, truth be told." Geoffrey shook his head. "Death has its sights on you, yet work you have busied yourself with over the last few years remains to be finished."

"You mean you can rid me of it?" McFarren asked him about the sickness.

Geoffrey looked skyward and laughed. "No! No, my newfound friend," he laughed while looking back at McFarren. "I am afraid that is beyond even my means. No, my friend. There is no escaping the sickness and its end result. You will die, but there is a way around it; such an inconvenience death can be," Geoffrey said after pulling a sheet of paper from his pocket. He gave the sheet to McFarren. "Ask someone to cite words on this sheet and say your name after you've taken your final breath. Do that, and life will revisit you so that you can finish your work. Might you be game?"

"That I might," McFarren replied after reading the sheet. "With another month of penmanship, I should be able to finish my greatest work, which has only now begun to come to fruition. This play may very well be my legacy. My something to be remembered by."

Geoffrey nodded and smiled. "Well, I am glad to hear that," he said.

"What is it that you meant by being game?" McFarren asked him.

"Just a figure of expression, my friend. A figure of speech is all," Geoffrey replied. "I just want to know if we have an agreement or not."

"I am in agreement," McFarren affirmed. "But what is it that you mean by agreement? What's in this for you?"

"Perhaps I might ask a favor of you in due time," Geoffrey advised him. "Now, don't be telling anyone, not a soul, about our meeting or the substance of our conversation. You are a good man, but some folks may not be inclined to have you back."

"I'm not sure what you mean by that," McFarren said. "I've not wronged anyone per my knowledge."

"No man has passed through this life without having aggrieved someone, intended or not," Geoffrey said. "But that's beside the point. You can come back to life to finish the work you are so close to completing, if so inclined."

"My soul I would offer if given a means of doing that," McFarren said.

Geoffrey smiled and winked at him. "Just give the sheet I gave you to your son or daughter and ask them to read the words aloud when you pass. They do not need to know about our meeting."

"How did you know I have a son and daughter?" McFarren asked him. "And how would you know of my character, calling me a good man as you did?"

"I know everything about you," Geoffrey replied.

"Very well then," McFarren said, curiously looking at Geoffrey, wondering how he knew so much about him. "It'll be a secret kept between us," he promised.

"Good," Geoffrey said while stepping back. "We shall meet again, my friend... Have yourself a splendid day!" Geoffrey went back behind the tree.

McFadden circled the tree, curious to find what became of the man who called himself Geoffrey. Geoffrey was gone. McFarren and his horse were alone. Alone save for the squawk of crows and ravens hidden within ancient oaks and other trees in the forest.

With sweat sticking a bedsheet to him, McFarren rolled onto a side after waking and vomited into a bucket. He dabbed a cloth into the bucket containing water and used the cloth to clear vomit from his lips and chin. He dipped a cup into the bucket and rinsed his mouth after filling the cup with water. After expelling into the vomit bucket, he filled the drinking cup and swallowed its contents. McFarren put the cup on the table his gloves were on and saw a sheet of paper with words written on it.

Words on the sheet matched those Geoffrey gave him in the dream. Perhaps he did encounter the man calling himself Geoffrey? Perhaps there truly was a chance to return to life? Otherwise, how could it be that a sheet with the words appeared in a physical form?

A moment passed of foggy blackness.

Aaron looked on as McFarren was in the throes of dying, the man's body trembling, and his eyes squinted to the width of hairs. His daughter repeatedly wiped sweat from his face and forehead with a damp cloth. McFarren looked at his son, haplessly standing nearby.

"Winston," he whispered to his son.

"Yes, Father," the younger man replied.

"Remember to read those words, as I have asked you. Make sure to read them aloud."

Winston held the sheet in his hands; his father gave it to him with a promise that each word be spoken.

"I will, Father. I will," Winston again promised.

McFarren began to have a series of seizures, each longer and more intense than the one preceding. He coughed and gagged. Blood streamed from his mouth, having repeatedly bitten his tongue. Death finally, at last, blessedly came.

Once again, time blinked.

Winston looked at his sister after speaking the words and saying their father's name. She nodded at him. After nodding back to her, Winston went to the front door and stepped onto the street. He posted a red cross on the door with the words 'Lord Have Mercy on This House' to notify the Deathman of his father's passing. Such signage was a standard way of alerting drivers of body hauling wagons that there was another corpse to be disposed of.

He returned to the room where his father lay. The yellow that complected Mr. McFarren's face had cleared, and his eyes were wide open. "Father is still alive," Winston's sister declared.

"Father!" Winston cried out. He hurried to the bed. "Father... I am so happy, but how could it be? You weren't breathing. This is God's doing, it was! It is He who brought you back! It's a bloody miracle."

"Please hand me the sheet," McFarren groaned after wiping blood from his chin with the cloth his daughter used to cool him with.

"Was it those words I read that brought you back?" Winston asked his father.

"No," McFarren glumly replied after taking charge of the sheet. "It had nothing to do with that." McFarren paused in an apparent effort to collect his breath. "The fever has left me. It's beyond explaining. A bloody miracle is what it is if that's what you care to call it."

The room grew dark. Tyler took him to another place. It was a different day.

Aaron found himself in a pub. People occupied stools in front of a bar and at tables as McFarren sat alone at a back table and drank away his sorrows. A bottle containing rye or scotch or something of that sort and a mug were in front of him. Aaron started toward McFarren, who had his back to the rest of the room, stopping just short of reaching him. Again, he could read McFarren's thoughts.

Alone in his drinking, McFarren listened in on a deep conversation the men at a nearby table were having. Barroom philosophers, so he thought of them, conversed about the plague as being a sign that God was not pleased with mankind's current state of affairs. One of the men surmised the plague was God's way of clearing the slate of those who dared to oppose Him. The practice of sorcery had become increasingly common.

McFarren consumed the contents of what remained in his mug and then belched loudly without concern of being overheard.

The room fell silent save for the crackle of the fire in a hearth as he studied a rat before it scurried into a hole in the baseboards.

McFarren looked behind him. Bottles and mugs were unattended, their contents at various stages of completion, on the table where the men had previously engaged in spirited conversation. Smoke rose from unattended cigars and pipes in ashtrays. The other tables were also empty as were the stools along the bar, and a man who tended it was nowhere to be seen.

McFarren wondered if the other patrons and the tender of the bar had left in a colluded humorous effort to leave him stumped as to why he was alone. Perhaps all would return after allowing him a moment to contemplate if he had lost his senses. They would share a laugh with him and treat him to a few pints of ale if class be within them.

Geoffrey, the man he met in the forest, approached McFarren's table after entering the pub.

"Good evening, my dear friend!" Geoffrey cheerfully bellowed upon reaching the table. "My, don't we look positively smashing, smashing for a dead man, that is?"

"What have you done to me?" McFarren angrily spat. He glared at Geoffrey with rage in his eyes. "I would have been better dead ten times over than to be in the dreadful state I find myself in."

"My, my, my, you are quite a crusty old sort," Geoffrey

remarked. "I have given you what you asked for... A second chance at life so you can complete your work. Use it, my dear man, use it! Complete your work." Geoffrey removed a fur coat, draped it over a stool, and then sat on one next to McFarren. "Write, my man, write… Does the world not await your work like a hungry hound its master bearing a fleshy bone?"

"I have no desire to write," McFarren declared. "My mind is too fogged for that. There is no desire within me to be here. I would be glad to find a hole to lay in, as I am nothing but a ragged bag of bones, as my spirit is dead."

"Your state is of little concern to me," Geoffrey said. "You and I have entered into an agreement. I fulfilled my part as you are alive and stirring… Plenty of others have accepted a similar offer and have rather benefited from having done so."

McFarren lunged at Geoffrey. "Die, you bastard, die!" he exclaimed while grabbing Geoffrey's throat. He squeezed it in an anger-fueled embrace. Geoffrey's throat had the firmness of a rock.

"You would be wise to remove your hands, my fine man," Geoffrey advised McFarren, in an unfettered tone of voice. His eyes glowed and turned red. "NOW DO IT!!" he yelled in a deep unworldly voice. McFarren obliged. Geoffrey ran a hand along the collar of his shirt to straighten it.

"How long will it be until I can leave this place?" McFarren asked him. "A day? A month?"

"Centuries might be a more accurate measure," Geoffrey said. He smiled at McFarren in a taunting manner. "You may very well live forever."

"What's the reason for this?" McFarren asked Geoffrey. "I don't want to be here in this place in this Godforsaken state."

"Oh, your ungratefulness is so utterly disappointing," Geoffrey said while shaking his head, accentuating his stated displeasure. "It's a good thing for you that I have compassion within me." Geoffrey rifled off a burst of booming laughter. He glared at McFarren as the man forsaken by death began to weep. "Oh, come now, you sniveling little worm!" Once again, Geoffrey flashed a taunting smile at McFarren. "You have caught me in a charitable state of mind. Perhaps I might consider amending our little Pact."

"Pact?" McFarren asked. "What Pact is it you speak of?"

"The deal, my man," Geoffrey said. "The agreement you and I have entered into."

"Agreement?" McFarren asked him.

"You sought my assistance to return to life, did you not?"

"I did," McFarren replied.

"And I presented you with those words, did I not?" Geoffrey asked him.

"You did."

"And your dutiful son spoke to them at your request, did he not?"

McFarren did not respond to his question.

"Well, did he or did he not, Zachary?"

"That he did," McFarren replied.

"I told you to ask someone to state the words and your name after you passed, and they did, and here you are," Geoffrey said.

"But what benefit is my being here to you?" McFarren asked him.

"Has a man ever done a favor without benefit to himself?" Geoffrey replied.

"Perhaps," McFarren muttered.

"Have you not?" Geoffrey asked him.

"I have, but I have helped others purely from the good of heart as well," McFarren replied.

"Still out of that, have you not had a benefit? A soul felt satisfaction from doing so? Had you not found satisfaction in such undertakings?"

"Some satisfaction," McFarren said. "Yes, I would say some was taken."

"A pleasurable experience, no doubt," Geoffrey surmised.

"It was," McFarren agreed. "Yes, it was."

"Well, perhaps you used those people you did a favor for out of some self-gratifying, unconscious, ingrained means to an end?" Geoffrey suggested. "I, on the other hand, bare no such deception. My motivation for helping you was for my profit. I would look you straight in the eye and say the manner of my profit if you had asked. But you did not. I merely said I might call on you in time to return the favor."

"Now, my mind is made," Geoffrey continued. "Power to rouse the dead from their slumber is yours through the words I have given you. Doing that will satisfy your end of our agreement, of our little Pact. But raising the dead is not mere words because it will be necessary for you to unearth a grave from time to time. I will let you know when that needs to be done."

"Digging out graves?" McFarren asked.

Geoffrey's eyes twinkled. "Not everyone is as fortunate as you when all the words are spoken. You were above ground, but if not, you would have woken to the blackest black and been there until someone dug you out."

"I will let you know when that time comes. You might see it in your head, a vision, you might say, of where you need to go, or I might come by for a visit and tell you myself. Either way, you won't be alone. You'll have the power to entice others to your will. I wouldn't expect a sick old man like you to have the strength to unearth the dead on your own.

"Let folks know not that you have means to raise the dead, but only means by which the living can communicate with them. Tell them the words are a means of conducting a séance and that they must be spoken aloud, along with the name of the person they wish to contact, so all the people present can hear. If you share the words, and they are used to contact the dead a certain number of times, and you release the dead as I ask, I will see to ending our Pact one day.

"Your knowledge of conducting a séance must be sought," Geoffrey continued. "It must be known but never offered. Your sickness will return when I am satisfied with the number of times the words have been used as intended, the Earth will be yours to lie in.

"So, might there be an agreement between us?" he asked McFarren, extending a hand in apparent anticipation of a deal-confirming handshake.

"How do I know that you're not deceitful as you have been?" McFarren asked.

"My man, I have not been deceitful with you!" Geoffrey replied. "I'm being completely forthcoming this time. You really have no choice but to trust me. Persevere in sharing the words, and I'll see to it that peace through death will find you one day."

"So, might we have an agreement?" Geoffrey asked him again.

"We do," McFarren warily said after accepting Geoffrey's hand. "We have an agreement."

"Splendidly, splendid... a toast to this noblest fellow," Geoffrey bellowed. A mug appeared in his hand. "If I may," he said while grabbing McFarren's bottle. McFarren nodded as Geoffrey filled the mug three-quarters full and then took a gulp. "Ah, scotch... Mmmm!" he said after gulping the mug. "This is fine-tasting scotch that you have here. Just the thing for warming the bones from that blasted damp and chilly weather." After taking another gulp, Geoffrey placed his mug on the table and dragged a finger across his lips. "You may very well have my company until the bottle is finished."

"Aw, but let us not distract from the subject at hand. Let people know you know of means by which to contact the dead. You know it's a means of raising the dead, but you will not state that point. You will tell them that it's a séance."

"Some miscellanea will be called for to make things look valid. Tell people a raised surface, somewhat of an altar, will be needed, that a table or chair will do. Say they need a black candle to be placed on the left, a red one to be placed on the right. Tell them a silver chalice needs to be between the candles. And this." A sheet of paper appeared in his hand. "Tell them that this must be hung against a westerly wall," Geoffrey said while handing the sheet to McFarren. A pentagram with a goat head was depicted on it. "A sheet with the words I gave you before and instructions on how to conduct the séance and this one with the pentagram and goat head will be supplied as replacements are required.

"Tell people to light the candles and to keep outside light from the room they do their séance in."

"Is that it, or is there more?" McFarren asked Geoffrey.

"Oh, there's more," Geoffrey replied. "Tell people their style of dress is important. Everyone attending your supposed séance must wear black."

Geoffrey glared at McFarren for the longest moment, the daggers that were his eyes rendering McFarren to a near-withering state. "Have you any further questions?" he asked the bewildered man.

"No," McFarren muttered.

"Very well then," Geoffrey said. "Ah, helping you finish the bottle is tempting," he said while looking at the bottle. "But I have other pressing matters to attend to."

Geoffrey rose from his chair and retrieved his coat.

"I do have another question," McFarren said.

"Very well then," Geoffrey said as he worked his coat on. "Ask away."

"Who are you?" McFarren asked him.

"My name is Geoffrey," the man replied. "You already know that. I told you my name when we met in the forest. You can call me Geoff for short if you like."

"No," McFarren said. "I mean, what are you? You show up in the oddest of places and know so much about me. After the first time we met, you went behind a tree and vanished. I went around the tree and didn't see a hair of you."

"That was in a dream you were having in your time of dying, my friend," Geoffrey said. "All is possible within a dream."

"So, how is it that I saw you in a dream?" McFarren asked him.

"I go where I go, and show where I show," Geoffrey cryptically replied.

"Okay, but what about here?" McFarren said. "I'm fully awake. I'm not asleep. What happened to the people? I come in here, and the place is full of people, and then they're gone having vanished into thin air. And you show up. And a mug, like those sheets of paper, appears in your hand out of sheer nowhere."

"That's all a trivial matter in the overall scheme of things," Geoffrey replied.

"What about those eyes of yours?" McFarren asked him.

"What about them?"

"They glowed red," McFarren said.

"Oh, you mean when you grabbed my throat?"

"Yes, it was then," he said.

"I get a temper about me when people put their hands around my throat," Geoffrey replied. He gave McFarren a stern look. "In answer to your question regarding what I am, I am whatever it is that you think I am."

"So, I'll move on from this place if I do as you ask me?"

"You will," Geoffrey assured him. "In good, due time. Please know as I have shown you by raising you from death, that I am a man of my word. Share the words I have given you, and let time tend to itself. And don't see dying by your own hand as a means of terminating our little arrangement. That will only send you back to where you started. Zero."

McFarren watched as the being who called himself Geoffrey vanished before reaching the door after starting toward it. He looked back at his table. The mug Geoffrey drank from was gone.

Conversation resumed as the pub returned to its prior, lively state. Patrons occupied chairs around tables and stools along the bar. The bartender, a stocky, no-nonsense type-looking man who could deal quite well with troublemakers, tended casks and bottles.

*****

Tyler stood a few steps away from where Aaron last saw her before embarking on the journey, she had taken him on. A grim expression appeared on her obscured, night-darkened face. A worried face of a person he did not know replaced the one of the fun-loving, full-of-life girl he once knew.

"Do you see what that séance is all about?" Tyler asked him. "It's about that Pact Mr. Farren made with that Geoffrey guy.

"Geoffrey is an actual demon; they really do exist. He wants people to do the supposed séance so he can take their souls. Mr. McFarren doesn't know it, but he collects souls for Geoffrey by getting people to say the words out loud, so other people can hear them. People there have to ask to be forgiven to keep their souls from being taken. That's what Abigail told me."

A prolonged silence fell between them as Aaron, mentally and emotionally, tried to digest the experience of seeing her and all that she had shown him. The combined experience, a collision of two worlds, the known and unknown, was difficult to process. He wondered if seeing Tyler and the journey she had taken him on was merely a dream.

"There are others," Tyler said after allowing Aaron time to compose himself.

"Others?" he asked her.

"Other dead people like me, who people tried to contact through the supposed séance, but stopped before saying all the words. The spirit of the person they tried to contact goes back to their body until the séance is completed or the Pact ends. Their spirit then goes to Heaven.

"People are dug out from their graves if all the words are

spoken, so we can tell people who spoke the words they need to ask God to forgive them. That person then tells others who tried the séance with them that the words are evil, and they need to ask forgiveness for hearing them.

"It's because of Abigail that Geoffrey has to give the people at the séance a chance to be forgiven. Abigail said that people who died before all the words were spoken, like our friends, or don't repent, will lose their souls unless the Pact ends before it's completed. But not everyone is going to repent because they may not listen to someone who claims they met with the deceased person they tried to contact. They might think the person is crazy.

"You and Wayne need to end the Pact. We'll never see Wayne again if the Pact is finished."

"Can I ask for everyone who ever tried the séance to be forgiven?" Aaron asked her. "Would that work? Wouldn't that save the guys?"

"No, that would be nice if it could, but Abigail said people can only ask for themselves to be forgiven."

"It would have been so much better if I didn't insist on trying the séance to talk with my grandpa," Tyler continued. "I feel bad that we all became a part of this. It didn't seem right. I should have followed my intuition and just let it go."

"You had no way of knowing," Aaron said. "And you weren't thinking straight. You were so upset about being unable to say goodbye, but then you changed your mind about doing the séance. Lots of people would have thought about doing it."

"Abigail said Geoffrey gives visions to people who didn't say all the words to get them to try the supposed séance again.

"Geoffrey wanted you to say all the words, so I could tell you what the so-called séance is about and warn you to repent. He doesn't want you to do that, but he has to because of Abigail.

"You saw a girl that looked like me when you visited with me at the cemetery," she said. "That girl you saw was a vision Geoffrey made up... Same thing with those kids you saw who looked like us, sitting at our spot beside Talbot Road when you and Shay passed it. He did that because he wanted to keep you thinking about me, thinking it might get you to try the séance again.

"You told Wayne you saw the girl who looked like me in the cemetery. Well, he saw the same girl, too, a few days ago. He was walking his dog in a park when he saw her standing behind a bunch of trees a ways away from him. The girl waved at him like she did at you and then walked behind the trees. He walked to where he last saw her, and the girl was gone.

"Wayne was convinced the girl was me but knew that was impossible... It worked because it got him to think about trying the séance again because he couldn't stop thinking about me. He doesn't know you kept the sheets, though. He's thinking about asking you."

"What do I do if he asks?" Aaron asked her.

"Just tell him you don't have the words anymore because you needed to destroy them," Tyler replied. "You should burn them. You can tell him about me and your meeting. It'll be interesting to see how he takes it. Maybe that will get him to see that there is an afterlife where he can be happy and at peace."

Tyler went on to say that the purpose of the other visions, like the one Wayne had of the dog in Oakwood Bush or Aaron had at Holy Redeemer, was to get them to think about the spirit world, which might prompt them to try the séance again. "Abigail told her that. Gregory would do anything to get you and Wayne to try the séance again," Tyler told him. Tyler and Aaron agreed that seemed to be a backward way of doing that.

Abigail also told Tyler that Geoffrey drove the truck that ran into Shay's car because he knew her death would upset Aaron. He wanted Aaron to feel sad and lonely, so he would try to contact Tyer again through the séance or Shay. And in Aaron's case, it worked.

"You know?" she hummed. "Do you ever wonder why it is

that our friends who tried the séance with you except for Wayne are now dead?"

"I think about that all the time," Aaron said. "About how our friends died so young."

"Strange, eh, how they died in such weird, bizarre ways?" Tyler asked him.

"You know about that?" he asked her. "About them dying and how they died?"

"I know they died, why they died, and how they died," Tyler matter-of-factly replied. "Remember, I could see things after I went back to my grave after you first started to say those words. Geoffrey killed them, because, like I said, he can keep the souls of people who die without asking to be forgiven, like our friends. McFarren doesn't know it, but he needs a thousand souls to complete the Pact, and he's almost done because he only needs a few more."

"Why does he have to wait? Why did he say a thousand? He could have asked for ten and ended it right then and there."

'Because of Abigail. The longer the Pact was meant, there was more of a chance to end it before it was completed."

"You've seen Geoffrey," Tyler said. "He was the guy on the horse at Holy Redeemer in the vision you saw when you were sitting where we sat the day I died. Other people have seen him, too."

"I read books on the supernatural to figure out what it was I saw there," Aaron told her. "I found a drawing in a book that looked like the man and horse I saw. According to the book, the man in the illustration was called Geoffrey!"

"I watched when you were looking through the books," Tyler said. "It's eerie that you found a drawing of him, but he's been around forever. Other people have seen him, so that's probably why he was mentioned in the book. I think you saw him for a reason. It just couldn't be by coincidence."

"So how come Geoffrey never came for Wayne or me?" Aaron

asked her.

"Because he needed one of you guys to say all the words to bring me back, according to Abigail," Tyler replied.

"Are you going to go to see Wayne? To tell him what you told me."

"No," Tyler said in a soft, mournful-sounding voice. "I wish I could, but I can't because Wayne didn't read all the words or say anyone's name to contact. It won't keep him from being lost or our friends. He needs to ask for forgiveness for himself, but he won't because he has no faith in God since he's soured on life. He's not happy inside. It's kinda like he died, even though he's living."

Tyler looked at her feet. Aaron knew she was thinking about something. That something bothered her.

"Are you okay?" he asked her, desperate to help her work through whatever it was that was on her mind.

"Aaron, there's something I did that I'm feeling absolutely horrible about," Tyler said. She looked at him. "I don't want our friends to be lost, and I want to see them again," she said through tears... "You know how I told you I had gone to Mr. McFarren's house before I came here? I went there for a reason... I snuck into his house, saw a knife when I walked through his kitchen, and used it on him. I wanted to kill him! That was my reason for going there."

His stomach knotted as Aaron contemplated the grimmest of thoughts.

"I stabbed him twice and would have stabbed him more if I could have, but I had to leave when a car pulled into his driveway." Tyler continued to cry. "And, and, I couldn't get the knife out of his shoulder because it, it was stuck," she stuttered. "It was starting to come loose when the car showed up."

"Oh, my God!" Aaron exclaimed, stunned and sickened by what Tyler told him and the thought of her hurting someone.

She put her hands against her face, upset by what she was saying. Aaron wanted to hug her. He stepped toward her.

"No, no, Aaron, I'm alright. Please go back," she begged, pointing a palm at him. "I'm sorry, but I don't want you to touch me... like I want you to, but I'm not what I was... Why does this have to happen, Aaron?" she said after she stopped crying. "I feel so sick about everything, everything is so sad, but that man has to die for Wayne and our friends to be alright."

"How did you get yourself to do that?"

"Abigail told me that (killing him) was a way to save our friends and God would be okay with it... Then when I started walking, I kept thinking about how I could do it, like how I would do it, but also how I could bring myself to do something like that. I was basically in a trance.

"I kinda blacked out when I went after him, and I don't remember everything, which is good because I don't want to... It was like something inside me was doing the stabbing, and I was just there watching. It was weird, like I was a puppet, because something took over me. Maybe it was rage that took over me with twenty years of anger inside me for that man. Even so, that wouldn't have made me do what I did, but it probably helped.

"I've been trying to feel better since I realized what I had to do by telling myself he's already dead," Tyler sobbed. "I hate talking like I'm a little murderer, but that's what I have to be... I know what I'm telling you is freaking you out. It's freaking me out, too." She looked skyward. "But it has to be done, Aaron. Abigail told me I should do it; the man had to die to save our friends and hundreds of other people... Maybe she was inside me, or she gave me the strength to do what I did because it takes a monster to do that, and I'm not a monster. Like I said, it was like I was in a trance, and someone else had taken me over... I can't explain it."

"I'm so angry at God that I had to do what I did and for everything that I've had to go through and everyone else that had to deal with me dying and what happened to our friends... I don't know why I have to go through this because I have always tried to be a good person. I never went out of my way to hurt anyone, so why does this have to happen to me? I don't understand," she tearfully said. "Abigail said I would one day, but I don't right now.

"Oh, Aaron, I have to do this, though. I have to make sure McFarren dies. I'll go to Heaven when he does and see everyone else and maybe Wayne one day.

"Mr. McFarren is vulnerable," she continued, looking back at the ground and dabbing at her eyes. "He's vulnerable because he can die again... As I said, he has to die before he gets his quota."

"All the people he has taken so far will be okay, and even McFarren will be okay. I kind of hate myself for saying this, but I care about what happens to him because I should. I forgive him... Geoffrey tricked him."

"Do you think McFarren is still alive?" Aaron asked her.

"He's still alive because I would have gone back to where I'm supposed to be if he wasn't," Tyler bluntly replied. "This is horrible. I can't believe I'm talking about, you know... doing that to somebody, but you know why I have to do it."

"I understand," he said.

"It's so hard for me, and I know it is for you to hear me talk like this."

"I'm so sorry, Tyler, that you've had to go through everything that's happened to you."

"I know... I'm sorry for everything everyone has gone through.

"God will forgive me, I'm sure," Tyler continued, confident He would turn a blind eye to what she had done and planned to do. Her goal was to save her friend who had strayed from God, and her other friends who had died. To give him a chance at redemption, not done out of hate. "Abigail said we would meet in Heaven, so I'll be there.

"Going after McFarren was so hard," she said. "I cried while I did it, especially when the knife got stuck inside him, and I couldn't get it out. I just wanted to get it over with, like I was in a trance, like I said, but I couldn't, and I didn't want him to suffer..." Tyler sobbed again. "And there was blood. It was coming out of him and streaming down the floor."

"Oh, Tyler," Aaron sighed. "That's so sad you had to do that."

"It's evil. I'm trying to kill, and I'm doing it to give Wayne a chance and help Allen, Andy, Carl, Steven, and Scott. That's what I keep telling myself. I know I'm doing the right thing, and God will look away. I'm just doing what Abigail said I should."

It was hard to fathom Tyler having it in her to attack the man. But the man had to die before the Pact was completed. That is how it had to be, and Aaron understood that.

"It seems so cliche, having a Pact with the devil," Aaron said.

"But that's kinda what it is, whatever the devil is," Tyler said. "We saw it happen... Geoffrey is a demon who tricks people to use them, and Abigail is fighting him. She's why people are given a chance to ask for forgiveness. It's because of her that people like you and Wayne aren't killed because people must have a chance to be forgiven, and that can't happen if the person who read all the words, who's supposed to warn the others, is dead. He hasn't come after you yet because you have to tell Wayne what he needs to do. Once you've done that, then you'll be next."

"Well, I won't tell him then," Aaron said.

"But if Wayne dies from a heart attack or something, then they'd be no reason for you to be here. Geoffrey would have taken your soul if you did not ask to be forgiven.

"You're probably thinking you're crazy or this is all a dream, seeing me and what I've shown you and what I've told you, but it's real," Tyler said. "I told you what's behind the séance. I have to tell you what I know, the best way I can explain it... You're probably thinking you're losing your mind, seeing me and what I just showed you; either that or it's a dream, but it's real. Everything I told you is real.

"But the main thing, for now, is I need to find McFarren. He might still be in his house or in a hospital if the person who showed up went inside and called an ambulance for him."

"I'll find him," Aaron promised. "I know lots of people who work at the hospitals. If McFarren was taken to one, I'll find out where he is."

"Being a doctor has its benefits, eh?"

"I guess you know I became a doctor because you've been watching me," he said.

"I'm so proud of you," Tyler declared. "You were always smart. You went on about wanting to be a lot of things once you grew older, but you talked about being a doctor forever."

"I was always proud of you, too," Aaron told her. "You were also smart. One day you wanted to be a teacher, and the next, you wanted to be a nurse like your mom before you finally decided you wanted to be a doctor or a veterinarian. You wanted to help people and animals… You could have been whatever you wanted to be if only you had had the chance."

"Oh, Aaron, that's so sweet," Tyler said. "But I do need you to tell me where to find Mr. McFarren. I need you to help me do that, and hopefully, you can find out tomorrow.

"I'll come back a few hours after dark, which I guess would be around eleven o'clock," Tyler said. "I should be here by then if I don't have to hide from people along the way and if I'm not misjudging my time. I've never been out wandering around after dark."

"I'll be waiting for you."

"It's better for me to come to see you than you come to see me, to not draw attention to where I'm going to be."

"Where are you going to go?" he asked her.

"I know of a place," she replied. "I have to spend the day hiding there so no one will see me… I'll be back if Mr. McFarren doesn't die."

"You can stay here," Aaron suggested. "You don't have to go anywhere." He noticed that Tyler appeared to be wiping away tears. "Are you okay?" he asked her.

"I am. It's just that I hate having to hide from people like I've done something wrong... I know you would want me to stay here. It's just I don't want you to get a good look at me. You need to remember me the way I used to be. "

"So, where are you going to go?"

"To an old house in the woods on the other side of that field and the forest behind your place."

"You're talking about that old house over that-a-way?" Aaron asked her while looking in its direction. He knew of the house she spoke of. One of a few buildings that remained of a decaying village abandoned decades ago.

"That's right," Tyler said.

"How did you know where the house was?" Aaron asked her.

"I passed by it on my way here," Tyler replied. "I was surprised we never knew about it, considering it's not that far from where Mr. McFarren lives."

"Me, too," he said. "But we never ventured past Sandwich West Bush, and no one ever mentioned it. We never thought of going through the field behind McFarren's place."

"It's weird that you ended up living so close to his house."

"I always liked that area. I like that it's out in the country but not far from where we grew up."

"It's cool that we lived close to the country," Tyler remarked. "It's cool that we had the bush to hang out in, too, and we had big yards to play in. I would have hated to grow up downtown where people barely have a yard and have no place nice to go to."

"We were lucky that way," he said. "So, how did you know where my house was?"

"As I say, I've been able to watch you," she replied. "I know lots about what's been going on with you. That's why I could find your place."

"That blows my mind that you were able to see me," Aaron told her.

"Aaron, there's so much I know that I just can't say, not because I don't want to, but I just can't put into words. But as I say, I'll move on when Mr. McFarren dies. The only thing is my body will be dead again."

"That's so sad to think about... about you being dead. You barely had a chance to live. Why is God so unfair? You were just a kid when you died."

"But dying brought me to an awesome place."

"This world pretty much sucks," Aaron hummed.

"But you have to live in it until you die," Tyler said, accentuating the obvious. "I always thanked God for my blessings and asked Him to help me with bad stuff when I played each night before going to sleep. I always prayed for you, my mom and dad, all my family and friends, other people I cared about, and for my animals. But I never asked Him to keep bad things from happening to me... I only asked for strength to deal with it and to be with people and animals who were suffering."

"I started praying every night after you died because that's when it hit home how hard this world can be," he told her. "Why does the world have to be so sad?"

"Because people choose to separate themselves from God is what I'm thinking," Tyler replied. "I don't want to sound all preachy, but God gave people free will to either accept Him or not.

"I never asked for bad things not to happen to me because Christ had bad things happen to Him. God created the Earth but allowed people to rule over it. That's why evil things like Geoffrey and his séance words and his Pact happen."

"I remember my dad looking in my little blue eyes and telling me how the world was a cruel bad place when I was a young kid," Aaron said. "I didn't understand what he was getting at because the world seemed to be good to me at the time. Things were all good until I became aware of the war in Vietnam, racism, and crime, and that people were living in poverty in houses only rats would want to live in and going hungry. I got it when I grew older, and especially after you died... But there are a lot of good things, too."

"That there is," Tyler agreed. "Life was mostly fun, at least for me."

"It's all about how you look at things, I suppose," Aaron sighed.

"That's what I always thought, but you and I had it pretty good because we never went without what we needed and lived in a nice area," Tyler said. "We were dealt a pretty good hand in life."

"No doubt about that," Aaron agreed.

"It wasn't good for me at all after the accident, except for seeing my grandpa."

"You died young and didn't really get into Heaven and had to be trapped like you were."

"Heaven is there, though, and next time I go there, I won't be coming back here."

"What was it like in Heaven?" Aaron asked her.

"It's beautiful," Tyler gushed. "I was in a field of the prettiest purple daisies I ever saw, right after the accident, in a place with meadows, forests, and the bluest skies you can imagine. There were tall mountains and streams so clear and clean you could drink from them. It felt weird, though, because I should have been happy, but I wasn't. I only felt sadness, seeing everyone here upset about me.

"It made me cry when I saw how sad you were and how horrible you felt, watching that truck hit me and wanting me to be alive... You think you'll never stop thinking about that truck hitting me, but maybe seeing me now will help you be okay.

"It broke my heart how you felt when you woke up the day after, listened to the doves and the truck noise coming in from the highway, and thought about how life carried on without me."

"Those doves seemed happy," Aaron said. "They just made me think how the world went on without you, and no one noticed, like you were nothing. As if you never existed.

"That tells how depressed I was."

"I get how you felt because that's what I felt when my grandpa died. I heard those doves, too. They nested in the trees in both of our front yards. It made me so sad. They still made me think of him until the day… well, you know."

"Did you see Jesus when you were in Heaven?" Aaron asked her.

"No, but I could feel His presence," Tyler replied.

"But I met my grandpa, though!! He hugged and kissed me and was so happy to see me. He took my hand and told me everything would be alright as we walked through a field with the most beautiful tall grasses imaginable. My grandpa said I would meet people I never met before, like my great-grandpa and great-grandma."

"Oh, I'm so glad you got to see him! That's what you wanted… You were so heartbroken when he died; you were so sad. You weren't your usual self for a while."

"It was the same for you, too," Tyler said... "You felt what I felt when I passed," she said. She seemed to smile, though it was hard to tell in the darkness. "He looked just like he did here, with his gray hair and his glasses with the big lenses in them, and his grizzled old beard."

"My grandpa said it would be different when I went back for good because he knew I wouldn't be there long. He said there's no pain or sadness, even though you can see and be with people you love who are still living and watch whatever is happening on Earth… I don't understand how you can be happy and not sad when seeing sad things.

"And then he took me to the most beautiful house imaginable. He said he lived in the house... That's where some of the people he wanted me to see were. I was only beginning to get to know them after we went into the house, and then all of a sudden, I was back in the field of daisies.

"The daisies smelled so nice! A bunch of them were in my hand before everything went dark while you read the words. The sky grew sinister looking, and the next thing I knew, I returned to my body.

"I got just a little taste of Heaven, but at least it's there."

Aaron felt his eyes well up. It was impossible to think they could return to what he was missing. That all this grief and loss were for not. Through a rush of feelings, the most pleasant feeling he ever experienced was knowing there was life after death. That it was possible to be with all the people he cared about. "Are our animals there, too?" he asked Tyler.

"Yes," she replied. "My grandpa had his little black dog with him that he had when he was alive. It was the same dog. I'm serious, the same one! She exclaimed. "So, that means I'll get to see Elvis and Cuddles again! And you'll get to see your cat Scamp, that you had when you were young."

"That's incredible," Aaron said.

"I need to ask you something, Tyler."

"You can ask me anything, Aaron. I'll try to answer whatever you want, the best I can."

"I want to know what it was like to die. Did you feel pain? Remember you were talking about dying on the way to Holy Redeemer? It's like you knew you were about to die."

"Yeah, it seems that way, but that's just because we were talking about my grandpa and death in general. But yeah, I never talked like that before. It seems weird that I was talking about dying and thought about doing a séance, and I'm glad I didn't. But again, it was all because of how I was feeling. I just wanted to say goodbye to my grandpa and seemed robbed of that chance.

"And yeah, maybe I knew I was going to die... It's funny that old people made me nervous about dying, and then I died when I was only thirteen. I should have just not worried about dying... Maybe something was wrong in my head for me to be that way. What do you think?"

"I don't think so. You were going through a phase. You would have forgotten about it soon enough, I'm pretty sure... You could have gotten old," he chuckled. "Wouldn't that have been something? You might have been afraid of yourself."

"That's funny! That'd be something. That would be like being afraid of your own shadow. You can't get away from it."

"You ended up dying in a way you wished you wouldn't have," he said.

"It wasn't as bad as you think, Aaron. You think that I suffered, but I didn't. It happened so fast. I remember feeling a horrible way I couldn't describe when I knew that truck would hit me. The last thing I remember was hitting the side of the hill alongside the highway."

"Did you know I was there with you?"

"No," she replied.

"I was holding your hand to try and comfort you, and I was telling you to hang on. You had to be in agony, the way you were moaning."

"Maybe I was, but I don't remember. If I did, you'd think I would recall."

"Are you telling me the truth, or are you just trying to make me feel better?"

"I'm being straight up honest," she said.

"I passed out and didn't wake up until the day after. The next day was the worst day I've ever had."

"I felt so bad for you then and felt terrible for you ever since. I'm the one who died, but it was quick for me. You've been reliving the accident and missing me since it happened."

Then they talked about how they both figured there was something wrong with Wayne because he wouldn't leave his house and missed school sometimes for no reason.

Through reading Wayne's thoughts and memories and watching him, Tyler learned the history between him and his father, that Wayne's father had beaten him, his sisters, and his mother a few times when he drank too much alcohol.

"Poor Wayne," Aaron moaned after Tyler told him what she knew. "Wayne never talks about his father or what happened at home when he was a kid. Wayne doesn't like his father, but he's never told me why. He just says they don't get along."

"Because it's too hard for him to think about the reason, let alone talk about it," Tyler said. "He never talked about it with me either, or anyone, because he's learned to keep things inside… His dad only did that when he was way too drunk. But that's not an excuse to hit someone."

Tyler then talked about Aaron and Wayne's relations, that Wayne thought the world of him and was always there for him.

"You know he's always been your best male bud," she said. "You guys were funny to me because you had a bit of a competition about whose father was better."

Wayne bragged about his dad owning that painting business his dad started and was doing well at it before he became an alcoholic. He was jealous of Aaron and Tyler because they did not have what he had going on at home. Meanwhile, Aaron was envious of Wayne for not having a curfew.

Tyler mentioned the time Wayne told her and Aaron how lucky they were because they had a curfew, which meant their parents cared about them, whereas he had no curfew. Wayne said he wished his parents cared about him. They both felt bad for Wayne after that and worried about him.

Tyler looked to the east. "I'll need to get going soon, Aaron, because it's going to start getting light in an hour or two," she said. "Before I leave, I have something creepy to ask you to do for me when I die again."

"I'll do whatever you want me to," Aaron replied.

"I want you to find my body and take it back to my grave," Tyler said. "That would be hard on you, but you would do that for me, wouldn't you? I don't want people to see my body, so I want you to take it back to where it's supposed to be."

"I'll take your body back," he promised her.

"I knew you would do that," she said. "But remember that it's not really me, that it's just my body. I'll be waiting for you in Heaven."

"But don't look at my body because I really, really want you to remember me like I was. Could you cover me with something? You have to promise not to look at me, please!"

"I promise I won't look at you," he said. "I'll cover you with a blanket. I promise you that."

"You'll find me at that house, probably in the basement because that's where I've been hiding," she said. "Oh, but if he dies while I'm on my way here, you'll find me along that path in the forest between your house and that house… I pray it doesn't happen that way. Anyone could find me."

"Are you scared of dying again?" Aaron asked her.

"No, because I've already died. I guess I would fall over, and that would be it. And then my spirit will be on its way."

Tyler removed a necklace and crucifix her grandpa gave her from around her neck. "I want you to have this," she said while gently placing them on the ground. "The cross will protect you from Geoffrey…" She took a backward step. "Aaron, I hate leaving you again, but I hafta go now… Just remember we'll see each other again if I don't come back."

"I will," he promised.

"Goodbye, for now, Aaron," Tyler bid him. She turned and started toward the field.

Aaron picked up the crucifix and cradled it in his palm.

He stared at where darkness consumed her well after Tyler left.

He gently placed the necklace and crucifix on a counter after going back inside the house and then proceeded to burn the sheets in a sink.

Chapter Eighteen
McFarren Survives

McFarren forced his eyes open, groggy from the anesthetic used to sedate him during an operation, to repair the damage Tyler inflicted. He lay in a bed in a post-op recovery room. People in an observation room looked at him.

McFarren recalled being stabbed by the girl who came to his house all those years ago with her two friends before passing out. His shoulder, upper torso, and neck were numb and throbbed with pain. Sweat pooled on his forehead. His lungs were full of mucus, and the hideous taste of anesthetic stained his throat.

Two men wearing respiratory masks and surgical gowns started out of the observation room and entered the recovery room. McFarren watched through blurry eyes as they began toward the bed. "How many times was I stabbed?" he asked both men in a strained whisper when they arrived at the bed.

"Twice," one of them told him.

"Why do I feel so numb?" McFarren croaked.

"Partly from sedation we used to knock you out during the operation to repair the wounds and from painkillers we're feeding you from the IV," the man replied. "It took three hours to stitch you up. You've been through a lot of trauma."

"How did I get here?" McFarren wanted to know.

"Paramedics brought you in," the man said. "Someone called 911 from a phone in your house. You're here all alone, as far as we know. Is there someone we can call? We'll call your wife or kids if you want."

McFarren shook his head. "I don't have any family," he hoarsely replied, neglecting to mention his daughter.

"Do you have a friend you would like us to call?"

"No, I don't have any of those either."

"My name is Mike," the man said. "I'm your nurse... Dr. Lang, who operated on you, is here with me."

"How long am I going to be here?"

"That's up to the doctors," Mike said.

"What you've gone through is pretty major, and you're doing very well for a man your age," Dr. Lang bluntly stated. "How old are you?"

"I'm seventy-five," McFarren said, seventy-five being the standard age he gave when asked. He could say going on four-hundred and eighty, and that would not be a lie. That got a few laughs out of people when he said that, but he was in no mood for humor.

"You lost three pints of blood," Dr. Lang continued. "It was touch and go before the team and I were able to stop the bleeding in the shoulder wound because it's deep. The track the knife took was right next to an artery. You would have been dead in minutes if the knife even nicked it, which it came close to doing."

"That's good, I suppose," McFarren weakly replied. He wished that he had died. "The pain medication you're giving me isn't helping because I still feel pain, especially in my shoulder. It's throbbing and feels worse than getting stabbed when I cough."

"You're getting 20 mg of morphine every four hours," Dr. Lang told him. "On a scale of one to ten, ten being horrible, what number would you give the level of pain you are in right now?"

"I would say eleven because I can't feel any worse," McFarren groaned. "I can't get any relief. No matter how I position myself when I'm awake, the pain throbs."

"Usually for elderly people, morphine dose range tops out at 15 mg, and you're already above that..."

"It doesn't help," McFarren said. "Give me 30 mg, please! Could you put me on 40 mg? I don't care. Put me under if nothing else works."

"Putting you into an induced coma is something we need to

avoid because that may be too much for your heart to take.

"Let's increase your morphine drip to 25 mg and see if that helps. It should, but if not, we'll go from there. You'll still feel pain, but it should be much less than you're feeling now.

"It took three hours to stitch you up. You've been through a lot of trauma. You're going to have pain."

"I get it, but this is unbearable," McFarren snarled.

"We'll help you the best we can," Dr. Lang said. "You pulled through surprisingly well, especially considering your age. But you have a significant infection based on your white blood cell count... Were you feeling ill before you were assaulted?"

"No," McFarren angrily muttered. Bastards, they were the people who tried to save him. If only they let him die.

"No touch of a fever or feeling dizzy and lacking energy?"

"No, and I just feel pain," McFarren declared.

"We're going to transfer you to the ICU to keep a good eye on you for a few days, deal with the infection, and manage the pain," Dr. Lang said. "We'll get you into a private room once the doctor in charge of your care over there feels that you're stable enough."

"So, when do I get to leave?" McFarren asked the doctor.

"That depends on your body and how well you respond to treatment," Lang replied. "I recommend you stay in the hospital for two weeks to monitor the wound, help with the pain, and ensure we kill that infection. We're pumping antibiotics into you right now through another intravenous line.

"To be straightforward, the probability of the fever becoming fatal should it get worse is high because of your age, so when you are discharged, I'm going to recommend that a nurse come to see you every day for at least a week to see how you're doing and then reduce it after that. You might not need post-discharge nursing for that long. It's hard to predict your recovery, considering your age and the stab wounds, particularly the one to the shoulder, and the fever."

"It's pretty serious, doc?" McFarren asked Dr. Lang.

"Yes, it is," Dr. Lang said. "Your stable right now, so let's see if we can keep it that way... I want you to rest. I'll be back in a few hours to check on you."

McFarren closed his eyes and pretended to fall asleep, wanting to be alone. Death would be welcomed if it finally came, a walking dead person ever since his son read the words. Anger seethed as he thought about his attacker. He did not know nor care what his actions had subjected the girl to. That the little tyrant tried to kill him was all that mattered. He would somehow find her and strangle the girl's scrawny neck.

A look of hatred in the girl's eyes while sticking the knife in him was seared into McFarren's brain. That the sweet, pretty, innocent-looking girl named Tyler, who came to his house decades ago with her friends, tried to kill him, alarmed him. How was it possible for that girl to be so vicious?

It surprised him that someone waited twenty years to complete the supposed séance. The girl's name and resting place came in a vision, just as others before and after her. He mused that leaving the girl in the ground would have been preferable.

No one who came back attacked him before. Why the girl? Maybe he was at the end of the Pact. Perhaps he might die again!

He did not know her goal was to save her friends.

Nurse Mike asked McFarren if he could hear him; McFarren reluctantly opened his eyes after falling asleep. "Zach, there's a person here that would like to speak with you," Mike said. "He's a detective with the LaSalle Police Department. Are you up to talking with him?"

"I guess," McFarren groaned. Perhaps the detective would provide information on the whereabouts of the lass who stabbed him, McFarren thought. If so, he would summon someone to dispatch her.

"Hello, sir," the man said. "My name is Stanley Simmons. I'm a detective with the LaSalle Police Department. I have a few questions to ask you."

McFarren looked the man over. He was dressed in a sand-colored leisure suit, wore a belt with a police detective badge on it, and bore a burly mustache like Yankee's pitcher Goose Gossage. He wore gold-framed sunglasses with light brown, square lenses, which McFarren found disrespectful to wear during a first-time conversation with a stranger.

"Please, take your sunglasses off if you would. I want to look you square in the eye."

"No problem, sir," the detective said, placing the sunglasses in the top pocket of his loud, multi-colored button-down shirt. "I want to help you," he said. "I want to find who assaulted you."

"So do I," McFarren sheepishly replied.

"Do you have any idea who it was?"

"Not a clue," McFarren lied. It would have been interesting to tell them, McFarren mused, ahead of meeting with the police, knowing that question would be asked. What would they think and say if he told them that a girl who died twenty years ago tried to kill him?

"Did you see them?" Simmons asked.

"I'm half blind without my glasses," McFarren said. "I didn't have them on, so I didn't get a good look at them."

"Was there anyone else in the house when it happened?"

"No," McFarren replied. "I live by myself." Pain rampaged through his body as he coughed. "No one was in the house," McFarren said after a few moments.

"Can you tell me what happened?" Simmons asked.

"I was sleeping," McFarren whispered.

"I'm sure you just want to sleep right now, but I would like to ask you a few more questions," Simmons said. "And you have no idea who it was?"

"No," McFarren replied. He feigned a puzzled expression.

"Have you had problems with anyone, a neighbor, a friend... anyone?" Simmons asked.

"No," McFarren said.

"You live at the end of a rural road, in a remote place," Simmons noted. "So, someone could go to your place to rob you, thinking you were an easy mark given your age. Especially if they knew that you lived alone."

"I suppose," McFarren moaned.

"But nothing major like your television and stereo were taken, and $200 in cash was in plain sight."

McFarren closed his eyes.

"Well, whoever the person was, you don't want them coming back and assaulting you when you get back home," Simmons said.

"Too sore," McFarren muttered, gesturing at his throat to suggest he could no longer speak.

"I'm going to let you get some rest," Simmons said, speaking in an emphatic tone. "I'll leave a card with my name and contact information on it with your nurse. I'll be back to see you in a few days when you're feeling better. Maybe you'll feel more up to talking then."

"Whatever," McFarren groaned to himself, not impressed with the man for not removing his sunglasses without being asked. McFarren found that to be rude.

* * * * *

That the encounter with Tyler occurred took several anxious moments to confirm after Aaron woke after a few fitful hours of sleep dreaming about it. He really did see her. Tyler's necklace and crucifix lying on the bed where Shay once slept were proof of the encounter.

So, it had to be as Tyler told him that she was trapped in her grave for decades. It had to be that after he tried the séance the first time, she lay conscious, alone and unable to move, interned in a wretched place of absolute darkness. Able to see people she cared about going on with their lives without her. That must have compounded her horrifying predicament.

He, too, was trapped in a grave, in an especially harrowing

dream he had during the night. Like Tyler, he watched life go on. Children became adults, adults grew old, and the already old that she feared went on to death. Years passed as people went about their living and dying, and through it all, he remained an unseen, ineffectual bystander. Long ago, having given up on calling out for help and pushing on the coffin's lid without hope of nudging it. It was the worst possible fate.

The horrid thought of Tyler trying to kill someone was lessened by knowing she intended to help Wayne and others. He would find out where McFarren was and kill him in her stead. Anxious to embark on the endeavor, he steeled himself to get killing McFarren over with.

Aaron turned a bedside light on, needing to reassure himself of his surroundings. The thought of Tyler being trapped in her grave occupied his mind after confirming that he was at home. That she suffered such an existence was beyond comprehending. And he could not stop thinking about her being in the abandoned house, terrified of being spotted should someone happen upon her place of hiding.

Geoffrey confronting him was a mortifying thought. Aaron picked up the crucifix, looked at it, and then grasped it in his palm. The crucifix would offer protection against evil, Tyler said. He looked at the ceiling and prayed to God to protect him.

A loud noise came from the kitchen downstairs. Aaron left the bed, put a bathrobe on, held the crucifix, and again asked God to protect him. He put the crucifix into a pocket of the robe and retrieved a rifle from a closet kept for protection should someone decide to intrude into his rural home. He lifted four shells out of an ammunition box with a shaking hand and struggled to stuff them into the gun's shell chamber. All the while, he wondered what effect the gun would have against Satan's soul fetcher if confronted by Geoffrey, the non-human entity that Geoffrey was.

Adrenaline on high, thinking an intruder had entered the house, he left the bedroom and began through a darkened hallway toward the first floor. He descended the stairs, each step taken, fearing it would be his last. Aaron began toward the kitchen.

No one was in the kitchen, Aaron was relieved to find after flipping a light switch. A broom lying on the floor had caused the noise, having fallen from where it had been loosely propped against a wall. Innocent though it turned out to be, hearing the broom fall heightened his sense of vulnerability.

Before returning to the bedroom, he turned a hallway light on and left its door open like a boy afraid of the dark. Fear of encountering Geoffrey kept him awake, every so often looking toward the hallway after returning to bed. Crushing guilt, returning to thoughts of the misery Tyler endured after first attempting the séance, mixed with fear.

Chapter Nineteen
Satan Rules the World

Guilt remained strong as sunlight filtered through drawn curtains in the bedroom, bidding a miserable good morning. Aaron thought constantly that Tyler would not be in this predicament if not for having bothered with the séance Blood-stained hands belonged to him, not her, he believed.

He tried to rationalize his reason for saying the words in a fault minimizing effort, to dull guilt, desperate to find a way to carry on living with himself. The thought of doing the séance would probably never have entered his mind if not for Tyler, like she said, having insisted on learning how to do one. Though something seemed wrong about the words, a self-indulgent need to contact her blinded him to his fears. If only he had heeded to instinct.

It seemed funny that Wayne knew about doing the séance and never mentioned it until Tyler talked about wanting to contact her grandpa.

A disturbing thought came while thinking about the boy Wayne's sister and her friends supposedly tried to contact. Would the boy not be in a predicament like Tyler had endured? Was the boy alive in a grave somewhere because not all the words were spoken, desperately hoping someone would say all of them so he could be released to seek out someone to help him?

Thoughts in his scrambled mind returned to Tyler, hiding in an abandoned house in the woods, alone and frightened. Had he not tried the séance, her body would be at rest and her soul at peace. Guilt for having caused her predicament intensified while entering the Florida room.

Aaron began an effort to find McFarren after taking a few

moments to collect himself. He went to a phone and called Windsor Western Hospital, the closest hospital to McFarren's place, assuming whoever scared Tyler away had found McFarren and called 911. A woman came on the line.

"Good morning, Windsor Western Hospital reception," the woman said.

"Good morning," he replied. "I'm calling to find out if you have a patient by the name of Zachary McFarren there."

"Please hold a moment, sir," the woman said. He crossed his fingers, hoping she would say McFarren had expired after being taken there. "We have a Zachary McFarren in intensive care," the woman informed him after coming back on the line. "I'll transfer your call to the intensive care unit. They'll be able to tell you when it's a good time for you to come and see him."

"No, that's okay," he said. "I'll call back in a few hours when I'm able to visit him. Have a good one."

"You as well," the woman replied.

A reckoning came that he may very well need to take McFarren's life. An overdose of succinylcholine, a muscle relaxant he had access to at the clinic, would do the job. He would wait until McFarren transferred to a private room should his condition improve. Claiming to be his doctor would give him access to the man.

In a melancholic state, he whiled away the day lying on a couch in the Florida room, aimlessly surfing through television stations. Guilt remained strong as he thought about Tyler alone and hiding in the woods and what she had shown and told him. At least it was a Saturday. The clinic closed on weekends so Aaron did not have to work; he had time to conjure the strength to kill McFarren if need be. To try to arrive at some manageable terms for it all.

Dreams began after drifting to sleep. At first, he was with Tyler when the brakes on her bike failed, but fate produced a better result this time. Instead of going onto the highway, Tyler rode onto the grass beside the path and once again fell from her bike. She remained alive and life, as they had known it, continued before he awoke to a reality where Tyler remained dead. Still feeling tired, he fell back to sleep after a period of tossing and turning. He was in Tyler's stead, in another dream, about to be struck by a transport truck as his life flashed by while preparing to die.

Heart pounding with adrenaline, again, he shot awake. He thought about Tyler trapped in her grave. The deeply entrenched sight of seeing her lifeless body played in his head. He remembered crying hard while watching her coffin lower into the ground, thinking that Tyler's fervent spirit and a dancing light in her eyes were extinguished forever. The moment driving home the reality that their life together and hope of what they wanted it to be had ended.

Night had fallen after waking again after having somehow managing to drift back to sleep. Panic set in, worried that Tyler was outside waiting for him. An irrational thought consumed him that she might think he had forsaken her before realizing there were forty-five minutes to go before they were to meet. He turned the TV on and remoted to Channel 4, a local station that carried Detroit Tiger games, curious to see how Tyler's beloved Tigers were faring. The Tigers were playing the Boston Red Sox, and the game was in the bottom of the ninth. Behind by a run, the Tigers had two players in scoring position. The next batter hit a line drive down the right-field line, cashing in the tying and winning runs. Tyler of old would have been overjoyed, but the Tyler of today couldn't have cared less, he surmised.

Time had reached a quarter to eleven. He shut the television off. Tyler would be near the house.

Hands shaking from nerves, he fumbled with the door's handle while going outside. Illuminated by a gibbous moon commanding a clear dark sky, the yard was brighter than the previous night. The wind played a soft melody on the metal chimes, stirring memories of when he and Tyler heard wind chimes in her yard, from inside the fort, on windy days. So interesting that such trivial background noise was now profoundly vivid.

He sat on the bench. An outline of a person formed in the direction Tyler had gone the night before. As the darkened figure continued toward him, nervous breaths intensified in frequency and depth. Geoffrey may have taken over her body, he began to think, in a disturbing thought. His heart raced with an unfounded thought the demon had assumed her being to gain his trust.

The darkened silhouette he prayed was Tyler reached his yard and continued toward him. He dismissed the notion that Geoffrey had taken her form as Tyler came into view — such an irrational thought it had to be. No matter his unearthly abilities, Geoffrey could never assume her lovingly warm and unique personality.

The figure reached a speaking distance from him. "Hi, Aaron," the figure said, speaking in Tyler's voice. A disheartened inflection tinged her voice.

"Hi," Aaron replied. It truly was Tyler; he was relieved to discover. "Were you okay today?" he asked her.

"I was as best as I could be," Tyler glumly replied. "Were you okay?"

"As best as I could be," he parroted. "I'm still having a hard time believing that it's you," he had to say. His eyes watered, and he began to quiver. "That it's you I'm talking to."

"I know it was hard for you when I came to see you last night," Tyler told him. "I feel bad about that. I love seeing you, but it should never have been like this. We should never have seen each other again until your time came when you died. It's sad, but that's the way it should have been."

"I don't want you to feel bad about what's happened to me, Aaron. You do, but it's going to be better one day. You just need to believe me... As I said, we'll be able to move on and then be with each other again when you pass on."

"This is hard," Aaron said. It saddened him that he could not fully see her face. "I understand, but it makes me sad that I can't be close to you."

"But it's not going to be the same anyway," Tyler said. "I've been to a few funerals, so I know what a dead person looks like… My face is probably paler that it used to be and unnatural-looking. It's better not to see me like this. It will never be the same, like it was here, anyway, and that is sad.

"I wish it could be different," she said weepily. "I don't like trying to hide from you."

They looked at each other silently for a moment as Aaron tried to peel away the dark. The best he could make of her face was similar to when he saw her in the dark when she was alive. She did not look much different, other than he could tell her face was paler; her face stood in strong contrast to her dark hair.

"Did you find out where Mr. McFarren is?" she asked him.

"He's in intensive care at Western Hospital," Aaron replied. "It's taking a chance as far as Wayne is concerned, but you should wait another day or so before you go to see him," he suggested. "He might be in his own room by then. There won't be as many people around."

"I suppose," she sighed.

"I'll call the hospital again tomorrow to see where he is," Aaron said. "Unless I have one of those black auras around me," he half-heartedly joked.

"There's no black mist around you, so you still have a few more days," Tyler said, chuckling softly. "You still have some time left, my man Aaron."

"That freaked me out when I saw you last night," he told her.

"It would have freaked me out too if I was alive, and you were dead and came to see me," Tyler replied.

"And it freaked me out when you said that you stabbed the guy."

"I know it did," Tyler moaned. "I never hurt anything intentionally before. I always felt bad whenever I hurt someone's feelings. Like, when I felt so bad after talking to my mom the way I did when she grilled me when we were inside the fort. When she gave me a hard time for not checking in with her... You know I only did that because I was hurt by how she and my dad seemed to have no interest in me."

"I didn't want to hurt the man, Aaron," she said. "I let this rage take over me. That was the only way I could do it. I kept thinking about how he did our friends and us wrong and told myself the guy did bad things when I went after him with the knife. Thinking about how I might have been stuck alive in the ground forever also helped me do it. But knowing the man has to die was the main thing."

A brief, awkward silence fell between them.

"I thought about you all the time," he told her. "My life turned upside down the day you died."

"I know it did," Tyler replied. "It's so sad for people when someone they love dies like it was for me when my grandpa died... "My parents were so upset and were never the same again... It's so sad, especially for parents, because they never expect their kids to die before them. And it was so bad for you because we were always there, and then I wasn't."

"My parents felt terrible about ignoring me, and I felt bad because I could have been nicer to my mom. We always thought there would be time to make things better, but it wasn't really all that bad between us... I'm pretty sure my parents planned our trip to Europe to help bring us closer. That's why they were only taking me and nobody else...

"I was going to try hard not to be mean to my mom. At least I got to apologize to her for being so rude the last time me and you were in the fort... One of many things I wish I did was apologize for not looking at the camera in her final picture of me. I feel horrible because I ruined it.

People were so upset, but I knew we would all meet again... I hope Wayne will be there."

Tyler then told Aaron how nice it was for him to call her mom on her birthday and to take her out for lunch to give her a chance to reminisce about the old days. Her mom appreciated that and told Aaron he was the only person she could talk about Tyler with because everyone else thought that would upset her.

Tyler said he knew more about her than anyone else because of their intimate friendship. Aaron learned things about Tyler from her mom, and she learned something about Tyler from him. Stories about Tyler helped them keep her spirit alive. Her mom loved to hear about things he and Tyler did, how she felt about certain things, what she liked, what her dreams were, what was her favorite anything, and on it went.

Most of the stories had been shared many times before, but that was okay for both of them; just talking about Tyler was all that mattered.

"That's gonna be weird next time you talk to her," Tyler chuckled. "It's not like you can tell her we met and talked about stuff and what we've been up to!"

"Same thing with people I run into who knew you," Aaron replied. "People mention you and talk about how long it's been since you passed away, what age you would be now, and what you would be doing. It's not like I can say I just ran into you the other day." Aaron chuckled. "And by the way, I never thought I would say this to anyone... You looked beautiful at your funeral."

Tyler chuckled. "Allen said I looked ladylike."

"You did, with the flowers your parents placed with you and the dress you were wearing... What happened to the headband they put on you?"

"I got rid of it," Tyler replied.

"You didn't like how it felt?"

"No, I just didn't like it. I left it at my grandpa's house."

"I had a dream about you that I didn't get to tell you about the night before you came to my house after your softball game."

"How come?"

He went on to tell her about the dream when he found her lying in a coffin.

"Why didn't you tell me about it?" she asked him.

"Because you were thinking about your grandpa and bumming about how you played," he said. "I didn't want to freak you out... You had enough going on without me telling you something like that... But I was going to tell you when you were talking about death. I was just about to tell you when you said you wanted to stop talking about it because it was depressing you."

"Yeah, I'm glad you didn't tell me. That would have freaked me out. It would have freaked me out whenever you told me, but right then wouldn't have been good."

"So, will you be back tomorrow?" Aaron asked her.

"I'll be back if Mr. McFarren doesn't die... But, like I asked you, I want you to take me back to my grave if he does."

"I will...," Aaron assured her. "If that doesn't happen, will you be back here at the same time?"

"Aaron, I love you." She turned toward the field and began to walk away.

"I love you, too," he called out to her.

Tyler started into the field. Aaron watched as she again disappeared into the darkness. Tears fell, saddened by her having to leave again, but also of joy. Joy in the miracle of seeing Tyler again and knowing for certain that life carried on after death.

Then a sense of dread set in. Was he capable of killing someone? Did he have it in him? What if he couldn't do it?

Chapter Twenty
Pick Any Age You Like in Heaven

Beside himself with anticipation, Aaron whiled away time in the Florida room while waiting to go outside to see Tyler. McFarren transferred to a private room, he was pleased to learn after calling Western Hospital earlier in the day. McFarren was in room 512, a room Aaron knew from having visited with patients of his on the fifth floor. It was located a fair distance from the nearest nursing station. Chances were, he could go into the room and leave without being noticed.

An article in *Time Magazine* about a plane crash in the Colorado mountains was initially an interesting read while killing time. In the article, a guide who led a group of hikers described watching as a DC-10 emerged from clouds and struck a nearby rock face. Aaron stopped reading the article, disturbed after the guide went into grizzly details of the deaths of two hikers who were struck by debris. The too vivid detail of their deaths stirred visions of watching Tyler die. He put the magazine down and blindly watched television until the time to see her had come.

Movement began in the field soon after he sat on the bench as a darkened figure appeared and continued toward his yard.

"Hi, Aaron," Tyler said softly as she stopped about thirty feet from him.

"Hi, Tyler," he said. "Were you okay today?"

"I guess whatever okay means," she said, her voice now wavering. "I'm not. All I do is try not to be seen and wish I wasn't here.

"It's so weird to have to hide from people... A man and his dog came down a path beside the old house, so I had to go away and hide. I watched as they reached the house from behind a fallen tree, where I went to hide. Fido looked at me and started barking, so I lay down and prayed that the man wouldn't come over to see what his stupid dog was barking at. It must have started coming toward me because he called it back, but I couldn't see it because I practically had my face buried in the ground.

"Thank God the dog listened to the man," she sighed. "I think Abigail is watching out for me because of that and because no one has seen me that I know of. You would think she must be watching over me if she came to visit me. Maybe she'll help us with Mr. McFarren?

"I'm so sad and scared and confused about being here. I don't want to be here, and it's so strange to have to hide like I've done something wrong... It's not fair! Being here is weird. I want to go to where I should be... Oh, I just wish."

"Wish what?" he asked Tyler.

"That this had never happened..." she said, her voice breaking. She wiped at her eyes. "So, so, tell me, what's happening with Mr. McFarren?"

"They moved him out of the ICU and into a room," Aaron told her.

"That's a good thing, right?" she asked him, speaking in the softest voice. Her voice and question were too sweet and innocent. "Do you think there's anyone else in the room with him?"

"No," Aaron replied. "He's in a private room."

"So, that's a good thing," she said. "Now, I can do what I must do without other people around."

"It is, but I don't want you to do it."

"But he has to die. That's the only way to end the Pact," Tyler reminded him. "I don't understand."

"It's my fault this all happened," he told her. "Let me deal with him. You had nothing to do with it."

"But I did!" Tyler squealed like she sometimes did when disagreeing with something he said. "I was the one who wanted to try the séance in the first place. You would never have thought about trying it if it wasn't because of me."

"But I was the one who tried it… It was my choice. You had nothing to do with that."

"But whatever," she sighed. "It is what it is. That man must die to make things right. That's the way it has to be, but you don't have to be the one to do it."

"I can deal with the guy," he said. "Have you thought about what would happen if someone saw you? You're afraid of me getting a good look at you, but you're not going to get into the hospital and go walking around without being noticed."

"I can be okay with that, as long as he dies," she said. "That's better than you, getting in trouble if you got caught."

"But what if he doesn't die?" he asked her. "You would be locked away somewhere, so people could study you… They would run tests on you and drill you with all kinds of questions."

"Why would they do all that?" she asked him.

"You know why," Aaron replied. You're a walking dead person, he wanted to say.

"I suppose I know the reason," Tyler said. She stared at him for a moment. "By the way, the sky's a little brighter tonight… You're not able to see me that good, are you?"

"I can almost make out your face, but I can't get a good look at you," Aaron assured her.

"Good," Tyler said. "I can't really see your face either. I just wanted to double-check."

"Getting back to if you got caught… Let me deal with McFarren. I'm a doctor. There are things I can do that people won't easily notice. I can give him an injection of something that'll stop his heart. You need to let me take care of him." Tyler stayed silent after he stopped talking to give her a chance to respond. "I can't stand the thought of you going after McFarren again, and I don't even want to think about how you're going to feel if you got caught."

"You know it's so horrible that you and I would ever have to talk about what we're talking about," Tyler said while looking at the sky. She looked at him. "Why did it have to go this way where we're talking about killing someone? I know the reason, but it just seems so unfair."

"That stupid old man and his stupid séance Pact," she huffed. "I don't mean to blame Wayne, but if he never told us about how his sister tried the séance with her friends, we never would have known about it. I would never have wanted to try one, and you guys would never have thought of trying it. I would have stayed where I'm supposed to be after the accident, and all of our friends might still be alive if not for that stupid séance."

"But I can't blame Wayne because he didn't know, just like you and I didn't know," she said while rubbing her right leg, something the Tyler of old did sometimes when feeling anxious.

"This will be the last time we see each other before your time comes if McFarren dies tomorrow," she continued. "When you die, we'll be with people who have already died. And everyone we know will die, so we'll be with them someday, too."

"I'm always going to wonder if you made it back," Aaron said. "I believe what you're saying, but…"

"I will send you a sign, so you know I made it back the night after Mr. McFarren dies," Tyler told him, cutting Aaron off. "You'll know because you'll see a star go across the sky." She pointed east. "It will go from where I'm pointing and go overhead and continue west."

"When?" Aaron asked her.

"At midnight or thereabouts," Tyler replied. "That's how you will know, Aaron. If you see the star, which you will, you'll know I made it back… I know it would be hard for you to do, but I do want you to take me back to…, you know? Where they buried me and put me in the ground again."

"I'll take you back there like I promised," he said. "That's why I wanted to know where you would be today."

"Thank you, Aaron... I suppose I better stay somewhere close when I leave your place to make it easier for you to find me. There are a few places in the field where I could hide."

"You can stay here," Aaron suggested.

"Where?"

"In the house."

"But again, I don't want anyone to get a good look at me," she reminded him. "Especially you."

"But I'll have to come and find you, one way or the other."

"Yeah, I suppose," Tyler groaned. "Wherever I am, please cover me with something and don't look at me."

"I promise not to look at you," he told her again. "And like I said the other night, I'll cover you with a blanket."

"As I told you, I want you to remember me the way I used to look," she said as her voice trailed off. "I... I don't want you to remember me as some kind of freak."

"It's going to be okay," he told her. "And you're not a freak."

"But still," Tyler said. "So, I would go inside your house?"

"You can go inside a few minutes after I do. That way, I won't see you."

"Where would I go?"

"Go through the same door you see me go through when I go back inside the house. Then go through another door that leads to my kitchen. I'll leave the door open. Once you go into the kitchen, you'll see another door on your left. That door leads to a staircase that goes down to my basement. Go to another door on your left after you reach the basement. That one leads to my recreation room. You can stay there."

"What if someone else comes into the house during the day?"

"There won't be anyone coming around. And I won't come and get you until it gets dark out. I won't be able to take you back until it gets dark anyway."

"Okay, but how will you find me without turning a light on?" she asked him.

"There's a couch in the room," Aaron replied. "I'll find you there in the dark if you stay on it."

"Okay," Tyler said. "If you say you can find me without looking at me, then that's what I'll do."

"This is so weird that you and I can see and talk to each other. I'm glad to be able to talk with you, but you know?"

"I know it is," Tyler said. She paused. "Like I told you the other day, I'm so proud of you for becoming a doctor. Your childhood dream came true! That's gotta feel so cool, being able to help people."

"You were the smartest kid I knew," Aaron replied. "You could have become anything you set your mind on." His voice trailed off, saddened that Tyler had been robbed of a chance to achieve her potential. He staved off tears to avoid upsetting her. "If only you were given a chance," he said in a quavering voice. "I often think about what you might have been if you had had more time."

"Who knows what would have happened to me?" she said. "But it is what it is."

"It's so sad you never had a chance to live, that you died so young."

"I had my chance to live here, and I'm still living, but just differently. My spirit never died."

"It makes me feel better about the star," he told her. "That way, at least I'll know that you made it back and that we're going to see each other again."

"That's the way to think," Tyler said. "Dying is the scary part, but once that happens, you go on to Heaven," she said, her voice soft and reassuring. It felt more like he was speaking to a kind, worldly, gentle mother than a thirteen-year-old girl.

"So, you'll be able to hear and see me when you get back there?"

"Just like now," she said.

"Were you close to me when you were there before?"

"I was close. I could see you and anyone else I wanted to. It's strange 'cuz like I say, I could be in different places and see different people all at the same time."

"Could you show yourself to me if you wanted?"

"No. I don't know why, but that's how it was," Tyler replied. "I couldn't show myself or talk to you, is all I know. I wanted to tell you and Wayne, my parents and brothers and sisters, my grandma and my English grandparents, and everyone else that I was okay but couldn't."

"I thought you might be a ghost when I first saw you the other night," Aaron said.

"But now you know I'm not," Tyler said.

"So, how close were you?"

"You know how you were able to go inside Mr. McFarren? Well, it was kind of like that. I knew what you were feeling, hearing, smelling, thinking, and seeing. I knew everything that was going on in your life."

"So, you'll always be nearby after you go on?"

"Always. You won't be able to see me, but I'll be close. I'll be there."

"Remember when we were younger?" he asked her.

"You mean when you were younger."

"Okay, when I was younger," Aaron said. "I never got close to anyone like I did with you. That's probably because we knew each other from day one. You and I could say anything to each other and accepted each other no matter what. We had the same interests and liked doing the same things."

"But you and Wayne are close. And you married that Shay lady."

"You're right about Wayne, but it wasn't like that with Shay over the last few years. Anyway, I never felt closer to anyone than I did with you."

"Same thing with me. We saw each other every day unless we

had gone away or were sick," Tyler said. "Your mom used to say we were like peanut butter and jam, and my mom called us two pieces in a puzzle that fit together."

"They were right," Aaron said.

"That they were," Tyler agreed.

"You know I was starting to fall for you, in a physical attraction kind of way."

"I was starting to see you that way, too."

"I think that's cool that we can be any age we want in Heaven," he said. It was unfathomable to think of him being his age and Tyler being the age she was. "It would be kinda gross if you couldn't be older, and I couldn't be younger."

"I want to be twenty-five," she hummed. "I always wondered what it would be like to be twenty-five, to be more mature but young at the same time. I'm going to be twenty-five. What about you?"

"I'll be that age, too, because we should be the same age as we were. Twenty-five was a good age for me. I loved being twenty-five. I was in med school, but it was a lot of fun. I loved learning and discovering things for the first time."

"Do you think we would have gotten married someday?" he asked her.

"Sure, we would have if we'd had the chance," Tyler replied. "We always said that we would."

"It was strange when I started to see you in a physically attractive kind of way," he said. "I was confused and scared about how I was feeling. I didn't want to lose you as a friend."

"That would never have happened," she assured him. "For me, and I know, for you… I would have been hurt and pissed if you started dating someone because I wanted you always to be my man. I told you that."

"It would have hurt me, too, if you started dating someone else," Aaron said. "It hit me after you died that I loved you a little more each day."

"Our hormones started kicking in," Tyler continued. "I liked it when we started making out after I told you about what my friends were saying. And they were right!"

"I could tell Wayne was jealous of us being close. Not so much as we got older, but he felt left out when you and I started hanging out without him when we were six there about."

"Part of that was he was hanging out with other kids, or he didn't come out of his house sometimes," Aaron declared. "Now we know why that was."

"So, by the way, to change the topic, whatever happened to our card collection? You better still have it!"

"I still have it. I sealed the cards in Ziploc bags, so they look good as new... Player cards come in box sets nowadays, not in bubble gum packages like they used to. I buy a set for baseball, hockey, football, and basketball every year. I put them away."

"You put them away?"

"Yeah. I don't even open the boxes they come in," Aaron said.

"Where's the fun in that?"

"It's not much fun. I do that so the cards hold their value."

"I don't get it. What's the point of having cards if you don't look at them?"

"Hockey and baseball cards are valuable now if you have a rare one. People pay lots of money for them. I just added a Mario Lemieux and a Guy Lafleur limited edition card to our collection."

"Who's Mario Lemieux? Is he a hockey player like Lafleur?"

"Yeah. Lemieux began playing in the 1980s for the Pittsburgh Penguins. He scored 199 points one year and won two Stanley Cups with them."

"The Pittsburgh Penguins won the cup?" Tyler yelped. "They were always a cruddy team. I remember when Montreal beat them twelve nothing after Pittsburgh ended the Canadien's fourteen-game undefeated streak the night before in 1979. Montreal was our favorite team."

"They're not a dynasty like they used to be," he said. "They've only won the cup twice since '79."

"That sucks! Hmm, so Pittsburgh won two Stanley Cups? Too much."

"That they did. I know that's hard to believe."

"And the Mario guy got 199 points!" Tyler exclaimed. "That's amazing."

"Wayne Gretzky was even better," Aaron said. "He had four seasons where he scored over 200 points."

"Oh, my God!"

"Gretzky scored 215 one year."

"Wow, that's amazing. I hope Gretzky played for Montreal."

"I wish," he groaned. "Gretzky played for the Edmonton Oilers, one of those four World Hockey Association teams that began playing in the NHL in the fall of 79."

"Oh, well, that's too bad," Tyler said. "So, how much did the cards cost you for Lafleur and that Mario guy?"

"Fifty bucks each."

"Fifty bucks each! Aaron, are you crazy? I thought you would say you paid like maybe five bucks for a big-time card."

"People spend lots of money on cards now. The most expensive card now is a rare Honus Wagner card that costs over $100,000."

"Well, that's just ridiculous! You didn't buy it, did you?"

"No," Aaron chuckled. "I don't have that kind of money. I like collecting cards, but I would never spend a stupid amount of money on one, even if I did."

"Shoot, you could buy a decent house for $100,000," she said.

"Maybe back in '79 you could. That would just get you half a decent-sized house these days. The average house costs double that now."

"No way!"

"Our card collection is pretty valuable," he said.

"You mean money-wise?" Tyler asked him.

"Yes, money-wise," Aaron replied. "But I would never sell

them, especially the ones we collected together. It's a nice feeling to know you have cards that are worth something... Remember that Al Kaline card you found that you liked so much?" he asked her. A star player for the Detroit Tigers in the sixties and seventies, the Kaline card was Tyler's favorite in their collection. "It's a rare one. It's worth a lot of money now."

"Yeah, well, you better not sell it or any of mine," she said. "I won't be happy if you do."

"I wouldn't even think of it," he told her.

"Well, that's good... So, that's too bad what happened to you and that Shay lady. It wasn't nice how she left you the way she did. You were nice to her. You treated her good."

"I always tried to, but her drinking got in the way," Aaron said. "She lost it after finding out that she couldn't have kids. I felt so bad for her... After that, she got drunk all the time and ended up losing her job because of it. Being with her was like walking on a razor blade after that... Man, could Shay be nasty... She wasn't fun to be around."

"I know about that," Tyler sighed. "I felt bad for you, and I felt bad for her."

"I came home one night this past January to find out that she left me," Aaron continued. "She was gone, and she took most of the furniture with her. I found a cute little note she left saying that things weren't getting better between us and that she wanted a divorce."

"That wasn't cool... You didn't see it coming when Shay left you."

"Like I say, she had a problem with alcohol," he grumbled. "We didn't have a major blow-up or anything. Nothing changed between us, so it was a total shock when she just up and left. I always wanted her to get herself together, and I still felt that way after she left. I was always hoping that we might get back together someday."

"She got killed when a cement truck hit her car," Tyler said.

"That blows me away that you know about that."

"I saw that only because that Geoffrey guy drove the truck. The driver was never found because no human drove it."

"But what would he want with Shay?" Aaron asked her.

"Nothing other than to wear you down, spirit-wise, I suppose," Tyler replied. "Geoffrey, no doubt, knew you still cared about her. He probably wanted to wear you down to make you feel bad enough to start thinking about trying to contact me again." "What time is it, by the way?" she asked Aaron while looking at the field.

Aaron pressed the illumination button on his dial watch and squinted to look at its hands, hour, and minute marks. "Ten after four," he advised her.

"That's cool," Tyler said. "We still have time to talk."

"Shay's parents said she stopped drinking a few months before the accident when I talked with them at her funeral," Aaron continued. "I think Shay probably would have gone back to drinking, but who knows? Maybe she would have stayed sober? She might have kept herself together, though I doubt it."

"Shay was like my Uncle Max," Tyler remarked, referring to her alcoholic uncle, who died a few years after she did. She had complained to Aaron about Uncle Max's erratic, alcohol-induced behavior and how some of her family members treated him.

"I bet Shay would win if they got into a drinking match," Aaron quipped. "If anything, she'd give your uncle a run for his money."

"I felt so bad for him," Tyler said, not responding to Aaron's comment. "My uncle was a sweetheart. Two aunts of mine and a few cousins laughed at him and said ignorant things about him behind his back during Christmas, Thanksgiving, and other family get-to-gathers. I didn't like it, and it made me mad... I wanted to tell them not to do that but didn't want to upset anyone and get them angry with me. My uncle slurred and stumbled around when he was hammered but was never mean or rude to anyone... Thank God, my parents and my sibs never talked bad about him, but someone should have told my aunts and cousins to knock it off."

"At least he's in a better place now," Aaron stated.

"That he is," Tyler declared.

As you probably know, I've been going to your grave every three months since I started driving. I bring purple daisies with me every time I go. Your favorites."

"I know you've been doing that, and that's so sweet," she gushed. "That made me happy... I wish I could have told you so."

"I met with a lady after the accident," Aaron said. "She was a therapist that helps people work through things that are bothering them."

"I saw you talking with her."

"My parents wanted me to talk with someone, and I wanted to because I was completely lost. And I couldn't stop having nightmares about the accident. But I would start seeing someone, and then they'd quit and go somewhere else, so I'd have to start over again with a new person, and they left. I didn't want to do it anymore."

"Maybe now that you know I'm okay, you'll stop having them," Tyler stated. "Because I told you I didn't suffer like you thought I did."

"I'm sure you're right. I wanted to stop seeing it and not feel so empty inside, but the therapist kept leaving, so I had to start over again, which was too much."

"So, are your mom and dad doing, okay?" Tyler asked him.

"Yep," Aaron told her. "They live in Florida in the winter and at the house on Askin the rest of the year."

"I know my mom and dad moved to east Windsor right after what happened to me. My dad died a year later, and my grandma on my mom's side died," Tyler said. "They would be with my grandpa right now... I would be with them if I weren't here." Her voice cracked like it did when she was upset. She paused a moment and then rubbed her eyes. "Well, I'll be seeing them soon enough," she hummed, looking at that sky. "Thank you, Aaron, for doing the séance."

"What are you thinking about?" Aaron asked her.

"That it must be blowing your mind to be talking with me… What were you thinking when you first saw me the other day?"

"I didn't know what to think when I first saw you. I thought you were a developmentally delayed girl living in my neighborhood who likes to roam around. Sometimes she gets lost and ends up in people's houses and backyards."

"What does developmentally delayed mean?" Tyler asked him. "Is that when a person can't walk or something?"

"That's a term for people who have intellectual deficits."

"Like someone who's retarded?"

"Mentally retarded is a better term," he replied.

"Oh, okay," Tyler said. "I watched you when you first saw me in your yard when you looked out your window. The look on your face was like you had just seen a ghost… Even though I'm not a ghost."

"What would you have done if I hadn't seen you?" Aaron asked her. "Would you have stayed in the yard all night? It's only because I happened to look outside that I saw you."

"Oh, I would have found a way to see you one way or the other. I was heading to your door when you came outside. I'm glad it didn't turn out that way, with me knocking on your door and you seeing me standing there. It was better you had a chance to get ready to see me if you know what I mean."

"I know what you mean, and I agree," he said. "At least seeing you in my yard gave me time to let the shock set in before I realized that it was you. If I had opened the door and found you standing there, I would have passed out."

"I'm glad it didn't happen that way, but that would have been funny in a twisted kind of way," Tyler said, giggling.

"Yeah, I suppose, but not really," Aaron replied.

"I know it wouldn't really be funny, but I'm just saying... I really didn't want to have to bother you in this, being that it's weird for you and all. But I'm happy we got to talk to each other."

"Me too," he said. "Obviously, I would never have thought this could ever happen a few days ago. I just wanted to contact you through the séance... I can't believe this is happening; it seems so unreal. It's like a dream."

"But it's not a dream, and it's not unreal," Tyler insisted. "It must seem so, though, to be a dream and unreal."

"I know it's not."

"I wish I never went to talk to Mr. McFarren to learn how to do a séance and that I dragged you along," she groaned. "None of this would have happened if I didn't."

"Try not to blame yourself," Aaron said to challenge her self-blaming thought. "All you wanted to do was to contact your grandpa. I wish that Wayne never told you that the man knew how to do a séance."

"But Wayne didn't know what the séance was about," she said. "He was only trying to help me feel better."

"That was Wayne, just being Wayne. Wayne always wants to be helpful. He helped me after you died and Shay left me."

"I felt so bad for you, Aaron, when Shay left you and after I..., after the accident. I don't know how I would have felt if it was the other way around. If you were the one who died."

"Part of me died with you."

"A part of me would have died too if it were you who ended up dying."

"It's just fate," Aaron surmised.

"Perhaps," Tyler remarked. "I think it's because some things are just meant to be like the séance stuff. None of us is guilty for what happened because of the séance. I think everything happened for whatever reason."

"Maybe you're right," Aaron said.

"Whether I am or not, what happened wasn't any of our faults."

"So, how did you know where to find me?"

"I know a lot about you because of being able to watch you. I knew what your house looked like, where it was and how to get here."

"I felt bad for McFarren after you took me to see what happened to him," Aaron told her. "This might sound dumb or strange, but I feel for the man."

"It doesn't sound dumb at all!" Tyler exclaimed. "I felt bad for him too… Poor old Mr. McFarren was tormented, and that Geoffrey guy took advantage of him… A walking dead person is what McFarren is." Tyler looked east, where the sky had brightened with the first light of dawn. Aaron's heart grew heavy. "Daylight is coming, so it's getting near that time."

"Tyler, I wish I could hug you right now," he said.

"I want that too, Aaron, and we could hug, but I don't want you thinking of me like I am now. I don't want you to see me because… I know what a dead person looks like. I can't, I can't, I can't let you see me up close, I just can't." Again, her voice cracked. "It's so hard, and I do sometimes feel angry at God for allowing this to happen to me. But like the priests would say, God only gives us strength. He lets Lucifer rule the Earth."

"My mom and dad, his dad, my grandmas and brothers and sisters, and you were devasted when that truck hit me. All of our friends and a lot of other people were crushed, too. My parents felt bad for not spending more time with me. That's why they planned the trip we were going to take, but that didn't happen.

"I felt so bad for my dad because he took it so hard. I wanted him to start getting better. He felt it would be wrong to stop thinking about what happened to me, that that would somehow hurt me, and be happy again because I would be hurt if he did. He thought he'd hurt me by trying to feel better because I might think he had forgotten about me.

"I'm so looking forward to seeing my dad, my grandma, and grandpa and all the rest when I get to stay in Heaven. My dad just could not get better.... He was never the same after the accident. I watched him when he would go off on his own, driving around thinking about aiming his car into a tree or something and asking God why I had to die. He was very angry at God, but I'm sure that won't stop him from going to Heaven."

"I was angry at God, too," Aaron said. "If you went onto the road a minute sooner or later, you would have reached the medium or could have gone onto the shoulder. There were no trucks or cars in front of it or behind it."

"My mom didn't do much better, but she managed to hold it together." Tyler took a deep breath. "She still stays awake at night now and again, thinking about me and what I might have become.

"She's had dreams about me and you, being married and having kids. She always said we were meant for each other, and I guess she meant it."

"Just like you've had dreams of us having kids. You had that one after you finished the séance."

"That dream was so vivid. There were the two little yours and the one little me."

"It was too cute!" she hummed.

"You were so beautiful. I got lost in your eyes a lot, trying to spot your pupils because they got darker depending on the light... Your eyes were always so full of life."

"You were so handsome, and your eyes were full of life, too," she said. "I liked it when you let your hair get long and loved how it changed from strawberry blond in the winter to platinum blond in the summer. When your hair was long, you looked like a rock star playing your guitar."

"I liked watching you play. You were getting better and better. And I was going to practice playing the piano. We could have had a jam session!"

"We could have had Wayne play, too," Aaron said. "He was getting good at playing the drums."

"It's too bad you stopped playing guitar," Tyler said.

"Medical school got in the way. I didn't have enough time to practice."

"Maybe you would have become a big old rock star!"

"Maybe we all would have," Aaron said.

"So, do you want to hear something completely cool?" Tyler asked him.

"Sure."

"Remember how I moped around feeling ignored and left out and would start thinking that I was an accident? Now I know I was my dad's favorite out of all my brothers and sisters! So even if I was a mistake, it all worked out!"

"Oh, Tyler," Aaron said, feeling his eyes ache, on the verge of happy tears. "I feel so happy about that! You always wanted their love and never seemed to find it; meanwhile, you were your dad's favorite. And I won't ever believe that you were a mistake."

"I'm going to miss you," Aaron moaned while dabbing tears away.

"Oh, try not to be so sad," she said. "The only thing than being able to try and end that Pact that made me feel good about being here was to see you. To be able to talk with you even though I fretted about freaking you out. Thinking about upsetting you bothered me all the way here the other night. I never wanted to upset you."

"But I'm so happy to see you and to be able to talk with you," Aaron glumly uttered.

"Same here," Tyler said. "Well, Tyler, this is it, I guess."

"For now. You'll see me tomorrow if Mr. McFarren doesn't die. If he does, the next time we see each other will be forever."

"I hope that's true."

"Oh, it's true," she told him, speaking in the sweetest tone of voice. "Just believe what I'm telling you because it's true."

"I believe you," Aaron replied. "I guess I should go inside now," he said while walking away from her. He slowly started toward the house.

"Things will work out, Aaron, you'll see," Tyler said when he looked back to take a last look at her. "I promise you that it's gonna be okay."

"I want to go to where I should be. I love talking with you, but I don't want to be here anymore… We'll see each other again one day. You just have to trust that it will happen and that we'll be okay.

"Goodbye until we see each other again, Aaron."

Aaron took a brief final look at Tyler after reaching the house. He forced himself to look away. Continuing to look at her would merely prolong the pain of their parting.

Faith that, in time, they would reunite in Heaven spurred him on.

He mused about how their lives had changed. One day they were teenagers, dancing, doing a daredevil romp in the pool where chlorine or Mrs. Page could have gotten them, tending to their card collection, and a few days later, trying to sort out the mess their existence had become. They had no way of knowing that day that she would die so young, and they would be involved in a Pact, a hapless man made with a demon. She would go to Heaven, return, and spend years alive in a grave, where a spirit would visit her, and many of their friends would die.

Chapter Twenty-One
A Moment in Hell

An effort to get a few hours of solid sleep proved futile, tossing and turning, burdened by the idea of murdering someone. Aaron thought what a heinous act to take another person's life would be, even if they were essentially already dead. A walking dead person McFarren was, Tyler told him. He prayed that God would look away, given the evil McFarren wrought in pursuit of selfish gain. Her promise that their souls would be together again and forever helped steel resolve to do what had to be done.

Hell, Tyler must have endured, alive and unable to escape her grave, pained Aaron's heart while thinking through his plan to kill McFarren. He planned to carry out the deed during his lunch hour. The drive to and from the hospital took ten minutes or less both ways. Time should be on his side provided all went well, that nothing unforeseen occurred.

'Got Me Under Pressure,' a ZZ Top song, played as an alarm clock radio next to his bed came to life. The song meshed with a dream in which ZZ Top played at Dirty Tom's pub, a pub where he and Wayne liked to shoot pool and down a few too many beers. With beers in hand, ZZ Top's Billy Gibbons and Dusty Hill were about to join Wayne and Aaron when the boys from Texas took a break when Aaron woke. Only then did he notice that the song played on his radio. He wondered if it stirred the dream or the song playing was mere coincidence. Disappointment came by realizing the close encounter with two of his favorite rock stars had occurred in a dream.

Then he noticed his stomach was hollow while he contemplated what the day ahead might bring. Surprisingly refreshed after only a taste of sleep, Aaron sat up, flicked on a bedside lamp, and gazed at his pillow and bed. Wondering... Thinking he may never sleep there again. That chances were the rest of his days would be spent in a place run by Hotel Corrections Canada if caught during or after killing McFarren.

Corrections Canada ran a chain of prisons across the provinces, but he would likely end up at the notoriously violent Kingston Penitentiary, given the region where he lived. Aaron, having seen photographs of Kingston Pen or KP, as people called it, could picture the prison with its towering limestone edifice, surrounded by barbed wire fencing. Gun-toting guards would be looking on from watchtowers when he and fellow inmates recreated in KP's yards.

Its cells had cinder block walls, concrete floors, and contained stainless steel toilets, sinks, and a small bed, he knew from photos. Mold and dust and body odor, vomit, shit, and piss stench were no doubt omnipresent. Rat-sized cockroaches and cat-sized rats probably overran the place.

He thought about Tyler while walking to his bathroom to shower and wondered how she was doing alone downstairs. After stepping into the shower and fiddling with its taps until the water temperature was just right, Aaron wondered if this might be his last comfortable private shower. The next might be taken in some dank communal stall, with water colder than preferred, he thought as warm water sprayed over him. Worse, there may be a need to fend off some crazed sex maniac. An average-sized guy he could fight off, but a monster-sized fudge packer, rigged with muscles honed by hours whiled away lifting weights, would be a different matter. Would such a muscle-bound, libido-driven beast with a crazed look force him to bend over and grab his kneecaps?

He inhaled a few pop tarts after showering while wondering if it might be the last breakfast at home. A man-sized breakfast consisting of eggs, bacon, sausage, toast, and coffee should be in order if only there were time and presence of mind to prepare one. Anxious to get on with what had to be done, he started toward the garage after eating quickly. He savored the comfort of its leather seats after climbing into the Lincoln.

Its engine never sounded sweeter, coming to life while thinking freedom to drive where he wanted could very well end after driving to Western Hospital. A push broom might be all he piloted henceforth, pulling janitorial duty at some token rate of pay, if so lucky. Perhaps money he earned could be used to buy pop or other trivial things from the prison canteen. Or pay in exchange to not become the sex-driven beast's special buddy.

He paused after reaching the street to take what might be a final look at his house. To rot in prison for killing McFarren in Tyler's stead was a price worth paying. McFarren had to die, Aaron kept telling himself while driving to work, so Tyler could go home and try to save Wayne.

Tyler and seeing to McFarren's demise stole his thoughts while seeing patients that morning, the last a young man dying from terminal brain cancer. Aaron wanted to tell him a better place lay ahead after death, according to a friend who died twenty years ago. But saying that would no doubt cause the man to question his attending doctor's sanity.

His lunch break began shortly after noon as time continued its perpetual course. No one noticed him remove a bottle of succinylcholine from a medication pantry. After handing the young man's file to Jen, he started into the parking lot with the bottle and a syringe stuffed into a pocket. A sinister thought prompted a wicked smile as distant voices chanted his name in a resounding chorus while walking to the car.

"You can do it, Aaron, buddy boy... there are lots of people counting on ya, boy," a familiar-sounding man's voice said. "You're the man, Aaron boy, don't let the bastard play you. You just finish him off and let us have him."

"Three cheers for Aaron," a woman yelled.

"Hip, Hip, Hooray..., Hip, Hip, Hooray..., Hip, Hip, Hooray," the chorus sang.

Aaron prayed to stay sane while climbing into his Lincoln. "There's no backing out now..., you've just got to do it," the man said as Aaron drove away. "Uh-huh..., oh yes, you certainly do.

"Oh, those glory days of yesteryear, singing songs and drinking beer," he sang. "Those days are gone, and things will never be the same. Our lives now so full of pain... Our boy Aaron will set things right and release us all from our hellish plight. Then the curtain can rise on our show. His name we will loudly cheer... and, in our hearts, hold him dear."

It was a catchy tune, but who was doing the singing? Aaron wondered until placing the voice. It belonged to Oscar Williams, the husband of a woman who owned a convenience store near Our Lady of the Lakes Cemetery, where daisies he left on Tyler's grave were bought. Oscar, who died two years ago, liked to sing while stocking shelves in the store.

He vividly pictured Oscar, a medium-skinned black man with salt and pepper hair and a similarly colored mustache and beard. Blue jean overalls and checkered long-sleeved shirts were Oscar's typical clothing of choice. He warmed a bench outside and smoked cigars when not stocking shelves and cleaning up around the store.

* * * * *

Roads, cars, buildings, trees, grass, the sky, and other things were on reality's wayside while driving to Western Hospital, Aaron, in another world. Clenched tightly with sweaty palms, sweat brought on by nerves, the steering wheel wavered between melting and its solid state. Voices talked, sang, and chanted while somehow reaching the hospital, guided by an inner radar through a maze of unreality.

Aaron shut the engine off after easing the Lincoln into an available spot in a parking lot. After fumbling for its handle, he pushed the driver-side door open and in his daze, fell against it while stepping outside. Seemingly determined to get their owner to his destination before having a change of heart, his feet moved of their own accord toward the hospital. But there could be no turning back. He was a soldier heading into battle in his abstracted mind, one that seemed doomed to end with his capture.

Voices continued after entering the hospital. "You can do it, boy... we're counting on ya," Oscar said.

He pressed an upward prompt after reaching a bank of elevators. A group of doctors, all but one Aaron knew, approached. "Please, just don't ask what I'm doing here," his inner voice pled. Not caring to engage in conversation, hoping to go unnoticed, he stared at an elevator and wished there was a way of becoming invisible.

"Aaron!" a voice belonging to his friend Dr. Walter Ford said. "Are you bowling this year?"

"Hey, Walt," Aaron looked at Walt and spoke. Both men bowled on the same team in a winter bowling league from mid-October through March. "Yeah. I just bought a new ball I had customized... I'm looking to lower my score." Initially not high on his things-to-do list, bowling was a hobby he got into to get away from Shay on Wednesday nights, six months out of the year.

"I'm having a get-together a week from this Saturday," Walt said. "I just left an invite on your voicemail.... I'll be barbequing steaks, pork chops, chicken, and frying fish. All you need to bring is any booze you want to drink... You can sleep over. I have plenty of space."

"Count me in," Aaron told him. "I'll make sure to bring an appetite," he joked.

"See you later, buddy," Walt said. "Come by any time after three."

"I'll be over at three," Aaron confirmed. "At least I hope to if I don't get caught doing what I'm aiming to do," he silently muttered while staring at floor indicators of the elevators.

Frustrated by one who, in his hurry, took their sweet ole time, he waited impatiently for passengers to disembark before entering after an elevator opened. A wavering voice asked to hold its door open while pressing the button for the fifth floor. An elderly woman using a walker waddled inside.

"Hit the seventh-floor button for me, would you, dear?" the woman asked him. She peered through thick glasses magnifying her eyes to the size of quarters. Aaron looked away to avoid conversation. The elevator began an upward trek.

"There's a lot of people counting on you, son," the old woman said. Aaron glanced at her, caught off guard by the woman's bizarre comment. He looked at the floor indicator and hoped that she, no doubt suffering from dementia or just plain crazy, would say nothing more. "Just do what needs to be done," the woman said as the elevator rose.

"You know that you might well be sharing the elevator with a crazed person," a man's voice announced. Standing where the old woman stood, Geoffrey looked at him with a penetrating stare. "Oh yeah, there's a whole lot of folks counting on you, my man," Geoffrey scornfully uttered. "For being a man of medicine, you're not the brightest sort. Understand that if you mess with my man McFarren that you'll be messing with me. I'll be coming for you, and it won't end well for you." The elevator abruptly stopped and went dark. A flat, barren, absent of color place with a hueless sky overhead came into view. "Would you like this, my dear friend?" Geoffrey asked Aaron, who stood flush against a wall, to put maximum distance between them. "Watch as such a fate might very well be yours." A man with half of his head blown off by a shotgun staggered before falling in a vision. What remained of his mouth was frozen in an agonizing scream.

"How about this?" Geoffrey said. Another image began, this one of a man curled in the fetal position in a rubbish-strewn alley. Vomit streamed from his mouth, and his eyes, bulging, looked like they were on the verge of exploding. A used syringe, a dried brown heroin-like-looking residue within it, lay nearby. Urine streamed from the man toward a storm drain.

Another vision followed. Muffled screams and fingernails scraping against a hard surface came from a place of absolute darkness. Perhaps the screams and fingernails scraping came from within a coffin, Aaron wondered. He imagined Tyler trying to escape the nightmare of being trapped in her grave.

In another vision, a man in medieval dress screamed wretchedly as an executioner's hood-wearing figure hammered a spike into his head.

"Hell is reliving your darkest moment forever," Geoffrey declared when the visions ended. "You'll find yourself doing that while trapped alive in a grave as you worry so much about, like your friend... Rest assured, watching your friend Tyler kissing that truck will repeat itself forever if you kill McFarren."

Geoffrey vanished. The elevator rose. Shaken by the encounter and Geoffrey's threat, Aaron steeled himself by believing he and Tyler would be together again.

* * * * *

The elevator opened across from a nurse station. A square with room 512 marked on it flashed on a panel indicating McFarren required immediate attention. Room 512's door was open, Aaron saw after arriving outside the room despite a sign on the door warning of a biohazard inside.

"He's gone," a doctor whose voice he recognized confirmed from inside 512.

The idea of Tyler having become a murderess was sickening.

"I'll call his time of death at 12:15 pm," the doctor announced to others in the room. "I'll talk to his family. We gave it our best, folks. We did what we could."

"He doesn't have anyone here, Dr. Brackett," a woman's voice Aaron recognized advised. "We haven't seen any family or friends of his and don't have a name and phone number of anyone to call."

"That's so sad," Brackett replied.

"Social Work has been trying to find someone," the woman, a registered nurse who had been practicing well over thirty years, said. Well-known and respected, given her length of service and expertise, people in the local medical community knew her simply as Nurse McCall.

"I'll keep you in the loop if they find someone, Nurse McCall," Brackett promised.

"Hey, Aaron, what brings you here?" he asked Aaron after leaving the room.

"Mr. McFarren was a patient of mine," Aaron replied. "I came by to see another patient and found out that he was here."

"I would have called you, but he didn't mention your name to me or anyone else, as far as I know," Brackett said.

"I'm not surprised because I only saw him twice."

"Do you know of anyone we can call? Nobody is here for him."

"My office is shut down for lunch, but I'll page my receptionist and ask her to check his file for any contacts he might have given," Aaron said.

"You have my number. Just call me when you get back," Brackett suggested. "Your patient had bubonic plague if you can believe it, according to toxicology results. Since a case in San Diego ten years ago, no one has died from bubonic plague in North America that I'm aware of." Aaron's spirit soared, pleased that Tyler's assault did not directly cause McFarren's death. "We did what we could to stem the infection, and he put up a good fight.

"Your patient was in critical condition and almost dead when he arrived in the ER the other night. Dr. Lang operated. Someone stabbed him pretty good with a butcher knife in the neck and again in his shoulder where they just left it, according to Ian," Brackett said, referring to Dr. Lang by his first name. "The shoulder wound was over six inches deep and oh-so-close to the subclavian artery and vein. He lost three pints (of blood). Ian and his team performed a miracle, stabilizing him long enough to suture his wounds."

"Your patient made it through surgery without complications, which was remarkable given his age after Ian worked his magic. The man had a fever on the low end when they brought him up after only needing to spend a day in intensive care. We were managing it with cefixime until his fever worsened. The plague is treatable, but none of my research-proven antibiotic treatments worked."

Aaron smiled as Dr. Brackett walked away, relieved the Pact was broken and that Tyler had not become a murderess. The thought of her dead in his basement and what lay ahead that night consumed him while driving back to the clinic. Somehow, Aaron managed fortitude to focus on patients and carry on through the afternoon.

Chapter Twenty-Two
A Lady in the Window

Aaron looked in a mirror after returning home from work at Tyler's crucifix, now hanging on his necklace. Overwhelmed by the prospect of finding her corpse, he stared into his eyes, at his soul, as an inner struggle ensued. He hoped that Tyler's body lay lifeless, struggling with and feeling ashamed for wanting that to be so.

There was time to waste, with four hours to go before sunset, before it grew dark enough to retrieve her. Too focused on Tyler to engage in comparatively trivial conversation, whiling away time with his parents, Wayne, or other friends, was not an option. He decided to drive to the Husky restaurant, part of a truck stop on Essex County Road 46 adjacent to Highway 401, in the outskirts of Windsor. After having dinner there, he would go for a long drive and return home by ten o'clock to ensue upon the dubious task of returning Tyler's body to her grave.

A parking lot beside the restaurant was its usual sea of tractor trailers, their drivers taking a break from the road. Truckers could get a bite to eat, shower and change clothes, sleep in the back of their rigs, and even wash them at the truck stop. They could partake with prostitutes plying their trade there if so inclined — lot lizards, the truckers called them. Truckers caught up on one another's doings and shared experiences along the roads, highways, and interstates of North America in truck stops like Husky's.

He eavesdropped while sitting in a booth on the conversation truckers were having at a nearby table. They talked about fuel prices, toll road costs, and discussed a new highway between Alabama and Florida and new truck stops in Kentucky and

Quebec. One of the truckers recounted avoiding a near head-on collision by swerving into an open lane to avoid a truck that entered his lane.

* * * * *

The Lincoln's tires squealed while jackrabbiting onto County Road 46 to avoid a line of oncoming cars after leaving the Huskies at 6:40 p.m. Aaron drove southeast until reaching Highway 3 ten kilometers later and started east. Highway 3 eventually paralleled Lake Erie and continued to Niagara Falls, should one care to drive that far. He would drive east until 8:15 p.m. and then turn around and head back home, which would get him there by ten.

Field gave to field, and hamlets came and went, where the speed limit dropped to 50kp/h, as he dwelled on Tyler. Though driving twenty over the eighty-kilometer per hour limit, not one car failed to pass; the speed limit as relevant as amber lights in a city at rush hour. Most drivers failed to obey it as road conditions and proximity to hamlets, where police were most likely to be watching traffic, dictated the speed.

Lake Erie, a hazy aqua slate stretching to the horizon beyond crop fields bordering its shore, came into view forty-five minutes into the drive. Familiar with the highway, having driven Number 3 many times, Aaron was surprised to see a faded sign he had not seen before indicating that a road, WEST BASELINE, was close. Overcome by curiosity, he slowed and turned onto the road to see where it led.

Despite driving only 45kp/h and at times less, the Lincoln felt each bump while passing cornrows on either side of the thickly graveled, heavily potholed road. Bored after passing kilometers of unchanging scenery, Aaron planned to turn around at the next field approach before spotting a sign announcing a town called Jacksonville, like the road, unknown before.

West Baseline Road became a paved, four-lane street after passing the sign and deciding to continue. Houses behind sidewalks and tree-shaded lawns flanked the street. Parked cars from a previous era lined its shoulder and were in driveways.

A glorious evening weather-wise, squirrels, dogs and cats, children playing, and adults in yards or sitting on porches were an anticipated sight, yet he was alone. Not a soul could be seen as he passed a police station, town hall, library, church, banks, and stores while driving through the central part of the town. He continued past other homes before turning around after noticing an oddly familiar iron, rust-coated fence on his left.

He pulled onto a graveled shoulder and stopped near an opening in the fence that was also familiar. Driven by a curious need to reach an unseen place, certain he had been to before, Aaron paused to gain his bearings before leaving the car. Someone was inside the house. It seemed that he was destined to meet.

Each step forward was challenged by fear after passing through the opening and entering a field of knee-high weeds. He trudged toward a cluster of trees as an abandoned mansion came into view. An odd feeling that something there knew of his presence began. A strong sense of a presence within it beckoned.

Though mindful of foot-slicing debris, snakes, mice, and whatever else might lurk underfoot, he continued forward in a trancelike state. Wooden, park-type benches, tops of their backs peering over weeds, came into view. Remnants of a brick structure, its circular shape suggestive of a decaying well lay to his right.

Crows and ravens cawing unseen in trees, the trees and field, himself and the presence, were the only living things about the mansion. Drawn by a faint rumble, Aaron looked skyward and noticed a jet flying far overhead, the only other presence of fellow humanity until a woman called out from the mansion. "Help me," she pleaded. No one stood behind gaping holes once containing windows when he looked to where her voice had come.

An archway of meshed wood provided access to a circle-shaped space bordered by a hedge to his right. A decaying iron table and chairs, rust-coated like the fence, were inside the space. Aaron pictured a stuffy wealthy gent wearing a pinstriped suit and his wife in a flowery summer dress at the table in days gone by, sipping afternoon tea. He imagined a servant standing nearby, waiting to heed their beck and call.

Such a couple appeared after taking another quick look at the mansion. The couple occupied chairs that were, as was the table, in pristine condition. Aaron listened as the couple talked about a nanny they hired to help care for their baby. The man questioned their nanny's child-caring competence.

"Over here!" the woman cried out. Again, he looked toward the mansion. Windows replaced gaping holes. A young woman stared at him from an opened, third-floor window.

Aaron looked at the couple curiously to see if they noticed the woman or if the mansion had changed. The chairs were empty. Wide gaping holes again replaced windows after looking back at the mansion that, like the chairs and table, had reverted to its prior decaying state.

Disregarding unsettling circumstance, anxious to help the woman, he began toward the massive house, worried about her welfare, and wondering where she had gone. He reached a fading driveway, a strip of crumbling asphalt well on its way to being consumed by nature. Wary of tripping, Aaron gingerly mounted five crumbling concrete steps leading to an expansive porch and reached a set of weathered, almost bare wooden doors, paint on them well faded. One door did not budge, but it's twin opened with an easy nudge.

Air mixed with sunlight, dust, and other floating particles as Aaron began across its foyer after entering the house. He climbed a grand staircase to its second floor and, after rounding a landing, ascended another flight of stairs to the third. Wood plank flooring in a rotting state creaked with each step while walking along a hallway until entering a room he assumed to be the one the woman cried out from. Cobwebs covered a bed and furnishings and stretched from the ceiling in spots. The nasal offending stench of mildew and must dispersed soon after going to a window, not noticing the woman, to gauge location referenced by eyeing where he saw her from outside. Beyond a doubt, he stood where she had.

A clean, cobweb-free room was before him after stepping from the window. Unnerved, anxious to get back to his car, Aaron hurried out of the room and into a hallway with blue walls and floorboards polished and solid. Tables topped by glowing lamps and a carpet runner ran along its length. Intricately carved polished wooden staircase posts shined.

Aaron hurried downstairs before slowing upon hearing voices below after passing the second-floor landing. Pounding footsteps descended from above while peering into the foyer after reaching where a wall ended. The woman who called out to him sat next to a man on a couch that faced the staircase opposite a shotgun-bearing man. The footsteps stopped. No one appeared behind him.

"Come on, Bob," she said to the shotgun-toting man. "Don't do anything crazy… Nothing happened between us. But I guess you wouldn't know that, being that you're never around."

"So, it's my fault, Leah?" the man asked her. "I don't give you enough of my precious time?"

"I'm not saying that!" the woman replied.

"So, what are you saying then?"

"I'm just saying you were the one who invited your brother to live with us. If you're so paranoid to think something might have happened between Denny and me, then maybe you should never have let him come and live here."

"So, you are saying that it's my fault?"

"Maybe I am. You let Denny live with us, and you're always going somewhere and leaving me alone with him."

"What is Leah talking about, Denny?" Bob asked the man beside her.

"I have no idea," the man replied.

"You know what I'm talking about," Leah groaned as she glanced at Denny. "He came into our room when I was watching television and sat on the bed. Your brother made me feel uncomfortable. He sat right beside me and began touching me. I moved away and told him I was tired and asked him to leave."

"You're such a liar," Denny retorted. He gave Leah a scornful look. "You asked me to massage your back." Denny looked at his brother. "Leah was trying to lead me on, but I didn't go for it."

"I never asked you to massage my back, and trust me, I didn't try to lead you on," Leah huffed. "You came into our room, sat on my bed, and began groping me."

"Now, you're saying that I was groping you!"

"I don't believe either of you!" Bob yelled as he smashed a vase against the floor. "How could you do that to me, brother?" he asked Denny.

"I didn't do anything to you," Denny replied. "Leah is full of shit. I was about to leave because she came on to me. If anyone was groping anyone, she was the one doing it."

"What were you doing in our room then when I came home and found you there? You had no reason to be in there."

"I was going to make dinner," Denny said. "I went up there to see if Leah wanted something to eat. That's all. I was just trying to be considerate."

"But I found you on our bed, man. Did you have to go and sit on our bed to ask my wife if she wanted something to eat? You couldn't have just stood at the door. Don't lie to me, brother."

"She asked me to come into the room and sit on the bed."

"No, I didn't," Leah grunted.

"You're both liars," Bob growled while leveling the gun at his brother. "You're both like little rats who got caught red-handed. How could you two do that to me? Screwing my wife, after I let you come and live with us? After I bent over backward to help you get on your feet by letting you live here and giving you a job that I had to fire your ass from because you're a drunk and kept screwing up. I got you off the street, gave you a job, and this is how you repay me?"

"And look at you, you witch," Bob roared at Leah. "I gave you everything you ever wanted, and still, you betrayed me by seducing my brother."

"It's not like that," she said. "Nothing…"

"Bullshit, it ain't," he spat, cutting her off. "Whether the two of you live to see another second is up to my little pinkie," Bob said while pointing the pinky of his gun-holding hand erect. "See my pinkie?" he asked Denny and Leah. Flame and thunder preceded a spray of dust and plaster as Bob fired a shot into a wall. "Ain't it ironic?" he said to Denny. "You, being six-foot-three and probably two hundred and ten pounds, that my little pinkie could drop you dead in an instant?"

"Remember those songs Mother would sing to us when we were little?" Bob muttered as he shoved another shell into the gun.

"Yeah, I remember that Bob, but come on," Denny replied. "Mom wouldn't be happy about what you're doing now."

"Maybe or maybe not, because she would not be happy about what you did to me either," Bob said, now directing the gun at Leah. "And no way would she be pleased with her whoring daughter-in-law."

"Nothing happened between me and your brother!" Leah insisted. "I never messed around on you with anyone, and like I'm telling you, I told Denny to stop harassing me and to leave me alone. I wouldn't do that to you."

"Oh, Leah, you act so sweet when I catch you in a lie. You almost make me want to believe you, but I know better because you're a slut and always have been. You were the class whore people warned me when we started dating back in high school, but I didn't want to believe them. But it was true. You were the flavor of the day for a lot of guys, people told me, and you proved them right because it was too easy for me to get into your pants. But I trusted you and put a ring on your finger and then come home and catch you and my brother on our bed... You tell me what I'm supposed to think."

"Nothing happened between your brother and me, and that's not fair for you to hold my past against me," Leah said. "Yeah, I messed around before I met you, but come on, Bob, we've gone through that before. We talked about how I was lost and didn't know what I wanted. My mom whored around, so doing that seemed to be okay. I didn't know any better until I met you... You've always treated me good, so why would I mess around on you, especially with your brother?"

"Maybe you're just not thinking straight," Denny suggested to Bob.

"Oh, I'm thinking straight," Bob replied, pointing the gun at his brother.

"Just put the gun down, Bobby. Let's just take some time to calm down and then talk later."

"There's nothing to talk about and don't call me Bobby, you condescending motherfucker," Bob angrily spat. "I always hated it when you called me that. You always thought of yourself as so much better than me, so fuck you."

"I never thought I was better than you," Denny insisted. "You're acting like you did when Mom had to put you in the hospital because you weren't thinking straight."

"Oh, you mean those horrible times when I ended up being locked up because of that crazy old woman? Is that what you're talking about? That never happened to you. How would you feel being locked up with a bunch of lunatics?"

"She had to do that for your own good because you were talking weird and seeing things that weren't real," Denny said. "Mom was worried about you. She just wanted you to be alright."

"So, what was your favorite, big brother?" Bob asked.

"What are you talking about, Bob? I don't get what you mean."

"Your favorite song that Mother sang to us."

"Come on, Bob, haven't you heard a word I said?"

"You're not answering my question."

"I don't remember," Denny said. "I guess I had a few, but that's not what we're talking about. You're pointing a gun at me and threatening to kill your own brother and your wife over nothing."

"You mean one little song didn't stand out, just a teeny-weeny bit? My favorite was the Piggy song... You remember when mom would grab our fingers and say this little piggy went to market, and this little piggy stayed home?" Denny offered a trembling nod. "Remember when you and I used to play hide and seek? You, being a little piggy, let's have a game of hide and seek for old time sake..., you, me, and that whore of a wife of mine! You both go upstairs and hide, and I'll seek. Only this time, I'm not going just to tag you and say you're it when I catch ya, which I will. Instead, I'm going to blow your cheating brains out."

"Come on, Bob," Denny said. "You're not doing well right now. You need to calm down, chill out, and give us some time to talk this out."

"No, brother," Bob muttered while shaking his head. "There's no talking now. We're past trying to work things out. Not with what you two have done."

"But we haven't done anything, Bob," Leah maintained. "Maybe Denny wasn't coming on to me. Maybe I'm was wrong by taking it that way. Like he says, let's chill out and relax and figure this all out. You're not thinking straight right now."

"Both of you can fuck off!" Bob exclaimed. "And stop telling me I'm not thinking straight, Leah, like I'm out of my mind. Don't play me as a fool... I've made lots of money. Look at the house we're living in. If we had to rely on the money you brought in, which there hasn't been any since I married your sorry ass, we'd be living in a slum somewhere. I might be a little off mental-wise, but I'm not stupid. I know what's been going on between you two, and now I'm done talking about it. Screw the two of you!"

"Well, Bob," Leah said. "I never thought that you were stupid or mental."

"That's just crap," Bob yelled.

"Come on, Bob, keep it down," Leah asked him. "My mom probably hears this."

"That's hardly likely," Bob replied. "She can't hear herself fart, she's so deaf."

"To bad if this bothers that poor old invalid mom of yours. And what the hell, you don't think that old bag heard the shot I sent into the wall, dumb twat! And, honey dear, don't think I give a shit about the hag because it's you and that betraying brother of mine I need to come to terms with. You guys are going to look pretty sexy when I blast your sick brains out. Nothing more I would like than to sit right here and watch your heads evaporate. I'll be coming after both of you after counting down from thirty, so you and that soulless brother of mine better go and hide."

"Come on, Bob, please stop this," Leah asked him, sobbing.

"I'm not stopping anything," he said. "You traitors liked to play, and so now I'm gonna play. My game is going to be giving you both a chance to whimper away before I come looking for you. Funny, eh, how things work out? You both doing what you were doing behind my back playing, thinking you're so clever. Time to pay the piper.

"Tweet, Tweet, Tweet," he insanely uttered.

"You both thought you played me, but now it's my little turn to play. You two think you're so clever, thinking that I would never find out what you two had going on. Don't even pretend and tell me tonight was a one-off. And I'm tired of hearing your voice, Leah... I'll shoot you dead right here if you don't zip your trap." Bob stood up and began to count. "Thirty, twenty-nine, twenty-eight…"

"There's no point in trying to reason with him," Denny said as he pulled Leah off the couch. He pulled her along, and she ran with him toward the staircase until breaking away from his grip as they reached the landing. Bob fired a warning shot a few feet in front of her, into a wall, as she started toward the door.

Leah stopped, the shot having its intended effect.

"Oh, Bob," she said after turning to face him. "Let's talk this out. Jesus! Come on, Bob. I've never done you wrong, babe. Why won't you believe me? Nothing happened with Denny and me. You gotta believe me. I've always been by your side. Bob, you know I love you. Please, you hafta know I would never want to hurt you."

"Blah, blah, blah," Bob mockingly uttered while stuffing another shell into the gun. "I don't want to hear it no more, so shut your trap and get going and don't even think about trying to go to that door again." He pointed at the stairs, directing Leah to where he wanted her to go. "Christ, woman, I could shoot your ass dead right now, so be thankful I'm giving you two lowlife's a sporting chance."

She caught up with Denny, who waited for her.

"I'm not going to let that happen. You've got my word on that," Bob said, apparently speaking to himself, internal voices or someone unseen. "I know… But what else could I do? Maybe I should… I will… You have my word."

Denny and Leah mounted the staircase as her demented, disenchanted husband resumed his counting. They stared ahead while approaching Aaron, without giving notice of him as though he were invisible. He followed them after they passed to the second floor and went into a room to hide as Bob's quarry continued down a hallway.

"One!" Bob yelled. "I'm done with counting, kids! Big bad Bob is coming now.

"I've decided that invalid of a mother of yours bedridden in her little haven on the second floor is gonna go." Footsteps pounded up the staircase. "Thanks for the idea, Leah... I was going to leave the old bat alone until you brought her up.

"You're both two peas in a pod, despicable the two of you are," Bob asserted. "God clued me onto your adultery... He told me that it was up to me to help clear His creation of wretched evil motherfuckers like you, and that's what I'm going to do. You're both about to get your brains removed.

"God says I should cut you down, and so help me, that's what I'm going to do when I find you," Bob continued. Bob reached the second-floor landing, Aaron could tell, based on the proximity of his voice.

Lights came on in the room. Aaron, hiding between a bed and wall, grimaced, preparing to be shot after thudding footsteps arrived behind him. Thankfully not shooting at him, Bob started away, ending a dreadful moment. Floorboards creaked with each step as he walked on.

"I'm coming for you," Bob yelled after reaching the hallway. "I'm going to find you two," he yelled from inside another room moments later.

Aaron, seizing an opportunity to leave, hurried out of the room and began toward the staircase. After returning uneventfully to the stairs, he descended them quickly, almost tripping while running. Desperate to get help for Denny and Leah, he picked up the receiver of a phone in the foyer and prepared to dial 911. There was no dial tone.

He tried to think of a way to help the couple while opening the front door. Perhaps, like the house, Jacksonville was now alive with people. That being so, he would stop at the police station and summon help for Denny and Leah.

The black-robed figure seen at Holy Redeemer stood on the porch. Geoffrey! The demon came to kill him, Aaron thought while closing and locking the door after stepping back inside.

What would become of Tyler's body, he wondered, if Geoffrey killed him, though Tyler said he had a few more days to live. Not returning her body to her grave disturbed him more than the prospect of dying as he ran back to the stairs.

Not surprised, certain Geoffrey could easily breach it, the door opened when Aaron looked back after reaching the staircase. He held Tyler's crucifix while ascending its steps and asked God and Tyler for their help. Covered in blood, Bob entered the hallway after shotgun blasts sounded from a room. Aaron looked for another place to hide after passing the second-floor landing. Bob rammed two shells into the double-barreled gun and pumped it while staring at him and uttering nonsensical things.

"Eeny, meeny, miny, moe, where did my stupid whore of a wife go?" The demented man sang as he resumed on his depraved way. "Fee-fi-fo-fum. You two had better hide because here I come!"

Aaron followed Bob, who eventually vanished. The hallway reverted to an abandoned state. Fear froze him in place as Geoffrey rounded the landing after ceding to a need to look behind him.

"This way, Aaron," Tyler's voice cried out from where Bob disappeared. He looked toward her voice. Glowing and wavering in a misty form, Tyler waved him toward her. "Quick, Aaron, run quickly!"

Geoffrey vanished after closing on Aaron.

"It's going to be alright now," Tyler said. "You won't see him again, and the next time you see me will be in Heaven... Goodbye for now." Her soul having returned to its rightful place, Tyler disappeared after he stepped toward her.

Aaron closed his eyes and shielded them with a hand as an intense, blinding light replaced Tyler. In a field, after reopening his eyes after blinding light subsided, he hurried toward the Lincoln, not caring about what lurked in weeds. A graveled road replaced the street. Crop field was where Jacksonville had been while continuing toward Highway 3. A sense of relief came upon seeing a stop sign where West Baseline ended. He looked behind after stopping at the sign. West Baseline, like the town, had been replaced by crop field.

He pulled onto Highway 3 after pondering whether he had lost his mind. The dream he had years ago, of being chased through an unknown town and a mansion, came to mind while driving home. Aaron wondered why the road, town, and mansion appeared from nowhere, how the visions and dreams were connected, and why Geoffrey and Tyler appeared.

* * * * *

Geoffrey, who had pacts with others like the one with McFarren, knew Tyler would tell Aaron the séance was a means of collecting souls if he completed it. Aaron needed to die to prevent him from warning people who considered trying the séance what it was truly about. Geoffrey knew Aaron would pray to be forgiven. Evoked by Geoffrey, the dream and visions were a means of drawing Aaron to his death by succumbing to a desire to once again connect with a godless world. Geoffrey's ability to harm him ended when Tyler appeared when he walked toward her.

Chapter Twenty-Three
A Child of the Grave

Twenty minutes remained to kill before retrieving Tyler's body after arriving home shortly after ten. He parked in the garage. That way, he could put her body in the car without being spotted by others.

Aaron closed his eyes after dropping onto his bed and dwelled on Tyler, lying lifeless in the basement. The song, 'The Rain, and Park and Other Things,' played in his head, the refrain, "I love the Flower Girl," playing over and over. He wondered where the emotional strength required to return her body to her grave would come from. Somehow, he would do what he promised, owing it to Tyler to put an end to what he had started twenty years before.

The dream he'd had so many years ago of being an intruder in a town before being chased into a mansion replayed itself in his acutely fragile mind. The dream, for whatever reason, had become a reality tonight. Perhaps it was Geoffrey who chased him, Aaron surmised. He wondered what would have happened if Tyler had not appeared and dreaded the possibility of encountering the demon again.

Reality was difficult to discern while contemplating how a road and town not noticed before appeared out of nowhere. And what about the mansion and seeing Tyler and Geoffrey? Tyler said that Geoffrey's influence would end after returning to her rightful place. Oh, how he hoped that she was right.

Time reached 10:15 pm per his watch after resting for a few moments. With a heavy racing heart, Aaron embarked on the task at hand. He grabbed a blanket from a closet to cover Tyler with and started toward the basement.

He began through pitch blackness after gathering strength before going into the recreation room and, as expected, feeling her body after reaching the couch. Aaron said her name, hoping she did not respond — that Tyler had returned to death, a desire that seemed odd and cruel. She stayed silent and still while he shook her and said Tyler's name aloud after draping the blanket over her. He held her right wrist to feel for a pulse. Not feeling one, he knew that she was dead.

Adrenaline summoned the emotional and physical strength needed to pick her up and place Tyler's rigid remains over his shoulder. A childhood memory played while starting upstairs, of carrying her when she pretended to be dead during a game of war they played with their friends. The memory numbed reality and allowed stamina to persevere toward the garage.

He dug into a pocket for the key to his car after reaching it. Undignified as it were, he placed Tyler in its trunk, wary of being stopped by police while driving to the cemetery. Aware of his rights, he believed they could not look inside the trunk without his permission or a warrant.

Sarcastic humor struck while entertaining a variety of responses to offer if pulled over and, for some inane reason, granted police permission to look in the trunk. No one would believe what really happened. Difficult to believe himself, telling the truth was not an option.

"Well, you see, officer, it's like this; I found the girl in a patch of brush in a field after stopping to take a leak," he fancied saying in an imagined scenario. "And being a good Samaritan, I decided to bring her to the nearest hospital wanting her body to be properly disposed of. Just doing my part for society, you know..., helping keep fields clear of dead folks. By the way, I knew the girl, and she was an absolute sweetheart... Her name was Tyler Page, and if you do some investigating, you'll find that she's been dead a good long time... After all the years, I was the one who found her because I happened to look where I guess no one else did… Her body should have gone to bones long before now, so it's mighty strange that she looks only a few days dead. Well, you know how some things are beyond explaining? This is one of them."

Or perhaps he might offer something more in line with the truth. "Well, officer, this girl here is Tyler Page, and we were best friends until she died in 1979. I missed her so much I got it in me to dig her up to spend some time with her... you know? I can't explain why skin and hair are still on her and why she looks like she only died yesterday. I'm on my way to take my friend back to her grave. Maybe you could see to let me go on my way. You'll find no trouble here. I'm just a crazy kind of guy, a doctor, by the way, who would never dream of harming someone. I just missed my friend so much."

He removed 'Bug the Jug' to make room for a shovel and a flashlight while feeling disgusted with himself for putting Tyler in the trunk like a bag of garbage. Logical and astute in her thinking, Tyler would have suggested that he put her in the trunk in case the police pulled him over. It would make putting her in the trunk easier to do if they had discussed the process of returning her body to her grave.

His father would have plenty to say if he were caught with her corpse. Mr. Richards wanted him to continue seeing a therapist, remaining concerned about Aaron's mental health with all the sleepless nights he had and anxiety, after the trauma of watching Tyler die and losing her. Dad would probably blame Mom for his misadventure because she took him out of therapy too soon.

Rattled, Aaron backed slowly toward the street after struggling to put its key into the car's ignition. His stomach churned, starting down Askin, on his way to do what had to be done. Life was unfair in many ways, he thought. Tyler would be alive and sitting beside him and not lying dead in a car trunk if it were.

Forty-five minutes passed before reaching Lake Erie while searching the radio for a song to bring solace to his situation, knowing such a song had yet to be written. He alternated between looking at a road's broken centerline, a road Tyler's funeral procession had taken on the way to the cemetery, and Lake Erie, to his right, illuminated by a full moon.

He thought about things he and Tyler did. The times their families would go camping together came to mind. Then he recalled when they went around the neighborhood selling expired raffle tickets Tyler found for her dad's soccer league, thinking they were helping him out. They sold a few tickets before realizing they were worthless.

* * * * *

What became of other undead who were subject to the words of the séance, Aaron wondered upon arriving at the cemetery. Did walking dead people, unable to find someone to return them to their proper place as Tyler did with him, look on from hidden spaces? Unaware Geoffrey's influence ended as Tyler said it would, as she had made it to her rightful place, fear of encountering Geoffrey and unearthed dead added to the fear of being caught with her corpse.

Security guards, local graveyards recently plagued by vandalism, no doubt patrolled the cemetery, so a place to park out of open sight was required. The end of a lane behind a mausoleum was the perfect spot. He retrieved the shovel and flashlight after parking and walked toward her grave, looking for approaching headlights and flashlights along the way. Aside from encountering security people, an encounter with Geoffrey or living dead released from their graves remained a constant, unnerving thought.

A man staggering out of darkness gave credence to his fears. Probably drunk, given his unsteady gait, the man passed a good seventy feet away before returning to the darkness. The man had taken a shortcut through the cemetery on his way home or was a walking dead person, Aaron thought, in the wilds of his mind.

Possessed by steadfast determination, he continued toward Tyler's grave. Maybe she was with him, Aaron wondered, while being brushed by a moderate wind coming off the lake and hearing waves breaking against the shore. A sense of Tyler's presence strengthened the resolve to carry on.

Death took someone's best friend, child, brother or sister, mother or father, husband, or wife in its unrelenting course. Children, Tyler's age or younger, died with every passing moment, somewhere in the world, Aaron knew. How selfish to think life unfair because Tyler died, he chided himself when guilt from having bothered with the séance began anew. She would have been left in peace if he had accepted fate. All the friends who tried the séance in 1979 might still be alive, and Wayne's soul would not be more at risk if he had not tried the séance. Shay would still be alive; perhaps they could have worked things out and resumed their marriage.

Numbed again into a trancelike state, he removed earth at a feverish pace after reaching Tyler's grave. Tired after clearing three feet of earth mixed with chunks of concrete, he rested to regain breath and strength. The shovel struck something hard another few inches down soon after beginning to dig again. A look with the flashlight revealed her white coffin.

He opened the coffin after clearing it of earth. Thank God her coffin was empty, he said to himself. If Tyler's body were in it, it would confirm that Geoffrey had disguised himself as his soul mate. To hell with undead walking people, Geoffrey, security, or anyone else, he thought while briskly stomping back to his car. Regardless of whatever was encountered, his soul mate's body would return to its proper place as promised.

In a fervent, determined, trancelike state, he draped Tyler over a shoulder and started back. Fond memories played again while trying to focus on positive things until tears fell while gently placing Tyler in her coffin. At least there was a chance to see her again, he thought after closing its lid. Hope enhanced resolve while mindlessly returning dirt to her grave.

Dawn broke after returning to the Lincoln. Light enough to navigate cemetery lanes without engaging its headlights and risk drawing attention, his timing was perfect. Proud to have done what needed to be done and relieved to have not been caught, he smiled after leaving Our Lady of the Lakes. He prayed that Tyler returned to her other proper place while driving home and to see the star the following night.

* * * * *

There was no time to sleep, arriving home two hours before having to be at the clinic. Exhausted and dwelling on Tyler, what they talked about, and the ordeal of having returned her to her grave, somehow, he managed to give his patients proper attention. Aaron prayed throughout a difficult day to see the star.

Chapter Twenty-Four
Take the Long Way Home

Perhaps souls of the dead roamed among stars, Aaron wondered, looking deep into a clear night sky while sitting on the bench in his yard. Tyler said she could be in different places. He glanced at where Tyler stood and imagined her looking at him through the dark.

The summer before she died, an evening they spent on the beach in front of his grandmother's cottage came to mind. They looked into a dark sky over Lake Erie, toward Cleveland, Ohio. Distance and the earth's curvature were the reason he said when Tyler asked him why lights from buildings on Lake Erie's opposite shore could not be seen. Perhaps, like Lake Erie's opposite shore, Heaven existed despite not being seen by the human eye.

A star moved in the east at the appointed hour. Aaron smiled, watching as it passed overhead and continued west before disappearing over the horizon. Tears fell. Tyler made it home. They would meet again.

He fixated on the heavens above that spot where the star left his view, happy but also with tears in his eyes from sadness, as he reflected on how tragic Tyler's life had been. No one is perfect. He thought about what she said all those years ago, about trying to give God good things to look at. She tried to live that mantra, and so did he after she said it. Yet she was, at times, as happy and confident as she was, a tortured soul who felt alone in a family of ten. Alone and unwanted, perhaps a mistake even.

It tore him up when she talked like that, for her to think she was nothing more than an ignored mistake. How could she hold onto a sense of meaning and purpose for existing if that's what she believed? Many people are born unplanned, but that becomes irrelevant; they are loved no matter what, and their circumstance is of little relevance. But for her, her parents' inattention made her think at times that she was unloved and not a blessing.

It was heartbreaking that she did not know or see when she was on earth that she was loved, appreciated, and very much wanted by her parents and family.

Some people say perception is more important than reality, Aaron thought. He did not believe that. The truth is the truth — it's black and white; it's as simple as that. But perhaps, he reflected, misperception in itself is real, based on shreds of reality twisted together by tangible evidence of what might be.

And then Tyler lost her grandpa. The man who had tried to fill the void her parents left. Then to die so young and violently. And to go on to being taunted by Heaven only to be sent back to a hole to stay alone for years, her only companion a spirit who visited from time to time.

Then she had to walk among the living, hiding, terrified to be seen on her way to doing the most horrendous things, forcing herself to kill someone to help her friends, and then see him.

But now she was in Heaven to stay. He was so happy for her now. Still, her early death and suffering made him angry and question things. Faith, whatever that means, is all there is to hold on to… hope, loss, and faith, and all of that. All she wanted was to live a happy life, to have fun and make something of herself, and to please God down deep, in her own personal, silent way. She did not deserve, nor would anyone, to endure what she had done for the past twenty years.

At least she mostly enjoyed her life, and he was there for her when she hadn't.

Tyler had to take a difficult way home, but now, finally, she was in a better place.

* * * * *

Eyes from elsewhere saw a black aura around him as Aaron peered through early morning darkness while driving on a fog-shrouded road, a month after seeing the star. He continued without slowing, despite the posted speed dropping where it curved along a river, to add excitement to an otherwise mundane drive. The Lincoln's right front tire plowed into thick gravel after Aaron swerved onto the road's shoulder to avoid a deer.

Unable to correct its course, the Lincoln struck a pumping station after continuing over a berm. The Lincoln flipped over upon hurtling a steep bank along the river until its roof struck water with a spine-shattering force. Unable to free himself, shock set in as water reached his forehead and then his eyebrows, eyes, and nostrils as the car sank.

Shock gave way to an overwhelming sense of absolute peace, falling unconscious during the latter stages of drowning after water entered his lungs.

A shadow put a hand on Aaron's shoulder. "Your time has come," a voice said. Aaron took his final breath as death took him.

A light at the end of a way felt soothing, warm, and embracing. The light became more intense while he moved toward it. Tyler and other loved ones who passed waited at the opposite end of a Heaven-bound path.

* * * * *

Aaron's father stood at his son's grave on a windy November day; swirling leaves wound past his feet. Aaron bought a plot adjacent to Tyler's after Shay left him. Today was the first time Mr. Richards had conjured the strength to visit Aaron.

"I was so proud of you," Mr. Richards told his son. "You were such a good boy... Oh, how I would love to wrap my arms around you and hug you."

A smile came while recalling an infant Aaron curling his hands and feet while laughing. The smile continued while thinking how cute it was watching Aaron and Tyler play when they were toddlers. What a sweet, spunky, vivacious girl Tyler was. He loved and cared about Tyler as if she were his child and remained haunted by her tragic passing.

"You were such a sweet girl," Mr. Richards said as he stared at Tyler's gravestone. "You were such a spunky little thing. You were just a baby."

Like anyone close to her, he wondered how far she would have gone in life.

A smile formed while remembering how frustrated her father got when dealing with his headstrong daughter. Mr. Richards respected Tyler's confidence, appreciated her fair-placed defiance, and knew Mr. Page was begrudgingly proud of her when she stood up to him. He and her mother were raising Tyler right, Mr. Page had said. Kind, loving, thoughtful, strong, and always respectful.

Mr. Richards smiled while looking deep into a crystal blue sky, certain that his son and his girl who died so long ago were together again, riding the winds of eternity. That somewhere above, they laughed out loud, their souls freed by death, no longer shackled by pain-saturated chains of earthbound life. That they had come to know what was to be known.

Music:

"The Rain, the Park & Other Things, i.e., The Flower Girl"
composer Steve Duboff/Jack Komfield, performed by The
Cowsills, released September 1967.

"Do You Believe in Magic?," composer John Sebastian,
performed by The Lovin' Spoonful, released November
1965.

"Boogie Nights," composer Temperton Rodney Lynn,
performed by Heatwave, released 1977.

"My Sweet Lord," composer George Harrison, performed by
George Harrison, released November 23, 1970.

"The Farmer in the Dell," composer/author unknown. Released
1820.

"Got Me Under Pressure," composer Billy Gibbons/Lyndon
Hudson, performed by ZZ Top. Released 1983.

"Nowhere Man," composer Lennon/McCartney, performed by
The Beatles. Released February 21, 1966.

"School,"co-composers Rick Davies and Roger Hodgson,
performed by Supertramp, released September 13, 1974.

"Listen to the Music," composer Tom Johnston, performed by
the Doobie Brothers, released July 19, 1972.

"Dust in the Wind," composer Kerry Livgren, performed by
Kansas, released January 16, 1978.

Television:

Baywatch, NBC, 1989.

Book Cover Picture:
"A Girl Close to Heaven," photographer unknown, royalty-free,
　　public domain.

Dark Winds
Show me a man without remorse, and I will show you one
　　without a conscience.

Could such a man lay his head in Heaven?

Perhaps not, yet all men sin.

Is sin not to be remorsed?

Disdained?

Repulsed like salt to an exposed wound, vinegar to the mouth,
　　or boring repetition to the senses?

Could not the greatest of sin be to repeat the same?

Time over and again.

Not holding oneself angled forward, tempted not to endure the
　　press of the howling dark wind.

Not trying with all that all have in them to keep a forward pace.

All the while knowing that to be so.

And then, when attended to, does sin not waver upon remorse?

Its purpose to wet the seed of divineness.